SECOND CHANCE

PRAISE FOR THE GIFTEDVERSE

This one kept me interested from the very beginning. With a lot of drama, intrigue and some magic, it's fast paced and entertaining.

— DOODLE BUG

...This trilogy is action packed from start to finish with love and loss along the way... From first book to last, the Owens women will keep you fascinated.

— SUNNI

Packed with excitement, danger, adventure and a roller-coaster ride of emotions. I couldn't put it down until I finished it!..

— CYNDEE MARLING

Wow. That is all I can say about this book. It kept me on my toes waiting to find out what came next. It was well-written with a lot of character and world building.

— SARAH COLEMAN

THE GIFTEDVERSE SERIES

In reading Order:

<u>The Owens Chronicles</u>

Prophecy

Destiny

Legacy

<u>The Gifted Chronicles</u>

First Life

Second Chance

Third Eye

<u>Companion Volumes</u>

Annabelle

Etta

Find out more at

www.giftedverse.com

SECOND CHANCE

THE GIFTED CHRONICLES

BOOK TWO

AMANDA LYNN PETRIN

To my dad, for always being there for me...

CHAPTER ONE

DELIA

"Those don't go there," Penny said when we got back from picking vegetables in the garden and found our delivery man placing our order right on the threshold. She could squeeze her tiny frame through and put her basket on the kitchen table, but I would have to open the other French door to get inside.

"If Miss Hill wants me to put them somewhere else, she'll let me know," Mr. Bosworth told the six-year-old as he continued piling my groceries in the most inconvenient way. It was a shorter distance for him and spared my floors his muddy boots, but the door would have to stay open until we put everything away.

This was my opportunity to stand up for myself and tell him exactly where I wanted everything to go, but he looked over at me with a smirk, like he knew I would never tell him how to do his job – or anything – and he was taking full advantage of it.

"I'm sure Mr. Bosworth knows what he's doing and considered every option before choosing to put a mountain of bulky, fragile items in the doorway. Rather than on the table, in that corner, beside the pantry..." I gave a multitude of better options.

"I've been doing this for thirty years," Mr. Bosworth shared, though he'd only been coming here for the last two, since his father retired. He'd seen where the order was supposed to go, yet it took a year to even get him to bring the groceries inside, rather than leaving them in the driveway.

I WROTE Mr. Bosworth a check and sighed when he left, staring at the mess of my kitchen. An old student had remodeled it for me, so everything had its place, but the floor in front of the door was not it.

"I'll get help," Penny decided, before she skipped down the hallway to track down other Rosehill occupants, her golden pigtails bouncing as she went. My pride wanted to tell her not to bother, that I would take care of it myself, but I knew that if Ben or Chris saw I was still letting Mr. Bosworth walk all over me, I would never hear the end of it.

I KNEW EXACTLY who she would come back with, so I went out of order and put away whatever would make the most damage if dropped; a carton of eggs, glass jars, bruisable fruit…

"Do you need help, Miss Delia?" Charlie asked as he burst into the kitchen a few minutes later.

Without waiting for my answer, he stared at the pile of groceries and made a loaf of bread travel across the room to land softly on the counter beside the toaster.

There were no rules against using your Gifts at Rosehill – Jackie used hers whenever she wanted, as long as she had the other person's consent – but until you could control your Gift, you weren't supposed to use it inside the house, or around other people. Charlie's telekinesis wasn't the end of the world when it got away from him, but there were a few close calls when students nearly burnt the place down.

"That's very kind of you boys," I said as Brandon followed his younger brother and used his Gift to put away a box of canned soups. The two of them were so alike, with bright blue eyes, dirty blond hair, and matching Gifts, but Charlie's locks were almost at his shoulders, while Brandon kept his in a buzz cut.

"It's our pleasure," Charlie assured me, tucking a loose strand of that sandy-blond hair behind his ear so he could have a better eye line of his target. His eagerness – both to help and for an excuse to use his Gift – was heartwarming, but it also made me nervous.

"The cereal boxes are a lot lighter," I pointed out when I realized Charlie was going for an industrial-sized bag of flour, which belonged all the way across the kitchen, inside the pantry. I was careful not to tell him to stop, or not to lift things he couldn't handle. I knew they could both lift even the heaviest of my groceries, and I wasn't the least bit worried about Brandon, but Charlie was easily distracted, and once he lost his concentration, everything he had up would fall to the ground.

"He's got this," Brandon assured me as I opened the door to the pantry so Charlie would have one less thing to worry about.

The flour landed softly in its place, while Brandon sent the laundry detergent out of the kitchen where he could no longer see it, listening to make sure it landed on the shelf in the laundry room. His Gift was stronger than any telekinetic I'd encountered at that age, and his brother had the same potential, but I often had a case of monkey see, monkey do, that ended terribly.

I washed the produce from the garden while they worked, careful not to get in the way of flying grocery items. Penny sat on the beige marble countertop and sampled everything, occasionally giving the boys orders and suggestions.

"A little more to the left," she guided Brandon with her mouth full of snap peas.

At seventeen, he was more graceful at putting things away in tight spaces, but Charlie was braver and faster, carrying way more than his fair share with the untouchable confidence of a fourteen-year-old boy who excelled at everything he tried.

Things were going smoother than I'd expected, until Lena came in through the open French door just as Charlie was adding a jar of cloves to the spice rack. I watched in a panic as Charlie lost his hold on the cloves and they crashed down onto the rack, launching a chain reaction that had dozens of glass jars falling to the ground – until Brandon caught them all with his Gift, leaving the lot suspended a few inches from the ground.

"Oh, thank God. That was almost—"

I was halfway through exhaling when a much bigger glass jar containing chia seeds crashed to the floor and exploded everywhere.

I immediately grabbed Penny, who was barefoot and inching her way closer to get a better look at the damage.

"I'm sorry," Charlie said. "I had it, but then…" I followed his gaze to the empty doorway, but Lena had vanished. Penny was convinced the fifteen-year-old had the Gift of invisibility, and while I knew that wasn't the case, I couldn't tell you if she'd retreated outside, or if she'd slipped upstairs while we were all watching the commotion.

"It's fine. I have tons more in the storeroom," I assured him.

"We'll clean it up," Brandon said as he dropped the telekinesis and grabbed a pair of brooms, handing one to his brother.

"I can help too," Mateo offered from the hallway, having no doubt heard the crash. The twelve-year-old took a step towards the dustpan before I saw his bare feet on the now-speckled white floor.

"Mateo, you're not wearing shoes!" I warned, harsher than I

intended. "This floor is terrible for spotting glass, and the boys are already taking care of it." I tried to let him know I was trying to protect him, that I wasn't mad, but he wasn't used to me yet. He'd been at Rosehill a little over a month, after bouncing around multiple foster homes, and that was more words than we got from him most days. While Charlie's long hair was a fashion statement, Mateo's was so he had something to hide behind.

"I'll get shoes." He turned to leave, but Charlie stopped him.

"Don't bother, we're almost done." He looked guilty and ashamed, which was the outcome I'd been expecting, but that didn't make it any easier.

"You were doing an excellent job today, Charlie. I was very impressed." I gave him an encouraging smile.

He nodded, then got back to the mess while I brought Penny to get shoes.

The kitchen was spotless by the time we returned, with even the counters sparkling, except for the addition of a rather large aluminum tray filled with lasagna noodles and meat sauce.

"Perfect timing," Chris said, coming out of the walk-in fridge with a head of lettuce, wearing his *Kiss the Chef* apron. "I was looking for someone to help me add the finishing touches to the lasagna." He was Michelin-starred and aspiring chefs would kill to train under him, but he spent his vacation days here, making kid-approved classics with underqualified sous chefs.

"You mean the cheese?" Penny's eyes got wide as she looked up at me with wonder, wordlessly asking if she could do the honors.

"As long as you've washed your hands," I assured her before taking out the plates and cutlery I would need to set the table for dinner.

"You put some underneath too, right?" Penny verified after

she moved the bench to the sink and started scrubbing the dirt from the garden out of her fingernails.

"Why, was I supposed to?" Chris teased, but quickly reassured Penny when she looked at the dish with horror. "Ricotta *and* mozzarella," he assured her.

"Thank goodness." She smiled, then poured an entire bag of shredded cheese onto the lasagna, tiny handful by tiny handful.

WE MADE a garden salad while the lasagna cooked, before everyone trickled into the dining room. I tried to get everyone together for lunch as well, but dinner was non-negotiable. Unless you were sick or away, you either ate with everyone, or… it wasn't like I would make anyone starve, but there was no going off to eat on your own. Even before Rosehill's completion, it was a rule I put in place with the construction crews and household staff. It seemed silly to keep up with old and stuffy traditions in the new world, with no one watching. Our friends nearly fainted when they came for a visit and sat down to an evening meal with the maids, butlers, and groomsmen all together, but everyone working at Rosehill quickly became family anyhow.

These days, it was moody teenagers I had to convince to leave their phones behind, rather than busy employees concerned with decorum. Charlie, Brandon, Jackie, and Penny sat down first and got along like siblings, catching up on their days and teasing each other as my brothers and sisters had done with me centuries ago.

Once the lasagna was ready, Chris put it on the table and took the seat next to Ben. They looked like brothers, an older version of Brandon and Charlie, only there was no relation, and Ben, though he looked a touch younger, was more like a grandfather, age-wise. They talked about cars and sports, two things I knew very little about. I understood the rules to everything one of my kids or students played, thanks to all the Sunday games I cheered them on at, but the only athletes I knew from the twenty-first century were the odd few who graduated from Rosehill, or happened to be Gifted.

Lena didn't trust us yet, but she'd quickly figured out that the best way to avoid suspicion was to play her part and pretend she did. It broke my heart to watch her do it, and to know there was a school somewhere, like Rosehill, where they trained little girls to become heartless killing machines. Luckily, I watched Lena in the moments she thought no one was looking and caught glimpses of the heart she kept hidden. Mostly with animals on the grounds who would never reveal her secrets. At least not to me.

"I made the cheese part of the lasagna," Penny told everyone.

"That's the best part," Jackie assured her. "It smells amazing."

"I made sure it was bubbling before Chris took it out, because I know you don't like cold cheese, see?" Penny leaned over the table to show Brandon how browned it was, because he only liked melted cheese. She dropped her doll in the process and Lena, without saying a word, got the doll from the floor and put it back on Penny's chair before she could notice. But I did.

"How was your day?" I asked Mateo, the only other person who was eating in silence. He always sat as far removed from the rest of us as he could and shoveled down his food as fast as humanly possible before asking to be excused.

"Okay." He shrugged.

"I heard you're acing math. At a college level. We might need to hire a new teacher next semester."

If I thought praising the twelve-year-old's skills would help get him out of his shell, I was dead wrong. The glare he gave me would have made me recoil if there wasn't so much hurt behind his brown eyes.

"Math is easy." He dismissed the compliment. "I don't need a teacher."

I had so many questions about his aversion to praise, but he was already on his last bite. He stood up the moment the food was in his mouth and tried to swallow so he could ask to be excused.

"We're making brownies for dessert. You can crush the nuts to put on top," Penny offered before he got the words out.

Mateo looked to Penny, then to the rest of us, who were all waiting for his reaction. It was easy to retreat to an empty room when you wanted to be alone, but Penny made it infinitely harder when she asked you to do something with her.

"I'm not hungry tonight, but maybe another time," he told her apologetically before turning to me. "May I be excused?"

The other kids sometimes asked that question as they ran out the door whenever something exciting happened, but as much as Mateo wanted to be on his own, he never left until I dismissed him.

"Of course. The brownies will be on the counter if you change your mind." I smiled until he turned away, wishing I could figure out how to reach him.

"GIVE HIM TIME." Ben came and put his hand on mine while I absentmindedly watched Jackie, Penny, and Chris making brownies.

"He's only been here a few weeks," I agreed, but Ben's smile told me he knew I was still worried.

"It takes at least a few months to get used to your over-bearing mothering." He shrugged.

"I can't tell if you're teasing or not," I warned as the house phone rang.

I went over to answer it, but Jackie moved faster than was safe for someone who couldn't see where she was going and beat me to it.

"Rosehill Academy, how may I help you?" The seventeen-year-old greeted in her version of my British accent, as if prospective students ever called that number. We didn't advertise, so most of our student body came from referrals, or we recruited them. "Are you on your way?"

Jackie dropped the accent, and I could tell from her smile that it was Tristan on the other end, even before she asked a bunch of follow-up questions about Alison and their trip.

"Tristan got used to it," Ben pointed out, stopping me from eavesdropping further. "And I didn't mean it like your constant care and attention is what's stopping Mateo from joining in."

"It just doesn't help?"

"He needs time to understand that he's safe here, that you won't send him away, and no matter how many times he turns you down, you will still be there, ready to welcome him with open arms once he's ready. It's scary when you've been hurt in the past, but time proves it's real," he explained.

"Then I'll keep doing what I'm doing." I smiled, but I wasn't sure if we were still just talking about Mateo, or if Ben was implying some similarities between me and the boy who was hesitant to accept my love.

"Sure, Delia's right here," Jackie said with an exaggerated sigh, handing me the phone.

"How are you? How's Alison?" I asked, nodding when Ben motioned to say he was going to take care of things outside. He'd arrived less than a century ago and worked his way up from the recruiter to teacher to my right-hand man. I was perhaps too reliant upon him, because I couldn't run Rosehill without him at this point.

"We're... okay." Tristan considered my question before answering. "Finally got on the road, so we should be at the airfield soon."

"Are you sure you want to go straight to California tonight? Rosehill is on your way to the airfield. You could spend a few days here and calm your nerves a bit before facing her family."

Not to mention my own nerves. That he'd come back to life did not negate the fact that he'd died on me. There was a weight in my chest that wouldn't go away until I saw he was okay.

"Alison hasn't seen them since this all started, which might only be a couple of weeks, but it feels like a lifetime. Do we still have people with them?"

"Of course. Until the threat is over, we will keep an eye on the Carmichaels. But they're all welcome here," I reminded him.

"I'll keep that in mind."

"For as long as they need," I added. I knew Tristan was rolling his eyes at my 'overbearing mothering', but I couldn't help it even if I tried. "I believe Jen is working in San Francisco for the summer, so if you need anything while you're there, I'm sure she and Peter would be happy to help."

"You have friends everywhere, don't you?" he called me on it. He'd met the two of them a few years ago, but had Jen left Rose-hill and settled on an island commune decades before I found Tristan. "We'll reach out if we need anything, but Alison's pretty eager to see her family, and she promised she would spend her time at the hotel or the hospital, so we won't be doing social calls."

"When the world stops making sense, you need your family more than ever. Will you let me know when you get there?"

"Of course." I could hear the smile in his voice. I knew it was a sad one, because he'd lost his biological family, but I was enough of a nagging, worrying mother that he never had to feel like he was on his own.

"Safe travels," was as close as I was going to get to telling him to be careful and drive safe.

"Always," he assured me before hanging up.

CHAPTER TWO

ALISON

Tristan ran his hand through his dark, messy hair before putting it back on the steering wheel. We were off to an airfield in the middle of nowhere because Tristan knew a pilot who could fly us to California under the radar. I would have felt safer on a commercial airline, but I had to get to my family.

There were a million thoughts running through my mind as I stared out the window, pretending I hadn't been listening in on his call. Now that we were driving away from the craziness of the past month, part of me wanted to forget all of it and start fresh in California as if I didn't know that I was a First Lifer with people trying to kidnap me so they could study my blood. Unfortunately, playing pretend wouldn't be much help. Not when I was the problem, with my rare Gift a built-in, very permanent reminder. No matter where I went, random objects I touched would show me their darkest, most traumatic memories. Every Gifted would temporarily lose their Gifts. And, worst of all, every person who got close to me would get sick, losing more and more of their health until there was nearly nothing left, like I'd been doing to my sister for over a decade.

Until I figured out how to control my particular 'Gift',

Tristan was the only person I was touching, and that was because he was the one who initiated it and refused to listen when I told him I would never touch anyone – or anything – ever again. He insisted we would figure it all out together, but to be honest, I mostly agreed with the people who'd kidnapped me. They believed that because of the part of my Gift that took away other people's Gifts, my blood could somehow turn Gifted back into regular humans. I probably would have stayed with them and helped them accomplish their goals if they didn't insist on administering it to all Gifted, whether they wanted it or not. Because given the choice, I would gladly get rid of my so-called 'Gift'.

"You're a million miles away." Tristan reached over the console to hold my hand. The sparks I felt when our skin connected used to give me butterflies, but now I knew it was just the remnants of his Gift that I was sucking away from him, however unintentionally. He didn't let go, but I knew he felt the sparks as well. Instead, he rubbed his thumb against my skin in a soothing back-and-forth manner. I loved him for showing me he wasn't afraid, and that touching me was worth it, but I was terrified of what could happen if we were attacked again while he was so vulnerable.

I could not watch him die a second time.

"Just processing." I gave him a smile, which he returned, before I went back to staring out the window.

"You are taking it a lot better than I did," he shared, getting my attention away from the trees.

"When you found out you were semi-immortal?"

I was fully aware that he was trying to distract me, but I welcomed the diversion. I'd been wanting to ask about his past since the moment I found out he was Gifted. Usually, when you die, you're dead, but if you're Gifted, you wake up with a supernatural ability and don't stay dead until you accomplish some kind of purpose. But how would you figure that out without someone there to tell you? All I knew for Tristan was that the doctors wanted to amputate his leg as a last-ditch attempt to stop the spread of his cancer, but he died before the surgery could take place. He'd never mentioned 'waking up'.

"Being a First Lifer – and being hunted for it – sucks," Tristan began, so as not to take away from my horrific experience. I'd drowned when I was younger, and it took just long enough for my dad's CPR to work that my Gift got activated, even if I didn't fully die. "But if you're not a First Lifer, then you don't find out you're Gifted until after you've died. When you wake up. If you're lucky, you stumble onto another Gifted who can explain everything to you before you get the chance to freak out."

"Is that what happened to you?"

"Not quite. The dying part wasn't bad. I was so tired of fighting that I wasn't even afraid of what came next. They kept giving me morphine to make me comfortable, and I drifted in and out with last goodbyes from the people I loved, and then it was over." He kept his eyes on the road, but I couldn't tell if he was seeing it, or if he was lost in his thoughts. I wanted to ask him what dying was like, but a shadow crossed his face. "Until I woke up." He swallowed. "I was in one of those…"

"A coffin?" I suggested.

"No. I guess you would call it a drawer? One of those things in morgues that only opens from the outside." I understood he knew the last part from experience, which made me reconsider whether I wanted to hear the rest of the story.

"I guess I'm lucky someone I trusted figured it out and sent me to Grace, who tried to teach me how to use it." Although it wasn't so lucky for either of them. Dr. Richards died alone after being tortured for information on me, and Grace barely survived a violent attack from the same people.

I took a deep breath and brought my focus back to Tristan.

"My luck was that it only took an hour of banging and

screaming before someone heard and let me out." He forced a smile, but there was nothing lucky about it, only less terrible than it could have been. "Unfortunately, it was the employee who'd signed for my body and just received hundreds of bookmarks with my face on them. He did not react well to seeing me alive."

"I am so sorry you went through that." I could only imagine how terrible that must have been for him. For both of them.

"I was confused and terrified, but the guy literally died."

"You killed him?!?" I was shocked, and the words came out before I could stop myself.

"Technically. But that was when I discovered my Gift. Not that I understood it at the time. I bent over him and tried to do CPR, but when I did my first compression, shocks of electricity travelled from my hands into him and restarted his heart. I called 911 and stayed with him until I heard the sirens, then I ran off into the night. It took me forever to slow down and realize no one was coming after me. I guess no one believed the guy, and the funeral director didn't want to admit they'd lost a body. But it begs the question of what they cremated for my mom's urn."

"You went home?" I asked delicately. I knew he hadn't spoken to most of his family in years, but I could only imagine how someone would react to finding their dead son on their doorstep.

"Eventually. I saw the pile of booklets from my funeral. Then I watched my parents sift through casseroles and cards through the living room window. I wanted, more than anything, to rush in amd tell them I was okay, that there had been some crazy mistake and they didn't have to be sad anymore… but even if I didn't understand it, I knew that I'd died. I'd seen enough horror movies to know no good could come from me coming back to life, so I was going to walk away and leave them alone, but Serena, my little sister, was crying on our backyard swing, looking so lost and scared, until she spotted me. Her face just lit up and… I couldn't leave her."

"You became her imaginary friend." I knew it wasn't nearly that simple, but I got a hopeful smile as he gave the back of my hand a kiss.

"I stayed close by and kept an eye on her, but I was mostly wandering the streets until Delia found me. The guy who found me hadn't let everyone calling him crazy stop him from telling people he saw a dead body come back to life, and eventually, it got back to Rosehill. Delia took me in and taught me what Gifted are, as well as how to control my Gift. I still snuck out to watch Serena play, or popped over for a chat when she was alone in the backyard, but as time went on… imaginary friends aren't so common once you hit high school."

"She was the only one you visited? Not your other sister?" I knew he had two of them, but he only ever talked about the older one.

"Serena was the only one I let see me. My parents would have freaked out and Izzie was afraid of me even when I was still alive." I gave him a confused look, so he explained. "She was born when I was in remission, like a fresh start for the family, but by the time she could walk, I was constantly hooked up to machines with loud beeping and tubes going everywhere… it was just best if I didn't cause her any more nightmares. I tried to stay away from Serena too, especially once she got older, but by then she knew to look for me, so eventually…"

"She asked you to stop coming, and you found me." I tried to add a happy spin to it, but I was painfully aware of how much trouble I'd brought into his life in such a short period. He'd come to Boston for a change of scenery after his sister told him it was better if he stayed away from her, and I immediately put his life in danger and asked him to stay away from me, before he saved my life and I watched him die. Though not in that order.

"My heart broke, and you put it back together," he agreed.

"I can't imagine—"

I had paused to let out a breath and gather my thoughts for something reassuring to say. Instead, I grabbed on to his arm and yelled, "Tristan!" in case he hadn't seen the pick-up that swerved out of nowhere and came to a grinding halt in the middle of the road, maybe twenty feet ahead of us.

I assumed the driver had fallen asleep, and I didn't want Tristan to smash into them, but he was more on the ball than I was, even before the people got out and faced us with a determination I found terrifying. Instead of stopping, Tristan had swerved into the field and drove as far as he could until it got too thick for us to keep going. He covered me a second before they launched something at us that shattered both windshields, raining glass everywhere.

"Run," Tristan commanded, opening my door so I could get out.

My brain was still trying to process what was going on, but luckily, my body was getting used to the adrenaline rush. We ventured through the field toward a wooded area. I made sure not to look back, but all I could think of was the truck's occupants, and how they'd looked like they wanted to kill me.

I SLIPPED on a muddy slope once we got into the trees, scrambling to get up because I knew they were right behind us, even if I could no longer hear them over the rumble of the nearby river.

"Are you okay?" Tristan asked in a whisper when he slid down and joined me.

"I'm fine," I said, but he already had me back on my feet and we were running again, though this time he held on to my hand.

We headed for the river, which was good since they wouldn't be able to hear our footsteps, or my heartbeat that was drumming in my ears, but I didn't like the idea of not being able to hear how close they were.

We followed it a couple hundred feet before we got to a clearing. I'd been hearing the river since the tall grass of the field, but this was the first time I saw it flowing about thirty feet below us. My stomach churned as I stepped back from the edge. I was not a fan of heights and felt that anyone who went cliff diving had something seriously wrong with their brain chemistry. And a death wish.

"Shouldn't we be moving? In the cover of the trees?" I suggested. We were completely exposed, and I did not want a closer look at whatever burst the windshield.

"Do you trust me?" Tristan asked, taking my other hand in his.

"Yes…" This wasn't the first time he'd asked, though I'd trusted him a lot more when it was a question of where we were going on a date. His face was determined, but I could tell I wouldn't like it.

"On three, we're going to jump."

"Into the river?" I whispered it, more because I was hoping I'd misunderstood than because I thought anyone would overhear us.

"I won't let go," he promised. "One, two, three…"

And we jumped.

CHAPTER THREE

DELIA

The mansion got quiet in the evenings, when the younger children went to bed, and the older ones enjoyed their free time. I could hear video games from Brandon and Charlie's room, as well as the occasional trash talk they would never use if they knew I was listening. We had more than enough bedrooms for them each to have their own, but while they made Rosehill their home as if the lives they lived before never existed, they didn't like being apart. I kept expecting them to change their minds once they got older, but we were going on four years, and it looked like they would be bunkmates until they moved out. Which I hoped wouldn't be for a while. Even if my job was to take care of them and teach them what they would need to excel in the world, I always dreaded the actual 'going out into the world' part.

Two doors down, Mateo made sure his music was just loud enough for me to hear it through the door, in case I had any inclination to go inside and start a conversation. He was going to go deaf if he wasn't careful, but it was better than the constant silence we got from him until a week ago. I would open the door to check on him after a quick knock and find him sitting on the floor in the corner, with his hands on his head, staring at me with so much hatred that I felt it to my core, until I realized he was looking through me. I didn't know it was possible to hate someone this fiercely that I had never met, but I did.

Jackie was listening to a book on tape – Jane Austen by the sound of it – which fit nicely with the classical music coming from Lena's bedroom. I could never tell if she was listening or playing unless I could distinguish more than one instrument. Even then, she often played along to recordings, creating her own orchestra. It was beautiful to listen to, but also incredibly sad.

No one needed me, so I went down to the kitchen to make myself a tea. It was too early for sleep, and I didn't have much luck with that anyway, especially not with Tristan being hunted and so much pain under my roof.

I filled the kettle and put it on the stove, then took out a mug with some tea bags to make it extra strong. My eyes burned for a millisecond, as they did whenever Jackie used them to locate me, so I took out an extra mug and a pouch of herbal tea for her.

"I was thinking we could all go horseback riding tomorrow," I said once I heard her in the doorway. "Mateo is too shy to come on his own, but if it's a mandatory group activity, he won't have—"

I stopped mid-sentence when I saw her face. Jackie often found me in the evenings for tea and something sweet, but tonight she looked scared.

"What's wrong, sweetheart?" I came over and brought my hand to the side of her face, so she could grab onto it and anchor herself.

"Someone's trying to hurt Tristan."

I had a million questions I wanted to ask, but the fear on her face told me we didn't have the time.

I went to the keypad and sounded the alarm.

CHAPTER FOUR

DELIA

"What did you see?" I asked Jackie, ushering her to follow me outside, texting Chris on the way. The alarm I triggered only went off in certain areas of Rosehill so the children wouldn't panic. Chris' bedroom, the same one he'd used as a child, wouldn't receive it, but I needed an adult I could trust to stay with the kids while I was gone. Rosehill was protected in many ways, and though we weren't currently under attack, it made me nervous to know that the magical barriers became less effective the instant I crossed the threshold.

"I wanted to see how far away he was, and I love looking out of airplane windows at the world below, but he was in the woods. If he was here, I would assume he just went for a run to clear his head, but it's getting dark, something is following them, and Alison looks terrified."

"Are they injured?"

"Not yet."

I loved Jackie with all my heart, but she was not an optimist.

"Are they still in Boston?"

"There are no trails or signs that I can see... but there's a river or a lake or something nearby."

"Is the water still, or..."

"I can't see the water, only that they're soaking wet."

I nodded encouragingly to reassure her, not that she could see it, but she had a knack for reading my emotions, regardless. I did not like the sound of her last statement.

"Find them and keep them safe," I asked three of the gargoyles perched above the front door. "Watch the school," I told the two others.

For a second, it looked like nothing was going to happen, but then all five gargoyles slowly broke free from their molds, breaking the stones that encased them as they spread their wings. Three flew off into the distance, one found a higher vantage point, and the other circled the school's entrance. They were originally carved to protect the mansion from evil spirits and superstitions, but I had a friend who was a witch and thought I could use someone to talk to without guarding my words. Over the centuries, they did a lot less conversing, but more of everything else. I often wondered if they did somehow communicate with each other at night, when I wasn't watching, but they had their own personalities and preferences as far as which tasks they liked to accomplish, which I tried to take into account. There was a limited radius they could reach outside the estate, but hopefully Tristan and Alison weren't too far away.

"I'll be back before you wake up, and if I'm not, Chris will take care of breakfast. Etta can come by and continue with lessons, if that's what everyone wants, or you can go on a field trip...or it's probably best if everyone stays within the grounds," I told Jackie, running through a mental list of things that needed to be taken care of before I left. I wondered if I should text Etta now, so she could see it when she woke up, or if I should wait and only bother her if it looked like I wouldn't be back in time.

. . .

THE TACTILE SCREEN analyzed my fingerprint before letting us into the war room. I hated calling it that, but there were only so many times I could remind everyone it was called the Supply Room before I gave up and joined in. I'd seen war, and what we did was not the same. We tried to make the world safer; to prevent wars and protect the people we loved. Unfortunately, we sometimes had to use a lot of weapons to get there.

"I'm coming with you," Jackie insisted, taking her training suit from the shelf. They were fire resistant and mostly bullet-proof, so I could keep everyone safe while they learned how to use their Gifts, but somewhere along the way, the kids decided they should use their training suits as superhero costumes.

"This isn't a game, sweetheart. No First or Last Lifers, especially not when they're underage." I reminded her of the rules.

"How will you know where they are if I'm not with you?"

"She has a point," Ben agreed, coming in to stock up on weapons for himself. He was already in his training suit, which made him look more like a black ops agent than a superhero, since he'd removed the white and red stitching of the school's logo.

"She's seventeen," I argued with him, but my eyes rested on her when she tried to put a grenade in her pocket.

"I'm an innocent, blind teenager. No one will see me as a threat," she pointed out, putting the grenade down so she could raise her hands in surrender.

"You thinking that scares me."

We never hurt children, no matter how vile their deeds, but not everyone had the same scruples. I knew from experience that some people shot first and asked questions later, no matter how young you were. Especially if you hung out with Gifted.

"I can stay in the car if it makes you feel better, but I can't stay here."

Jackie was a couple of inches taller than me, but she usually slouched to take up less space in the world. Tonight, to push her agenda, she stood to her full height, as uncomfortable as it made her, and urged me to listen.

"He's family, and I can help."

I loved her fierce determination when it came to protecting those she loved, but not when it put her in danger. I weighed the risks against the benefits, looking to Ben for support, but he just shrugged, reminding me I knew his thoughts on the matter. I would never forgive myself if Jackie got hurt, but I would lose her if anything happened to Tristan. Not that I would forgive myself for that, either. Unfortunately, if Alison's Gift could actually remove Giftedness, then the Damned would never stop looking for her. A large majority of Gifted might join in as well if they believed her to be the cure to their immortality. We didn't have time to grid search an entire forest to find them when a handful of Gifted were already hot on their heels.

"I am trusting you to stay in the car and listen," I relented, grabbing extra shields and protection for her. "Not until you get your license." I took the handgun from her and replaced it with a taser and pepper spray. Not that I wanted her using those, either. The last thing we needed was her shooting herself, or someone else.

By the time Jackie and I got outside, Chris and Ben were waiting with our presidential-grade Navigator, while Caleb and Etta pulled into the driveway behind them.

"I'm not a kid anymore," Chris reminded me with his arms crossed.

"But you're in your first life, without a Gift, and you're the person I trust the most with the children sleeping upstairs," I reminded him he wasn't just staying back, he was protecting the people we had to leave behind. "I made a promise to your mother—"

"I'll stay for the kids," he cut me off, then sighed to let me know he still didn't like it. "But if you don't come back, they're getting dessert for every meal until they rot their teeth and child services take them away," he warned.

"I'll be back," I promised. Technically, no one could promise such a thing, not even with my Gift, but even if I died, the chances were that I would wake up at Rosehill, like nearly every other time my luck ran out.

"MIDNIGHT STROLL?" I turned to Caleb and Etta, who I could now see were armed and ready, with Caleb looking every bit the soldier as Ben. Etta was wearing her training suit as well, but she adorned it with a red bandana around the neck. It was an unnecessary fashion statement for now, but she would use it to tie up her waist-length jet-black hair once we got to fighting.

"Your bat signal tipped us off," Caleb explained, pointing to the spotlights on the roof, which I doubted he could see from their house. We were technically neighbors, but there were acres of wooded land between us.

"And he paid the security guy to hook us up to your alerts, in case of emergencies," Etta ratted her husband out. An affluent father who wanted to make sure his daughter would be safe in our care digitized the security system, so I couldn't blame him for jumping at the opportunity to add an extra layer of safety.

"It's an honor to have you both by my side," I said instead of reproaching him, taking them both in for a quick hug.

THE FIVE OF us piled into the vehicle so Ben could follow Jackie's directions through back roads and forests to get us as close as we could to Tristan and Alison. Jackie kept bringing her fingers to the space between her eyebrows, trying to stave off the migraine that came when she used her Gift too much. She could see through one person's eyes continuously, only stopping when it got too uncomfortable for the other person, but switching back and forth was hard on her. Luckily, her connection to Tristan was one of her strongest, so the distance wasn't nearly as difficult as it was with Alison. We just had to hope it was enough, and that we weren't too late.

CHAPTER FIVE

ALISON

It felt like we had been running for hours, but judging by the sun that was still setting, it hadn't even been one. My legs were burning, and I'd twisted my ankle on the uneven terrain at least a dozen times. I only walked into branches twice, but I could feel the blood coming down from the cut it made above my eyebrow. I was still soaked from our jump into the river rapids, so I couldn't tell if it was blood or water until it got into my eye and tried to blind me. Not that there were actual rapids, but there was a strong current that carried us miles away from the car, and civilization. I'd seen one of the others jump in after us while we drifted away, but we'd been alone since we got out of the water and into the forest. Or at least I hadn't seen anyone.

There were five of them after us, and while I had tried not to slow us down by looking back, the few times I had, they'd looked like trained killers who could chase us for days without getting tired. I would have given up miles ago if it weren't for Tristan holding my hand and dragging me along, encouraging me to keep running just a little further. I didn't know what he thought he was guiding us to in the middle of nowhere, but a part of me felt like I could follow him to the ends of the earth, so I pushed forward.

AFTER FIFTEEN MORE MINUTES, I heard movement in the woods behind us. Or maybe I imagined them, but it got to where I was half-wishing they would just find us already, before they could pop up when I wasn't expecting it and give me a heart attack.

"Here," Tristan whispered, guiding me into what I thought was the opening of a cave, but I quickly realized was a hollowed-out tree.

I panicked and nearly cried out to Tristan when he didn't follow me inside, but he was covering our footprints leading to the tree. He ran past it a dozen feet, turned, then took off his shoes and came back to me in his socks, making much less noticeable tracks.

"How did you know to do that?" I asked.

"Delia and Ben taught me a bit about covering my tracks, but it won't fool them for long," he warned. Jackie had been watching us through Tristan since we got out of the river, but I had no clue how far away she was, or if she could find us in time.

Tristan wasn't saying anything, but I knew it was all my fault. Tristan's Gift allowed him to shoot bolts of electricity out of his hands, which could have given us a fighting chance if my Gift hadn't sucked his away from him.

I went to apologize for stealing his Gift, for putting him in danger, for everything, but he brought his finger to his lips. Which was fine, because there wasn't anything I could have said that wouldn't have fallen short.

NOW THAT WE weren't running anymore, my breathing slowly returned to normal, but my heart was still pounding against my chest, the fear making me feel like anyone could hear it from a mile away.

Tristan took me in his arms just as I heard someone coming. I was vaguely aware that I was holding my breath, but it wasn't even the Gifted who'd been following us. Two bears the size of minivans slowly made their way up the path where Tristan had tried to cover our footsteps, and planted themselves in front of our tree's opening, all nonchalant, but also like they were guarding us for their next meal.

I was still on restricted breathing when two of the Gifted hunting us came through, commenting on the bears, but showing no fear. Which terrified me about as much as the bears. I was sure they must have noticed us as well, but they kept walking. Tristan held my hand, as if he could comfort the fear out of me. I appreciated the effort, but until the bears moved on and the Gifted gave up, I couldn't relax.

Two more Gifted walked right past us twenty minutes later, and I was almost glad the bears were there. As long as they blocked the entrance, the Gifted weren't coming near us.

That is, until one of them on their own looked right past the bears, straight at me. He was taller than Tristan, and muscular, with dark eyes that somehow reminded me of wolves.

"Looks like someone's got a bit of Dr. Doolittle in them," he said before whistling to summon his friends.

CHAPTER SIX

DELIA

"They're hiding in a hollow tree, but I can see the people who are after them. At least one, but there were more earlier," Jackie said once we got as far as the vehicle could take us.

"They'll be okay." I squeezed Jackie's hand before getting out. "And you—"

"I'll stay right here with Etta," she assured me, possibly an attempt to cut me off in case I was about to use my Gift on her. I would never, but she didn't know that. As far as she was concerned, I would break a promise and risk her hating me if it meant she stayed alive.

"Thank you. I really appreciate it." I sighed, hoping I wouldn't regret letting her come, before running as fast as I could, followed by Ben and Caleb. Etta would join the fight if we needed her, but her healing Gift was best kept away from danger if we could help it, especially when First Lifers were involved.

Ben and Caleb ran past me almost as soon as their feet hit the ground. Their legs were much longer than mine, but I had

30

endurance on my side, from a lifetime of being slower and weaker than those against me.

I'd been trained by the best the Guardians had to offer, to fight those more powerful than me. It didn't always work out, but I never backed down from a fight I believed in, whether it was to defend myself, someone I cared about, or even a stranger. Unless, of course, my fighting put someone else's life on the line.

I'd also learned to hunt, and to track people by the footprints and cracked branches they left behind. I wasn't as talented as the one who taught me, but I still would have expected to see a lot more damage to these woods from a group of people running through them. Most of what I found was from Caleb and Ben, plowing through ahead of me, with no regard for the evidence they left behind. I could make out maybe two other sets of footprints, tops.

"I think they're over here," I called, leading the guys through a clearing they'd overlooked.

I could say it was the way a branch was bent at Tristan's shoulder level, or how there was a half print from a woman's sneaker, but there was something else pulling me to the clearing. I couldn't put a finger on it, so I attributed it to a mother's instinct, even if Tristan wasn't really mine.

The guys caught up to me just as I encountered a group of people. They were Gifted, judging by the way a tree's roots tried to wrap themselves around my ankles. I chopped away at them before Caleb found the woman responsible. She wrapped vines and branches around his arms to hold him back, but he broke through them almost as quickly as she summoned them.

Ben looked like he was being tortured by a man with a shaved head and a baby face. He couldn't be over eighteen, with none of the wisdom in his eyes that usually hinted a Gifted had seen more than their looks implied. I would have compared his youth to Tristan, but there was a cruelness to this boy's actions.

I couldn't see anything in his hands, but every time he made a fist, Ben cried out in agony, shaking uncontrollably.

The man facing me could cover himself in scales at will, using them both as a shield whenever I tried to strike, and as a weapon at the end of his arms whenever he took the offensive. Thank God I was fast, because they looked like they could slice through me like I was nothing.

I could see Tristan and a young blonde woman in the distance, facing off against two men who looked ready to pounce, but they were prevented from it by about a dozen wolves, and a couple of bears, who stood between them. It was a testament to Ben's strength, determination, and selflessness that the animals stood their ground, because every time he screamed, they howled, and he had to stop them from rushing to his aid.

ONE MAN TRIED to fight the animals, but the other held him back simply by putting his arm out, telling me he was the one in charge. The subordinate searched for another way through the wild animals, and I got a fleeting glance of his face. He was older and harder than the teenager I knew, but I could have sworn it was "Potts?"

As if to answer my whispered question, the leader tensed up. He turned away from Tristan and Alison, so his ear was towards us.

"Wait," he growled, and every nerve ending in my body responded.

His people froze with such precision that it was like I'd used my Gift on them. Caleb and Ben stopped as well, because we weren't the type to strike an enemy when they weren't fighting back, but only I was literally frozen in place, unable to move a muscle, waiting to see if I'd imagined it. Him. I was acutely aware of how loud my heart was pounding, not to mention my breathing. Luckily, no human could hear such things from that distance. Unless it really was him.

THE PAUSE GAVE me more time to look around and assess our situation, while our opponents did the same. We were five against five, except Alison was a First Lifer not even old enough to drink, and the man beside the leader, who looked both exactly and nothing like Potts, might be able to destroy us in one fell swoop.

The woman who controlled the trees had green hair, like when a blonde spends too much time in a chlorinated swimming pool, only I think she did it on purpose. To be honest, I couldn't tell if it was a dye job, or if her entire body had a greenish tint, as if her Gift was in the process of turning her into a plant.

BEN AND CALEB turned to me, waiting for our next move. Ben had a look in his eyes I could only describe as fear towards whatever that man had done to him, but there was also a fierce determination. He was ready, bracing himself for the fight. All three of us were prepared to die for the cause, for this girl none of us knew.

The group's leader stepped forward in the darkness, letting the new moon's light touch his face, but it was enough. Any shred of denial I was holding on to disappeared. The bridge of his nose, the crook of his chin... I would know his profile anywhere, even in the barest of lights. If I was closer, I would know it by touch, by the very sound of his breathing.

James.

But I couldn't go close. Not when lives were on the line.

James' eyes scanned the forest we were all standing in before they locked on me.

"Lilah," he said under his breath, but the wind had no trouble carrying it to me. It was just one word, my name, but my legs grew weak, and I knew I would let them kill me before I lifted a finger against him.

POTTS – it had to be him – came up from behind James and checked us all out, landing on me with guilt and surprise. "We just want her," he said, putting his giant arms up as if to say he meant us no harm. There was a gleam in the eyes of the man facing Ben that told me Alison wouldn't be so lucky.

"Over our dead bodies."

Caleb had found his way to Tristan, and they both stepped forward, as if hiding Alison would make anyone forget about her. The wild animals stayed close, but their job had been to protect her until we arrived, so it was of their own volition that they stood between Alison and James, but I could already see him winning a wolf over. Knowing him, the others wouldn't be far behind. Which was strange, because you would think hunters would be feared by the animals they hunted, but he'd always had a way with them.

I quickly summed up the group in front of us and tried to guess how many casualties there would be if we fought each other for real. If it was just me, I might have let it happen, but Tristan and Alison were defenseless, with Jackie in the vehicle less than a mile away. She was staying inside, for now, but as soon as she saw the battle going against us, she would be out here – guns blazing – and get herself killed.

I couldn't be responsible for any more children dying.

CHAPTER SEVEN

ALISON

I was grateful that Tristan and a tall blonde boulder stood between me and the men chasing us, implying you would have to go through them to get to me, but I got the feeling these guys wouldn't mind a few dead bodies to get what they wanted. They were inching to come closer, either to kidnap me or tear me apart, and I wouldn't survive either.

I was personally of the opinion that we should run to whatever vehicle Tristan's family came in as fast as my feet could carry me, then keep driving until there was no chance the others could catch up to us, but Delia had a scary determination that I wouldn't want to cross. For the split second she looked at the giant beside the leader, meeting his eyes without a trace of fear, I could swear I saw him flinch.

I held on to Tristan's hand, hoping Delia could broker a truce that didn't involve giving me up, or somehow trick them into letting us go, because we would not survive an actual fight against them. Even if you counted me and Tristan, who I rendered more useless with every touch, they still had at least an extra person worth of height and muscle against us. Not to mention turning themselves into literal scaly weapons.

When Delia stepped up to the leader of the group, I held my breath in expectation of what she was going to do or say, but there was no discussion or arguments. She just…whistled.

I looked around us, expecting armed soldiers to run out of the trees, but the woods were quiet. Maybe Delia had gone mad. Or was using this as a diversion for us to run away? But we weren't.

I tugged on Tristan's sleeve to ask him to run off with me while everyone was distracted, but suddenly, colossal beasts rained down from the sky. One of them was breathing fire, and to be honest, a dragon at this point wouldn't be so far-fetched, but when they got closer, I could see they were made of stone. Or some kind of really flexible stone-like substance that could fly.

The man with the scales tried to slice into the one that came close to him, but the gargoyle was unfazed. When the one who caused pain every time he made a fist realized that his Gift had no effect on them either, the five Gifted who'd run us off the road started running. The leader was the last to go, but I heard screams as they went off into the distance.

Relief flooded me as I went to thank the woman, Delia, but a guy with wavy blond hair yelled, "Back to the vehicle!" and led me to an SUV with the thickest doors I'd ever seen.

"WHAT THE HELL HAPPENED?" A teenage girl with long blonde hair was waiting inside, but she opened the door when she saw us coming. Or heard, I guess. Her eyes were unfocused, staring into the distance between Tristan and I, but seeing nothing. She wore the same black suit as the others. Now that we were close, I could see a logo on the right breast; a red rose over a white mountain range.

"Language," Tristan warned her with a smile.

She adjusted her position based on his voice and rushed into his arms. They were almost the same height, which was surprising, because she'd looked a lot shorter when she got out of the SUV.

"You must be Jackie," I concluded. His blind 'sister person' who sees through other people's eyes.

"Alison! I'm so glad to meet you!" She pulled away from Tristan and reached out to take me in for a hug before I could stop her.

"There'll be time for that once we're home," the guy with wavy blond hair warned, ushering us inside.

Delia looked at the trees as if she expected more people to jump out at us, or for the others to double back. Maybe she was concerned they would track us from the logo on their suits. Then again, after tonight, I was starting to think I had a neon sign attracting them to me.

"You didn't even mean to do that, did you?" Jackie asked once I was sitting between her and Tristan in the back seat. There'd been blankets waiting for us, as if they knew we'd gone for a swim, but it was Tristan's arm pulling me into his body heat that finally got my teeth to stop chattering.

"Do what?" I asked, finally allowing myself to take a breath now that we were relatively safe and driving away from the danger.

"I haven't felt this blind since before Delia," she shared, reminding me she used her Gift to see, and I'd just robbed her of it. Tristan had mentioned she was also a First Lifer, which was another reason I shouldn't get too close to her. It was bad enough I sucked the health right out of my sister; I wouldn't do it to Tristan's.

"It'll come back," he assured her, though we didn't have any specifics. Tristan hadn't been away from me long enough to regain his Gift since he rescued me from the Damned. They were a group of Gifted who would give anything to perma-nently remove their Giftedness, including my life. The Gifted we'd just faced were probably a part of the organization as well.

"I'm sorry. I should have warned you." This was precisely why I'd decided not to touch anyone or anything ever again. Clearly, it was easier said than done.

"Don't worry about it. Tristan warned me about your Gift, I just thought you had to, you know, touch me on purpose."

"Nothing I do is on purpose these days," I argued.

"We can fix that." Jackie smiled confidently. "By we, I mean other people, but they're the best. My Gift used to be nightmare flashes of places and things I didn't recognize until I figured out how to make sense of it all and use it to my advantage."

"You're two for two on using it to find damsels in distress, so it clearly worked." Finding us in a forest in the middle of nowhere would have been nearly impossible without her.

"I see no damsels," Tristan said pointedly, putting his thumb beneath my chin to lift it for a kiss.

"Considering you had already escaped by the time Tristan found you at the factory, and you lured the bad guy away while he was unconscious…you definitely don't qualify as a damsel in distress," Jackie agreed.

"How much do you see?" I asked her. "Have you been watching us since yesterday?" I knew she'd found us by using Tristan's eyes, but I didn't know what made her look in the first place.

"On a day-to-day basis, I'll try to get by on my own. Some people, like Tristan and Delia, will let me use their eyes to watch TV or read a book, since they can do those things too and it's like a bonding experience, while others will let me steal glances if they're in trouble. I like to ask permission first, which I couldn't do with you, and I am so sorry about that, but Tristan, who is usually pretty unfazed, was freaking out and really desperate. He'd also just been dead, so I couldn't say no."

"I would still be in a cell if you hadn't," I assured her, giving Tristan a grateful smile for his part in it.

"Other times, like tonight and when you were kidnapped, I use constant contact, so I can keep track of what's going on and make sure everyone's okay."

"What does it feel like for you?" I knew my eyes burned when it happened, but I was happy to keep the focus on her for a while.

"It feels the same as seeing does for you, only it's weird, because it's not my perspective. I can see all these things I know aren't really in front of me, which is especially confusing if they're on a plane or in the water, anything really different from my reality. But even if the person is right in front of me, it's still off. Like if someone was wearing a head camera, and you were seeing it all through a virtual reality headset. I can't hear what the person is hearing, or their thoughts, but I am getting better at figuring out the big stuff. Like blurred vision usually means someone is crying, people look down when they're sad, constantly look over their shoulders when they're afraid…"

"That's impressive."

"She's being modest. When she's using my eyes, she can tell if I'm lying by where I'm looking, with no idea what I'm saying. And she's usually good at figuring out relationships."

"When you're using their eyes, or…"

"You two are obvious no matter whose eyes I'm using. Even listening to you now, I can tell from your voices when you talk to and about each other… but if you were trying harder to hide it, that probably wouldn't work once I was seeing through your eyes. We look differently at the things we care about, whether it's constantly finding them in a crowd, or looking away so you're not making it obvious…I can tell what you're focusing on, even if it's way in the peripheral."

"But you can hear how much she likes me?" Tristan smiled at me, but he only got a half-hearted one in return.

"When I'm not using my Gift…it's not like a superpower, but my other senses do sort of compensate for the fact that I can't see. Just like people who are hard of hearing read lips. Although, to be honest, I'm pretty crappy at being blind compared to everyone else who does it all the time. I'm good in the dark for familiar places, but if I'm somewhere new, I'll usually cheat."

I found her – and their entire group – fascinating. I knew one of them could control or at least communicate with animals, and the big one literally pulled a tree out of the ground when it tried to hold him prisoner, but I hadn't figured out the other Gifts yet.

"This is the rest of your family?" I asked Tristan, but it was loud enough for the row in front of us to hear.

The boulder-sized human in front of me looked back at Tristan as if he was debating whether he wanted to claim him, before nodding. "I'm Caleb," he told me with a smile.

"Were you the one who sent the bears?" I asked. They were roughly the same size as him, although from up close, with his goofy smile, he looked more like a giant teddy bear than a grizzly.

"No, that was Ben. I'm just really big and strong."

"Which are admirable qualities." I recognized the voice to his right.

"Etta?" I was so frazzled I hadn't recognized her in the training suit, but back in Boston, she'd saved one of my friends with her healing abilities. She'd also made sure Tristan's insides didn't come out of the huge slice he took to the abdomen while protecting me.

"I see you've met my better half." Caleb looked at her like she was the most amazing creature on earth, and she looked at him the same way, before turning back to me.

"Here, let me get that for you."

Without waiting for a response, Etta leaned over to put her hand over the gash above my eye, that I'd completely forgotten about. It felt like when you put your hand a little too close to a fire, where it doesn't burn, but it's almost uncomfortable…and then it felt like nothing at all.

"Thank you," I told her. "Again. For everything."

"You're family now." She shrugged like it was no big deal, but I turned to Tristan. They were either the most welcoming in-laws in life, or they were crazy.

"Because of him too, but more because you're Gifted. A First Lifer," she corrected herself. "We look after each other. At least the good ones do."

While I was talking to Etta, Tristan asked Jackie about other people from Rosehill, and how she worked her way onto this rescue mission when it was against all of Delia's rules. I tried to listen in, to find out more about this strange place I was going to, but the exhaustion from the past week, and today's excitement, knocked me out before Jackie could give him an answer.

CHAPTER EIGHT

ALISON

When I woke up, I was at the front door of what looked like Downton Abbey. There were sweeping grounds and wooded land as far as the eye could see, multiple wings, and more windows than I could count.

"This is Rosehill?" I verified before noticing the plaque beside the double doors. I had pictured a small schoolhouse or community center with a bunch of people crammed in, taking care of each other... not a mansion at the top of the hill on a sprawling estate.

"Delia's family owned the land and built it for her, but it was too much space for one person, so she takes in all the Gifted and First Lifers who don't have a home," Tristan explained. "I wasn't exactly a kid anymore by the time she found me, but I was lost and had never been on my own. Some parents don't understand the Gifts, so they're afraid, some are orphans..."

"We're a band of misfits," Jackie summed them up.

Delia was looking towards the top of the boarding school, where a stone gargoyle landed and took its place on the roof. There were three similar spots that were empty, probably the homes of the gargoyles still chasing our attackers through the woods.

"They'll be back soon," Tristan's surrogate mother said, coming over to me. "I'm Delia, and I am so happy to have you in my home. I promise I will do everything in my power to keep you safe here with us."

"I'm not staying," I argued, seeing her face drop as I did. "Tristan and I...I'm leaving as soon as I get my phone."

"I wouldn't recommend flying in the middle of the night with a pilot who's had no sleep." Delia gave me a conspiratorial smile, then added more when I didn't join in. "I messaged him once we had you both safe. I'm sure he'd be happy to take you once you're ready, but in the meantime—"

"I can find a motel and...I don't want to put you in danger. Or everyone you're already sheltering," I argued. Not that I had a better idea of where I could go, especially not this late without a car or my wallet. I did not want to bring this kind of attack to my parents and little sister, so California was out of the question, but there had to be somewhere I could go that wouldn't put others in danger. I couldn't stand anyone else dying on my account. I wasn't even sure if Tristan should come with me anymore, now that I knew it was nowhere near over. I'd thought Gabriel locking the people who kidnapped me up in a special prison would give us at least a brief respite, but either the FBI was losing their touch, or this was bigger than I'd imagined.

"I won't tell you what to do, but I think the safest place for you is here. We're used to keeping First Lifers safe, and the entire property is protected to varying degrees. No one will get in without my knowledge."

"Protected by the gargoyles?" I asked. They were terrifying to watch, but from what I could see of Rosehill, it was massive, and one touch from Logan – if he ever got out of the FBI's prison – would make Delia's gargoyles crumble into sand.

"By wards and enchantments, but the gargoyles are also a much later line of defense. We even have an ultra-modern, very complicated security system I was forced to learn how to use. I can show you everything in the morning if you concede to stay here for now and make your decision after a good night's rest."

"I hopefully won't stay long enough for you to need any of those." I could leave while everyone was sleeping, under the cover of darkness, while I knew my pursuers were otherwise engaged. But I suspected her security system would work both ways, which meant I wouldn't be able to leave without her knowing. The question was whether she would stop me. And whether I could betray Tristan to keep his family safe.

"I would love to discuss all of this in the living room." She smiled. "I'll go make tea," she added before walking into the house, followed by the others.

I TURNED TO TRISTAN, trying not to judge this woman I knew he looked up to and cared about, but she was weird, and no one else seemed to notice.

"Her Gift is really powerful, so she chooses her words carefully," he explained, but my expression was still blank, so he elaborated. "If she tells you to do something, you have no choice but to obey her command. It goes by intention, so even if she adds words or makes it seem like a question or a request, if she wants you to do it and the words are there, you will."

"Which is why she tells you what she's going to do and hopes you'll read between the lines and follow along," Jackie explained.

"That sounds exhausting." I thought of how much harder life would be if you could never ask for what you wanted, or make suggestions...her whole life was reliant upon other people hopefully wanting to help her.

"Most people love and respect her, so they see what she's asking and do it, no matter what she says. Others fear her and do what she wants because they know she can make them if they don't."

"That's terrifying." I changed my mind about who had the shorter end of that stick.

"It would be, only I've known Delia for almost seven years, and I've never seen her use that Gift."

"Same," Jackie agreed. "And I've been with her for over a decade."

"How are you sure she has it?" It would be an incredibly ballsy move, but Delia exuded enough power and control that no one would question her. It was a weird mix with the warmth she gave off as well.

"One look at anybody who has seen her use it." Jackie gave an involuntary shiver before heading to the giant wooden doors. They bore elaborate carvings, the likes of which I'd only ever seen in old churches, or at the museum. The doorknob was so intricately made that I almost thought it was a real rose left there as a decoration, until Ben, the guy with wavy blonde hair who'd been all business and no nonsense in the woods, used it to open the door.

WE FOLLOWED THE OTHERS INSIDE, where I was once more blown away by Rosehill. The entrance revealed one of those giant, winding staircases that split off at the top, with a larger-than-life painting of hundreds of faces in a crowd. In front of the painting was a suit of armor that the old me might have wanted to get a better look at, but after the gargoyles, I couldn't be sure the knight wouldn't come back to life send attack me. Or show me its tragic death. I planned on keeping my distance.

BY THE TIME we got to the sitting room, I was half-expecting a row of butlers with silver trays of snacks, but it was just us, surrounded by enough art pieces to fill an exhibition. They were all placed on shelves and tables in a way that I wouldn't have even noticed them if I hadn't spent my teenage years working at a museum. It wasn't just for the benefit of the others that I was going to keep my hands to myself while at Rosehill. I could only imagine all the memories contained in the furniture, the art, the books…the walls.

Tristan, Jackie, and I sat together on a giant couch covered in pillows almost as big as me. Jackie brought her legs up and let herself sink into the back of it, while Tristan kept a firm grasp on my hand.

Delia and Etta emerged from the kitchen within minutes, carrying trays of tea and freshly baked croissants for everyone. I felt like I should help, but the last thing I wanted to do was intrude. Or accidentally touch anyone.

Once everyone settled, it was Caleb who asked, "Who were those people?"

"Are they the same people who hurt Grace and took you?" Etta sounded confused. "Gabriel said they arrested everyone who was there." While she and her husband focused on me, the other man in the room hadn't taken his eyes off Delia.

"I would guess they're the Damned?" I looked to Tristan, even though he hadn't been there for most of the explanations when I was kidnapped. I was still foggy on the details, but the Damned were a group of Gifted who felt it was a curse, and wanted to die in peace without constantly coming back to life. The ones I met also wanted to keep me locked up in a lab for the rest of my life so they could experiment on me. "They think my blood contains the cure to Giftedness."

"They're not Damned," Delia said with certainty. "But I assume the Damned hired them to bring you in."

"Because you knew him." Jackie's voice was weak and tentative. I'd assumed she was watching through Tristan's eyes, but our earlier conversation hinted that she'd used Delia's point of view, and that she'd seen something.

"Centuries ago, when we were both very different people," Delia agreed. I thought she would have denied it, or blushed at being found out, but all I saw in her face was pain and regret. "His Gift is hunting, or rather tracking people down with heightened skills and the utmost precision. In my experience, he always gets his target." She said it calmly, just laying down the facts, but my heart was about to pounce out of my chest from how terrified it was. "Which is why the safest place for you is right here."

"If what you say about him is true, having her here endangers every single person under this roof. The boys, Penny…all of us."

I don't think Ben meant it in a mean way. His inflection implied that he agreed with Delia's conclusion and was just making sure she knew what she was getting everyone into, but boy, did the words make me feel like a terrible person.

"Ben," Delia warned, with a glance in my direction. He sighed, but immediately stopped arguing.

"Can you talk to him? Maybe if you ask him to leave us alone and explain that Alison isn't a threat…" Jackie suggested, shifting the focus onto Delia.

"Mercenaries are usually paid to accomplish a task and don't stop until it is done," Etta said gently, offering Jackie another croissant. Unfortunately, I'd put them all in a position food wouldn't fix.

"That's perfect. We have lots of money." Jackie was undeterred, and if the rooms I'd seen were any indication, Delia could purchase a few small countries without financing.

"Based on the ones I've met; their honor is worth more than whatever you pay them. If they gave their word, they'll die rather than break it. Especially if they're Gifted, and their death means nothing," Caleb spoke up.

I gave an involuntary swallow at the thought that these people would lay down their lives to get me, and even if we killed them all, they would keep coming back until I was dead. Or as good as.

"How certain are you that the magical protections will hold against them? Or that their Gifts can't come through?" It was Tristan who asked, and at first, I rolled my eyes at the seriousness with which he said 'magical protections', but then I remembered Ben screaming in those woods while one of my assailants tortured him. I swallowed again, magic no longer sounding far-fetched or funny.

"I have complete faith in them. I just need to verify their limits, to know where is safe from what. They were designed to make Rosehill a haven where First Lifers and Gifted could find refuge, and have withstood more than you can imagine."

Tristan looked at me, then around the room. I did too, expecting at least some of them to glare at us in a 'we don't want you here' way, but I only saw resigned determination as they nodded, with Jackie even going so far as to reach out and find me to give my arm a reassuring squeeze.

"I'll worry less having you here," Delia added.

"If you're out there, I'll just be constantly in your eyeballs, making sure you're okay," Jackie warned. "That is once I get my Gift back. But it's not like you can leave until Tristan can shock people again, so I've got time."

I looked down and saw Tristan's hand still held mine. My instinct was to pull my hand away, but his was to hold me tighter.

"Maybe I should just go on my own. That way, everyone is safe, and no one has to worry." I wished my voice sounded more confident, but it was the best option for them and the people already sheltering here from the outside world.

I knew Tristan would be upset at the idea and argue with it, but I wasn't prepared for absolutely everyone in the room to talk at once; a combination of letting me know it was the stupidest idea they'd ever heard, and at least three people volunteering to accompany me instead of Tristan if I was too afraid of losing him. The consensus was that there was no way in hell I could go off on my own.

Tristan's pressed lips and flared nostrils told me both that he understood why I suggested such a thing, and that he felt betrayed.

"I only *look* seventeen, Allie, and contrary to how I make it seem when I'm around you, I can take care of myself," he told me while Ben and Caleb argued about who would be better at protecting me if I insisted on leaving Rosehill.

"I can't lose you, and I would rather die than hurt more people." I knew it sounded like something people said without meaning it, before they encountered real danger and changed their mind, but while I was far from seasoned, I had the very vivid images of Grace on the floor in a pool of her own blood, and my sister fighting for her life in a hospital bed to remind me I absolutely meant it.

"Then let's just stay while we figure out where to go and make a game plan."

Ever since he'd found out I was in danger, he'd wanted to bring me here, so I knew he wanted to stay, but I could see he would still follow me to the ends of the earth if I decided not to.

"If you're sure you can keep everyone safe, we can stay a few days, until the coast is clear," I relented, bringing an end to Caleb's long list of reasons why he was better suited to protect me than someone called Rosenberg.

Delia nodded at my acceptance, but the unspoken truth behind her smile was that she wasn't sure she could keep anyone safe, and unless the Damned got what they wanted, my coast would never be clear.

I made the mistake of looking out the window, at the hypothetical 'coast', and found a grotesque stone carving staring back at me. We had a sculpture back at the museum whose eyes were carved in a way that it seemed like they followed you, no matter where you stood, but this creature was literally watching our conversation. I jumped, first because it had not looked that big out in the woods, and then because it blinked.

I caught Delia watching the gargoyle as well, but instead of being startled, she smiled and nodded her head, giving it permission to fly away. I didn't know how long I was staying at Rosehill, but it would not be long enough to get used to that.

"I think it is high time to get some sleep," Delia suggested. I had no idea what time it was – other than before sunrise – but my eyes did not want to stay open. "You know where the spare bedrooms are, but she might feel more comfortable with you." She turned to Tristan, who nodded.

"They won't come back tonight, right?" Jackie verified, trying to sound like she didn't care one way or the other, but I could hear the fear behind her nonchalance.

"I'll ask the gargoyles to keep watch, just in case," Delia assured her with a motherly smile. She pressed her hand to the teenager's cheek, then took her in for a goodnight hug that sent a terrible pang straight to my chest. I missed my mom something fierce and wanted more than anything to borrow someone's phone so I could hear her voice, but I was old enough to know that a call in the middle of the night when I was scared was a thousand times worse than no call at all. Another thing to figure out in the morning.

"We'll keep you safe."

Either my exhausted eyes were playing tricks on me, or mopey Ben – who had yet to smile – had just winked at Jackie, hinting there might be a softer side to him after all.

"How do you feel?" Tristan brushed the hair from my face and smiled once we stood up and he saw how tired I was.

"A million things you can't fix. But sleeping might help a bit." I tried to be encouraging, because I would feel better than I currently did once I slept, but then I would also be able to think clearly and realize there were people sent to kill me, who wouldn't stop until they had me, and if any of them bothered to look into me, they would go straight for my parents and Sybill.

"Most of the visitors get a room in the South wing. Some of them are taken, waiting for their occupants to return, but you could have your pick of the ones that are left. Those of us who live here on a more permanent basis stay in the East wing." Tristan talked as we walked, holding my hand as he led me up the stairs, stopping on the landing with the suit of armor.

My mind was too busy going over my options – and being wary of the suit – to realize he was waiting for me to give him an answer.

"I'll sleep better knowing you're safe with me…but I don't mind if you'd prefer your own room to process everything," he assured me.

"I don't expect to actually sleep tonight, or any night as long as I'm a danger to everyone I come close to, but the only place I feel safe right now is in your arms."

"Then in my arms you shall stay," he said, pulling me close. "But I don't have a couch," he warned, getting the tiniest of smiles out of me. Back at my house, I felt like it was too big a step to sleep together in my childhood bed, so we spent the week on the living room couch.

"Your old bones need a proper bed, anyway." I shrugged.

"I'm only twenty-four, all things considered," he reminded me.

"Are you sure it's not slowly killing you? Being this close to me. You haven't been able to use your Gift since…since yesterday." I wasn't about to go into specifics on the time he died trying to protect me, then came back to life.

"I rarely use my Gift, and I feel fine. If it's a question of using my Gift or holding you, you win. No contest."

It was sweet, but also stupid. I didn't know what protections Delia had in place, but the moment they fell, Tristan and I would be sitting ducks, unless someone else risked their life for me.

For tonight, I was too tired to argue.

I got a thrill at the idea that I could explore his bedroom and maybe discover a secret or two, but almost as soon as I sat on the bed, I was out.

CHAPTER NINE

DELIA

I headed upstairs with everyone else, but I passed my bedroom and continued to the servant's staircase at the other end of the hall. Not that we'd had servants at Rosehill in over a century, but kids loved discovering secret passageways, and sometimes, you just needed to get around without encountering prying eyes.

Instead of getting off on the main level like I usually did, I took the second staircase to the basement. No one ever went down there, unless something broke or, God forbid, we had to use a car from the back garage, which were neither insured, nor particularly roadworthy. Penny called it the dungeon, and even Brandon was reluctant to go down on his own. We used to use it all the time to get to the carriage stables, but it became pointless once we moved the horses to the larger, more comfortable barn.

Behind the main stairwell, there was a door that usually hid cleaning supplies, or whatever one keeps under one's staircase. I had to dust away a few cobwebs and was careful to make as much noise as possible to scare away any rats without waking those sleeping upstairs. After squeezing through a few more doorways, I found the underground tunnel to be just as it always was. Cold and dark, but ready to guide all Rosehill's occupants to safety.

I walked with purpose to the chamber where we had nonperishable supplies, blankets, first aid kits, and anything else we might need if there was a siege keeping us locked in. I was not the best at keeping it stocked, made painfully clear by the canned peaches from 1982. I made a mental note to order extra supplies from Mr. Bosworth, then continued along the stone walls, using a lantern from the chamber to light my way instead of my cell phone.

I got to the end and found the old wooden chair intended for the guard, or whoever would let everyone in. I had vivid memories of old Frank, who sat guard during the Eclipse, or little Timmy, who spent an entire summer standing on that chair to get a better look at every person going in or out, to make sure they weren't a changeling. I'd warned James about age-appropriate bedtime stories, but the two of them always told me, "The scarier the better!"

I'D WANTED the gargoyles to get the threat away from the people I cared about, but I hadn't intended for Lorcan to burn them alive. Unlike my Gift, that I was happy to keep buried, my gargoyle adored using his, often helping the students roast marshmallows, or lighting up the skies instead of a bonfire whenever we spent the evening on the beach. I checked my watch again and saw it was an hour since Lorcan had returned, which gave someone ample time to drive to the path's entrance and dig up what must be at least a century of weeds and thorn bushes since we last used it. Though I suppose he would have tried the greenhouse first, unaware of the magical protections that made it off-limits to non-guests over a century ago. They'd tried to seal off the tunnels as well, since they were the only part of Rosehill that left us vulnerable, but the tunnels had their own secrets and protections that didn't need wards or enchantments.

AFTER A HALF AN HOUR, I wondered if maybe he wasn't coming. Maybe he'd forgotten the way, or they were gone to get reinforcements first. I went through the traditional, "I'll give him five more minutes," twice before I decided to seal the tunnel off like I should have done in the first place. It was equipped with various points at which you could pull a lever and cause the tunnel to cave in; a last line of defense if the entrance was breached. It pained me to destroy something that stood for so long, but the enchantments didn't span the length of the tunnel, and I couldn't risk my family upstairs.

"Lilah."

I heard his voice and froze, my heart pounding faster than if I'd just run a marathon. He was the only one to call me by that name. Gabriel had tried a few times in the beginning, but he settled on Delia after he saw my heart breaking every time James' nickname for me came from someone else's lips.

I'd been hoping for this moment since I recognized him in the woods, and was disappointed when I thought he hadn't come, but now that he was here, I wished I was back upstairs in my room, safe from all the things this conversation could lead to.

"James." I swallowed before turning around to face him in the shadows. He raised his torch, and while his face was the same as always, the darkness of his eyes shocked me. They'd been black for centuries, a telltale sign that someone is Gifted, but every time I looked at him, I always expected them to be blue, like the first time I saw them. "You came alone," I pointed out.

"So did you." He looked down the hallway to verify that fact, but then his eyes rested on me, taking in every inch, from the hair I'd tied in a high ponytail and the Rosehill training suit, to the combat boots I was more used to seeing on him. The clothes he wore were different as well; a relaxed pair of jeans and construction-type boots, with a fitted gray Henley. It suited him better than a lot of the 'costumes' he'd worn with me at court, or at least he looked more comfortable.

He'd left the buttons at the top of his shirt open, revealing the St. Christopher's medallion my mother had given me. I'd given it to James when he was protecting us, hoping it would somehow keep him safe. I felt a pang in my chest that he still wore it, but it wasn't like I'd removed the wedding ring that now lived on a chain around my neck.

I put my hands into fists when his eyes got to my fingers, searching for the ring. It was easy to imagine what went through his mind as he inspected the modernness of everything I wore, but it was the way his eyes lingered in certain places, trying to see how much I had changed, that made me nervous.

I waited until his eyes came back up and settled on my collarbone to respond.

"What are you doing here?" My intention was to stare him down and let him know he had no business being here, but I was failing.

"I came for the girl," James said, breaking my heart a little. He swallowed hard when he saw my reaction, which was stronger than it should have been. Than I wanted it to be.

It wasn't in James' nature to be cruel, but if there was anything harder than seeing him out of the blue after this long, it was the fact that he wasn't even here for me.

"But then I saw you and…" He trailed off, his glassy eyes pleading with mine, though I don't think even he knew what they were asking for.

He was close enough that I could smell the alcohol on him.

Not like he'd had a beer with friends after work to take the edge off, but like he'd made it a habit to finish a bottle of Jack before bed. It hurt to see him like that, when he'd spent so long giving second chances to other men who'd lost themselves, helping them find their way back. Then again, he'd been much worse the last time I'd seen him.

"And what?" I pressed, willing my face not to betray me.

"You protected her." His face was hard, but then it softened. "In your matching super spy outfits."

The corner of his mouth lifted into a smirk. I wanted to reciprocate, but it had been too long, and as much as I wanted to, I couldn't let my guard down. Not completely.

"We're a team," I defended my outfit choice, then turned it on him. "Since when do you work for the Damned?"

"I'm a gun for hire, Lilah. I work for myself." Even as he said the words, his thumb reached for the golden signet ring on his left pinky, which designated the leader of an ancient order known for their goodness and bravery; a reminder that he represented more than one person.

"So much for Guardians living to protect." It was a low blow, and I hated myself for taking it, but maybe he needed the tough love.

I'd hit a nerve, obvious from the way his breathing changed, in and out through the nose to calm himself, while to the person he was arguing with it would sound like he was a wild bull about to charge. It was incredibly effective on most people, but I'd always defused the situation by laughing at his overly serious expression. Sadly, we weren't those people anymore, and convictions backed his anger rather than stubbornness.

"Protecting means eliminating threats as much as defending the hunted."

"You used to only kill the ones who deserved it," I reminded him.

"She does."

The fire in his eyes reminded me of the last time we had this argument, about the difference between killing in cold blood and killing to protect people.

"She's a twenty-year-old college student who spends most of her life helping others," I argued. "What part of that warrants her death, other than a Gift she never asked for and has yet to figure out how to use? The James I knew would protect her from an army trying to bleed her dry for their own purposes. Especially the Damned," I reiterated. The only thing worse would be if he had banded with the New Order.

"That isn't…I'm not doing this for them, Lilah, this is for me. She's…" I could see the anger behind whatever he was about to tell me, but he made himself take a deep breath. "She's a Carmichael," he admitted.

The look on his face was desolate, his head tilted and lips pressed together. He hadn't wanted to hurt me, but he expected this to change my mind. It didn't, but at least it explained his interest.

"Yes, Alison Carmichael," I agreed. My calm shocked him in a way that made me feel guilty. He looked as betrayed as I felt.

"I wish I had your forgiving soul." The words were like acid from his lips as his anger returned.

"She's done nothing wrong except for being born into his family. If you go back far enough, no one is innocent."

"It's not the same thing. Her bloodline is poison, no matter how hard she tries to fight it."

"You sound just like *him*."

James looked at me like I'd cut him, but he had to know it was true. The mentality that people can't change, or grouping them together and assuming they're like the worst of their kind…those were New Order principles, not ours.

"I'm still coming for her, Lilah, and I won't stop until I have her," he warned instead of attempting to defend himself.

"I know," I said simply. In all the centuries I'd spent with him, not a single person got away once he was after them, unless he let them.

"But you still choose her?"

"From where I'm standing, it feels like you're doing the same."

"I can smell him on her. That man who—"

"She's just a child." I cut him off. "And a First Lifer, which Rosehill is here to protect."

He shook his head at me, then sighed, both of us aware that not even the soundest of arguments could sway the other when we were like this.

"I won't show this to them," he told me softly. "I will get her, but this is ours, and using it…betraying us to get her defeats the purpose. I will not back down, but I won't use us against you. You're not my enemy. You're just in my way."

"If only I could trust you."

The hurt on his face would have been anger if he hadn't found the same pain on mine.

"I never break a promise," he reminded me.

"I won't bury you on your way out."

He gave me the tiniest, saddest of smiles before turning to leave. He'd barely taken a step before he turned back and reached for me. You didn't need Tristan's Gift to feel the sparks when he touched my hand, traveling deep into my soul.

"Lilah…" His eyes locked on mine, asking me to come with him. A request I wanted so badly to entertain, if only I could listen to my heart and ignore everything else.

"I can't," I said, my hand shaking as I pulled it away.

"Be safe." He stood to his full height, over six feet of pure muscle, and exited the tunnel, letting in the early morning light.

. . .

I STAYED THERE LONGER than I should have, watching the door. I told myself it was because I needed to make sure he stuck to his word and didn't come back with his friends, but I knew the real reason was because a large part of me wished I had gone with him. Not against Alison and Tristan, of course, but that delusional part of my head, or heart, that believed if I had followed him, I could have convinced him to leave them alone.

But if I wasn't enough to stop him back then, there wasn't much I could do now.

I CLOSED and barricaded the door, then made my way back through the tunnel, ignoring the voice in my head that told me this was a liability. That the levers were put there for a reason. But the tunnel was too.

I eyed the last lever and debated it. We would be safer from James and his friends if the tunnel was gone, but it was also our last resort escape route, and there were people outside who could use it to get to us if they needed to. More importantly, I trusted him. James was by no means perfect, and he'd done his fair share of terrible things, but he'd never broken his word if he could help it, especially not to me.

I left the tunnel as it was, but before leaving the basement, I went to the keypad and armed it. There was no reason for anyone else to come down without my knowledge, and at least we would be warned if I was wrong.

I TOOK the normal route back to my bedroom, rehearsing the lies I would tell if anyone was up early enough to run into me, but Rosehill was blessedly quiet this morning, probably because most of us got in late, and Tristan was my only early riser out of the younger ones. Not that he was a child, but just like Chris, I could never see him the same way I saw Ben or

Caleb, no matter how many years he spent with us, or how old he got.

The hallway to my quarters was empty, so I breathed a sigh of relief as I shut the heavy doors behind me. Not that I didn't love Penny rushing in occasionally to see if I was awake, but while I wouldn't be able to sleep much this morning, I did want to process the jumble of emotions that made me want to either scream or burst into tears. Perhaps both.

I went to rest my back against the door and nearly jumped out of my skin when I found Ben waiting in the sitting area before my bedroom. By the looks of him, he'd been sitting there since I called an end to our family meeting.

"What's wrong?" I asked as innocently as I could.

"What's the deal with you and their leader?"

He didn't seem to know where I had been, or even that I'd gone anywhere other than the greenhouse – my usual haunt when I couldn't sleep – so I relaxed. He sounded more hurt that I hadn't told him than reproachful of my involvement with the enemy.

"What do you mean?" I played dumb. Jackie had seen James through my eyes, so an accusation from her would be harder to deny, but Ben wasn't a mind reader. All he had was doubt.

"He looked at you like Caleb looks at Etta," he argued. I knew he wanted to say that James looked at me the way he does, but neither of us wanted him to go there.

"He looked like he wanted us dead," I corrected him. And it was true, until he'd realized I was there. Then he just looked betrayed.

"Most of the time, yes. He looked like an angry, wild animal. But not when he saw you. Or rather, smelled you." He sounded disgusted at the thought, but it made sense that Ben, who could communicate with animals, would notice James' somewhat animalistic tendencies when he was hunting his prey.

I knew lying would hurt him more, and depending on how

long James stayed on target, it might all eventually come out, but I couldn't face him knowing the truth. Not yet.

"We were close once, but it was centuries ago, and I hadn't seen him since we parted ways. Not until last night."

"He was before Gabriel?" Ben asked, a hint of their old rivalry resurfacing. It was hard for people to understand that while Gabriel and I spent decades with each other, we had been completely devoted to our past loves. We were siblings rather than lovers, helping each other shoulder centuries of pain. Had this reunion occurred under different circumstances, I would have called him immediately, but it felt selfish to complain to Gabriel about my heart, when James had come to harm Alison.

"Long before," I agreed.

Ben looked like he wanted to ask more, but love had always been a topic we skirted around to the best of our abilities. There was nothing to be gained from Ben finding out that although it was forever ago, it also lasted for centuries. That James was the man who had loved me so fiercely that losing him broke me. The one my heart still belonged to, which prevented Ben from getting his happily ever after.

"If they come after her here, and we have to…will you be okay?" he asked instead, making me wish, not for the first time, that I could be the woman he wished I was.

"I'll be fine," I assured him with a smile so convincing I almost believed it myself.

"I hope he doesn't. For your sake," Ben said, getting up and heading to the hallway.

"For my sake?" I asked.

"If he so much as thinks of hurting someone I care about, I'll kill him," he explained. I couldn't even consider James hurting any of the younger Rosehill occupants, but the way Ben was looking at me implied breaking my heart was included in that threat. "And so will Tristan if he touches Alison."

My heart tightened, because I knew they would both try to

live up to that threat. Ben mistook my sadness and left the room without another word, but it wasn't James I was worried about. It was Alison, Tristan, and Ben. Because I'd seen what everyone could do, and was grateful I'd never been on the opposite side of James' wrath. I wasn't going to lose him to one of them, but I would not be able to forgive James if he hurt them.

CHAPTER TEN

ALISON

I woke up in a four-poster bed with heavy hanging drapes that were open to let in the bright sunlight. The spot beside me was empty but still warm, which meant Tristan wasn't too far away. I considered going back to sleep, but if I had to guess, it was already past noon, and I had a lot of figuring out to do.

The floor was freezing on my bare feet, but Tristan had thought ahead and left me a fluffy pair of slippers, along with a plush housecoat, to tempt me away from the covers.

His room was decorated more like a college dorm than a childhood bedroom, although the antique desk and wardrobe looked like they belonged in a museum. I assumed most of it was there when Tristan arrived, but he'd added his own touches as well. There were framed photographs of his family on the bureau, with his parents and sisters all boasting the same thick mess of dark hair. His mom's eyes were dark brown, almost as dark as his were now, but I could see that once upon a time, he and his sisters had inherited their father's bright green eyes. I had forgotten that Gifted didn't age, and expected Tristan to look younger in the pictures of his family at the beach, but the major difference, other than his eyes, was his body type. In the photographs, he was clearly the weakest link, beaming at the camera while withering away at the same time. He was Captain America before the super soldier serum. Not that Tristan was anywhere near as bulky as Caleb now…but he was built. He hid it under multiple layers and jackets, but he could easily carry me up flights of stairs if he had to. Or wanted to.

There was one picture that wasn't like the others, taken more recently at a black-tie event in a fancy ballroom, possibly at Owens Manor. It showed Doctor Black and his fiancée, Caleb and Etta, Delia and Ben, Jackie and Tristan, and a bunch of people I didn't know toasting something with the brightest smiles I'd ever seen on the Rosehill gang. Though I hadn't exactly met them under the best circumstances last night.

"Spying on me?" Tristan asked, coming in with a neatly folded pile of clothes.

"Trying to." I turned to face him instead of the row of pictures. The rest of the room would have to wait, though there wasn't much to it.

"I figured you might want some clean clothes, since we abandoned our bags with the car." He handed me the pile, which contained a pair of shorts, a tank top, a light button down, a pair of sweatpants, and a sweatshirt. "I tried to get what I thought you might wear, but I also got something really comfy in case you would rather stay in here and try to feel safe and cozy for a bit."

"It's perfect," I assured him, although 'safe' felt like a distant memory from lifetimes ago. I wondered if the clothes were Delia's, or if Rosehill had a room full of items for runaways like me. There were no tags to say the clothes were new, but they looked it, even the sweatsuit with 'Rosehill Academy' on the front. I ran my fingers over the logo's stitching, recognizing it from their outfits from last night.

"An old student designed the school uniform to make everyone feel like they were a part of something," Tristan explained. "The lounge wear wasn't as popular as the training suits, but Delia was very proud of her *budding fashionista* – who has now graduated from a fancy design school in Los Angeles – and ordered everything in bulk. She's very supportive of all the alumnae."

"Is that usually what happens? The kids graduate and move away like a regular boarding school?" I asked before realizing he might take offence, or feel weird about the fact that he was no longer a kid, yet still lived there.

"It depends on whether they're Gifted or First Lifers, why they came here, who they have waiting for them…"

"How many people live here now?" I made sure not to call them students, or kids, because he was neither.

"Rosehill has twenty-odd students and half a dozen teachers during the school year, but most of them go home for the summer. We're nine in the 'family' who live here full time, but even if you live somewhere else, like Gabriel or Caleb…once you're in, your bedroom is always there, waiting for you to come home."

I felt a tightness in my chest at the word, because all I wanted to do was go home. I nodded instead and went to get ready in the en-suite bathroom.

WHILE THE HOUSE itself was ancient, the bathroom was not. There was a large, clawfoot bathtub I could not picture Tristan ever soaking in, as well as one of those showers that's like a waterfall, coming at you from above, in addition to the regular shower head. I was just going to change my clothes, but a chunk of dried mud on my forearm quickly changed my mind.

I WOULDN'T EXACTLY SAY the waterfall shower washed away my worries, but I felt a lot better after I'd showered and slept for a few hours. The clothes Tristan chose fit perfectly, and although I didn't know what my next move would be, I was ready to figure it out.

"Are you hungry?" Tristan asked when I got out and braided my hair to keep it out of my face. The bed was made, and the windows were open, letting in a warm summer breeze.

"Starving," I said as my stomach grumbled.

"Delia's waiting downstairs." He came over and tucked a tag into the back of my shirt, his fingers brushing my neck in the process. It sent shivers down my spine that made me want to spend the day in the room with him instead, pretending I'd never heard of Gifted, but it also reminded me of the sparks, and how that touch was enough to strip him of his powers. Ignoring my problems would not make them go away.

"For us?" I asked.

"She was hoping to show you around Rosehill after we eat."

"Just me?" I tried not to be nervous, or at least not to show him, but right now there was a very short list of people I trusted, and Delia taking me in was very generous, but not something a sane person would do when they had a family and people were trying to kill me.

"I can come if you need me to, but Jackie asked if I could—"

"No, of course, you should hang out with your sort of adopted sister," I assured him, using his terminology. "Delia is nice. And she's literally risking the life of everyone she cares about to keep me here safe, so I'm sure I'll be fine." I knew the words were true, but they weren't as comforting as I wanted them to be. I would feel a lot better with Tristan there, which he could tell.

"I can hang out with Jackie another time. It's not a big deal," he assured me, leading me out the room.

"No, I'm teasing. It'll be nice to get to know your people, maybe find out some secrets." I forced myself to give him a convincing smile. "And it's only fair I let Jackie have you this morning after I blinded her last night."

"Her Gift is back. As of at least five minutes ago. She texted to see where I was, then checked in before I could reply."

"Checked in as in saw through your eyes to find out where you were?" I asked, to which he nodded. "And you let her do that whenever she wants?"

"During the day, when she knows I'm up and about," he argued. "And you can block her out if you know how and work at it. It's like how you can put walls up so people have trouble getting into your mind, only it's with your eyes. And I'm not someone with a vital piece of information she needs to save the planet, so if she tries and there's resistance, she won't push."

"You say all that like it's normal and you have experience blocking people from reading your mind. I'm having trouble wrapping my head around any of it."

"I've had years to adjust. You're going on a month."

I shrugged, not sure I would ever be that comfortable with it. "Did you say she texted you? As in phones work here and you found yours?"

"This is not a prison. It's secluded and protected because you're not the first First Lifer who needed a safe place to hide, but everyone can come and go as they please. And Delia has a stash of cell phones because, back in the day, I fried a lot of them." He handed me an iPhone. "Yours is on the charger in my room, but feel free to let everyone know you're okay and that Malcolm doesn't have to make good on his threats."

Lying had never been my strong suit, so I texted my mom and told her I dropped my phone in the bathtub, but everything else was life as usual, then wracked my brain for Malcolm's number. I'd programmed it into my cell phone, which meant I'd had no reason to remember it anymore.

"Try Gabriel," Tristan suggested, waiting at the top of the stairs so I wouldn't fall down them with my eyes on the screen.

"Because of his FBI connections?" It would probably be quicker to call the precinct and ask for Detective Malcolm Cortez.

"Because Grace wasn't getting discharged until Monday…"

"Of course!" I shook my head at how silly I was. Even if Malcolm wasn't in his mother's room, Enrique would know how to get in touch with him. I didn't want to write a novel, so I just reminded Gabriel who I was and asked him to tell Malcolm that there was a change in plans, but I was safe.

"Good morning!" Delia said when we finally got to the kitchen. Her smile was fake, like the ones Tristan used to give me when he was upset and didn't want to ruin my day, but her warmth was real. "I can whip up some breakfast if that's what you're in the mood for, but Chris made Tristan's favorite when he found out he was home."

"Kraft Dinner?" I raised an eyebrow when I saw the orange noodles in her bowl.

"With the cheese powder sprinkled on top." Tristan was thrilled.

"I tried recreating it with fancier, less radioactive ingredients, but he likes the one from the box best. Comfort foods." A man defended himself as he put the bowls in front of us. I would put him at mid-to-late thirties, but his hair was already more salt than pepper. "I'm Chris," he told me, wiping his hand on an apron before putting it out to shake mine.

I went to oblige, but I didn't want to take anymore from Tristan's adoptive family, so I held my hand back and bit my bottom lip, wondering if he'd just forgotten, or if I had to warn him about my 'Gift'.

"Oh, I'm not one of them." He read my reluctance. "My parents were. They fought alongside Delia, then taught at the school, so when they died in a car crash, my godmother took me in." He gave Delia a warm smile before turning to me. "I know, a car crash, of all things, but my dad got used to driving like he would never die."

"I'm Alison." I shook the hand he still had outstretched for me, although after the damage I did to Sybill, regular humans weren't safe with me either.

"I'm not the help, so I don't clean, but I cook most of the meals when I'm here. If there's something you like, or anything you're allergic to, please let me know."

"Will do," I assured him. He gave Delia's hand a squeeze before going back to the kitchen, where there was a lot of banging around with pots and pans.

"He was young when his parents died, and furious because, up to that point, he believed superheroes couldn't die," Delia shared while we ate. It tasted just like when my dad would make it, but the extra sprinkle on top added a nice kick.

"He owns a really fancy restaurant in New York, but spends his summers here. We weigh significantly more at the end of August than we do in June," Tristan added between bites.

Delia gave him a look like she was about to defend herself and her cooking, but decided he was right and let it go.

"Are you guys still eating the radioactive cheese imposter?" Jackie asked when she came in with her arms full of jars. Some looked empty, while others had fireflies inside.

"We were just finishing," I assured her. Tristan's bowl was nearly empty.

"Alison, I would love to show you around, introduce you to everyone, and answer any questions you might have about Rosehill?" Delia offered. "We try to be a home, not a prison."

I wondered if she didn't know Tristan had already warned me, or if she just felt it was more polite to ask and pretend I had a choice.

"That sounds great." I tried to hide my nerves.

Tristan kissed the top of my head before going off with

Jackie, and while I didn't think he was using her as a replacement Serena, he definitely enjoyed having a little sister to get into trouble with while he was here.

"It's so good to see him truly happy."

Delia was watching me watch them. She had her hair back in a French braid and wore a bright yellow tank top with a flowy white skirt that made her look less like a headmistress and more like the lead in a romantic comedy. Until you got to her feet, where she wore combat boots.

"He's been through a lot." I had every intention of explaining to Delia why I had to leave as soon as possible, but she saw right through me.

"We all have, and so have you," she reminded me. "I know we think it's better to go off on our own and deal with our troubles, so they won't affect the people we love, but I've always fared better when I had help. And it's nice to not have the added problem of worrying about the person who ran off to save you from worrying about them."

"I'm not sure it's the same thing when your problem is that people are after you and won't hesitate to kill anyone who stands in their way."

"Which is why I am going to show you Rosehill."

"I would love to see it," I told her honestly, but I doubted the sprawling grounds would change my mind.

I EXPECTED her to bring me to a massive weapons room, or to show me a secret army she was holding in the basement, but she just grabbed a Tupperware full of chocolate chip cookies and headed outside. I could see a beach in the distance, with crystal clear water that would be so refreshing on this hot summer day, a barn with wild animals grazing around, and what looked like an obstacle course in the distance. Delia ignored these and ventured into the part of the estate that was covered by trees.

We went through an opening in a brick wall to follow a path deeper into the woods. There was an ornamental wrought-iron gate, but it was left open, and wouldn't stop anyone from getting in.

After a few minutes, we reached a single-story house with lots of windows and wind chimes that gave it a dreamlike, ethereal quality.

"Delia!" A little girl with big brown eyes ran up to her from the side of the house, followed by an Indian couple.

"I brought cookies," Delia shared, bringing her eyebrows up as she handed over the Tupperware.

"Appa's favorite!" The girl ran over and handed it to the man, whispering something in his ear that resulted in him handing her a cookie.

"Alison, I would love to introduce you to Mohinder, Sakina, and Krishna Patel."

"A pleasure to meet you," Mohinder told me, stepping aside so I could enter their home. The main room looked a bit like a yoga studio, only instead of yoga mats, there were piles of cushions in every color you could imagine.

"Likewise," I said quickly, realizing I was being rude, but their place was distracting. Besides pillows, there were targets and practice dummies, some of which were covered in holes and burn marks, but I didn't see any weapons.

"When I first discovered my…Gift," Delia swallowed like that wasn't the word she wanted to use, "my father sent me to Sakina so I could learn how to control it."

"How long ago was that?" I asked before I could stop myself. "I'm sorry if that's not okay to ask, I just—"

"It's fine." She cut off my rambling with a smile. "It was a little over five centuries ago."

"She was just a little girl, so lost…I wanted to hold her close and never let her go." Sakina looked at Delia like she could still see her that way.

"You were a First Lifer too?"

"Back then we called her Blessed." Sakina smiled, but Delia waved her off.

"That wasn't the only thing they called me." She let out a breath. "A lot has changed since the 1490s. Though some of it has stayed the same."

"Let's not remind me how old I am," Sakina warned. "I don't know my year of birth, which I believe means I am ageless."

"You don't look a day over twenty-five," I assured her, hoping that was a good number. In truth, I would guess early forties, as her black hair was going gray at her temples.

"I like her," Sakina told Delia, putting an iron kettle on the stove.

"What's your poison?" Mohinder asked me.

"I don't really drink, but tea would be lovely." Considering I was underage, I didn't drink at all, except for a few mojitos with my boss back in Boston. She'd been under the assumption I was Gifted and only pretending to be twenty, but I'd needed it with the First Life bombshell she'd dropped on me.

"He means your Gift, but he thinks he's funny," Sakina explained.

"I get memories when I touch things," I said loosely, looking to Delia, who gave me an encouraging smile. "But when I touch people, they lose their Gifts. And get sick."

Mohinder nodded in understanding while Sakina gave me a look of sympathy.

"What's your Gift, if you call them poison?"

"Empathy."

"Like empathizing with people?" I wonder if I had the wrong definition for that word.

"I can feel people's emotions, which is great when it's someone who is happy and excited, or full of wonder…"

"But not so cool when they're depressed. Or evil," I understood.

"Or stressed, or exhausted, or simply having a bad day." He gestured with his hand to tell me the list went on and on.

"Does it happen all the time, or do you have to be touching the person?"

"I can feel for miles without effort, but If I'm touching you, I can choose to take your emotion away. I can absorb your pain into myself and deal with it for you."

"Can you turn it off?"

"I've mastered the art of turning it off during the day, but when I'm sleeping…let's just say my dreams depend heavily on my surroundings."

"Is that why you don't stay in the mansion with everyone else?"

"One of the reasons," Sakina agreed, pouring us each a cup of tea. Darjeeling if I had to guess. "We like a quiet life, and wanted Krishna to grow up as normal as possible."

"She's not Gifted, is she?" She looked happy, but my heart still broke at the idea that she would forever be that small. It was a visual that made me want to give myself up to the Damned, no questions asked.

"Not Gifted." Sakina brought her hand to her heart.

"But the children of First and Last Lifers will often inherit their parents' Gifts," Delia shared.

"So she's like me without the briefly dying part?"

"Yes, only we don't know if she also has a purpose, or just the genetics. Had you fully died, you would have come back to life as Gifted, but we don't know what would happen to her."

"That would mean that you've achieved your purposes?" I realized, since that was how you became a Last Lifer. It meant that once they died, they wouldn't come back to life like other Gifted. They were simply humans with supernatural abilities.

"I still don't know what I did, but my beautiful wife wonderfully avoided a world war at the turn of the century." He looked at her with pride, but she rolled her eyes at him.

"Alison is going to stay with us for a few days, and we were hoping we could find someone to teach her how to control her Gift." Delia explained the reason for our visit.

"I'd be more than happy to help you with that. I have appointments in the afternoon, but my mornings are free once Krishna is off to her Summer Camp. We can meet here tomorrow at nine."

"Or you can take me with you to the school!" Krishna exclaimed, her eyes going even bigger with excitement.

"I can take her to camp on my way to work," Mohinder assured his wife before using a cookie to bribe away his daughter's pout.

"There's a group of Gifted who are after her. Who know she's staying here."

"The old barn then. It should have everything."

"The three of you are always welcome at Rosehill. Even if they aren't after you, it could get dangerous."

"We appreciate that Delilah, and will come straight to you if we hear anything."

They didn't seem concerned, so I was trying to explain what we were up against without scaring Krishna, but Sakina caught my eye.

"There's ancient magic and very expensive security systems protecting us here as well. Delilah just enjoys having her people where she can see them in situations like these."

"I'm learning that."

"Caring and wanting to make sure you're safe are not crimes," Delia defended herself.

"They are a testament to your caring soul," Mohinder said, emphasizing the last word.

"Blood of my blood." Delia brought her hand to her heart before giving them each a hug.

. . .

"I FORGOT to ask what Sakina's Gift was," I realized once we were outside, headed back to Rosehill.

"She hears thoughts. Krishna is brilliant for her age, but it's an overwhelming burden she doesn't need. They lived in the mansion until she was born."

"Krishna hears the thoughts and feels the feelings of everyone who comes near her?" I asked, actively trying to remember everything I'd thought while I was there.

"She's working on controlling it, but I imagine she was curious about you. Jackie isn't the only one who missed Tristan while he was away." She smiled.

"Does that mean that if ever I were to have children with someone like Tristan, they'd have to figure out how to control his electricity and my power suck?" I was naïve enough to believe that if I figured out how to control my 'Gift', everyone around me would be safe. It didn't seem fair to put that same burden on an infant. By the time they got old enough to figure it out, I would be on my deathbed.

"If he achieves his purpose and you stay alive, then yes, that would be the most likely outcome."

It was a nasty twist of fate after saying I wouldn't wish my 'Gift' on anyone.

"But if we're both Gifted, they wouldn't inherit anything?"

I thought of Malcolm, who had no Gifts, even though his mother was a human microscope.

Delia looked troubled for a moment before she said, "Tristan can't have children right now. If he reaches his Last Life, he would be able to, but Gifted don't age, and they can't procreate."

"But Mohinder and Sakina…"

"Had Krishna once they were Last Lifers."

"You've known them since the fifteenth century?" I changed the subject. Delia was looking at me with a combination of pity and pain, which wasn't good for anyone.

"I've only known Mohinder a few decades, but Sakina saved

my life. It was not pretty, or pleasant, but I worked hard, and I figured it out."

"You still don't use it though," I argued, worried I might be overstepping, but it didn't seem like she had a handle on her Gift so much as she monitored everything she said to never accidentally use it.

"No, I don't. But that's because I don't want to. I wouldn't want someone to take away my free will, so I won't take someone else's, unless I can't help it. But usually I can."

"If the gargoyles hadn't shown up last night…"

"I might have. We weren't so unevenly matched that I would give up, but I couldn't risk you or Jackie getting hurt. Your lives would have been more important than their freedom."

"Would you just tell them to leave and never come back?"

"That's too general. It needs to be simple, but specific enough that it can't be misinterpreted. People look for loopholes to avoid things they don't want to do, and it's the same with my Gift. We value our free will and our right to choose, so when it is taken away, we rebel. Rebellions are dangerous, so I make sure whatever I make someone do is specific and temporary. And only on Gifted."

A shadow crossed her face like that was a lesson she had to learn the hard way.

When we got to the opening in the brick wall, Delia put her hand out to warn me to stop. I froze, terrified she'd heard something and someone was about to attack us from the trees, but she just bent down and grabbed a rock, not the least bit concerned. That's when I remembered that telling me to stop would have been an order, so it was easier for her to stop and use a hand gesture in the hopes that I would understand.

"The estate continues at least a mile past the Patels', but it isn't technically a part of Rosehill, so they don't have all the same protections. The main building has the heaviest protection, because it's easiest to control, but I think most of them extend to this wall as well."

She took the rock and threw it through the opening, but when it got to the line of the wall, there was an electrified sheet of plexiglass. Or at least that's what it looked like.

"That goes all around Rosehill?" I asked, to which she nodded.

"The magic does. There isn't always a wall to indicate it, though. A couple hundred feet that way, the wall collapsed, and there's absolutely nothing on the shore, but we put extra there for the boats."

"How did we get through it last night? How do we get back in?" I was sleeping for the drive and only woke up when we were at the front door, but I felt certain I would have reacted to being zapped by a magical barrier on my way in.

"I choose who comes past the wall. Although I guess the barrier does too. It was put in place to protect the occupants, but I made the school for First Lifers seeking refuge from the outside world, so they are always welcome. If the barrier deems you a threat, it won't let you in. But if you're in trouble, running from something terrible, it might welcome you without waiting for my approval."

"So I passed a test of sorts when it let me through?"

"It isn't foolproof, which is why I usually have final say, but the barrier didn't have any objections to you," she assured me.

She walked right through the opening with confidence, but I was cautious, putting one hand through, then a toe, before pretty much hopping onto the other side.

"I don't want you to stay here so I won't feel bad about sending you to your death, or because I want to put the other people who live here at risk. I would never put my family in danger like that," Delia said with a fierceness I found terrifying. "I want you to stay because I truly believe you will be safe here, more so than anywhere else. And not just from them, but from the parts of your Gift that scare you. Sakina can teach you how to control it so you only use it when you want to, however often that may be. I want you to be able to hug your sister without weakening her, and to let Tristan hold you without it leaving him defenseless."

"I've told him not to, but he insists…"

"I'm not reproaching you for it. While you're here, comfort is more important than his fighting skills. As long as the breakers don't blow, we're good." She smiled, implying that was all she needed his powers for.

TRISTAN HAD POINTED out where the other bedrooms were, but Delia turned down a different hallway on the first floor and opened a door for me. I expected a study or maybe a library, but I was standing in the middle of a science lab. It was like the ones I had in high school, only there were big, expensive machines in the corner, like the ones at the precinct, and those medical fridges that either held vaccines or live cultures. Ben was with two teenage boys at a long metal table, poring over a beaker filled with a milky substance.

"This is our science classroom. We teach all the core subjects, but follow more of a homeschool curriculum, where you can do independent study and go deeper into the subjects you like. Not that you'll need to take any classes while you're here, and it is their summer holidays, but—"

"Miss Delia," the younger boy cut her off.

"Yes, Charlie?" she asked with a smile.

"You're not allowed in the science lab while we're doing experiments if you're not wearing your safety goggles."

"My apologies, boys. I was just showing Alison around."

"Hi Alison," they said in unison, more so we would leave than because they had any interest in meeting me.

"Now you can add the phosphorous, but just a tiny drop," Ben warned, looking ridiculous in his white lab coat and thick safety goggles. Maybe my first impression of him made me biased, but he had looked like he belonged on a SWAT team, not as a high school science teacher.

No one moved, so I waited for Ben to repeat himself, at which point I would offer to get the phosphorous, which was in a dish on the table closest to me, but just as I was moving forward, less than a pinch of it floated up in the air and travelled directly on top of the beaker.

"Is this good?" Charlie asked.

"About half of that," Ben corrected. "But don't measure it out on top of the beaker, in case it spills."

"Got it," the older boy said, looking at the powder that separated itself from the rest and went back into the dish.

"Excellent control, Brandon," Ben encouraged.

"Miss Delia." Brandon looked at us apologetically, but the message was clear.

"Safety first," Delia said before leading me into the hallway, so we could watch from outside the window. As soon as the powder touched the liquid, it fizzed up and burned a hole into the bottom of the beaker, which one of the boys quickly sent to the sink.

"Are they wizards?" I asked, realizing how it sounded, but she'd brought up magic long before I did. "They can move things with their minds?" I rephrased it.

"They're telekinetic," she agreed. "Very powerful, but sometimes a little over eager."

"Do a lot of Gifted have the same Gift?"

"They definitely repeat, some more often than others, but when it's genetic, it's much more common."

"Their parents were Last Lifers?" I guessed.

"Their father was. He didn't know that he would pass it on, so he didn't warn their mother. They've been with us since he passed away," she explained, not explicitly saying it, but I got the impression their mother was still out there, living her life without her cursed offspring. "I'm not sure if they enjoy science, or simply the fact that Ben allows them to blow things up in there."

"Is Ben qualified to be a science teacher?"

"Reluctantly so. He was a chemist in his First Life. He still likes to tinker around with stuff and publish if he finds anything interesting. I'm afraid they do a lot of these experiments. So much so that the lab has its own set of sprinklers and can be sealed off if need be."

"Good to know." I made a mental note that if danger came to us, Plan A was to lock them in the science lab while we got away, and Plan B was to lure them into the science lab after me so everyone else could get away.

"This is Mateo." We stopped outside a room where a young teenager with shaggy brown hair was working hard on Physics vector problems. His concentration was laser-focused, and I got the impression he would bite our heads off if we went too close.

"Is that look because he's very serious about his studies?"

"He hasn't been with us very long and hasn't quite adjusted to an environment where he doesn't have to be constantly on edge. He's used to being on guard to defend himself and those he cares about. I truly believe he has a huge heart, but so far, he has kept it very well hidden."

"Is he Gifted?" It was the easier way of asking if he didn't have to defend himself anymore because he died, or if she rescued him.

"A First Lifer," she shared. "We get a few Gifted children and teenagers at the school every year, but Tristan is currently our youngest Gifted, looks and time-wise." Her look implied she knew how tight my chest got each time I asked if a child's life had been cut short, and the relief I felt when she told me they were still in their First Life.

"I thought we were really rare?" I in no way wanted to be special, but I was getting the impression that First Lifers were a lot more common than originally implied. Delia had a collection of them.

"You are. But Rosehill is the only school of its kind, so we make it our business to find the ones who are lost or need guidance. And there are different kinds of people who have Gifts in their first life, like Krishna."

"They don't all have to die and be brought back to life before it takes hold." I let her know I understood.

"That in no way means they've had it easy," she warned. "Gifts don't work on Mateo, so they used him as a human shield. He inherited it from his mother, so I imagine she suffered a similar fate."

"Would that mean she was protective of people before she became Gifted?"

"You can't always read that much into Gifts. Some are spot on, but there's a cruel irony to others. Mine represents the thing I hated most about myself when I was alive."

"That people listened to you?"

"That people didn't have a choice but to listen to me. That kind of power can corrupt even the kindest of souls."

We got to another large window that showed a combination of a dance studio and a James Bond training facility. One side had a bar mounted on a mirrored wall, but the other had one of those heavy torsos and a corkboard with knives sticking out of it.

A girl was alone inside it. She looked maybe sixteen years old, with purple hair and angry eyes. She carried herself like she had all the confidence in the world, but it clearly frustrated her that whatever she was trying to do wasn't working. She emanated so much power and anger that I wouldn't be surprised if she screamed out in frustration and caused the entire building to blow up.

"She looks like she could kill me with her bare hands," I said without thinking.

"In hand-to-hand combat, Lena could kill all of us," Delia agreed.

I watched, waiting for a smile or some kind of indication that she was joking, but she was dead serious.

"This is the training room. It's the size of an Olympic swimming pool, but we can section it off as needed. Once the walls are in place, each room lets you practice magic or your Gift, but nothing leaves the confines of your room."

As she explained it, the girl, Lena, brought her hands up and covered the window in front of me with ice. When I brought my hand to the glass, it wasn't even cold.

"That's incredible."

"We need safe spaces to practice our Gifts without hurting others. We mostly use the individual rooms for private study, but once they're competent enough to not hurt each other, we allow students to train together."

"To become superheroes?" I asked with a smile, not sure if it was a silly question, or exactly what they were doing.

Instead of answering, Delia sighed. "A long time ago, I used to wander around town at night, trying to help the helpless. Gifted, of course, but mostly women walking home alone at night, or anyone who was being mistreated…It's how the school came to be, really; a place to protect the people we saved and keep them safe. I spent less time patrolling outside and more time looking after everyone inside, but while many people with Gifts want to forget them and live a normal life, many believe that if you have a Gift, you must use it for good, to help others. It was a losing battle when I tried to stop them, so I established ground rules instead. No First or Last Lifers, but especially not under eighteen."

"How is that working out for you?" I asked. Jackie had been there last night, and I distinctly remembered Tristan quoting

Delia the night I first met him, something about how selfish it was to deprive the world of your Gifts. I thought it was just about pursuing my love of archeology, but it had a whole new meaning now.

"I have a lot of eager teenagers waiting to turn eighteen, but at least the gray hairs they give me don't show." She smiled before heading back to the school's main entrance. "People come and go here all the time, but Jackie, Brandon, Charlie, Lena, Mateo, Tristan, and Ben are the ones who live here all the time. And Penny."

We'd arrived at the front doors, that had potted plants on either side. Each one had a steady stream of water cascading onto it, as if it were raining indoors.

"How did you know it was me?" A little girl came out from behind one of the trees. She was about as high as my waist, with big blue eyes and honey-colored hair in French braids.

"I don't remember installing a sprinkler system for our fake trees," Delia explained, taking the girl's outstretched hand, and motioning for me to follow them to the living room we'd had the meeting in last night.

"I'm showing you how responsible I could be if they were real. I would water them every day. We could get gumdrop trees."

"I second that," Jackie agreed as Penny rushed to tickle her while she was lying on the ground. Tristan was beside her, reading a comic book. He closed his eyes and shook his head when Jackie tickled Penny back.

"How were the fireflies?" I asked, sitting on the floor a safe distance away from the three of them.

"Turns out it was the electricity that attracted them to him, so we'll have to try again once he gets his Gift back. There are probably still a few in the old garage," Jackie shared.

"Oh, I found a family of skunks in there this morning, and they left their mark on the way out. It would probably be best to avoid the entire basement for the time being," Delia shot her down.

"The barn usually has some," Tristan suggested, reminding me that Delia had shown me what she needed me to see today, but there was still a lot of Rosehill to discover.

"I smell an adventure," Penny announced.

"It'll have to wait until later because dinner is served," Chris came in to tell us, making a silly face for the little girl.

I turned to see Tristan already had Penny on his shoulders with his work cut out for him, trying to stop her from putting her hands over his eyes.

CHAPTER ELEVEN

ALISON

We made our way to the dining room, where a giant dish filled with meatballs was sitting on the table, waiting for us.

"Do we just take a seat and serve ourselves?" I asked Tristan, going to the closest chairs with place settings.

"No, we wait." He put Penny down and guided me to a couple of chairs near the end while the girls continued to the kitchen. "Dinner is a family affair, and I saw Caleb outside with Ben, so there will probably be a discussion after."

"Because I'm complicating everything?"

"This isn't the first, and it won't be the last time they face something like this."

"What about you?"

"I'm not a First or Last Lifer. And technically, by the time I moved here, I was eighteen."

"They let you be a part of their dangerous operations?"

"They used me as a decoy for Gabriel. Doctor Black," he shared. "We—"

"Did you fight?" I cut off whatever story had him smiling and regretted it the instant his eyes went dark.

"Not when I was his decoy, but there was a battle to take down Lucy's Big Bad." It sounded like some silly urban legend only children believed in, but his clenched jaw and furrowed brow told me whatever the monster had been, it deserved the title and all the fear that came with it.

"I never want to be the reason your face looks like that," I decided.

"I was born with this face," he teased. "And we went by Delia's rules. Mostly. Lucy isn't Gifted, so she's technically in her First Life, but she was of age, and the fight was to protect her, so she was going to be there either way."

"But the fighting didn't come here. To your family."

"At the risk of scaring you off, you are my family now, so if the fight comes to you, it came to my family."

I knew what he was trying to do, but I could tell he also got my point.

"And your fight is our fight." Delia came in like she'd been a part of our entire conversation.

"I appreciate you taking me in like this—"

"They're not after you because you slighted them or some silly feud. The Damned want to eliminate their own Giftedness, but if that kind of technology is known to be available, the New Order will be after it. If they get their hands on something like that…we're all dead."

"Me too?" Penny asked, coming in at the worst possible moment with a bowl of freshly grated Parmesan cheese. I could smell the garlic bread Chris was carrying long before he put it on the table.

"All the Gifted who've already died," Delia amended. "No one will ever hurt you."

I got the feeling she was trying to make her Gift apply to those words, but it was impossible, even with Gifted magic.

"The rest of us are safe here?" Charlie asked, like he was just confirming something he already knew, but there was a hint of fear in his voice. I didn't blame him; I was terrified.

"Everyone is safe as long as they stay at Rosehill. The bad guys can't get in."

"Are we sure about that?" Lena asked, obviously doubting her, but I didn't sense fear. It was more like she wanted to know what she was up against and didn't trust anyone else's word for it.

"We are," Ben backed Delia, taking the seat beside her.

"But we can't stay here forever," Brandon pointed out.

"Afraid of what will happen with me in charge of physical education for the rest of the summer?" Caleb came in with Etta.

Everyone took their seat and, after a cursory glance around the room, started piling meatballs onto plates and passing them around.

"We need to figure out who is behind this and why. Then we can get rid of them and go back to our lives," Etta said like it was the simplest thing ever, and I almost believed her.

"You mentioned the New Order?" I asked Delia.

"What's left of the Knights," she agreed.

"I've heard the name, but I still don't know what it means."

"Like in fairytales," Penny told me, scooping meat and cheese onto her garlic bread, then taking a huge bite. "They're the ones who rescue the princesses and live happily ever after with them."

"What did I tell you about princesses?" Delia asked over the bridge of her nose.

"They can save themselves." Penny sighed. "But that wouldn't be a fairytale."

"It would just be history." Ben shot Delia a smile I couldn't decipher, but I was still waiting for an answer.

"This food is so good we should enjoy it while it's nice and hot. But I would be happy to fill you in on Gifted history after dinner?"

"It is delicious." I read between the lines. "Thank you, Chris."

"My pleasure," he assured me.

"Do I have to marry a prince to become a princess, or can I just get kidnapped by a dragon?" Penny asked with her mouth full.

"I definitely need to teach you better table manners if princess is your career choice." Delia shook her head, but she was smiling, so Penny did the same before swallowing more carefully.

"I can go to princess school?"

I watched everyone around the table while Penny asked silly questions, either completely unaware of how we dropped the topic for her protection, or so sensitive to the current situation that she made it her job to get everyone smiling. Either way, she excelled at it, roping everyone into her princess training, except for Lena. Mateo shrugged his agreement to be one of her knights, but Lena looked like every aspect of this etiquette school made her skin crawl.

Once all the plates were clean, Jackie put her hand on Tristan's and whispered something in his ear before offering to tell Penny fairytales in bed.

"What did she say?" I asked him while the older kids tried every trick in the book to stay and listen, each shot down by the adults.

"Made me promise to tell her everything later." He kissed my temple and didn't even flinch at the sparks. I'd been so careful since I got back from Delia's tour, not to accidentally brush my hand against his at dinner so he could get his Gift back, but he just lost it all over again. "Worth it," he told me before bringing our plates to the kitchen.

I helped clear the table, then followed the others to the room from last night.

"The Order of the Knight were knights, like in the fairytales, but their goal was to protect the world from evil beings, notably

Gifted who used their dangerous Gifts for selfish reasons," Delia explained once we were all sitting.

"Gifted Hunters." I swallowed. That did not sound good for us.

"Only the bad ones," Delia assured me. "The Order was created with the best of intentions and did incredible work for decades until some members failed to make the distinction between good and evil. They just saw different and sought to eliminate it. As did parts of the population."

"So, in the sixteenth century, Johannes Van Bergen abandoned his Knights and created the Guardians, to protect Gifted from angry mobs with pitchforks," Chris spoke up, passing around a tray of homemade rice crispies treats. It happened centuries before he was born, but his face was hard, like he knew about it from experience...or maybe firsthand bedtime stories?

"And from the members who branched off and called themselves the New Order of the Night, with a mandate to eliminate all Gifted," Caleb said with his mouth full, getting a stern look from Etta, that quickly turned into a laugh.

"Can't you not die until you achieve your purpose?" I asked. "Otherwise, I know a few people who would gladly submit themselves to the New Order."

"Eliminate can mean many things."

A darkness came over them. It hadn't occurred to me that there were ways to prevent Gifted from regenerating without letting them die. Logan was one of the Damned whose Gift was to turn whatever he touched into sand. I wondered what would happen if you put that sand in different boxes...I turned to Tristan and shivered, taking his hand in mine.

"Not everyone is as humane as what Gabriel created for the FBI."

"If the Damned find me, they'll bleed me out to find a cure, but if the New Order get me, they'll do their best to eliminate me, unless they figure out why the Damned are after me, in which case they'll also try to bleed me dry so they can eliminate more Gifted in a permanent capacity?"

Tristan, Chris, and Etta all looked like they were about to tell me that wasn't what they were saying, but Delia looked me dead in the eye and said, "Yes."

"And you're Guardians?" I ignored the shocked look on the other faces and concentrated on her.

"Sometimes," Delia agreed. "There are official members who date back to the original Knights, but there are also pockets of people all over the world who were trained by them to protect themselves or other Gifted and First Lifers at safe houses across the globe, so you are never far from help."

"Caleb's one of those," Etta explained.

"Rosehill mostly caters to children and First Lifers on a long-term basis, but every safe house is equipped with more safety measures than a presidential bunker."

Delia probably thought she was being comforting, telling me they designed the school for this, but Caleb and Tristan exchanged a glance, and I knew that even the safest of safe houses could fall.

"Should we send me to one of those safe houses, then? I'm not a child and this is a home, not just a safe house." I turned to Caleb, assuming he was the most knowledgeable on the subject.

"Officially, I think Hawai'i and Texas are the only ones left on American soil," Caleb admitted. "But I don't know how we would get you to them. From what little I saw of those guys last night, they would find you before you left the state."

"I doubt they would attack me in a public place with hundreds of witnesses," I said, looking to Delia for confirmation. She knew him more than any of us did, even if it was a long time ago.

"There's always a way. And if they hired mercenaries to bring you in, I doubt he's the only one they'll send." At first, I thought she was trying to scare me into saying I would stay at Rosehill forever, rather than just until I got my Gift under control, but she looked apologetic, like she was just being honest.

"You have to remember they aren't regular people," Ben warned. "They're Gifted, which means they don't have to touch you to get to you. They don't even have to be in the same room. You would need a team of us to keep you safe, and even then...I like your chances better here."

"The barrier makes a clear division between Rosehill and the outside world, so he can't track you inside here, but the second you went outside, he would find you. It's not a question of if, but when."

"But they know we're here. Our suits with the school logo were basically calling cards, even if he wasn't a super tracker. Shouldn't they be at the doors by now?" Jackie asked, coming to sit beside Tristan on the sofa.

"I thought you were staying with Penny?" Ben asked.

"She was either exhausted or my story was boring."

Delia and Ben exchanged a look, ultimately deciding Jackie could stay, possibly because they knew Tristan would tell her everything later.

"They're smart. They would want to see what they were up against and come up with a plan before trying anything," Delia explained.

"And what is our plan?" Tristan asked. "Because we can't stay here forever. They're either waiting out there watching us, or they'll find a way in."

"We don't have one. Other than helping Alison get a handle on her Gift and figuring out as much as we can about the people that are after her. The more we know, the better we can plan." I was still having trouble wrapping my head around the fact that Ben was a science nerd when he looked so much like a soldier. Not just his build, but the way he carried himself, like he was just waiting for details so he could strategize an offensive strike to eliminate the threat.

"Did you have any suggestions?"

I looked at Delia, to see who she was talking to when no one answered, but she was looking at me. Genuinely asking for my opinion. On something I knew nothing about. But it was my life that hung in the balance. They were all just collateral damage.

"I guess it's too late for me to leave and hope they won't bother you if I'm not here?" I sighed. "I'll do whatever keeps everyone safe."

I knew it wasn't really an answer, but I didn't have a better one. I wanted to go back to when I wasn't weird, and people weren't trying to kill me. To when everything made sense. It would also mean that I wouldn't meet Tristan, and I would still be slowly killing my sister, but then again, people close to me were dying, and I didn't know how to keep anyone safe.

"Gabriel asked Terrence to pay a visit to the people who kidnapped you, so that should give us some insight."

"Who's Terrence?" I asked, while the others nodded in agreement.

"He's very good at getting people to talk," Tristan explained.

I wrapped my arms around myself to stop the shiver, but I couldn't get over how okay everyone was with torturing people for information. Especially Tristan.

"No, not like that." He took me in his arms. "It's his Gift. You literally spill your secrets out to him. One minute he's asking you where you grew up and before you know it, you've told him about every childhood trauma. Always the truth, but not just the one you tell yourself, the real one that scares you."

.   .   .

"Tea?" Jackie asked me once the older ones brought up other friends they might reach out to for information on this group of the Damned and the mercenaries they were hiring. They hadn't told us to leave, but we weren't contributing much.

"No, I think I'll go FaceTime with my parents to let them know I'm okay."

"I'll come with you." Tristan stood and gave Jackie a hug.

"No, you have tea and catch up with everyone. I'll feel guilty lying with you there knowing the truth."

"Are you sure?" He took my hand in his and searched my eyes to see if I meant it.

"Normal parents freak out when you run away from home to live with a band of weirdos in the middle of the woods," Jackie told him with a wink I knew was directed at me, even if I was already in the doorway.

"I won't be long," Tristan promised, so I gave him a grateful smile and headed for the stairs.

I hadn't really ventured around on my own yet, especially not at night. The dark hallway, illuminated by the moon through the many windows, made me feel like I was walking around a haunted mansion, but I shook it off and kept going. The classical music coming from a bedroom didn't make it any less spooky, but then Brandon and Charlie were playing Mario Kart, and the upbeat racing music reminded me of home.

Tristan's room was pitch black and didn't have a central light on the ceiling, just a bunch of lamps scattered throughout, so I felt around in the dark to turn them all on.

My new phone was plugged into the wall beside the bed, an iPhone, so I just had to enter my login to have all my contacts, including Malcolm, who warned me his mother would file a missing person's report if I didn't write to them daily. I knew I had to give my parents more than one-word responses at some point, but I found myself hoping they wouldn't answer.

"Hello?"

I was surprised to see Damian, my sister's new boyfriend, when I called her number.

"Is everything okay?"

"They're playing Twister, because, you know, and I was the only one with a free hand," he explained, showing me the smorgasbord of limbs that surrounded him. I hadn't had the chance to tell Sybill what I'd found out, so she was still under the impression that her miracle recovery was a placebo effect from the drug trial, and that her illness would be back with a vengeance as soon as the trial was over. I was both dreading it, and excited to tell her she wasn't sick. I was just sucking the life out of her.

However unintentionally.

Damian usually looked so much healthier than Syb, but tonight, he was the one who appeared pale and out of breath from a high-intensity game.

"Allie!" Sybill exclaimed, keeping her arm and one leg firmly planted, while trying to wave with the other foot.

"I was just calling to check in and say hi." It was easier to pretend everything was okay when I saw them all smiling and happy, but I also felt like a claw was compressing my heart. I would never be a part of that again.

"Did the rice work?" my mom asked. I couldn't see her face somewhere behind my dad's elbow, but I saw the top of her red curls.

"Yep, good as new." I smiled. They didn't need to know that this was the second time I got a new phone since they'd left for California so my sister could attend a clinical trial.

"When does your internship end?" My dad asked, turning his head almost all the way around so he could face me.

"A few more weeks," I lied, catching Sybill's eye. She knew I hadn't been doing the internship since Grace, my supervisor, had been stabbed and left for dead in the hallway outside our office.

"Do you think you'll be able to come here?" My mom was hopeful, but she looked worried, like she was maybe transferring some of her Sybill concern onto me. That was the last thing I wanted.

"Maybe the last weekend, but I'll probably just see you when you get back."

We had mere days to get rid of this threat so I could go home and leave my parents none the wiser. Or I had to come up with some prestigious program that justified me living here and them having random people following them around. Unless I told them the truth. Which was maybe scarier than another face to face with the hunter. It was like everything happening now was some messed up mistake I could write off, but as soon as my parents found out about it, it would be real. And I didn't want this to be real.

"Anything interesting going on?" Sybill asked awkwardly, like she didn't want to force me into another lie, but still wanted to know what was happening.

"They're giving me extra training starting tomorrow, so that should be…fun." It was as close to the truth as I could give them, although I wasn't expecting any of it to be fun.

"Enjoy yourself, sweetie. And be safe."

"I'll try my best."

"We love you," my dad said.

"I love you guys too." I smiled and hung up, hopefully before they saw the tears.

. . .

I GOT ready for bed and huddled under the thick red comforter. It felt abnormally cold for summer, but Lena was a few rooms away, and some of it might be in my mind.

I tossed and turned until Tristan came in and wrapped his arms around me. It wasn't like all my problems melted away and I was fine, but I felt safe, like as long as he held me close, the bad couldn't get in.

CHAPTER TWELVE

ALISON

Tristan had planned on taking me to the barn once I was ready, but he looked so peaceful now that he had managed to sleep in. His dark locks were sticking up at odd angles while his face was completely relaxed.

Sakina wanted me to meet her on the second level of the barn so she could see what I could do. It wasn't like I had the power to blow anything up, so I didn't need to suggest the training rooms, but then again, I didn't really know what I was capable of.

The bottom level of the barn looked like it was a venue for rustic weddings. There were chairs instead of hay bale benches, but fairy lights lit my way to the staircase when I couldn't find a switch.

I expected a second level like the first, but I found centuries worth of storage. And not just extra chairs and tables. There was a corner filled with what looked like paintings covered by white sheets, vases, old cribs, and toys I couldn't imagine letting a child go near.

Sakina was sitting in the middle of the room with a tea set. Her mug was made of clear glass, with a kind of metal cage, but the one she set out for me was plain ceramic, gray and modern.

"I'm afraid this set has taken in a lot of bad memories, but I'm still quite partial to it," she explained, motioning for me to take a seat.

She waited expectantly, then relaxed when I dropped my weight on the rust-colored cushions and nothing happened.

"Is this the chair of horrors?" I guessed at her expression. Unless it was booby-trapped, she'd thought I would get a memory from it.

"I tried my best to choose items that would bring you powerful happy memories until you get better at not feeling them. Then again, most of the stuff up here isn't mine, so I don't know what you might find."

I cautiously reached for the cup, keeping my eyes on her.

"I bought it years ago at a department store and didn't take it out of the box until this morning," she assured me.

I still touched it gently so I wouldn't scald myself if there was an unexpected emotion, but she was right, and I felt nothing.

"I thought we might begin with you showing me how your Gift works, and then we can focus on controlling it."

"As in not using it?" I verified.

"That'll be easier once you have a handle on it. And since we don't want to leave ourselves defenseless, we can wait to work on people until you've mastered objects."

"Just how long do you expect to keep working with me?" I knew it wouldn't happen in a day, but I thought a few lessons with Sakina would fix me. I would have to work with her for years if I had to master one thing before even starting on the next.

"It depends on you. I've had students master their Gifts in a matter of hours, while others have been working on it for centuries and still haven't fully mastered it."

"Like Delia," I ventured.

"Delilah can wield her Gift with an accuracy and precision others can only dream of. If she wants you to do something, she will make it happen."

"But she said—"

"Giving people the right to choose gives them the right to refuse, or to rebel. It's when she half uses it that things get misinterpreted, or when she wants something she doesn't fully ask for."

I digested this information while finishing my tea.

Sakina went over and collected a tray filled with a variety of objects and placed it on the table in front of me.

"Pick your poison," she encouraged, borrowing her husband's expression to put me at ease. I appreciated it.

I had no interest in revisiting weapons, so I dismissed the daggers and the arrow. I hesitated at the long golden chain with a locket on the end, but necklaces had been depressing for me of late. Instead, I chose a long piece of blue ribbon that had seen better days, but was so carefully preserved on the satin cushion that I knew it must be a lot older than my first impression.

Sakina nodded when I brought my hand toward it, so I picked it up and held it between my fingers. My heart immediately swelled with love and pride as a pair of hands wove the ribbon through long black hair, thicker than Tristan's. Like Sakina's, only there wasn't a trace of gray.

"What did you see?"

"Someone making a braid with it in long black hair."

"What did you feel?" she pressed.

"So much love. And pride."

"When a girl in my family turns eight, we hold a special cere-mony. Krishna's was last month."

I smiled, still feeling her love for her daughter, but it gave me an ache as I thought of my mom, miles away, maybe in danger, with no clue what was going on with me.

"Can you usually see more than one memory?"

"Sometimes, but it's easier if I know what I'm looking for." Like when I knew whose memory I was trying to see.

"Can you single out the woman whose hands you see?" she suggested. "Find her strongest memory."

"I can try."

I held the ribbon in my hand again, which conjured the same memory. I had to concentrate hard before I saw two hands tied together with a blue ribbon. The feelings were coming at me from both hands; fear, apprehension, relief, frustration, love, devotion…It was an avalanche of emotions. I concentrated harder on Sakina, trying to single out which ones were hers.

"It's like you were going to your death to honor your family," I shared.

"It felt that way," she agreed. "My first marriage was chosen for me by my father. I was terrified, but I would have done absolutely anything he asked."

"What happened?"

"What was he feeling?" She asked instead of answering. The last one had been a test, but this time she was curious, like she didn't know the answer.

"Relieved. Nervous. I think a little excited," I said, digging into the other person.

"He was happy I wasn't ugly. I was quite the sight when I was younger."

"When was that?"

"You'll be here a lot longer if you ask for stories," she warned with a warm smile. "I died about a decade before Delilah's father hired me. I was going crazy with all the voices in my head, so I tried everything, including a lot of meditating and retreats, until I got a handle on it."

"I can't imagine what it's like inside your head."

"After centuries of perfecting it, my head is empty." She let out a grateful breath. "Unless I don't want it to be."

"Did it really take centuries?"

"Why don't we try not getting a memory?" She kept me on track, but I worried it was more because she didn't want to discourage me than that she didn't want to share.

OVER TWO DOZEN times I touched the ribbon, and each time I saw one of the memories, no matter how hard I tried not to.

"Interesting," Sakina said after my next failure. "Do you like samosas?"

"I can't say I've ever had any."

"Come for lunch. We can work on clearing your mind afterwards."

I hadn't realized the time, but my stomach let out a growl as if I hadn't eaten third helpings of garlic bread last night.

THE SAMOSAS WERE ready and waiting when we arrived at Sakina's, taking the same path from yesterday, which I now saw had a strange red plant growing along the side of it.

Krishna had me sit beside her at the table, leaving her parents across from us. Mohinder was left-handed while Sakina was right, so they held hands while they ate, demonstrating an enduring love I could only hope to find. I wondered how many centuries they'd been together, because he definitely wasn't the husband from the memory.

When the meal was over, Mohinder told Krishna to play outside while Sakina sat me in the living room on a pile of pillows. I got flashbacks from yoga sessions with my parents and Sybill, but Sakina didn't have me do any stretches, or prove my flexibility. At first, she had me chanting with her, a few good ohms, then she made me lie down so she could chant and run silk materials over me. I was half-convinced she was pulling my leg by the end, but after an hour she dismissed me, saying we would try again the next morning, same time and place.

Delia was waiting for me outside the Patels' house. She looked around the woods, attuned to every sound. Not quite nervous, but she did not trust what might hide within the forest.

"I can move her studio to the lower level of the barn. We won't be having events for a while," she said with a reassuring smile I didn't trust.

"You think they're here? Watching us?"

"I'm sure they came here as soon as they were free of the gargoyles," she agreed.

I quickened my pace until we were safely past the stone wall, but even then, I couldn't relax.

"If only my Gift was to fly. Or be invisible." I sighed. It was infinitely more of a curse, at least for now.

"So you could slip out without us noticing?" Delia looked concerned, but I shook my head. "Things aren't going well with Sakina?" She jumped to her next conclusion.

"Not if the goal is to control it," I shared. "But even if I figure it out, they'll still want to bleed it out of me. I'm putting everyone in danger just because my Gift takes away other peoples'."

"They'd still be after you if your Gift was invisibility. You'd just be harder to find. And though I warned you not to read too much into them, our Gifts aren't arbitrary, which means there's a reason you can do what you do. Sometimes it's based on personality, but often it's linked to whatever your purpose will be."

"What do you mean, they would still be after me?" I asked, not wanting to get into why *I* was given a Gift that hurts people. "They want me because they think I can take away their Giftedness."

"And that kept you alive when you were kidnapped. Otherwise, they'd have taken your blood and been done with it."

"My blood would be useless to them if I was dead."

"You said they told you about the Magnum Finis?" Delia looked confused, especially when I met her with a blank stare. "The jewel-encrusted golden blob," she elaborated.

"Yes." I hadn't realized the artefact had a name. Even the museum they stole it from had been in the dark on its purpose and origins. "They thought I could open it and that something to help them might be inside."

"That's not because of your Gift, it's because of your blood."

"Because I'm a First Lifer?" I tried to remember everything they'd told me when I was kidnapped. I should have had Grace take my hand to read me with her microscope-like Gift, but then again, I would have sucked her Gift from her. It would have told me way earlier that I had the power to do that, rather than having my kidnappers tell me about it.

"Because you're a Protector of the Magnum Finis. Before my time, the Protectors would keep the Magnum Finis for special ceremonies where Gifted who had served their time could choose to move on."

"Without accomplishing their task?"

"Some people have tasks they'll never fully accomplish, that are too big for a single person. Gabriel, for instance, promised to protect someone's family without realizing it meant all her descendants, for centuries, until the threat was neutralized. Some protectors lived thousands of years before passing down the torch to a suitable replacement, by which point their task wasn't complete, but someone else had taken over...we would have a big ceremony, honor their service, and let them go."

"What changed?"

"The Damned mobilized, believing themselves to be cursed. They wanted an easy way out, without even attempting to find their purposes. The Protectors were mostly Masters of Ceremony until that point, but they suddenly had to fight and protect the Magnum Finis, keeping it separate from the key, only coming together for ceremonies, which grew too dangerous for everyone involved. The Protectors' sole task was guarding those two items against those who wanted to use them to get rid of their Giftedness altogether."

"And my blood is the key?"

"It's a part of it. There's a physical element, which only works when you activate it."

"Because I'm the Protector?" The crazy never stopped.

"Because you're in the Protector's bloodline. The actual position is given to someone chosen by the previous Protector before they move on. Everyone in the bloodline has the potential and can activate it, but the actual Protector gets the job of guarding the physical key."

"That's why it let me in when I cut myself," I realized.

"Your blood would be called to it, and vice versa," she agreed.

"Is this something you can tell from looking at me, or is my name on a list somewhere?" I asked, worried about the rest of my family. Was it a beacon Gifted could follow to Protector blood, or did they just have to look up Carmichael in the phone book?

"I knew from your name, because I've tried to keep tabs on your family. Although I must admit, I never properly introduced myself to your father. He wasn't very interested in any of it as a young boy, so Philip decided not to push it."

The tiny part of me that thought she might be making this up, or confused, died when she used my grandfather's name. "You know my dad?"

"We've met, briefly," she corrected. "I knew your great-great-many-times-great-grandparents. I was lucky enough to witness a ceremony when the Protector passed it down to his granddaughter. She's the one who told me all about the history and traditions."

"So the Carmichaels have been doing this for thousands of years?"

"The Bennetts," she corrected with an edge to her voice, as if she did not like the Carmichaels very much. "But the first Carmichael who gave his name to your branch of the Protector bloodline is the reason I try not to judge a man by his ancestry."

"But the rest of the Carmichaels…"

"Every family has good and evil in it. I take them on a case-by-case basis."

"Am I living up to expectations so far?" I asked.

"If I didn't know any better, I would call you a Bennett." She winked at me before walking ahead.

Delia left me at the staircase so I could go find Tristan. He was lying in the grass while Penny was under a sheet that appeared to be floating in mid-air. She made dandelions fly into his face with bursts of wind, and he pretended to be surprised and flustered every time it happened. Her giggle, so pure and full of joy, made the charade worth it.

"Do you have homework?" Tristan asked me, raising an arm so I could cuddle into him. As soon as he took my hand in his, the tent-like structure Penny was hiding under collapsed. *Static electricity*, I presumed.

I felt terrible, another thing my Gift destroyed, but Penny's laughter burst through the blanket as she shouted, "Again! Again!"

"Not that I know of." I answered his question. I could practice, but without knowing how to control it, or clear my mind, I would just be spending the evening touching everything at Rosehill and seeing things I probably wasn't supposed to see.

"Perfect. Let's go find you a bathing suit."

"Is there a pool?"

"Yes, but it's indoors. We only use it in the winter."

"Because in the summer you…"

"We go to the beach. You mentioned you loved splashing around in the waves when you were little."

"I did," I agreed. Now that I knew I got my Gift from nearly drowning in a river when I was little, the rough waters brought a cold sweat to the back of my neck, but I pushed it aside and focused on Tristan.

"I convinced Chris that today would be a great time to try out his paella pot."

"Paella?" I asked.

"It's a Spanish dish with rice, saffron, and a bunch of seafood. I tried hamburgers, hot dogs, and the pizza oven, but it took paella to get him on board."

"House outing?" I concluded.

"Figured we could all use a night of fun."

"You're pretty awesome, you know that?" The damage from touching him was already done, so I leaned in and kissed him.

"Starting to," he agreed, while Penny pretended to be grossed out.

CHAPTER THIRTEEN

ALISON

I wished we could have gone somewhere just the two of us, but it was nice seeing Tristan surrounded by his adopted family. They actually made an effort to have a sit down, family meal every night, no matter what was going on around them. To watch a bunch of Gifted hang out together and use their Gifts without fear…and not just about being discovered. Penny was barely old enough to ride a bike, but she used her Gift of controlling the weather with more confidence than I had for anything.

There were some Rosehill residents who had yet to warm up to me, though I wasn't sure they ever would. In my defense, they didn't seem overly fond of anyone. Mateo sat in a corner as if someone had forced him to come only to put him in a timeout. He was determined to glare at us without participating in any of it, though some – mostly Delia – tried. Lena took everything in like she expected every one of us to be hiding a knife up our sleeves. The only one who got her out of her shell was Penny, who kept climbing onto her lap to whisper secrets in her ear. Lena kept a straight face the first few times, but then the smile stayed even when Penny was gone.

The adults put on a good show, but they were weary, constantly looking into the distance, surveilling the water line. I imagined Delia knew the limits of her property, but tonight seemed like the kind of thing she allowed against her better judgment.

Penny pulled Tristan by the hand to the shoreline with her, where they spent nearly an hour finding shells. I was touched when she brought some of them to me, but I felt a pang seeing how good he was with her. Not that I was in any kind of hurry, but I always knew that someday, I would be a mother. To find out that Tristan wouldn't be able to have that, at least not in my lifetime...but then again, unless I got my Gift under control, I wouldn't want to be near a baby, let alone hold one in my arms or carry it in my womb.

WE SWAM in the water and splashed around, but stayed close to shore so as not to give Delia heart palpitations. I knew she was worried about how far the protections went, and I didn't want someone – or something – grabbing me while I was in the water. It would be equally twisted and poetic if I died by drowning thirteen years after my father saved me from it.

"I was completely off the mark with this one, wasn't I?" Tristan asked, lifting me up in his arms when the bottom got rough and murky. I couldn't tell if there were creatures or just slimy rocks beneath my feet.

"Not completely," I argued, but he gave me a look, like I wasn't fooling anyone. "When you suggested it, my thoughts were that I'd rather be alone with you, and that rivers aren't on my good side anymore."

"Because of the jump," he said, like he'd been expecting it ever since I reacted so unenthusiastically to his suggestion.

"It didn't help," I agreed. "But I drowned in a river when I was little."

"Oh my God," he said, fear and realization dawning on his face.

"No, it's fine. I got over it and still loved the water. Until I found out that's what gave me my Gift."

"When you died," he understood. "We can go back. I think Delia's having a panic attack watching us all out in the open."

"We can go in if you think she'll worry less, but I really needed this…" He'd brought us to a deeper part, where I couldn't reach the bottom, so I let myself drift back into the clear water, with the sun beating down and warming my skin.

"You enjoy revisiting bad memories?"

"I don't want to be afraid of something that used to make me so happy." I came back into his arms. "You're right, this afternoon I wasn't sold on the idea, but next time you ask, I'll remember you holding me in your arms and keeping me warm while the waves crash onto us, and I'll be excited to say yes."

"You're sure you're happy?" he asked, looking into my eyes like he was trying to see into my soul, not just talking about if I was glad we came to the beach, but whether I was happy as a whole, here with him.

"I'm a mess, and nothing has made sense since I found out about my Gift, but right now? In this moment? Definitely," I assured him.

"Next time, I'll plan something fun for just the two of us."

"I'd very much like that." I smiled. "But I also like getting to know you through them. How you are as a big brother or hanging out with the guys or trying to take care of Delia. It's a lot of new sides to you."

"And?"

"All the more to love." I leaned in and kissed him before remembering that at least half the people on the beach were probably watching us to make sure we didn't get attacked or taken out by the current. Before I had the chance to confirm my theory, Penny called out as she swam to us, splashing more water on our faces than she moved underwater to propel herself. Every time she ran out, she came back with another victim, so this time Jackie was shivering along with her, looking uncomfortable with the coverage her bathing suit gave her.

"Here," Penny encouraged, using her Gift to magnify the sun. Or at least that's what it felt like.

I looked to Tristan, wondering if I should be worried she was going to fry us, but Delia was on the lookout.

"Penelope Margaret Bingham!" She called out at the water's edge.

"I'm not allowed to use it on anything more than my immediate surroundings," Penny explained to me, rolling her eyes. "I thought you might come in if it was warmer," she called to Delia, the picture of innocence.

"I didn't bring a bathing suit, but next time," Delia assured her, but I knew there wouldn't be a next time, at least not this visit.

PENNY, Tristan, and I stayed in the water until the sun was setting and the night air grew cool. Tristan ran out first to get us towels, so Penny and I stayed up to our necks in the water, which was slightly warmer than the air.

Penny spun around in circles while we waited, but I watched Tristan, my eyes wandering to the rest of the people on the beach. Delia was talking animatedly to Krishna, some story that involved lots of gestures and had Krishna in stitches. She'd joined the festivities with her parents, who were talking to Jackie about something a lot more serious, and way less entertaining. I studied all the tiny groups, but it was Ben who caught my eye. According to Jackie, the Patels, Caleb and Etta, as well as Tristan and I, were the only couples at Rosehill. Etta even mentioned that Delia had been single for as long as she'd known her, except for rumors of a brief affair with Gabriel that she thinks probably never happened. But Ben's eyes found Delia across the room, across the beach…wherever she was, he found her. And he looked at her like my dad looked at my mom, at least until he felt someone watching. Ben said he'd been at Rosehill for sixty years now, but I wondered how many of them he'd been in love with Delia for.

LORCAN, the gargoyle who'd hunted my hunters through the woods, made us a bonfire to sit around while eating.

"Ew! Ew! Ew!" Penny exclaimed when she realized the shrimp still had its shell on in her paella. "Take it off."

She brought the plate to Tristan and sat on his knee, burying her head in his chest while he dissected all the pieces of shrimp so they no longer had eyes or legs. She thanked him, but didn't leave her new seat on his knee.

"They're more flavorful that way," Chris defended himself.

"It's delicious," I told him.

"Glad someone notices." He surprised me by sticking his tongue out at Penny, who reciprocated before laughing her head off.

"It tastes good. It just looks gross," she assured him.

I WAS STUFFED by the time Jackie and Brandon came out with graham crackers, marshmallows, and chocolate bars. It was less noticeable in the darkness, but Delia's concerns about our beach party were doubling by the hour.

"Bedtime?" she asked a little too eagerly when Tristan yawned.

"I'm not…" Her look, the fear more than the reproach, stopped him mid-word. "That sounds like a great idea," he decided, grabbing his plates.

"I've got them," I assured him, since Penny was half-asleep in his lap.

"And we've got whatever is left," Charlie told me with a wink as he and his brother looked around the beach, gathering all the dishes and garbage into the air and making it follow us back to the main building.

"I will never get used to this." I shook my head at the scene of a gargoyle-made fire, flying dishes, and a path illuminated by the moon, while darkness covered the rest of the landscape.

"You think that, but then it becomes second nature, and you don't understand why you would ever get up to grab a drink when you can just make it come to you," Brandon told me with a shrug, but I had a long way to go before I was using my Gift willy-nilly without a specific purpose. Rosehill was a treasure trove of memories, but I was carefully avoiding every artefact and doing my best not to come into direct contact with the furniture, just in case.

"PENNY IS IN LOVE WITH YOU," I told Tristan once he'd carefully tucked her in, making my heart burst.

"She's an actual six-year-old," he pointed out. "Although, by the time she's seventeen, I'll still be—"

He was teasing, but I didn't like the joke, nor what he was implying.

"You'll be turning gray." I cut him off. I'd also been teasing with my comment, because I meant it in the way little girls have silly crushes on older boys, but he was about to tell me he wouldn't get any older, so their age difference would technically shrink, until it got bigger again, with him on the younger side. Like ours was already doing.

"Allie…"

"You already like helping people and making them smile, so I say you keep doing what you're doing, and figure out what you're meant to do."

"That's easier said than done. I could just as easily do it tomorrow as I could—"

"How long does it normally take a person?" I asked before he could tell me it could take centuries.

"I don't think there is a normal. Some people just need a little more time, some students aren't even here a year before they start aging again…but you can figure out how long it took Sakina, how Delia still hasn't found hers."

"But that would be cruel," I argued.

"That's why I tried so hard to stay away," he reminded me, with a kiss to prove he wasn't doing that anymore.

"You've given up on that ridiculousness, right?"

"It was a stupid idea," he agreed. "For good reasons, but it was game over the minute I went over and talked to you." He smiled and brought me in for a kiss, longer and deeper than his earlier reassurance.

"I'm okay with being a cougar," I told him. "But I won't be a puma." I wasn't sure if that was the proper terminology, but I held my ground.

"I'm not following."

"It means you need to figure out your purpose so we can grow old together," I told him, more vulnerable than I wanted to be, but I figured we were past playing coy.

"Or else…" he asked.

"There's no or else." I shrugged, trying to sound more confident, while wondering if it would work if Delia told him to find his purpose and do it. I would assume she'd thought of that, but it would probably take some convincing to get her to do it.

"Then your wish is my command." Tristan kissed me again, probably to distract me from the blatant lie he was telling me, but when I was in his arms, I no longer cared.

.   .   .

Once we were alone in his bedroom, I told him all about my first lesson, and the weird meditation exercises Sakina had me doing afterwards.

"Do you think you're improving?" he asked, running his fingers along my arm, giving me shivers.

"I'm getting better at pinpointing parts of memories, but the goal is to get rid of my predicament, not strengthen it."

"The goal is for you not to unintentionally hurt people, but I think your Gift could be pretty cool if you decided what you saw when. For someone who loves history and archeology, just imagine everything you could discover."

"They usually frown on guests touching the pieces in museums," I pointed out.

"Rosehill is like a museum," he reminded me.

"But how many of the strongest memories are happy ones?"

CHAPTER FOURTEEN

ALISON

"Who else is there?" Sakina asked after my tenth time watching a girl's fingers weave through the harp. There was laughter and dancing, with some very off-key singing, but none of the shapes were close enough for me to see them in focus.

"Delia," I tried.

"Because you see her, or you assume it's her house, so she should be there?"

"We've been at this all morning, and I've told you everything I could see. Shouldn't we be trying to have me touch the harp without seeing anything?" I'd expected a nervous musician before a grand orchestra, but the million-dollar harp was only ever used in Rosehill's library by a girl who didn't want to be playing it.

"The first time I was able to control my Gift perfectly was with a little girl I met in Peru. She shared absolutely every thought that ever crossed her mind, so even if I listened in, there was nothing new for me to discover. You can touch that harp and try not to see anything, but while you are still curious about the shapes and the other voices, you won't get very far."

"But Delia was there, right?"

"I wouldn't know that unless I was also one of them," she pointed out.

We tried the harp a few more times, which was easier when I decided Delia was one of the people and focused on finding her rather than figuring out who was there. I still had other shapes to figure out, but Sakina insisted progress was progress. She'd also brought some personal items, knowing exactly which memories they would bring up, and she was right, that knowing the answers to all my questions made it easier to stop the memory from flooding my mind, but it still wasn't consistent.

I tried to clear my head while walking back to the main building from the barn, but I had never been good at meditation or focusing on nothing. A good book or an artefact, sure, I could stare at it for hours. But I wasn't one to do nothing without letting my mind wander.

I saw Tristan, Delia, Jackie, and Penny with a couple of horses and debated if I wanted to try my hand at horseback riding or check out some books from the Rosehill library. Sakina was giving me lessons, but I was curious about what the other students learned regarding Giftedness and their history.

I turned away from the others before they could spot me and headed for the front doors, nearly jumping out of my skin when the phone in my pocket rang. So far, I'd only received text messages with it, so the FaceTime ring tone was unexpected.

"I finally got a minute alone," Sybill said as soon as her face popped up on my screen. "What the hell happened to you? Why aren't you here yet?"

"How are you?" I asked instead. "Still feeling good?"

"Al, you can't have me dig up information on stabbing incidents where you work *and* murder victims, then radio silence for over a week."

"I talk to you every day," I argued.

"With mom and dad, about ice cream and the internship I know you're not doing anymore. And where are you?"

I was beside the solarium, facing the front gates to make sure no one was coming for me, which meant her view was of the mansion behind me.

"This is Rosehill. It's the boarding school Tristan went to."

"A pit stop on your drive to California?"

"Syb…"

"I keep quiet on the calls because I know you don't want to worry them, but I read your police file, Allie. I know you got kidnapped and rescued and I don't understand why you haven't called us to say you're safe now, why you're not here. I'm worried, and whatever you're up to is probably a million times better than what I'm imagining."

"I'm not sure about that," I argued.

"Try me."

I took a deep breath and tried to find the words. It wasn't even that I didn't want to tell her; it was that I didn't know how. "Grace woke up and told me that the people who attacked her were trying to find me…"

I told her everything. About the men who killed my security detail and chased us until they killed Tristan and took me. I winced at the shock and pain on her face before assuring her, "He's okay. That's part of why I didn't reach out…" I explained how some people who die before accomplishing an important task become Gifted, how they get supernatural powers and keep coming back to life. I told her how Tristan was one of them and he rescued me. Then I told her everything Logan told me about why they wanted me; how I'm a First Lifer and my blood was the cure for their cursed existence. "I thought it was because of my Gift, which is more of a curse, but apparently our entire bloodline could be useful to them as well, if my blood fails."

"What is your Gift?" Out of the million questions she could have asked, that was the answer I least wanted to give her.

"When I touch an object, I can see its most powerful memory, like a part of your essence lingers inside of it."

"That's why you always say the old things speak to you. That you can practically see the battles that were fought…it's because you can."

She was accepting my predicament a lot easier than I had.

"And why Dr. Richards thought I would be great at solving cold cases."

"That must have been so hard for you." The compassion in her face broke my heart, because she didn't know what I'd done. "How would that help them get rid of their Gifts?"

"They think I see the memories because I suck out the lingering essence. That I do that all the time whenever I touch people as well."

"As in you take other peoples' Gifts?" Her eyes widened, like this was a new superpower she'd discovered with endless possibilities.

"I do."

"Can you use them?"

"No, I just strip them away from the Gifted person. It lasts anywhere between four and twelve hours, but we haven't really been testing it."

"And if they want the effects to be permanent, they would have to reverse engineer something with your DNA?" she asked, but her science was better than mine.

"That seems to be their plan."

"I can cover with mom and dad a little longer, but you need to tell them eventually. They'll probably just treat it the same as my illness, as something we can all get through together." She rolled her eyes at how supportive and optimistic our parents were, before catching on to my look. "You have a plan, right? You're not just going to hide there forever and never see us again?"

"It's more like they're coming up with a plan, but you're all invited to move in if it goes that far." I tried to make light of it, but my joke fell flat.

"What's the bad part you're not telling me?" she asked, making me wonder if she was also Gifted to know when people are hiding something, like that Terrence guy who was supposed to be grilling Logan for us.

"It works on normal people too," I mumbled.

"But they don't have Gifts," she argued.

"It's not a placebo effect that you're feeling better, Syb. It's because I'm not there. I'm the one who's been making you sick because every time I touch you, I literally suck the life out of you. It's all because of me."

"Syb, who are you talking to?" I heard my mother in the background, but Sybill was white as a ghost, looking as ill as she had when she was spending her days with me killing her.

"I have to go," she said, her voice completely flat, or numb, but it made me feel like I'd broken her, even more than my Gift had.

"Syb..."

"I...I'll call you."

She hung up before I got the chance to say goodbye, or make sure she was okay. I wrapped my arms around myself as the tears fell. It was some twisted irony that all I wanted to do was take her in my arms, which was exactly how I was hurting her.

"There you are!" Penny exclaimed, rounding the corner with all the excitement of a child riding a pony. "The barn was empty, but we thought you might want to go riding. Or at least I did. They're big and scary at first, but it's fun. And you can try my pony to get used to it." She said all of this before noticing the tears running down my cheeks. "Did Sakina show you sad memories today?" she asked, trying to dismount on her own.

I didn't want to touch her, but I couldn't let her fall from that height either. I wrestled with myself, moving closer so I would be there in case, but Tristan ran over and caught her.

Then he saw me.

"What happened?" he asked, putting Penny down and rushing over.

"I'm fine, just a bad memory," I lied, putting my hands out to stop him from coming any closer. "I think I'll go try that claw-foot bathtub of yours."

"There's bubble bath in his bottom drawer," Penny told me. Tristan was so concentrated on me he didn't even reproach her for snooping around his room.

"That sounds perfect." I gave her a smile, as convincing as I could manage.

"Can I…will you be down for dinner?" Tristan changed gears when his attempt to come with me led to me taking a step back. I wanted his arms around me more than anything, but something inside me would die if I felt those sparks right now.

"Of course," I said, but I mustn't have been convincing enough.

"I'll bring you something in case you doze off," he covered for me, but the look in his eyes was the one I always had when I looked at Sybill in pain, knowing there was absolutely nothing I could do. I attempted a reassuring smile, then hurried inside before they could both see the fresh tears it triggered.

CHAPTER FIFTEEN

DELIA

"Where do you want me to put this?" I asked Penny as she read the directions for me. Baking with her was always an adventure, as she liked to give you higher measurements of the things she liked, and lower ones of the things she didn't. It wasn't so bad for cooking, but when it came to baking and you only used one egg instead of three, or left out the baking powder…you got a very depressing cake. She became the picture of innocence if you confronted her about it, reminding you she was just learning how to read, so you couldn't hold it against her.

When it came to decorating, she used the utmost precision. Or rather, had you decorate with the utmost precision for her, because her tiny hands couldn't recreate the visions she had in her mind. Neither could mine half the time, but she was nice enough to blame our ingredients when that happened, as opposed to her vision or my lack of skills.

"On top of the vacuum," she said with confidence.

"This is for Alison?" I verified.

"She sucks things away, but it makes her sad. Vacuums do

that too, and Jane loves to vacuum," she said of one of our cleaning ladies.

"We stay outside the house on cleaning days," I reminded her.

"But sometimes I can help. She doesn't see me, but I can blow the dirt outside for her."

"That's very sweet, but I'm sure she likes to do that on her own," I suggested. The last thing we needed was for a contractor to go crazy after seeing something they shouldn't, and set child protective services on us.

"But you told Tristan we should always help people whenever we can."

"I did say that," I agreed. Penny was inquisitive, caring, and remembered almost every word I told her. She was going to be the death of me. "But it's dangerous if she sees you. For you, for me, for everyone in this house. Sometimes, helping people doesn't look like we think it will."

"Like I'm helping Alison when I tell Tristan I don't want to go for a walk with him, even though I really do."

"Sometimes," I agreed. "But hopefully not all the time. He loves hanging out with you."

"I like him too," she shared. "And Alison," she decided. "When I'm older, I'm going to show her my mommy's locket." She looked down at the necklace she always wore, even when she was sleeping. It was the only personal item she had on her when she was left on our doorstep as a baby. She lost it once and acted like the world was ending until Charlie found it for her.

"Why would you do that?" I asked.

"Just to hold it," she assured me. "I don't think I'm ready for it just yet."

She went back to the icing she was turning a shade halfway between purple and brown. That girl was wise beyond her years sometimes.

"Good morning," Alison said, coming in with Tristan. She looked a lot better than Penny's description of her from yesterday afternoon, but there were dark circles under her puffy eyes.

Like every other morning, she consciously avoided any skin-to-skin contact with Tristan, but he made no such effort. He generally had her in his arms by the time we finished dinner, and as far as I was concerned, she deserved comfort wherever she could find it.

"How are your lessons going?" I asked, giving her an opening, although Sakina assured me Alison was fine when she left the barn.

"I'm learning a lot about Sakina. And whoever played the harp you have in the barn."

My attempt at stealthily gathering information on her mental state died then and there. I closed my eyes, vividly remembering the sound of Cadence playing that harp for hours on end, with James singing along to songs he knew none of the words to.

"Such as?" I smiled to cover the tears that welled in my eyes, terrified of how much she might see in those memories.

"They hated it." She shrugged.

"But her father loved to listen to it, so Cadence pretended to enjoy it for years," I shared, not ready for the rush of emotions that came with it. I took a few steadying breaths, like Sakina had first taught me to channel my anger, but it worked for pain as well.

"At first, I thought it was you playing, but Sakina had me focus on finding you, and you're the one laughing."

"Delia, laughing?" Tristan teased, getting a slap from Penny when he tried to stick his finger in her icing.

"I forgot we kept the harp." I focused on the instrument, the only part of that scene that didn't rip my heart to shreds.

"I don't think it works anymore music-wise, but it looks like solid gold."

"I'm sure it's just gold-plated," I said without thinking. It was a reflex to downplay the things in the house that would reveal too much, or simply make people jealous. It was always a cycle, where people were intrigued, then they found out more about me and I became this larger-than-life, historical figure, until they spent enough time with me to realize I was just plain old Delia with an interesting background. I'd long ago learned that the longer it took for them to know the full extent of my past, the less time to get rid of the weirdness.

"This probably isn't the time, but your house is beautiful. The artwork and ornaments you have…it's amazing."

"My naïve attempt to recreate the places that made me happy when I was younger. But thank you for saying so."

"Your sitting room reminds me of an exhibition we had at the museum I worked at in high school. Not so much now that I know it wasn't just my wild imagination, but some of those rooms were my happy place when life got to be too much."

I wanted to reach out to her, but I don't think she would have let me, even if it weren't for her Gift. "Some of my favorite pieces are in that room." I smiled at her, but also at the memories I got from certain books and vases in the sitting room. You didn't need Alison's Gift to see the lingering fragments of your heart that stayed behind, you just had to have been there.

"But Delia likes us better," Penny piped up. "She would trade every single thing in this place for one of my smiles."

"Absolutely," I agreed, getting a raised eyebrow from Alison. "I told her that and I meant it. Money means nothing in the grand scheme of things, and memories can't compare to the living person." I knew it didn't mean much coming from someone who'd always had more money than I knew what to do with, but if money could have saved any of the people I'd lost, I would gladly trade every last dime.

"Don't tell Penny anything you don't want repeated," Tristan warned.

"I can keep secrets," the six-year-old defended herself. "I didn't tell anyone about—"

She made a show of covering her mouth in horror, as if she'd been about to reveal some terrible secret. With her, it was most likely a joke, but she could also be sitting on any number of secrets, with all the sneaking around she likes to do.

Tristan brought Alison into the dining room for breakfast, so I brought Penny back to the cake. "Where does this go?"

My last decoration was a wedding cake topper, which might make Alison feel like we were coming on too strong, but Penny was in charge.

"In the middle, so they're safe."

"Here?" I asked, placing them at the center of the cake.

"Inside," she argued, standing on the chair so she was tall enough to push them into the cake, so the tops of their heads barely poked out.

My eyes burned before I heard banging on the walls from Jackie guiding herself to me, not taking the time to be careful.

She paused in the doorway when she sensed I wasn't alone.

"Hi Jackie!" Penny said excitedly. She made it a point to speak up whenever Jackie arrived, so the teenager would never be surprised by her presence.

"Hey Penny bug. How's it going?"

Penny looked to me, smart enough to know something was off.

"What is it?" I asked Jackie, letting Penny come up into my arms as Tristan and Alison came back in to see what was going on. I wanted to tell Penny she was being silly and there was nothing to be afraid of, but Jackie looked almost as worried as when she told me Tristan and Alison were attacked on their way to the airfield.

"You asked me to let you know if *they* moved?"

"Are they leaving?" I was hopeful, but a tiny part of me was reluctant to see James go. Even if I knew it was best for everyone, including myself, if he left.

"They're coming closer."

"Where?" Last she saw them, they were camped out in the old hunting cabin at the end of the property. It had been abandoned long before the barriers went up, so security was minimal, with locked doors to avoid squatters instead of magical wards and enchantments.

"The front gate."

I put Penny down and was going to suggest she show Alison her room, ensuring both of their safety, but as soon as Penny's feet touched the ground, she followed the others outside.

I pressed the alarm button on the keypad and met them in the front yard.

"No one underage, and no First or Last Lifers," I reminded them of the rules, putting my arms out when Jackie and Mateo tried to follow me past the front steps.

"Where do you want us to go?" Jackie asked. The rule was normally that kids and First Lifers stayed home and couldn't come with us on the dangerous adventures; we weren't used to the trouble finding us here.

"Inside," Ben answered for me with his dogs, Bear and Brutus, at his heels. "What is it?"

"They're coming," Jackie shared.

Mateo was the only one who walked back to the mansion, taking Penny by the hand. I made a mental note to tell him how grateful I was that he listened, and that he took her with him.

"How close?"

Before Jackie could respond, the surrounding skies went dark. It was raining, with thunder and lightning as far as the eye could see...except within the stone wall. It was dark above us, but only at least a hundred feet above the highest tower, where it looked like the storm was just rolling off an invisible barrier.

"Woah," Penny remarked.

I turned to plead with her to get inside, but Mateo had already taken her up in his arms to move her along faster.

"Guess that's your answer." Ben pointed ahead, where James and his friends had scaled the fence, but could not get down the other side. I'd been wondering if the protections were more like a dome, or a barbed-wire fence, and it seemed like it was the former. Potts lingered slightly behind the others and was definitely avoiding eye contact with me. He'd chosen his side, but that didn't erase decades of us being family.

The one who'd tortured Ben the other night locked eyes with Tristan and balled his hands into fists, trying to take him down, but his Gift wasn't working on us. The one with scales pounded against the invisible barrier, to no avail.

I let out a sigh of relief, carefully avoiding even a glance in James' direction, just as the earth shook. James was standing by the wrought-iron gate with that woman who controlled the trees. Roots rose around her, covering the gate and all the cement of the fence, crushing it by sheer force as she kept her eyes locked on Alison. I wondered what made her hate her so much, or if she just blindly followed James' every word.

Someone screamed behind me when the vines ripped the gate off its hinges, sending it crashing into a nearby tree that absorbed it into itself, as if the tree had grown around the gate for centuries.

"Do you want me to freeze them?" Lena offered, coming out of nowhere. I spotted Charlie and Brandon beside Jackie and sighed at the lack of control I had on my teenagers.

"I don't know if it'll bounce back on us," I argued, gesturing for them all to stay back, but not stupid enough to believe they would listen longer than a few minutes.

I stepped forward, keeping my hand out behind me to warn the others, including Ben, not to follow. I stopped just before the indentations from where the gate used to be, and locked eyes with the woman, trying to convey that if she came after my family, there would be hell to pay.

She broke eye contact first, so I turned back to look at my gargoyles.

"Take the intruders to the Northern Border, please," I asked of them.

Like the magic that animated them, they broke free, spread their wings, and flew down upon James' people.

His team used their Gifts and their strength, but they were no match for the gargoyles made of magic and stone. Persephone went for James, but stopped when she recognized him. There was a momentary stare down before Persephone flew off with the woman, leaving James behind.

I knew it looked like my gargoyles were fallible. Like this man had somehow bested them without lifting a finger, but I knew the truth. I'd chosen my words poorly, as they didn't see James as an intruder; he was the master of the house. While witches put the magical protection up in 1843, when I turned the mansion into a Boarding School, the gargoyles came centuries earlier, back when James would climb the side of the building to cover them in candles and wreaths around the holidays – showing off when I could just ask them to fly down – because he knew it would make me happy to come home and find the house all lit up and covered with snow.

That was the man they bowed down to. The one in front of me wore his face, but it was not the same.

James walked off, keeping his eyes on me, then switched to a run, to meet up with his friends. Or maybe to get reinforcements. All I knew was that he would be back.

I breathed another sigh of relief once he was out of sight,

because the threat was gone, at least for now. I nearly even smiled, until I saw Sakina standing in the distance with Mohinder, ready to fight. He looked relieved they wouldn't have to face the enemy from the wrong side of the magical barrier, but Sakina had her eyes on me.

CHAPTER SIXTEEN

DELIA

Chris had the DVD for one of those superhero movies the kids were into these days, the kind I never encouraged them to watch, because it gave them the wrong idea of what it meant to have Gifts, but everyone was shaken, and we needed a break. It was a temporary Band-Aid on all the questions and fears that this morning brought, but for now, I needed a minute where everyone was in the same room, safe and sound. I'd slightly encouraged Penny to force Lena and Mateo to sit on either side of her, because no matter how grudgingly Mateo complied, at least they weren't off doing something reckless on their own. Jackie and the boys were used to the safety of Rose-hill, so they wouldn't dream of venturing out on their own into the unknown, but Mateo and Lena had survived in much harsher situations far longer than anyone their age should have. Not that I thought they would leave us to fend for ourselves if we needed them, but if the attacks kept coming, I didn't know how long I could convince them to stay put without getting involved.

I pulled the knitted shawl tighter around my shoulders, but the chill had nothing to do with the temperature in our home theater, especially not with the popcorn machine running, and more guests than we'd had since the premiere of Finn's directorial debut.

"You've been keeping secrets," Sakina reproached as she took the seat beside mine, leaving Mohinder up front with Krishna.

"I would have told you if you'd asked," I argued.

"If I asked who was after her, or if I specifically asked if it was James?" She clearly didn't believe me. "I take it you knew before this morning?"

"When they attacked Tristan and Alison the other night, we went to rescue them and...I sent the gargoyles after them. And defended Alison against him."

"Explains the betrayal," she stated without judgment, but I could feel it. "I hadn't seen him since...not since he found me in Italy."

"That was in the sixties?" I asked, knowing it was in 1963, that he cornered her as she was about to go into the Vatican and talked to her less than fifteen minutes before leaving her with a twelve-year-old First Lifer who needed protection. Laurel wasn't the first child James had sent my way since I opened the school, but she was the only one he'd personally delivered to someone I could grill for information on him. Not that Sakina had shared more than his mustache looked ridiculous and she wondered where he'd found his leather jacket.

"I doubt he's changed that much in fifty years."

"Over two hundred years and he's still driven by the same thing," I argued with the point she was trying to make, that he was still my James. "Alison's last name is Carmichael. And it's not a coincidence."

"Does she know?"

"Some of it," I admitted with a sigh. "The Damned are after her, but I doubt he plans on giving her up."

"I could ask Mohinder..."

I knew her offer was genuine, but I couldn't, not when I

knew how his Gift worked. James' pain and anger wouldn't disappear, they would just be transferred to Mohinder, and he didn't deserve that.

"Is vengeance a feeling or an obsession?" I pondered aloud.

"Both are fueled by James' pain."

"He won't break his promise."

I wanted, more than anything, to ask her what she heard in his mind, for Mohinder to tell me what emotions drove him, but I'd already betrayed James enough in the past few days, and it would probably be harder if I knew.

I tried to concentrate on the movie, but I'd missed the beginning, and it was more comforting for me to watch the way Tristan kissed the top of Alison's head once she got comfy leaning into him, how Mateo smiled at some jokes before he caught himself and looked around to make sure no one saw, and Lena turned Penny's fruit punch into a popsicle for her. It didn't even bother me when an explosion on the screen made Charlie drop the bowl of popcorn he'd been summoning, that Brandon quickly sent to the garbage before I would notice. Seeing them happy was better than a thousand films.

"CAN we go for ice cream after dinner tonight?" Krishna came to us once the movie was over, eating the last of her popcorn. She let me pull her into my lap, so she sat on my knee while waiting for her mother's response.

"I don't even know if you'll be able to eat your meal after all those sweets," Sakina argued. The evidence was more obvious on Penny, who had a ring of red around her mouth, but Krishna's lips were artificially colored enough to let us know she'd partaken in the popsicles as well.

"If I finish my food?" she tried.

"We'll see." Sakina rolled her eyes, but she was smiling.

"I thought for sure you would stay here tonight, after what

happened. Your rooms are ready for you to stay as long as it takes to get rid of them."

"We can take care of ourselves," she assured me with a reproachful smile.

"Sakina," I pleaded, keeping my own smile so as not to worry Krishna.

"James won't hurt me, or my family," she said under her breath, taking me in for a hug. "As much as he is known for always getting his target, he is known for his precision," she said, reminding me that he never left unintended casualties.

She was right, but I didn't like it. Not her family staying alone and poorly protected in the vast expanse of the grounds, or me worrying about James threatening the safety of my family when he was the one who used to protect it.

"Mrs. Patel? I was wondering if we could keep working tomorrow, even if it's the weekend?" Alison came over and interrupted any excuses I could have come up with to convince them. "I just…I don't want to be a sitting duck next time that happens. Tristan's first instinct when there's trouble is to take my hand, but that just knocks out his Gift. And I'm afraid of even touching Penny, because I don't want to hurt her, but sometimes people could get hurt if I don't touch them, and…I don't want to be this helpless."

"Eight am sharp," Sakina assured her before heading out with her family. "I have some ideas."

THE THEATER ROOM made it seem like it was nighttime, but the sun was still shining when we came out. I was grateful that even Mateo and Lena stayed inside the manor for the rest of the afternoon, though all I got was a shrug when I thanked him for taking care of Penny earlier. When everyone said they were too full from the snacks to have dinner, I wanted to remind them that dinner was a family thing, about the company as much as the food, but it was more about me wanting to have eyes on them, and not be alone.

"Of course." I smiled instead, with absolutely no appetite myself.

I WAITED until they were all in their rooms, with Penny sound asleep, before going up to my bedroom, where I turned off all the lights. My room was designed so I was surrounded by memories of those I loved and lost, with photographs and knickknacks, but I couldn't bear to look at them tonight. I'd given Alison free rein of the manor, like everyone else had, but I purposely avoided having her anywhere near my rooms. If her Gift was half as powerful as Tristan and Sakina claimed, every inch of my quarters would tell her my secrets and announce my betrayal to the others. Not that I was lying to them, or that it was any of their business...but I hated secrets and lies. They tore families apart. Unfortunately, there was no way I could protect anyone if they knew the truth.

CHAPTER SEVENTEEN

ALISON

"I made muffins," Delia said while cradling a large mug when I got downstairs the following morning. "The berries are fresh from the greenhouse."

"You must have been up dreadfully early," I pointed out. I'd woken up earlier than Tristan so I could beat Sakina to the barn and get in some extra practice. I wasn't expecting anyone to be up yet.

"I've always had trouble sleeping," she brushed it off. "I can make you breakfast if you'd prefer. Eggs or pancakes or…"

"The muffin is perfect, thank you," I assured her, heading for the door.

"Isn't Sakina meeting you at eight?"

"I thought I might get a head start."

"I can walk you," Delia offered, before Penny rushed into the kitchen, straight for her arms.

"There you are," the little girl exclaimed before climbing into her lap. "I had a nightmare, and you weren't in your room."

"I am so sorry love, what was the nightmare about?"

I gave Delia a tiny wave and slipped out before Penny woke up enough to notice I was there. The sun was barely visible over the hill, especially not through the mist, so it was a chilly walk to the barn, but the muffin was perfection. Every bite was like an explosion of fruit on my taste buds. Maybe I would convince my mother to start a backyard garden once it was safe to go home.

THE BARN'S upper level was just as we'd left it, with the table of old objects and the harp in the middle of the room, waiting to be played. If Sakina was right and the key to touching the harp and seeing nothing was to know everything I could about the memory, I needed to figure out who was doing that awful singing. I'd compared the voice to everyone I'd met at Rosehill, especially Ben, but there was the hint of a Germanic accent in the singing, and I had never seen Delia look at Ben the way she looked at the man in the memory.

I took a few deep breaths to clear my mind like Sakina had taught me, then carefully placed my fingers on the cords, as if I were about to play. I was prepared to hear the music, to focus on the singing, but the memory didn't take me to a vibrant room full of joy where my heart wrestled with my distaste for the instrument and overflowing love for my family. I stayed where I was, only it was darker; both emotionally and literally. It felt like I was in an ocean of despair, and I would never reach the top. My tears – mixed with the ones from the memory – were suffocating me so I couldn't catch my breath. I had yet to feel a memory so strong, even back at the precinct. This one was fresh.

I pulled my hands off the harp and took a step back, placing my hand on my heart and trying to calm my breathing. I had an overwhelming urge to call my mom, or rather, for her to comfort me like Delia had comforted Penny this morning. But it was too early, and I didn't want to worry my family when there was nothing they could do.

Sakina insisted she didn't know who the girl playing the harp was, nor who her parents were, acting as if she'd popped in and out of Delia's life, which was always full of love and laughter. She'd tried so hard to make sure everything I touched in here held happy emotions, but what was once happy could easily turn depressing when an immortal woman revisited objects from her past, clutching them to her chest and mourning the loss of what felt like a child. It was my fault, really. Delia's reaction when I mentioned the harp yesterday had all but confirmed that she was the laughing voice, and that the daughter was hers. She also mentioned the girl's father, which told me Delia had not always been the lonely matriarch to a band of unwanted children, as Etta had implied.

"Are you alright?" Sakina asked. She came close, but stopped herself before she reached me.

"I wanted to solve the harp, so I could stop seeing it—"

"Don't worry about the harp, I shouldn't have you working on questions I don't have the answer for," she said before seeing the guilt on my face. "The harp did this to you?"

"I accidentally stumbled on a very fresh, very raw, gaping wound of a memory," I agreed. "I mentioned the harp to Delia, and I'm guessing she came here this morning to torture herself, or relive a happy memory, but all I could feel was her heartbreak and an emptiness in the pit of her stomach."

"I brought some tea." Sakina gave me a look of sympathy before setting it up. "That always helps."

"Do you know a Cadence?" I asked, my hand still pressed to my heart, trying to dull the ache I felt the echo of. "Delia told me she was the one playing, but that didn't feel like the pain of losing someone from natural causes after a long and happy life…it felt like having your child devastatingly ripped away at a young age, long before—"

"Parents aren't supposed to bury children, and Delilah has

buried many. It doesn't matter how you lose them, or how old they are; it rips your heart out all the same."

"The girl from the ribbon…it isn't Krishna, is it?" I asked delicately. Might as well get all the grief in at once.

"Neela," she said wistfully, taking a sip of her tea and motioning for me to do the same. "Ninety-six when I lost her, but I was nowhere near ready."

"I'm sorry."

"Thank you." She gave me a sad smile. "I followed my daughter's children for generations, coming in and out of their lives when it got too hard. We settled here before Krishna was born because we wanted her to have a family where she was safe to be as she is, but Neela's descendants live in Boston and go to summer camp with her."

"That's sweet."

"They don't know, but it makes me happy," she shared. "The harp, were you looking for Delilah, or…"

"I was listening for the singing, to figure out who it was, but this new one hit me like a ton of bricks."

"If you touch an object with a powerful enough memory, it will come to you unbidden, even if you are looking for something else? You don't have to dig for it?" She brought it back to my training, which was what I was here for. I just felt like she and Delia were the most tight-lipped women I'd ever met, considering all the life and experiences they'd had.

"The only times I had to work at it was for the weird Magnum thing, and a knife that had recently been used to kill someone," I shared. "The knife was self-preservation, though. Delia's memory was an emotional punch in the gut, but with weapons, I can feel them slicing into me, and it stays for hours after I'm no longer touching it."

"For all weapons?" Her eyes went wide.

"Just recent ones. I think objects are like people, in the sense that time heals their wounds. Or at least dulls them for me."

"The older, the better," Sakina declared.

"Until I figure out how to block them out," I agreed.

"Well, as far as actually using your Gift, you can see memories from the surface, you can dig deep to find the buried ones, locate more than one memory in a single object, focus on specific details and reveal more if you have something to go on…I'd say you're doing pretty well."

"These are all things I was working on with Grace, my supervisor at the precinct, to solve cold cases. Right now, I'm more concerned with not accidentally reliving painful memories every time I touch something here."

"Then why don't we try touching emotionally charged objects and not seeing anything?" Sakina looked excited, but I knew this meant I was going to spend the day being bombarded by memories and feelings of failure. "We can start with the objects you're familiar with, because I know curiosity is a big motivator. Then you can decide if you want to move on to new objects with heartbreaking memories, so you won't be tempted to see them, or happy memories while you figure it out."

"I'm leaning towards happy," I said, shaking off Delia's heartbreak while Sakina brought her blue ribbon over.

"We want to get to a point where you can touch anything and have to will your Gift to work, rather than having to concentrate to not use it," she reminded me of the objective. "But we can start with something familiar."

I nodded and took a deep breath before gently brushing my fingers along the blue fabric. I concentrated with all my might, but I still saw that little girl.

BY THE END of the day, after constantly reminding myself to breathe like Sakina taught me, and to concentrate like Grace suggested, I could touch the ribbon without seeing anything, and an old rocking chair only showed me a memory half the time, which was probably because the person who'd used it was usually sleeping, and the strongest memory was of them staring down at an infant and saying, "I can't believe you're all mine, my beautiful baby boy." Apparently, Chris also used the barn as storage for his parents' old things.

"This is amazing, Alison." Sakina beamed with pride after I touched the chair for a second time in a row with nothing happening.

"It's two objects whose memories I know by heart. And I had to start all over again with the chair like I hadn't just mastered it with the ribbon."

"It's progress. And a mind needs rest for things to sink in. We'll come back to it and try more things tomorrow."

"I'll stay here and keep working for a bit." I tried to sound enthusiastic rather than defeated, but it was hard when everything was difficult, and every object presented the same challenge as the one before.

Sakina hesitated in the doorway before leaving with a sigh. As soon as she was gone, I turned back to the chair. If I could touch it ten times without seeing anything, I would consider it two items down and infinity to go.

It was less than fifteen minutes later that Mohinder came up the stairs and sat across from me on the old couch. He watched me work on the harp, but didn't say a thing.

"Does it look as fun as it feels?" I asked, only realizing after the words were out that he had the unique perspective of knowing both.

"Every object is a new obstacle because it shows you something different." He sighed. "The hardest part of stopping the emotions is that there are so many that I want to feel. When someone is filled with joy and excitement, I want to bask in that. Every first that a child experiences is like magic. And no matter how Krishna and Sakina feel, I want to know it, so I can either share in their happiness, or try to make their pain go away. It is one thing to fight against your Gift, but it's a whole other bucket of worms to compete against your Gift *and* the part of you that is curious and wants to know."

"I know the harp's memories by heart, and it didn't help," I argued.

"But you must accept that you won't find more clues about Delia within it. I bet part of you was trying to see nothing, while part of you was still trying to pull another memory from it."

"Maybe if Sakina was more into gossiping, this would go faster," I defended myself, getting a laugh in return. It was pure and happy; I wanted nothing more than to bask in it.

"She loved to gossip when she was little."

"Your wife?" I didn't believe him.

"She wanted to know everything about everyone, hated it when people whispered, she listened at closed doors…her dad called it curious, but she was a gossip."

"I can't picture it."

"Too much of something is rarely a good thing. She went from wanting to know things to being able to hear everything. No matter how overwhelming that can be, no matter how good she is at controlling her Gift…she must actively resist using it on me. And Krishna."

"That would almost be torture," I argued.

"Not like our thoughts are pushing their way in and she has to keep them out…controlling your Gift is not the same as not using it."

"You think I want to relive the same memories over and over again? To have my heart torn to shreds by Delia's pain?"

"No, but you want to know the answers to your questions, that might be in these objects."

"Did Sakina just go home and tell you I was in trouble?"

"No, but Krishna lets her curiosity win far too often, especially when someone new is exploring the mysteries of Delia's past. She hopes you only learn how to control your Gift after you figure out who the man is, because she has never seen Delia get that close to anyone except for Ben, and we know Delia isn't in love with him."

My thoughts exactly.

CHAPTER EIGHTEEN

ALISON

"Another early start?" Delia asked when I got to the middle landing of the staircase. She had a mug in her hands, but she'd been staring at the tapestry of faces.

"Things aren't going so great."

"It's always hardest in the beginning, when you have to learn everything, but once you master the basics, everything gets so much easier," she assured me. Her smile was warm, but her eyes were a million miles away.

"Was this painted by one of your students?"

"Many of them. I received a family portrait as a birthday present, but it was after I became Gifted, so they had the foresight to know they'd need a much larger canvas as the family expanded."

"Are these all of your students, then?"

"Most." She brushed her hand against the fabric in a way that told me I did not want to go anywhere near it. "Anyone who stayed long enough got added in as soon as we had an artist in our midst."

She pointed over to a spot maybe five feet above our heads where I could see Jackie, Tristan, Charlie, and Brandon smiling back at me. Jackie was with a girl I didn't recognize, while the boys stood together. My eyes traveled along the many faces I recognized. Gabriel, Caleb, Etta, Lucy…

"That's Mr. Aetos," I said when the owner of the Greek restaurant Tristan took me to on our first date was smiling at me. He looked younger than he had back in Boston, but it was unmistakably him.

"You met Cy?" Delia's face lit up.

"We went to his restaurant. Tristan mentioned he was an old friend of yours, but I guess he couldn't tell me about the school."

"Cyrus' family moved to the States just before the war. His grandfather enlisted and his grandmother was Gifted, so she trusted us to take care of her boys while she went to be a guardian angel at the front."

"Did she…"

"Every single member from his company came home," she assured me. "Meropi and Stavros came back after the war and opened that little restaurant. I try to go every time I'm in Boston, but it isn't nearly often enough."

"Then he knows about…all this?"

"It was hard not to. I'd bet you any money Meropi was in the kitchens, making your food. She loves being hostess and talking to everyone that comes in, but she can only do that a few years every half-century before she has to move on or hide behind the pots and pans."

"Tristan did leave me for a while to hang out in the kitchens," I remembered.

"She would have blown her cover in ten seconds if she came out. Some Gifted act the age they look, because it's how people treat them, but Meropi is a badass matriarch who was probably pinching Tristan's cheeks and would have gone full grandmother on you. Especially young love. We live for that stuff."

I could see a sparkle in her eye, either because of Meropi or all the young loves she'd witnessed, but her comment had me thinking about the people at Rosehill, and the dynamics.

"You look about my age, but I don't think I would ever treat you like it," I admitted, not sure if that was rude, but it was the truth. Grace had been my superior at work, which had given her an air of authority, but it was only when she interacted with Malcolm, her son who looked decades older than her, that I got the feeling she was more than a couple of years older than me.

"I'm a bit of an old soul." Delia shrugged. "Even as a young child, I was raised to be very polite and eloquent, a picture of decorum. It wasn't until I'd been here over a century that I stopped talking like a Queen of England." She rolled her eyes at herself.

"You still…" I stopped myself and wondered if maybe she couldn't hear her own accent.

"I sound British, but I've dropped the fancy, posh part, right?"

"Right," I agreed. "More or less."

"I assure you; I sound much younger, and more hip now than I did the first time I was this age."

"You're doing an excellent job."

I put on the sarcasm, which got her to laugh, before Penny jumped from out of nowhere to scare us. Tristan had warned me she liked to do that, especially with the secret passages throughout Rosehill, but I hadn't been expecting it on the staircase this early in the morning, so I momentarily lost my footing.

I saw Delia reach out to catch me, but I'd already grabbed on to the suit of armor to steady myself, without thinking. My reassuring smile vanished as the memory took hold.

I'd been so careful to avoid touching it every time we went up the stairs, knowing that weapons, shields, and armor had seen more battles and injuries than I ever cared to experience. I expected to feel a moment from inside the suit, some terrified soldier riding out to his death, but instead I got a child, waiting in excitement and confusion. My stomach rose to my throat, thinking of an overzealous child believing the fairy-tales rather than the harsh realities of war, but instead of a battlefield, I saw an elegant dining room through the mouth opening. The room was similar to the one here, but much smaller, with yellow curtains.

Lucy, Gabriel's fiancée, came into my view, wearing a gorgeous pink gown, looking like she'd been on her way to a ball from a Jane Austen novel, but now had a very pointy metal rod in her hands.

"Everything is okay, sweetheart, just stay in here until Daddy gets home."

"Where are you going?" The voice sounded feminine, but it was hard to tell at that age, with the fear making her voice crack.

"I'll be right back; I just need to take care of something first. You be a good girl and no matter what happens, don't make a sound until Daddy finds you."

"But Mummy—" the little girl pleaded.

"No matter what," Lucy insisted. I could feel the girl nod, but I doubted Lucy could do more than sense the movement of the armor. "I love you, sweetheart. More than you can imagine."

"ARE YOU OKAY?" Delia asked with concern when I got back to the landing.

"I'm so sorry," Penny apologized, her big eyes filling with tears.

"That's what I get for being clumsy." I smiled at her, hoping I hadn't scarred her for life. "That was an excellent scare, if I do say so myself. I had no idea you were there."

"I came from the other side, behind the tapestry," she explained, lifting it to show me there was room for a small child to slide across the landing unnoticed.

"Very clever," I praised her.

"I think Chris made cinnamon buns last night, and I'm sure

Ben would love one," Delia said, obviously trying to get rid of Penny.

"Maybe I'll bring him two in case." Her eyes went wide as she ran down the stairs.

"We'll be lucky if there are any left," Delia said as she watched her go, before turning to me. "What did you see?"

"Lucy," I admitted, the fear still constricting my chest. "And I thought it was Clara, but…"

"But what?"

I wondered if maybe Lucy had a secret love child I wasn't supposed to mention, but if they'd been near this suit of armor, then Delia must know about it. "She called her mummy. And Lucy was dressed funny, like she was in costume."

"Cassandra." Delia gave me a sad smile.

"The little girl?" I was relieved it wasn't another secret I had to come clean about, but I hated the sadness in Delia's eyes, even worse than when I first found her staring at the tapestry.

"No, the woman you saw was Cassandra. Her daughter's name was Corinne."

"Was?" I asked quietly, my heart sinking.

"No, Corinne lived a long and happy life. She just happens to have been born in 184…4." She had to think about it.

"And Cassandra?" It was horrible of me to press, but I could have sworn it was Lucy.

"Cassie wasn't as lucky. She was one of Lucy's ancestors, another Bearer of the Crescent Moon." She noted my blank expression, but didn't elaborate. "I'm not sure what you saw, but Cassie spent most of her life helping the helpless and protecting anyone who needed it. And no, she was not Gifted, or a witch. She just had the means to help, and so she did."

"Like Batman." I shrugged my shoulder, hoping to lighten the mood.

"She was definitely one of my heroes."

"I was hoping I'd catch you." Tristan came down the stairs to join us, so Delia gave me a nod and a smile before taking the other staircase up towards her room.

"Everything okay?"

"Just wanted to walk you to class." He took my hand in his, which I knew I shouldn't allow, but I'd been wrapped up in him less than an hour ago, so it wouldn't make that much of a difference.

"And leave love notes in my locker?"

"You're joking, but I would have killed to have someone like you when I was in high school." He smiled before remembering how his high school career ended. "Actually, if I knew you in high school, I wouldn't be able to see you now, so I take that back."

"If it's any consolation, no one walked me to my classes in high school either. And the closest I got to love notes was Sybill letting me know she went home without me." I smiled, thinking of how she used to come up with insane reasons for her absences, like a magic carpet ride with Aladdin or having to run tests in Racoon City because Umbrella Corp had a promising cure for her unknown disease. Then I remembered I was the true cause of her disease, which was why she was avoiding me.

"She's probably just busy with your parents. This isn't a conversation you want anyone overhearing." Tristan saw he lost me, so he took it upon himself to reassure me that my sister didn't hate me, and if she did, it wouldn't be forever. Not that it helped, but I loved him for trying.

"I wish they'd been home. I'm sure I would have told her what was going on as it happened, so by the time this part came out, we would be in it together and it wouldn't be some terrible confession I had to make."

"It's not like you were willfully hurting her. You were going to let them experiment on you for the rest of your life to keep her safe."

"But I didn't. I escaped and am currently running away from

the people who, although severely misguided, have her best interest at heart."

"You don't mean that," he argued. "And if your sister is anything like me and mine—"

"Alison," Sakina exclaimed when we got to the barn at the same time as her. "Looks like we both wanted to get a head start."

"To be continued?" I asked Tristan.

"I've got all the time in the world," he assured me with a kiss on my forehead before he went back to the mansion, and I followed Sakina up the stairs.

As soon as I was up, we got right into it, revisiting every object we'd worked on so far. I was grateful when I could hold the ribbon in my hands for minutes without seeing a single thing, but I saw the chair memory once before I could keep it at bay. It went that way with most of the items I touched; one last look at the memory before I was free of it. Even the harp held its emotions back if I concentrated hard enough on not seeing anything. By the end of the afternoon, as long as I'd seen the memories a few times, I could control myself enough to see nothing.

"Tomorrow we can introduce new items, rather than ones that have nothing left to show you," Sakina said while packing up her things. She carefully wrapped the ribbon, and I got the feeling I wouldn't be seeing that keepsake from her past ever again.

"Then we can work on people?"

"Once you have complete control over powerful objects you've never touched before, we can introduce people. Following Delia's rules, of course." She smiled and possibly winked, but it seemed so out of character that I might have imagined it.

"So I might be able to touch people by my thirtieth birthday?"

It was sarcastic and Sakina didn't deserve my sass.

"Would you rather try it now, when you're still learning, before we know the damage it causes?"

"I know the damage it causes," I argued, pressing my lips together to try not to think about Sybill, but she was my Gift's greatest victim, a million times worse off than I was for having it.

"Then why would you want to try that before you know how to stop it? One of my biggest regrets was making Delia test her Gift before she learned how to control it."

"You're right. I'm sorry."

She reached over to put her hand on my jacket sleeve. "You're doing great, Alison, and you will get there. I am sorry this is happening to you, but I believe with every fiber of my being that you will do incredible things with your Gift. This is just a detour in the magic of your life story."

It was oddly optimistic for my taste, but Sakina believed it with her whole heart, and that meant the world to me.

"Same time tomorrow?" I asked, hoping the more hours I put in, the faster it would work.

"I'll be here," she agreed. "And if you want to get ahead of yourself, you can try not to take away Tristan's Gift, since we know he'll be getting close to you either way."

"I will work on that," I assured her.

TRISTAN, Jackie, and Penny were all waiting for us when we got to the barn's main level. Or rather, they were capturing fireflies in the corner and didn't notice our presence until Bear started barking for Sakina to play with him instead of leaving.

"Is Krishna coming to Rosehill soon?" Penny asked excitedly.

"She has summer camp, dear. But we can have a play date on the weekend."

"Why doesn't she come here instead? Jackie's teaching us about bugs." Penny sounded both fascinated and grossed out by this.

"Her school friends are there. And I don't believe Krishna likes bugs," Sakina argued, but I knew it was more than just school friends who went to camp with her.

"We can set something up for Saturday. Maybe camp out in the backyard," Tristan suggested, putting his hands on Penny's shoulders when she was about to ask another question.

"I'm sure Krishna would love that." Sakina smiled before saying her goodbyes and heading towards the woods.

"And Brandon thinks *I'm* a suck up," Jackie said once Sakina was gone, putting her hand on Tristan's shoulder, and shaking her head.

"What did I miss?" I asked, looking from one to the other while Penny's focus was entirely on the jar of fireflies we were bringing back with us.

"At lunch, Delia was saying she wished they would stay at the house and not go out so much."

"Is that why Penny…"

"Nope, Penny just wants a friend more her age, and Krishna has been asking to attend Rosehill since she could talk," Tristan explained.

"But camping would bring everyone close?" I understood.

"I think their house is probably safer than a tent, mind you," Jackie pointed out.

"Not if they camped in the courtyard."

"Sneaky," she clearly approved.

"Is Ben's dog spying on us or for protection?" It nuzzled up to my leg, so I scratched behind its ears, before realizing I had no idea what my Gift could do to animals. I was incredibly eager to control it, but Sakina was right that I had no idea what I was capable of.

"Bear!" Tristan called, sending the dog to his side instead. Thankfully, he was letting me keep my distance from him as well, since he was the only one who could entice the fireflies when Penny declared they lost their luster.

"I'm pretty sure he has something following us every time we leave the house, since you arrived at least, but Bear doesn't like hiding in the shadows when belly scratches are an option."

"And I had bacon in my pocket," Penny added.

"For him, or in case you got hungry?" I asked her.

"We shared," she assured me.

"Is everything okay?" Tristan asked me once we were alone inside Rosehill. "I mean, relatively speaking, based on whatever happened today?" he amended before I could respond.

"I'm good," I said with a smile, careful to follow him up the stairs at a safe distance. "What about you? Looks like you've got your hands full; distracting Penny, reassuring Delia..." On the surface, I was asking him about his day and his troubles, but I was also finding out just how badly I'd disrupted all their lives since I arrived.

"You say that like I don't usually spend my time here distracting Penny. And the only difference with Delia is that I usually have those conversations with her before the sun's up, when neither of us can sleep."

"You haven't had any problems lately," I pointed out.

"It's a lot harder to leave the bed when you're in it." He tried to come close, but I took a step back. "Allie, I know I'm not imagining that you're—"

"No, it's...I've been dying to rush into your arms since I saw you in the barn—"

"Then why do you keep pulling away?"

"Because Sakina says I'm not ready to work on people, which sucks because I don't want to use my Gift, I just want to not hurt people anymore, but she pointed out that I would hurt people while I was figuring it out…" I put my hand up when I saw he wanted to argue. "But you refuse to stay away from me, no matter how many times I ask you to, so she suggested I might as well use that."

"As in…" Tristan cocked his head to the side, but I took it as a good sign that he was still smiling as we entered his bedroom.

"You still have your Gift?"

"I do…" He brought his hands together and created lines of electricity between his fingers when he moved them away from each other. It was like those globes at the science center. It occurred to me that other than the few times he'd used his Gift to protect us, I'd never really been able to see what he could do.

"That's really cool," I told him, trying not to dwell on how I take it away from him.

"Yeah, all the girls love it," he teased.

"Thank God I get rid of it then," I played along.

"Did I mention the girls I'm referring to are Jackie and Penny?" He dropped all cockiness. "And I happen to be in love with someone who couldn't care less about the theatrics."

"You're making this so much harder," I warned.

"My apologies. I'll try to be repulsive now."

"Pretty sure that's impossible."

We settled on his bed with about a foot between us, where I placed a pair of gloves, a sheet of paper, and a pashmina.

"I'm all yours," Tristan said, running his hands against his jeans in anticipation.

"Being this close doesn't do anything, right?"

"Nope." He demonstrated his Gift again, this time just a ball of sparks in his right hand.

"I figure the gloves are thickest, so I'll try those first."

"When I pictured myself experimenting in the bedroom, this is not what I had in mind."

I looked over, and his smile was warm and genuine, but entirely for my benefit. I hadn't realized my hands were shaking.

"The worst that happens is I lose my Gift, which is exactly what will happen when I take you in my arms once this experiment is done. You've got nothing to be nervous about."

I took a deep breath, then asked, "Take my hand?"

"With pleasure." He reached out without an ounce of fear.

"Guess the gloves work," I stated when he held my hand in his right one, and made sparks with his left. He locked eyes with me and made the sparks go bigger, then let them die when I pulled away.

"What's next?"

"The scarf." I took off the gloves and placed the pashmina on his hands, still folded. "Sakina touched my arm, but I was wearing a jacket, and…"

"You want to know how much clothes you need before you need to pull away."

I looked at him from the corner of my eye because he said it way more suggestively than the situation warranted. I wasn't nervous anymore, but I wasn't going to tell him to stop.

"Is it only with your hands?" I asked, putting mine on top of his.

"I've yet to try shooting it out of my toes," he said, wiggling them through his socks. "But…"

I heard the humming first, like an old fridge. I realized it was coming from him about a half a second before every strand of hair on his head stuck up as if he'd just been electrocuted.

He was looking at me as if he wasn't aware he was doing anything, as my face broke out into a smile I couldn't stop. "Is that how you usually style it?"

"When I run out of gel," he agreed. "Do you like it?"

"Love it," I assured him. "Once I figure this out, you can wear it like that every day."

"You'll be Penny's favorite person. She's been trying to convince me it's my look since I accidentally showed her I could do it."

"She has great taste." I'd unfolded the pashmina down to a single layer, and his hair was still standing, so I moved on to the sheets of paper.

"Pretty sure the scarf was thinner than this stack," he pointed out as I removed one at a time, until it was just a single sheet of paper between us. "Can I kiss you now?"

"I need to concentrate to not use it. That won't work if you're kissing me," I argued.

"Are you saying my kiss does things to you?"

"You're taking this way too lightly."

"I've got my priorities straight," was his rebuttal.

"Stay still," I asked of him, bringing my hand up to his hair. I let myself run my fingers through it, like I'd been dying to do since he made it go up. I was careful not to touch his scalp, but other than a lot of static, nothing happened.

"It's addictive, that's why I do it all the time," he assured me. "Do you have any other tests? Hand creams, sanitizer gels?"

"Excellent ideas for tomorrow night." I got a smile as he shook his head at me. "I'm just going to brush my fingers against your hand really quick, and then if that works, we can count how long it takes for your hair to go flat with my hand in yours."

"Sounds like a plan."

He straightened his shoulders and put his hands at the ready. I closed my eyes, took a deep breath, cleared my mind, and—

I'd barely even brushed the tip of my fingers against the palm of his hand, but I felt the sparks. I opened my eyes and saw his hair was lying, not quite flat, but not sticking up anymore.

"Hey." Tristan took my hands in his and tilted his head until he found my eyes and made me look at him. "I promise you someday very soon, the only sparks you'll feel when you touch me will be the butterfly chemistry kind."

I nodded and pressed my lips together, trying not to cry, but I'd really expected to last at least a second.

"You're perfect, you know that?" I asked him.

"I'm just crazy about you," he argued, bringing me in for a kiss. "And hey, now we get to do this," he said, kissing me again. "And this." He brushed the hair from my face, running his fingers against my cheek.

"All the touching," I agreed with a sad smile.

"Come here."

He brought me back on the bed, with my head on his chest and his arms around me.

"I have complete faith in you Allie. You'll figure it out and we'll all get through this."

I let him run his fingers through my hair, soothing me as much as his words were. I knew I was being impatient, and everyone said this took time, but I didn't know how long I had until me and my 'Gift' drove everyone away.

CHAPTER NINETEEN

ALISON

"Nope." Tristan pulled me into him when I tried to get out of bed the following morning.

"Sakina is expecting me," I argued, but I didn't make another attempt to leave the warmth of the bed.

"It's too dark to be morning," he pointed out.

"Looks like it's raining." I strained to see through the opening in the curtains, but it was dark and gloomy outside, with not a trace of sunlight. "Do you guys have umbrellas?"

"Five more minutes and I'll carry the umbrella for you."

I could tell that his eyes were closed throughout the entire conversation, and I knew I should get up to go to the barn, but I had zero interest in leaving the safety of Tristan's bed.

FIVE MINUTES TURNED into ten before my phone buzzed. I'd been halfway between sleeping and awake, so I jumped, utterly convinced I was late, and Sakina was asking where I was.

I was right about the provenance, but the message read:

. . .

"Change of plans. Scavenger hunt starts in the kitchen at eight."

"What do you think she means by scavenger hunt?"

I looked to see if Tristan had read it over my shoulder, but he'd apparently received a similar invitation.

"Like an Easter Egg hunt?" I guessed.

"You don't look excited."

"This house is a minefield of antiques. Anything I touch will be a struggle." I remembered my reaction to the coat of armor.

"Trial by fire...I think Sakina's got a lot more faith in you than you do."

"Or she hates me," I argued.

"Only one way to find out." He kissed me before going to get dressed.

"Now you're good to leave the bed?"

"The day seems a lot brighter now that I get to spend it with you." He smiled.

"Did you hear?" Penny asked with her mouth full once we got downstairs, already halfway through her pancakes.

"Were you invited too?" Tristan asked with fake surprise, like this was an exclusive adventure and she must be pretty cool if she was allowed in.

"Everyone is. Delia said she was too busy, but Sakina knew she was lying."

"Is it teams, or every man for himself?" Charlie asked, taking a seat and a piece of bacon from the plate in the middle of the table. There were similar plates with sausages, pancakes, French toast, and buttered toast.

"It's always more fun in teams," Ben shared, going straight for the espresso machine.

"You're doing it too?" Penny was surprised, but her mouth curled into a smile like this was going to be the best day ever.

"Everyone means everyone," he agreed as Chris came from the kitchen with Sakina and Krishna, while Delia brought in Mateo and Lena.

"You'll be in two teams," Sakina informed us. "I saw the rain and thought it would be fun to organize a scavenger hunt within Rosehill. You can learn about the history, yourselves, each other…"

I was slightly dreading it, because I was going to be exhausted just from having to avoid everyone all day, but the faces in front of me also revealed a mix of excitement, apprehension, boredom, and mistrust.

"What do we win?" Jackie asked, biting into an apple like she had the competition in the bag.

"Eternal bragging rights?" Delia suggested.

Jackie considered it a moment before nodding.

"Do we pick our teams?" I asked, grateful for Tristan's arms around me, but I usually tried to give him the day to recover from being so close to me at night.

"I thought it would be fun to let the newest residents choose their teams." Sakina was smiling, but Mateo swallowed, looking slightly green, and Lena shot daggers at Delia. Through her eyes, obviously, but she gave the impression that had she been holding actual daggers, she would have thrown them as well. Sakina pretended she didn't notice. "But Delilah vetoed me so you can all pick a number from this hat."

ONCE WE'D all picked our numbers and gathered into groups, I found myself with Charlie, Lena, Penny, Ben, and Chris.

"Why are you smiling?" Ben asked Penny when that was her reaction to our list. We needed to find something from every continent, from the year each of us was born, something as old as the house, something that scares us, something that makes us happy, and some surprise in the training rooms once we found everything else. "Delia's on the other team."

"Because I know the secret passageways." With that, she took the list and headed for the pantry.

"Are we supposed to follow her in there, or is she getting a snack?"

"Unfortunately, we are following." Chris sighed before going after her. "I fit a lot better when I was Penny's age," he warned Ben, the biggest of our group by far.

I let the others go first so I could keep my distance, and while Ben gave me a look like he would rather tie up the rear, this was a hidden hallway within the residence, so it was one of the safest places we could be.

IT STARTED off as a literal hallway with cement walls on either side, light fixtures, and everything, but as we took different turns – and even a staircase – it got narrower, darker, colder...scarier.

"Where are you taking us?" I called out to Penny after about ten minutes. The house was enormous, but it didn't take that long to walk from one end to the other. I was okay in the back, but since Penny was apparently the only one who used the secret passageways anymore, anyone taller than her had to deal with decades worth of cobwebs.

"The trophy room." I could hear the smile in her voice.

"Like for the school?" I asked. It was established in the nineteenth century, so there could be trophies dating back that far, but the library probably had books spanning much farther.

"Delia has another one for non-academic medals," Ben shared.

"And newspaper clippings," Chris agreed.

"Does she let people see it normally?" I was beginning to

think the secret passageway was less of a shortcut and more of a hiding from Delia tactic.

"I've never seen it," Charlie admitted. "But Delia always says that unless it's locked, it's for everyone."

It took another five minutes before we emerged in a hallway I hadn't seen before, but I assumed we were around the student dorm rooms. It was like the wing where Tristan and the others slept, but I could see through open doors that some had two beds, while others had bunk beds, and there was a dry erase board on every door, some with names and others with a greeting for new students.

"We're just above the training rooms," Penny told me. She held her own hands, possibly to stop herself from taking mine, but she stayed by my side.

"Have you explored every part of Rosehill?"

"Pretty much," she said in the way children like to pretend they know a lot more than they do, but she probably knew more about it than anyone who hadn't grown up within these walls. "I'm too young for regular school, so I hang out with Delia a lot. Or Chris when he's here. Or Ben if they're busy. Or Tristan, because he doesn't have to go to school either."

"Why did you choose the trophy room?"

"It has everything in there. From everywhere."

We passed the school's trophy room, with the usual sports teams and spelling bees, but the room behind it was almost like a shrine, only without the candles and stuff that makes it obvious the person died. There was a bookshelf with alphabetized scrapbooks, then various shelves and stands with ribbons, medals, trophies, and tiaras.

Without thinking, I picked up what looked like an Olympic Silver Medal and immediately saw the view from a podium, with thousands of people cheering. If I had to guess, I would assume a woman won it for something involving horses. Unless they allowed them as spectators.

"That must be Mary's." Charlie came over to see what I'd unceremoniously dropped on the shelf.

"Is she Delia's only Olympic medalist?"

"The only equestrian. That I know of," he amended, showing me the engraving. "She came last summer to see Delia and taught us some tricks."

"You're fourteen, right?" Ben came over and asked him.

"For the next few months," he agreed.

"Then that medal is as old as you are."

"Cool."

Penny came over and took a picture with our team camera, then spent the next few minutes taking pictures of awards and newspaper clippings from all over the place.

"Here," Lena called Penny over, pointing to a pepper mill-sized queen from a chessboard.

"Where is that from?" Penny asked.

When I leaned in closer, I could see the writing on it was not in an alphabet I could read. Russian or Romanian or one of those Slavic languages.

"Russia." Lena sighed. "But it's also as old as I am."

"There's no numbers on it," Penny argued.

"Sometimes they spell it out to be fancy," Ben shared.

"I didn't realize you were Russian. Are you flu—"

"I'm not," Lena cut me off. "It's just another language I learnt."

"For fun?" Penny asked.

"Why else?" She kept her face neutral and her eyes on me, giving the distinct impression that it was a lot of things, but not fun.

"How old are *you*?" Penny turned to Ben. He was the only one who didn't have something as old as he was, but I also think Penny was better at reading us than we gave her credit for.

"How old do you think I am?" He raised an eyebrow.

"I would think…fifty-five."

"I look that old, or because you know I'm older than I look?"

She shrugged her shoulders like she had no idea.

"How old do you think *I* am?" I tried. After the Olympic medal, I took deep breaths and concentrated before touching things, so I wouldn't see anything, but the Miss America tiara had the year on it.

I was so excited by my progress that I was only a little crushed when Penny guessed, "Forty?"

"Kids are terrible at guessing ages," Chris said to make us feel better, but she'd said thirteen for him earlier. "How long have you been thirty for?"

"I was thirty-two," Ben owned his age. I assume that once you kept getting older without aging, you held on to every last bit of normal that you had. "The World War I medal is as old as me."

"Really?" Charlie was surprised. "I thought...you seem very wise."

"Thank you," Ben said as if he didn't know that wasn't where Charlie was headed. "How many continents are we missing, Pen?"

"Just Australia," she shared. "I have a kangaroo upstairs."

"A live one?" Charlie teased, ruffling her hair.

"Did that girl with all the boots take them with her?" Lena asked as if she couldn't care less, but she wouldn't have said anything if that was the case.

Without bothering to answer, Charlie and Penny ran out of the room, to a dorm with butterflies and horses stuck on the door. Though, to be honest, it kind of looked like unicorn stickers with the horn cut off.

"Uggs?" I asked, seeing them in black and brown, long and short...even slippers.

"She lives in them," Charlie agreed.

"Do we think Sakina didn't realize how easy she made this,

or she's giving us some wins before the hard part?" Chris looked to Ben, as did we all.

"I was summoned by Sakina and told nothing," he defended himself. "What was next?"

"We need to find something as old as the house," Penny read off the paper.

"How old is it?" I asked.

"It was completed in 1631," Chris shared. He was turning out to be quite the historian.

"Why don't we split up and cover more ground?" Lena suggested. I suspected she wanted to get away from us more than anything, but I also got the impression that as stupid as she found the activity, she wanted to win.

"Teams of two," Ben said, raising an eyebrow in case she tried to argue. She didn't, but there was a very severe eye roll before she walked off, quickly followed by Charlie.

"After you." Chris smiled and gestured for me to show him the way, since Penny was already on Ben's shoulders.

"Any thoughts?" I asked Chris, following him down hallways with large paintings ranging from a bowl of fruit to a battle recreation to a young woman in a white dress, so pale that she might have been a ghost.

"These were the first rooms they occupied, and I believe there's an old sitting room full of junk from back then."

"They might have moved it to the barn." I thought of his mother's rocking chair.

"The big, bulky stuff no one will ever use again, yes, but after centuries, instead of a junk drawer with things you need some-times but don't have a place for, Delia has an entire room."

"Show me the way." I grinned.

He talked as he walked, telling me about the things he'd seen in the junk room when he was younger, how he assumed it must be the same now, but he hadn't explored Rosehill like that since he was Krishna's age.

I listened to every word until I felt a tightness in my chest that convinced me to turn the corner. It was a familiar feeling that I couldn't place, but my heart beat with fear as I wondered if it was Kazimir's Gift I was remembering. How he could slow your heart until it stopped completely. I shuddered at the memory, but my heart was beating way too fast for that, and the hallway was empty. Or rather, nothing greeted me but a life-size painting of four children: three girls and one boy. It was ancient, probably as old as Rosehill, if not older, but it was the necklace on one of the smaller girls that stopped me. It was a string of pearls with a solitary teardrop ruby, that I'd seen before at the museum. If I had to think back on the first time an object showed me a memory, it was that necklace that called to me from across the room, and showed me the pain I would feel if I lost my sister.

It could be a coincidence. Maybe one of Delia's students, or adoptive children, painted the portrait of the royal family at some point, but the girl wearing the necklace looked so much like Delia. Her eyes were green instead of Delia's black, but she had the same dark brown curls, the burgundy lips, and powerful attitude.

I still felt that same pull from years ago, so against my better judgment, I followed it into a dressing room. I could tell it was Delia's from the racks of dresses and arrangement of boots, but there was an entire section filled with jewelry. Rosehill held many priceless artefacts, but that necklace belonged in a museum, and I couldn't imagine Delia stealing it.

"I DOUBT you'll find what you're looking for in here."

I nearly jumped out of my skin at the sound of Delia's voice, dropping my cell phone with a deafening clatter. I had no interest in finding out if the screen shattered. I wanted to sink into the floor and die. Instead, I turned around and faced her.

"I'm so sorry, I didn't realize it was your bedroom until—"

"I'm not upset." She stopped me, sadness the only emotion on her face. "Just curious, since you showed no interest in the different bedrooms during the tour."

"I was, um…called to it?" I couldn't find a better way of explaining it.

"I thought you'd mastered not getting memories from random objects?"

"I can stop myself from seeing things if I concentrate. That's what I was doing earlier, but…I was going to turn back when I realized where I was going, but then I saw…"

"The painting," she realized. "I chose that one because we're so young in it hardly anyone ever recognizes Henry, but I'm assuming you saw the necklace." Delia sighed. "I heard you telling Penny about it when she asked how you first discovered your Gift, but I didn't think the pull would be that powerful."

"You're a princess?" I asked her, focusing on my discoveries rather than the snooping I'd done to get to them.

"What did the necklace show you all those years ago?"

"I hadn't figured out how to focus on anything, but I just remember so much pain was inside it," I shared. "I thought it was from the Princess who lost her sister, but now I'm guessing most of it was yours, in the centuries since you lost her."

"We each got a piece of jewelry when my mother died, to ease our pain. It didn't help, but it became a sign that when one of us was wearing our mourning jewels, the others knew to be kinder and more affectionate. When I died, she wore my necklace to honor me, and as a beacon so I would know when she needed me to come out of the shadows and visit with her. By the time I lost her, there was no one left for me to use it as a secret symbol with, so I just clutched it whenever I missed them. Which, the necklace can attest, was all the time."

"I'm so sorry," I apologized. Here I was, unable to imagine

losing Sybil, but I knew that Delia, like many Gifted, had lost every single person she had ever known and loved.

"You remind me of Margaret. She was strong, stubborn, and always trying to give herself up to spare us pain. She knew all our family history and every time we accidentally knocked over something fragile while playing indoors, she let us know exactly what we'd destroyed."

I wanted to tell her I wasn't that bad, but I could tell that she loved this person she was comparing me to so much that centuries hadn't dulled the loss, so I took the compliment.

"When you say Margaret and Henry, with the roses and… you're not really…"

"Elizabeth Tudor, named after my mother and grandmother. Delilah was my middle name, so I used it after I died, until it eventually turned into Delia."

I suddenly understood exactly why she was given her Gift. When she was alive, she had the power to make a castle full of servants do whatever she told them to. It reinforced the Damned idea that we were cursed.

"Does everyone know?"

"The adults do. Penny knows I'm a princess, or rather was. The boys either don't know or couldn't care less. I think my past intrigues Lena, but I'm waiting for her to open up enough to actually ask about it. Mateo's read enough of my books here that I'm sure he's pieced it together, but he hasn't mentioned it either."

"When Tristan said your family was spread over Europe if ever we needed to lie low, I didn't think he meant…do you know the current royal family?"

"I know the Queen. When her son takes the throne, we will be introduced, but that's more for political reasons. Lilibet loved hearing stories of her ancestors, and I think when you lose people, it's nice to talk about them with people who knew them. Otherwise, I try to keep a low profile."

"When you say political reasons…"

"Yes, certain members of all governments know about us. There are liaisons in some places and Gifted in power in others. There's a Guardian whose principal job is to coordinate with British Parliament, but whenever the royal family is concerned, I am called. It used to be because I was already involved, but now, before the crown is passed down, I am introduced as an ally and loyal subject."

"Does that make it easier for them? Like yes, there are people who come back to life when they die, and they have magical powers, but don't worry, here's your great-great aunt so you know they're friendly?"

"Probably not, but I enjoy keeping an eye on them. And while there have been elected leaders who found out about Gifted and thought the best course of action was to eliminate them all, no British monarchs have ever suggested such a thing."

"Allie, we found it!" I heard Penny calling from what sounded like miles away.

"Someday, when there isn't so much going on, I would love to hear all about it. Your life, your family…you're fascinating." It came out ridiculous, like she was something I wanted to study, but I'd just discovered so many layers to her that explained a lot, but introduced a million questions as well.

"I would love that," she told me with a sad smile. "I can show you my private collection and let you know which ones shouldn't be heartbreaking."

I gave her an equally sad smile before we both went off to find our teams for the final challenge in the training rooms.

THE ROOMS WERE PITCH BLACK, but we had to take the objects on the table and figure out who they belonged to. There was a single light in an upper corner, but it was so high and dim that you couldn't see a thing unless you were glued to it. Not that the light would be that helpful, considering we faced a mountain of gloves.

"This one's mine!" Penny exclaimed. "And this one smells like you."

"What do I smell like?" Ben asked her with a touch of apprehension.

"Like Bear and Brutus."

Chris burst out laughing, but Charlie had already placed a glove in the Chris box.

"I had to move it before the cologne spread onto all the other gloves," he teased. I couldn't make out his face, but I knew he was smiling.

"Better than dog," Chris insisted.

"And I think this is yours," Charlie pressed, awkwardly handing Lena something. "It has the hole at the finger."

"I need new ones." Her words implied she was over them, but she clutched her glove like Penny clutches that doll of hers.

"You still feel the cold?" I asked without thinking. It was stupid, because she spent most of the time I was watching her trying to sink into the background and show how she was not a part of our group and not interested in changing that.

There was a pause which I assumed was her holding back a snarky remark before she admitted, "I don't feel my Gift, or anything I make with it, but normal cold gets me like everyone else."

"I'm sorry. I'm curious by nature."

"We have three gloves left," Chris pointed out, saving us from the awkwardness of that conversation.

"They don't smell," Penny dismissed her contributions.

"Are the dogs allowed to help?" Ben tried.

"I can try," I offered.

"Does it hurt when you see things?" Penny asked me. "Sometimes it hurts Krishna when she uses her Gift, but she does it anyway."

"Sometimes it makes me sad, but it rarely hurts," I assured her.

"By all means, go ahead," Chris encouraged.

"That's easier for you to say when yours is in the box," I pointed out, turning to Charlie in the dark.

"I don't think I've done much wearing gloves, but just in case…"

"I won't share what I see."

Charlie nodded, so I touched the first of our mystery gloves and was brought to the memory of a snowball fight. It looked like the happiest of memories, and all I could hear was giggling, but what I felt was pain and longing. I also knew, the moment it pulled me in, that the memory belonged to Tristan.

The second glove could easily have fit Jackie or myself, but I put them on and saw a maybe ten-year-old Jackie building a snowman with whoever was wearing them, which meant they had to be Delia's.

"Tristan and Delia, but I'm getting nothing from this one."

"Is it black or blue?" Penny asked.

"I can't tell without more light."

The words were barely out of my mouth before the glove flew out of my hand and floated steadily to the light source. I'd seen Charlie's Gift before, but I don't think I would have been able to hold on to the glove, even if I'd tried.

"Brandon's," Charlie shared once we saw it was a dark blue. "He never wears gloves, he just leaves them in his pocket," he told me.

"Sakina!" Penny yelled. "We won! Sakina!"

"Not so fast," Sakina warned, turning on the lights.

She came over and inspected our glove handiwork, as well as the pictures on the camera.

"Did we?" Penny pressed.

"Excellent job," Sakina told us. "I just have to check on the others."

She went outside and turned another light on, showing us the other team in a similar training room with the same glove arrangement.

"So close, but the blue gloves were Brandon's," she told them after reviewing everything. "Penny, you do win."

"Yes!" Penny rushed to Krishna, and the two of them celebrated as if they'd both been on the winning team, while Tristan came over and kissed me.

"Congratulations," he said with a smile, wrapping his arms around me.

"Why thank you." I smiled instead of focusing on the sparks I'd been unable to prevent.

"Charlie, Brandon, Mateo, and I all have the same pair of gloves. Should I be touched or concerned that you recognized mine more than I did, without ever seeing me wearing them?"

"Definitely touched." I nuzzled my head into his chest. "Charlie recognized his brother's glove in the light, but I saw nothing when I touched it."

"Because you've mastered your…."

"Because Brandon never wears his gloves," I admitted. "Although I was pretty good at only seeing things I wanted today. Mostly."

"I'm sensing a story."

"One I haven't fully heard yet," I agreed. "You forgot to mention you were living with a princess. Which might make Rosehill a castle."

"She told you?" He was surprised. "Or you saw?"

"A bit of both. And I am so curious about Lena," I shared, because it was easier than dealing with Delia and my concerns about Sybill right now.

"Get in line," he agreed, kissing the top of my head before we followed everyone to the dining room.

· · ·

Most of us hung out in the sitting room after lunch, with Penny and Krishna comparing pictures, while others took advantage of the time to recharge from all the morning's social interactions. Sakina and Delia went off to another room once everyone was settled, so I couldn't have asked her questions or continued my lessons even if I had wanted to.

Tristan told me all about their morning, and how Jackie knows their clothes by touch, but a lot of my brain energy was on Delia, her family, and my sister.

"Do you want some tea?" Tristan offered out of the blue. I'd been in my mind, so I wasn't sure if he'd said something I hadn't responded to, or if he just got a craving for hot beverages.

"And hot chocolate?" Penny perked up from her spot on the floor.

"Whatever you want."

"With marshmallows?" Her eyes grew as wide as Krishna's.

"With marshmallows," he conceded, rolling his eyes at me before leading the girls into the kitchen.

Jackie was on the opposite couch with headphones on, listening to an audiobook, lost in her own world. I was debating interrupting her for a conversation, but my phone rang with Sybill's picture.

"I'm so sorry," I said instead of hello, walking out into the hallway so I wouldn't disturb anyone. And so they wouldn't see me cry if things went badly.

"It's not your fault, Al," she assured me. "I'm sorry, we're getting to the end of the trial so it's a million tests and Mom is staying super close in case I get worse when they wean me off of it, because she doesn't know...."

"It's not my fault, but I still did this to you," I argued.

"I've spent my entire life feeling bad because I thought me being sick was ruining your life. Did you ever hate me for it?"

"No." I wasn't sure if she knew that question made me feel a million times worse, not better in the least. "I hated that you were going through that and wanted you to not be sick, but I never blamed you for it."

"Exactly."

"But now we know it was my fault."

"That's a bad example, but the point is that it wasn't my fault I was sick, so you never hated me for all the crappy things that came with it. Your Gift or curse or whatever, it isn't your fault, so I won't hate you for the things that happened because of it that were out of your control."

"Over a decade of your life, Syb," I reminded her.

"But you won't do it anymore, right? You're learning how to control it, and healthy should be my new normal?"

"I won't go near you unless I can control it," I agreed, taking a seat on the steps when my own pacing was making me nervous.

"Then we're good, Allie. I thought I had a mystery disease that was slowly killing me. Now I get to live and discover the world with a whole new perspective. And I have a dark, tortured past that is basically a get out of jail free card and makes me irresistible."

"Did you tell Damian?" I asked delicately.

"No, because I know how he'll react. But he sees how much better I'm getting. Knows something is up."

"I'm not a fan of telling people, but I don't want to have secrets from the people I care about."

"Do you plan on telling mom and dad?" She sounded uncertain.

"Once you guys get back. And it's no longer dangerous."

"When you find the right time?" she suggested.

"I think it'll all come pouring out of me once I see them in person, but it wasn't something I wanted to do over the phone. I just couldn't not tell you when it affects you as much…or rather more than it affects me."

"I can't wait to see you, Allie. I'd kill for one of your hugs right now."

"Right back at you," I assured her.

"They'll be wondering where I went, but I wanted you to know none of this is your fault, and I know that."

"I don't deserve you, kid."

"You have the next hundred years to make it up to me."

I FELT like a huge weight had been lifted from my chest, and I could finally breathe. I brought my hand to my cheek and waited, so I could wipe the tears before going back to the others. I placed my palms on the step to push myself up and cursed myself when a memory caught me off guard. I was doing so good today, but wasn't expecting the stairs to be memorable.

"Oh God, I don't think I can make it up the stairs," Delia said, looking the same as now, only her eyes were so much happier, before she took her seat on the steps beside the person whose memory I was feeling.

"You wanted to dance until the sun came up." I could hear the smile in his voice, but the familiarity of it shot shivers up my spine.

"I did. And thank you for following me. I know this isn't your favorite."

"You're my favorite," he argued. "And I would follow you to the ends of the earth. Or, in this case, carry you."

The memory ended when he was no longer touching the stairs, but I knew the voice belonged to James, the man who drove us off the road and would have killed us – for money – if Tristan's family hadn't intervened. Delia had admitted that she'd known him centuries ago, and I guess it wasn't our business whether they were friends, acquaintances, or lovers, but his laugh had been the same one from the harp memory. From the man who was singing. I think we'd all suspected she'd had a dalliance with James when she said she'd known him, but the man from the memory was more than a casual romance. Delia had raised children with him, which didn't seem like the thing you did with someone you later tried to kill.

I WANTED to get back to the barn to make sure I was right about it being the same voice in the memory, but it poured all evening, so getting there was a lot more trouble than it was worth. Instead, I planned to be extremely early for my lessons in the morning. Which was good, because after verifying my theory with the harp, I was probably going to spend a lot of time inter-rogating Sakina.

CHAPTER TWENTY

DELIA

Tristan and Allie were in the kitchen when I came down and made myself a tea. I took out a second cup when my eyes burned, then turned to the young couple.

"Would you like a refill?" I offered.

"We're good," Tristan assured me. "Are the cookies reserved?"

"You can have as many as you'd like." I smiled, trying to discern how Alison was taking the news of my ancestry, and how much she saw in my dressing room. Sakina once told me I was a hoarder, but my house had so many rooms that it didn't show. I was both grateful, and absolutely despised the fact that cameras weren't a thing when James and I were together. "I made extra, if you want to bring some to Sakina."

"Of course," Alison assured me. I was probably imagining it, but she sounded overly polite. Like Tristan had been when he found out, only he'd added a teasing, "Your Majesty" at the end.

"We should get going," Tristan decided, his mouth full of cookie.

"I spoke to Sakina yesterday about maybe using one of the

training rooms instead of the barn. The wall is the limit for the enchantments, but the farther you stay from it…"

"The safer we are." Alison reached out like she was about to put her hand on mine, but even if I wasn't going to use my Gift, I wasn't ready to leave us that vulnerable. The only thing that got me to sleep some nights was the knowledge that if everything else failed, I could send the bad people away. I just had to betray my principles and the other half of my heart to do it.

"I'll be back soon," Tristan assured me before they headed out.

I brought both teas to the table and looked out the window. It offered a beautiful view of the back yard, all the way down to the water. I would assume the enchantments went out to the wooden platform that used to hold the diving board and slide, but I wouldn't risk any more beach parties until James, Potts, and their friends were gone. No matter how much I thought about it, I knew we only had two options; we could stop James in a way he would never forgive me for, or I could convince him to stop hunting Alison. Reason wouldn't help, I knew because I felt the pain and hatred in my own heart, and there was no amount of reason that could make it go away. An ultimatum would have been my plan if this were a few centuries ago, back when I believed James would do anything for me. I didn't blame him for what he'd done, but I couldn't forgive the way he didn't regret it. The way he betrayed everything he stood for, then defended that decision.

"Should we go horseback riding today?" Jackie suggested, pulling me from my thoughts.

"I'm not sure today is a good day for something like that." I put my hand on hers and rubbed it with my thumb. I appreciated her effort, but the last thing I wanted was anyone going past the stone wall.

"We could stay on the property, like the other day. I found some of those old mini fences equestrians hop over."

"Mary left them here for the next – how did you find them?" I cut myself off.

"You're the one who told me not to let my blindness stop me," she warned.

"Not to stop you from living a full and wonderful life. I wasn't expecting you to look through discarded sports paraphernalia that was boarded up decades ago."

"I was looking for something that might explain what's going on."

"And the stables were your best bet?"

"I heard you come up from the basement the other night. The only reason to be down there is to get to the old stables. So, I checked it out. But then you told us not to go into the garage—"

"Jackie, you know you can always ask me anything. You don't need to sneak around and try to figure things out on your own. Especially not now."

"You said we're safe as long as we stay on the property," she called me on it. "And you're obviously not that worried if Krishna is still out there. I know how stubborn Mrs. Patel can be, but they would never do anything to put their daughter at risk. When you were on that 'secret mission' to help Gabriel, all three of them stayed upstairs with us, in case someone followed you, or tried to get to you through us."

"What are you trying to ask, Jackie?" I was calm on the outside, but dying on the inside. I knew exactly what she was hinting at, and a huge part of me wanted to just lay it out there so I wouldn't have any more secrets, but I couldn't stand the look she would give me. I would lose her respect, her confidence…maybe even her.

She took a deep breath before asking the question that had probably been on everyone's mind lately, but hers ever since she watched the encounter from my eyes. "Who is he to you?"

"James is—"

I wasn't sure how much I was going to tell her. All I knew was that I wouldn't lie. But then Penny screamed, and my heart filled with terror because it was coming from outside.

"Where is she?" I asked instead, halfway to the door before Jackie answered.

"She's following an injured deer just outside the gate. They're heading for the woods."

I ran faster than my legs could carry me, through the kitchen's side door and down the long driveway that led to what remained of the front gate. I was out of breath before I reached the end of it, held up by adrenaline and sheer force of will. None of James' people had controlled animals the other night, and Ben would never do something so reckless and irresponsible. It was possible this was just a regular deer that she was following without being in any kind of danger, but James would be watching. Even if he would never attack a child, I knew they would come for anyone who ventured out to bring her back inside.

I saw her about twenty feet from the gate, about to veer off the drive into the trees that surround most of the property. I bridged the distance and scooped her up in my arms as soon as I got close.

"Are you okay?" I asked, checking the reaction of her pupils before looking around us. The woods were oddly quiet today, which could be because it was early, or rain was coming, but was more likely because our enemies had scared off the animals and were lying in wait for us.

"He's hurt," she pointed out, going close to the deer that let her touch it. No one had hunted in these woods for over a century, so the animals were less fearful of people, but this one was acting more like a pet than a wild animal. "Can Etta heal animals too, or just people?"

I saw it wasn't blood, that there was no wound underneath, just before a man came out of the woods, holding a silver whistle between his lips. I didn't recognize him from James' group, but it made sense to call in reinforcements after the other day's pushback. But then again, James rarely worked with so many people.

"Why don't we go inside and ask her?" I already knew exactly what Etta was capable of. She could heal everything except for a broken heart, but I didn't want to scare Penny if I didn't have to, and I needed to get her behind the wall as fast as possible.

I stood and started walking, holding Penny in one arm while I whistled with my right hand before leaving it out at my side, ready to strike.

So far, the man was just watching, with the deer now at his side, nuzzling into his leg, but I could feel the tension. He was waiting for something, and I didn't want to be there once it happened.

I was twenty feet from what used to be our front gate when the air around me changed. It suddenly felt cold and ominous, in addition to gray.

"Where's the other girl?" the man with the deer asked, though he was now joined by at least a dozen others. Some were holding weapons, all kinds of medieval assault items, but others held their bare hands out, ready to unleash all kinds of misery with their Gifts. I always found it ridiculously outdated how the New Order – and even the Guardians – insisted on using axes and swords instead of guns and grenade launchers, when one was clearly a thousand times more powerful and effective than the other, but now that I was against a group using them, I was incredibly grateful.

"I have no idea what you're talking about. This is a boarding school for orphaned children."

"We don't have to kill all of you." He didn't even acknowledge my response. "A deal can be arranged if you give up the key."

"You won't hurt her," Penny warned them with all the confidence of a child who believes her heroes are invincible and all-powerful.

"That's adorable." The man laughed, but there was a gleam in his eye when he looked at her that made me want to gouge it out. And I was a peaceful person. I looked around at the other faces watching us, many of them laughing with that same evil stare, but I couldn't see James, or any of the people who'd been with him the other night.

"Now's not a good time," I warned Penny when she balled her hands into fists, but she'd already summoned a storm, with thunder and lightning raging around us.

"This makes things much easier." The man took a step forward when a bolt of lightning ripped a branch off the tree. "We try not to kill the innocent, human type of children, you see?"

"She isn't Gifted." My heart pounded in fear.

"I'd beg to differ." He motioned to the thunder that was drowning out his words.

I looked once more at the faces and knew it was no contest. Penny's life was more important than anyone's free will or possible overreactions.

"Leav—" I started, but my gargoyles showed up with Ben and Caleb, who threw me my shield before standing between us and the unfriendlies. Persephone took Penny and I in her arms, then all three gargoyles flew into the air at the same time. I could hear attacks landing on our shields, Ben's grunt when one of them got him, and the vibrations when Persephone twirled to absorb a shock on her back to protect us, but we made it back onto the grounds and across the wall in one piece.

. . .

"You're okay now, they can't get in," I reminded Penny, feeling her heart beating against my chest while I held her in my arms. "You're safe here."

I looked around at the dozens of people surrounding us outside the magical barrier, and all the people behind me I had to protect. The man with the deer had followed us and stood where the gate used to be, watching us with hatred while brandishing a knife.

"We're safe inside the wall," I reminded myself as well as Penny, when a man, probably in his forties, walked towards the barrier with purpose. He closed his eyes at the threshold, but then he just walked through, like there was nothing there. Others tried, but only one other person made it.

My mouth froze, unable to formulate a sentence that didn't order everyone I cared about inside the house, especially not without including the men rushing at us.

"In the house, now!" Ben screamed as I held on to Penny and ran.

Luckily, we were close enough to the front door to reach it long before the men could catch up, but they didn't seem to follow us in any kind of hurry.

"What the hell was that?" Jackie asked, locking the door behind us as if the deadbolt would stop them.

"Rosehill is a sanctuary for First Lifers. I have final say for the house, but First Lifers are always allowed on the grounds, in case they're being chased and no one is here or....it's like the cemetery is hallowed ground as much as the church is."

"You said they couldn't get in," Penny reproached, searching my face for reassurance.

"The building is safe," I promised. "And most of them can't get past the gate. We're all safe in here for as long as it takes for them to go away."

Ben's face was hard; his lips pressed, and his brow creased. He did not approve of lying here in wait for them to attack, nor did it look like he trusted my judgment at the moment, as he turned to Jackie before resting his eyes on me, itching to say something. I gave him a reassuring smile and nodded as if to say, "I've got this," when in reality, I did not have this. The only thing I had was a magical barrier between everyone I cared about and the people who wouldn't think twice about killing us to get what they wanted.

I was so relieved to see Tristan and Alison had made it back inside that I almost broke down in tears. The commotion had been enough to bring Chris, Mateo, Lena, Brandon, and Charlie from their rooms, so I had eyes on everyone in the house, safe and sound. At least for now.

The thought comforted me long enough to allow me to take a breath, before I remembered that not everyone was safe within Rosehill's walls. The Patels were still at home on the grounds, thinking they were safe because James wouldn't dare hurt them, but the men outside my doors were mercenaries paid by the Damned to deliver a teenage girl to her eventual death, which told me they wouldn't hesitate to get rid of any Gifted obstacles in their way. Mohinder knew how to shoot, and Sakina had been taught how to defend herself, multiple times, but they were both pacifists who would always try to talk things out first. And Krishna…Krishna was as innocent as they come, having only known kindness and love from the world around her.

I tried to hide the terror in my voice from the children. "The Patels!"

CHAPTER TWENTY-ONE

DELIA

"They're gone," Charlie shared, staring out a window.

I joined him and saw that the front yard was empty. While some men who'd been outside the gates had dispersed, most of them had come to the wall's opening, watching us, waiting for an opportunity to make us pay for escaping them.

"Lorcan probably took him away. Or Persephone," Penny said, nodding while looking to me for confirmation.

"They're not gone," Lena argued. "They're almost at that old guard post."

I wrenched open the front door to get a better view. There were four of them inside the walls now, one of them holding back the gargoyles with a force field, like the ones Lucy could conjure. He had to keep bringing it back up, but it was at irregular intervals, and the other one who kept shooting at my gargoyles made sure they never got the chance to take advantage of it.

"There's no one in there, right?" Alison asked, looking between me and Tristan.

"That's where the wards are," I explained, as Ben and Caleb rushed out to stop the men. "The wall was enchanted for First

Lifers, I control who comes into the house, but the grounds at large are protected by wards at all the property limits."

"What happens if they reach the wards?" Brandon stood tall, ready to fight to protect us all, but the last thing I wanted was any of them getting involved.

The First Lifers had stopped and two of them crouched down while the others kept fighting off the gargoyles. Ben and Caleb were running across the grass to get to the guard post while I tried to figure out how certain I was the grounds and house would be protected, even if the wards fell. The mercenaries could get from the opening to the house far quicker than I could get back from the guard post if we failed.

"We can help," Jackie assured me.

I was about to send them to the training rooms while I went to protect the wards, but the two men on the ground, that I assumed were injured, stood up with a rocket launcher. I ran out, but the blast struck the tower just as Ben and Caleb tackled the men to the ground. Once the force field was gone, the gargoyles lifted the intruders and carried them off, but one look at where the tower used to stand told me there was no way the wards survived.

I spun around to see what happened at the opening, ready to use my Gift to hold them off while the children escaped, but the barrier was holding. Gifted were throwing themselves at it, but no one got past the invisible barrier, and the ones who used their Gift in the attempt got launched a dozen feet away when it bounced back on them.

"They can't get to you *inside* the house," I warned when Brandon and Tristan came down the front steps to join me.

"What does this mean?" Tristan reiterated.

"The grounds aren't safe anymore. Inside the house is the only place I can control."

"But what about Krishna?" Penny asked from the doorway

while I contemplated which exit would have the least amount of people.

"They'll take you apart if you try to get to them," Ben warned, jogging over with Caleb. He put his hand out to stop me in case I made a run for it. "You're better off sending the gargoyles or catching a ride with them." He accurately sensed that I wouldn't stay back and wait.

"Let's take the car. It'll be less obvious." Caleb had his determined look, as if he knew he was going to die, but would do everything in his power to accomplish his mission before he did. And he was right. Even if the gargoyles stayed below the tree line once they were over the wall, there was no hiding them. Not that the car would be much better, aside from being bulletproof.

I bit my bottom lip, trying to think of a solution that would keep us alive long enough to reach the Patels. I was willing to die, but not to lead those men right to them, or leave everyone at Rosehill vulnerable without us.

"There's a secret tunnel," I admitted. If the mercenaries hadn't found the house yet, I could sneak over and bring the Patels back with me. If we were going for stealth, it would be better on my own, but if there was trouble, it would be better to have Ben and Caleb with me, to ensure at least one of us made it there to protect them.

"The escape tunnel. As a last resort." Caleb nodded, and I gave him a sad smile, remembering all too well the time his muscles pushing against the door were the only thing that stopped the New Order from getting in.

"It lets out a couple hundred feet from the Patels' house. If there's any danger, they'll already be on their way to it," I said, like I expected to find them in the basement by the time we got there, although I knew they weren't even in the tunnel yet. I had the sinking feeling something was wrong, but kept reminding myself their house was in the middle of nowhere and wasn't obviously a part of the estate. The mercenaries had no reason to attack our neighbors, so the Patels should be safe.

"Lead the way." I couldn't read Ben's expression, but I knew he wasn't happy that I'd never told him about the tunnel. It was something I only thought of when we needed it. Or when I wasn't sure I trusted old friends.

"We need someone who can stay and make sure…"

"We've got it," Tristan assured me. "We can hang out in the training rooms if things go sideways." I could see how painful it was for him to not be able to come with us, when he fit most of my criteria, but Penny had latched onto him as soon as I put her down, and although Alison was keeping her distance now, he couldn't make a spark if his life depended on it.

I WALKED with purpose through the house and down the stairs. I imagined the men outside would watch the house, trying to find a way in, wondering why we weren't attacking or fleeing, but I doubted they would scour the grounds further away from the house. Unless James had betrayed everything and everyone he ever cared about, they wouldn't know about the Patels or the tunnel. As long as they didn't stumble upon the house, or Sakina on her way to the barn, they'd be fine.

I kept repeating the words to myself, but they lost their meaning the more times I repeated them. I had the gnawing thought that the First Lifer knew he would get through the barrier, and he came prepared with the means to destroy the wards. James didn't even know about that tower.

We didn't have time to grab more than what we'd had on us, but Lena came running after us with a bag full of armor and weapons.

"Thank you," I told her as we took what we needed. It was the most team-like thing she'd done since she arrived, and the only silver lining to this attack.

"If we want to have a fighting chance, we'll need all the help we can get." She put her own armor over her head and tried to follow us.

"You're underage and in your First Life. That's two strikes," I argued, but we didn't stop walking.

"And I've trained for a lot worse than whatever they can do to me."

She said it without emotion, but I flinched and swallowed hard at the thought of everything that had been done to this girl before she got to us.

"I can't have another child's death on my conscience." I knew she would argue and not care about my feelings when it came to keeping her safe. She'd been trained to believe her life was expendable as long as the mission succeeded, but she wasn't Gifted like Caleb, and had yet to even graduate high school. Sure, she had a Gift, but if Lena died out there, I had no clue if she would come back robbed of the chance to grow up, or if I would lose her forever. She could have inherited her Gift from a parent, or even accomplished whatever she was meant to do in the years since her Gift first manifested. It wasn't worth the risk.

We reached the end of the tunnel, so I turned to her, knowing she would find another way to follow us if I didn't convince her.

"We designed this tunnel as an escape, or for people to reach safety, so I don't know which of the magical barriers protect it." It was a partial lie, but it was accurate enough. "If they see us come out, I need someone on the inside who can make sure they don't get inside."

"You're trying to treat me like a child and give me a stupid task to feel useful when we both know I am more than capable of helping you fight."

"I know you are. I hate it, but I know you can hold your own and give more damage than you receive, but this tunnel leaves us vulnerable. I need someone I can trust not just to watch the door, but to fight them off, and seal it only if need be. I could get anyone to pull the lever after we go through and eliminate that risk, but then we would be out there without a safe way back in."

She looked at me and sighed, pissed off because even if I was driven by an ulterior motive, I was right.

"I'm giving you twenty minutes to bring them back, or I am coming after you," she warned.

"I'll take what I can get." I put my hand on her shoulder, smiled when she allowed it, then led Ben and Caleb outside the barriers.

THE WOODS WERE QUIET, like the calmness you find early in the morning, when the grass is wet with dew and most of the forest is still asleep. It would have been comforting if it wasn't nearing lunchtime. I looked to Ben, but he just shook his head before I could ask. Something in the woods made the animals flee, or he would have called them to us by now. One of the mercenaries did have a pet deer, but it had seemed like he used a whistle to control it, not a Gift. This was something much more ominous, and I was terrified of what we would find.

The house looked the same as it always looked, but even from a distance, I could see that the front door was open. I hurried my step and saw the screen door was still shut, as if they needed the breeze on a warm summer's day, but didn't want the bugs to get in. Caleb and Ben followed behind me, not because I was the fiercest or strongest, but because I wouldn't stay back, no matter how much they might want me to.

We made our way up the steps slowly, careful not to alert anyone to our presence, but when I heard Krishna scream, all bets were off.

. . .

I RAN straight to her bedroom, where the noise was coming from, and found a man with long, scraggly hair reaching for her as she hid in a ball shape at the bottom of her closet. Without thinking, I struck him on the back of the head with the handle of my dagger and rushed to Krishna before he hit the ground.

"It's okay, I've got you." I held her as Ben and Caleb dealt with more mercenaries I hadn't seen from other rooms. "Where are your parents?"

"We were in the backyard, and Amma was going to meet Alison, but then she heard something and told me to come inside and hide. I wasn't to come out or make a sound unless it was them, or you, but then the man found me and I screamed, and…"

"It's okay, love, you did nothing wrong. We found you and you're safe now," I assured her, but the look I exchanged with Ben was not so certain. If the mercenaries – other than the ones that wandered in – hadn't known about the house before, her screams ensured they would now. "We're going to go up to Rosehill. Maybe you can help me make some snickerdoodles with Penny." In my mind, no one talked about baking when they were about to die, so saying such trivial things to her would hopefully make her feel safe.

"With Amma and Appa?" she verified, looking up at me with her big brown eyes.

"Of course. Caleb can bring you back while I go find them."

"I want to stay with you," she argued.

Caleb nodded, to say I should go with her, and he would stay, but he didn't know the woods like I did. He didn't know the secret hiding places and all the paths to get back to the wall…then again, my knowledge would be just as useful getting Krishna to the wall as for finding her parents.

I carried her to the front door. She was at least two feet taller than the ideal size to be held in that way by someone as short as me, but it ensured that I could keep her safe and that she wouldn't see anything beyond the creases in the fabric at my chest.

Once we stood in the doorway, I saw our debates were useless. There had only been those three men inside the house, but it was now surrounded by at least twenty men, women, and children – most likely Gifted – waiting for us.

"She's not Gifted," I said out of habit, knowing it rarely made a difference once they realized she had Gifts, or just from her associating with us, but I would try anything on the off chance it might influence their decision. Especially considering how well-hidden Krishna's Gifts were.

"That's okay. We're looking for something to trade. The younger the better, but this one can work too." I spotted the man who'd lured Penny out with his deer earlier. He had what looked like blood on his sleeve, the fear from which elevated my heart rate, but I already knew that he wasn't above creating fake injuries to mislead us.

I weighed my options and decided once more that without contest, stripping these people of their free will was more than worth it to save Krishna, as long as none of them overreacted. And I had to make sure my words went to the mercenaries, but not to Mohinder and Sakina, who I hoped were somewhere nearby. I was formulating a command when the man with the pet deer suddenly fell to the ground.

JAMES WAS STANDING BEHIND HIM, his long sword covered in blood. His shirt was too, but it looked like that was from being gutted himself, not from damage he'd done to someone else.

"Do you remember where all the jars were?" I knelt down to Krishna while Ben and Caleb moved in closer to shield us, braced for the fight.

"All the different shapes and colors?" she verified.

"I will find you there," I promised her.

Their cellar connected to an old bomb shelter that was further from the tunnel than I would have liked, but right now I just needed to get her away from the angry mob.

"With my parents?" she asked again.

"I would never leave them behind." It was as much of a promise as I could give her, though she deserved so much more.

Ben and Caleb had already started fighting when I joined in, after covering the secret door with a rug. There was no way Caleb would have fit inside, which removed it as an escape option, but I found that comforting, since most of the people against us were closer to Caleb's size than mine. Even the first woman I came against was at least a foot taller than me, with braids in her blonde hair that made her look like a Viking. An angry Viking, but her Gift seemed to be changing her own appearance, which allowed her to be taller and stronger than me, but I was trained to fight people larger than Caleb. It also helped that while she was looking for a payday, I was defending my home, and there was no way any amount of money motivated her as much as the little girl cowering beneath us motivated me.

The Viking woman charged me with an ax she looked ready to stick into my gut, but I moved to the side and threw one of my daggers. It landed in her chest, and she fell before her blade could touch me. I winced, but I didn't have time to feel bad for her death before the next assailant came for me. It was one after the other, and while some of them had impressive Gifts, many of them either had passive ones, or weren't Gifted at all. I understood the Damned's attraction towards human soldiers, as they were much easier to manipulate and control, but I still couldn't risk using my Gift until Krishna was a safe distance away.

Through the fights, I was slowly making my way to the backyard. I could see James coming for me, slicing through mercenary after mercenary, which made little sense, since he was currently on their side. Unless the reward was so great that he needed to cut down the competition, but that wasn't likely. I knew the warning look in his eyes, but I rarely listened when he used it. He wanted me to stop and wait for him to get to me, but I couldn't. For a million reasons, and only one of them being that I had to find Mohinder and Sakina before the other mercenaries got to them.

My current foe looked like he was twelve or thirteen at the most. I knew being Gifted was misleading, that he could have centuries on me, but my first instinct would always be to protect him. James was the first, but far from the last, to get exasperated when I would rather die accidentally protecting an evil Gifted with the appearance of a kid, than to risk hurting a child.

"Lilah." James used my name as he got closer, but the skies had gone dark and the battle was thinning out around us, the mud making it hard to stand once you reached the side of the house, where almost every inch was devoted to an overrun vegetable patch. Mohinder's squashes were always twice the size of mine, and ten times more flavorful. I wanted to concentrate on that, to figure out what their patch had that my garden didn't, but Krishna was scared and alone, and I needed to find her parents.

There were only two mercenaries left between James and me, as well as the teenager in front of me I would need to dispense with before I could round the corner to the backyard. I didn't know what the kid's Gift was, until he fell back and his hand touched the ground, burning the surrounding grass to a black crisp. I could easily understand how someone would want to get rid of their Giftedness, no matter the cost, if they couldn't control it and everyone they touched died. He and Alison would have a lot to talk about.

If I'd met him under any other circumstance, I would have brought him into Rosehill and introduced him to Alison and

Tristan, proof that if you worked hard, you could figure it out. I would have welcomed him with open arms, but today I couldn't risk it. I still swung to miss, making sure I pushed him back and brought him down without killing him. I was used to never going for the kill, but I kept thinking that if we could just teach him to control his Gift, I was sure he would be less angry and not want to kill people anymore. I couldn't get close enough to subdue him without getting burned, so I pushed him back down a row of turnips where I'd spotted a forgotten shovel. I lunged for it, then knocked him out with the handle. He might have a concussion, but he was no longer a danger, and he wasn't dead.

I got to the backyard and saw them just before James' hand landed on my shoulder. I grabbed it and threw him to the ground, resting my blade against his throat. I could pretend I didn't know it was him, but in that moment, he was just as guilty as every other person paid to accomplish the same task. I had half a mind to knock him out as well, if only because I thought he might let me, but I walked away instead, rushing to the colorful piles of fabric I knew were Mohinder and Sakina, even before I got close enough to tell them apart. Blood covered her orange sari, while his entire body was coated in boils.

I brought my fingers to their carotids, knowing Etta could save them if there was even the faintest of heart beats.

There was nothing.

I wanted to scream, and to yell at every single person in those woods to leave and never come back, but words yelled at large, especially in anger, were a recipe for disaster.

"Lilah…"

I turned and glared at him, my heart pounding in my chest. I wanted to claw at it and rip it out to make the pain stop, but I took a deep breath and got up.

"What are you doing here?"

"I saw them, and…I never would have…I never meant for any of this to happen."

I knew the blood on his shirt wasn't because he'd done this, that he probably had the lowest rate of civilian casualties in the history of the world, but he was still a part of this, and he would have fed Alison to the lions, maybe worse.

"Great people you're working for."

I walked past without looking at him, even though I could feel his eyes on me. It killed me to leave the Patels alone in the yard like that, but I couldn't risk bringing more attention to myself until I was away from the mob and Krishna was safe within Rosehill. I walked away from the cellar, deeper into the woods.

"You're not wanted here," I told James when he followed.

"They had a child."

"That your friends just orphaned."

"They are no friends of mine."

"Colleagues then. It doesn't matter." We were far enough away from Krishna's hiding spot that I yelled once for help, hoping Persephone would bring Lorcan and Dashiel with her.

"I'm not like them."

"Right now, you are."

Persephone arrived with the others, as if they'd been waiting for my call, flying low and cutting through the trees so they wouldn't be seen more than they had to.

"Mohinder and Sakina are about a hundred feet that way, in their backyard. Please bring them to Rosehill and keep them out of sight from the children. Chris will know what to do," I asked of Dashiel. I hated what this would do to Chris emotionally, without any warning. I wanted to tell them to go to Etta instead, to have her at least try, but I knew what it took from her when she attempted to use her Gift on a corpse.

"Caleb and Ben are still fighting in front of the Patel house, if you could offer them your assistance?" I asked of Lorcan, aware that James was watching me silently. He was completely torn up, devastated, but I couldn't be easy on him. I would either fall apart in his arms or leave us exposed, and neither were options.

Persephone looked from me to James expectantly, not sure if we wanted a ride home, or if I was going to order her to take him away again. Not that she would listen.

"Krishna is hiding, but I'll need your help to get her home as fast as possible, before they notice."

"That's their daughter?" James asked, which got him a very sharp look from me.

"Don't you have somewhere else to be?"

"I'm not leaving until you're safe behind those walls with Sakina's daughter."

He didn't have my Gift, so there was nothing supernatural to make his words come true, but when he made statements like that, promises, he always followed through.

"I don't need your help."

I considered getting rid of him to protect the secrecy of her location, but even without knowing that we'd connected their cellar to the bomb shelter, James knew where our old escape shelter was, and would have found her eventually.

We walked in silence, James probably fearing that I would try to send him away again, this time without leaving him a choice, but I was worried that I would break down if he so much as touched me again.

I went ahead of him, with my jaw set, determined to ignore him, but when we got close, James was the one who lifted the branches and opened the door to the shelter. He didn't have Caleb's superhuman strength, but the way his muscles bulged when he forced it open, I probably would have needed Persephone's help, and she did not have the appropriate grip to get into it without busting down the door. Still, I did not thank him.

"Did you find them?" Krishna asked me immediately.

"I did," I told her, trying my best to smile as she sought refuge in my arms. "Persephone is going to take us home to Rosehill."

I saw Krishna eyeing James, and the blood that soaked his shirt, but I didn't address any of it. There would be plenty of time once we were behind the stone wall, but my priority was her safety.

I had just gotten Krishna onto my back when a band of mercenaries came from the trees, ready to attack us with both weapons and Gifts.

"Close your eyes," James told Krishna, knowing I would have struggled to find the words. He used to do that a lot for me, but today I was equally grateful and angry about it.

I sliced into the first man who lunged for us, but they were smart, and weren't coming one at a time to make it easy on us. They were a steady slew of attacks, both sharp and supernatural, directed at both of us.

"Get her out of here," James told me. "I'll hold them off as long as I can."

He took a slice above his right eye, causing blood to leak down, but I knew it was our best hope.

"You don't care what happens to me anyway, right?" he pressed when I didn't leave.

I knew it was to encourage me to go, not to make me feel guilty, but the falseness behind the words tore at my heart.

"Take us home," I told Persephone, so she wrapped her arms around me from behind, cocooning Krishna between us.

She flew low at first, using twirling maneuvers to deflect the attacks they threw at us, but then she flew high above the trees and darted right over the stone wall.

An explosion resonated through her just before she crossed the threshold, blasting off one of her wings, but she landed and released us safely before crumbling.

Dashiel scooped her up and brought her to the roof, while Krishna turned to me.

"Where are they?" she asked.

"Dashiel brought them back here," I started, trying to find the words, but also trying not to think of it, so she wouldn't overhear it from my thoughts. Not that it helped when she could also feel my heart breaking.

"I peeked," she admitted in tears. "I think that's how the man saw me, but I had to know they were okay when I didn't feel them anymore. But they didn't look okay," she told me. "Are they okay? Can Etta help them?" The tears and the look in her eyes told me she knew the truth, but was begging me to tell her something different.

"I'm so sorry, sweetheart."

I took her in my arms, but I could feel her heart breaking with mine, even without her Gift, which I knew only made her pain a million times worse. "I'm so sorry."

CHAPTER TWENTY-TWO

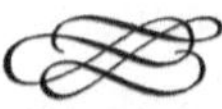

DELIA

Krishna insisted on seeing her parents with her own two eyes.

I didn't think it was a good idea, but at that point, there was nothing I would deny that child. After sending Etta to bring Lena back, Krishna and I sat with her parents in the courtyard for what felt like hours, in silence, Krishna holding a hand from each of them, while I tried my best not to leave any of my thoughts or emotions exposed.

By evening, Krishna looked sick and exhausted, so Chris made her some broth that she barely ate, and I went up to bed with her.

"Where would you like to sleep tonight?" I asked when she stopped dead a few feet from the room she usually shared with her parents whenever they stayed over.

"Can I stay in Penny's room?" she asked, as the six-year-old came up the stairs with Tristan, carrying a teddy like I hadn't seen her do since she got Matilda. I guess children take care of dolls, but bears comfort them, and we all needed comfort tonight.

The right thing to do would be to ask Penny if she minded, but my concern was more about having someone so close to Krishna, who was also going through something at the moment. Then again, Penny was dealing with her fear after being in danger, and I couldn't even tell how I was feeling from the sinking depth of emotions that plagued me. I wanted to hold Krishna close and make sure she was okay, but I was probably the least suited to it out of everyone at Rosehill, except maybe Alison. But that one was a toss-up as well.

Luckily, Penny nodded and came to take Krishna's hand, so I followed the girls into the bedroom and obliged when Penny asked me to lie in the bed with them until they fell asleep.

WHICH TOOK THEM FOREVER. At first, they listened to a dozen bedtime stories without Krishna uttering a single word, then Penny coerced everyone who came to say goodnight into staying, so before long she'd orchestrated a group sing-along. Except for Mateo, who stood there and moved his mouth to pretend while fooling no one, everyone sang. Lena's voice was even better than her instruments, but she shut down the instant Chris complimented her on it.

Penny fell asleep not long after that, but Krishna stared at the ceiling in silence, gripping my hand, until she eventually asked, "Am I an unwanted child now?"

"No, sweetheart, you're mine now. We just happen to live here."

"I want to go home."

She cried into my chest for a good forty minutes before her breathing finally calmed down and I could tell she was sleeping.

· · ·

THE CHILDREN WERE in their rooms for the night, but some adults, especially Ben, were waiting for Krishna to be settled so they could have a word with me. I wasn't ready for that conversation, and my entire body was stiff from trying to hold in every thought and emotion over the last six hours, so I slipped out and took the hidden staircase.

For the first time in forever, it wasn't my painful memories that were pulling me to the greenhouse. I went down to the kitchen as if I was having trouble sleeping and wanted to make myself some warm milk and honey. Or at least that's what I would have told anyone who'd stopped me and asked before I made it out the door.

Now that the grounds were exposed, I couldn't chance being seen, so I took the less direct, more complicated route, but it also bypassed the marble swan whose stony stare would have judged me as much as I was judging myself. Although who knew if Francis' masterpiece would have judged me for coming out here in the dead of night to meet up with James, or for not letting him inside.

We grew our own fruits and vegetables on the property now, along with many other spices and natural remedies, but when Rosehill was first built, the garden held nothing but roses. Red, white, and pink ones as big as my head.

For over a century, the greenhouse was where I would find James when he couldn't sleep. I would wake up in the middle of the night, find his side of the bed empty, and come down to watch him tend to the herbs under the light of the moon. He had a green thumb for gardening, but was always too busy during the day. He would know that I was there before I even laid eyes on him, so he would pick a rose and hand it to me when I came up behind him and wrapped my arms around his waist.

When I saw him tonight, he had his back to me, like all those times before. It felt like a dream to see him there after centuries spent wandering the rows of plants, now that I was the one who couldn't sleep at night. Instead of picking a rose for me, I watched him place his thumb on a thorn and press down hard, barely wincing when the pop let me know it had pierced his skin.

"Why did you do that?" I asked, resisting the urge to move closer.

"The thorn? Or this afternoon?" he asked, turning to face me.

"They got you." I took a steadying breath when I saw the blood at his temple.

"It's nothing," he dismissed it, keeping his eyes on mine, boring into me like he had no right to do anymore.

"It's still bleeding." I kept my focus on the wound, because his eyes were stirring up feelings I could not entertain. There was a first aid kit beside the door, so I brought it to his side.

I could hear Ben's voice inside my head, calling me stupid and careless, every name in the book if he could see me, but if I had to be afraid of James hurting me, then I might as well be dead.

"You can't help it, can you?" He had a sad smile that broke my heart, but I willed myself to stay strong and unaffected.

"Taking care of idiots? Apparently not."

"They came to make sure I was doing my job. Or I guess it's our job, and they finally caught up to me."

"I never thought I would see the day you allied yourself to men who would use a child to kill a teenager."

"They'll use anything to get her. The reward is worth it."

I flinched and poured the antiseptic directly onto his cut instead of dabbing it on with a cotton ball. James breathed in sharply and clenched his fist. He never liked to show people when they hurt him; it added to the illusion of being cold and invincible, but neither was true.

"To them," he specified.

"Not to you?"

"They're offering more money than those men have ever seen, and the chance to end it all for good. I know a lot of decent, caring people who wouldn't hesitate to give her up if it meant ending their suffering."

I knew he was right. It wasn't everyone who was like me, believing that every human life should be valued and protected above our own, but even the ones that were…I'm not sure which side they would land on in the debate between one human life versus curing Giftedness and finally finding peace.

"Is this where you convince me to end my own suffering? To give her up for the good of the Gifted community?"

"No, this is where I warn you we are not the same."

"Not anymore," I agreed.

"I meant the people who have been arriving by the handful since this morning. I live by a code, and I don't want anyone else getting hurt. I avoid casualties at all costs, but most of them will kill anything that gets in their way."

"I appreciate the warning, but I doubt we'll be venturing outside again."

"Lilah…"

"You gave up that right a long time ago. The minute you agreed to pursue an innocent child…"

The disgust in my voice, and on my face, must have gotten to him. He grabbed my wrist and looked into my eyes, forcing me to do the same.

"I'm telling you I'm after one girl whose blood has been tainted since the day she was born. But they will burn the place to the ground to get to her, with all of you still inside. They won't stop coming, and I can't protect you from that."

"I'd like to see them try," I said with more confidence than I felt, ignoring his last statement. Protecting me hadn't been his responsibility for a long time.

He pressed his lips together and looked at me like I was the most infuriating creature in the world. He took a few calming breaths before his demeanor changed entirely. "Why didn't you just compel me in the forest? Or in the tunnel after?"

"We promised," I said simply. It was the same reason no one was coming in through the tunnel, or going after the other people I cared about who weren't safe inside Rosehill. "But I will break that promise if you so much as try to hurt her," I reminded him.

"I would expect nothing less." He sighed, then looked up at me with a tenderness that broke my heart. "It's not the first time you're misguided about who you try to save."

I could have argued with that statement. Sure, I'd been betrayed, but I never regretted choosing to help instead of harm. And this wasn't about that.

"Or the first time you lose your way," I turned it on him.

I could see the pain in his face then, because whenever he'd get lost in a task or a mission he no longer believed in, he'd say it would all be okay as long as he always found his way back to me. Which he had, only we'd never been on opposite sides before.

He looked into my eyes, the words unspoken, and for a second I thought he was going to take me in his arms, either to kiss me or comfort me I wasn't sure, but in that moment I didn't care; I would have let him.

"Take care of yourself, Lilah."

His gaze lingered on me for seconds that felt like a lifetime before he left. My heart was pounding in my chest, and I knew he heard it. He heard everything, like a hunter with his prey. Only he knew what my breath sounded like, and could tell how I was feeling from miles away, just by the rhythm of my heartbeat. Jackie could look through my eyes and Sakina could read my mind, but James saw into my soul, and it terrified me.

CHAPTER TWENTY-THREE

DELIA

I casually prepared a pot of tea, then brought a tray into the sitting room and waited. Ben was there within an instant, having clocked me as soon as I got inside, but Caleb and Etta, Tristan and Allie, Chris, and Jackie all took their seats long before I took my first sip. Caleb and Ben had each given up a life this morning, but Caleb regenerated faster than anyone I knew, other than James, and Ben had been back in time for our evening singalong with Penny. Lena would be upset she wasn't included in this, since she clearly saw herself as one of the warriors, but the rules were in place to protect her from danger, not to be thrown out the window as soon as something could hurt her. I never wanted Rosehill to be anything like the place she came from.

I was composing myself, coming up with the words to accept their blame and the consequences of my actions, but I didn't know where to start. Ben and Caleb had seen James fighting on our side, so keeping our past a secret at this point was more of a lie than simply leaving some details out.

They misconstrued the workings of my mind as me waiting for something, so Caleb poured out teas for everyone. I could feel their eyes on me, waiting, but I knew the moment I started speaking, so much was going to change.

"So?" Chris asked, speaking up when no one else was.

"Rosehill isn't the safest place for everyone to be anymore. And I can't stay safe inside these walls while the people outside are dying." I knew that my initial plan wasn't working. Sakina and Mohinder's deaths were my fault, and I would never be able to forgive myself for that.

"Are there other tunnels? Ones that lead farther away, maybe off the grounds?" Tristan suggested.

"The one we used to get here lets out in the woods behind our house. I doubt they'd be expecting us there, and we could take cars to—"

"There are lots of escape tunnels," I cut Etta off. "But James knows all of them. We would all be safe, but he'd get Alison. And leaving you here alone is out of the question," I warned before she could suggest it.

"When you say you knew him centuries ago…how well did you know him?" Jackie finished her questions from this morning.

I looked to Ben, knowing this would hurt, but he had described it perfectly.

"Once upon a time ago, I was James' Etta."

As expected, Ben did that thing where he tries to slow his breathing and calm down before speaking when he is really upset. I was grateful. Any words he used for me now would slice deeper than a knife.

"We were together a long time, until he chose vengeance, and that was the end of it. I was heartbroken, but I found Gabriel and I had Rosehill, then all of you came along and I truly hadn't even had a passing glance of him since."

"By a long time, you mean…" Jackie pressed.

I considered lying, or dismissing the specifics, but that

defeated the purpose of coming clean. "Two – almost three – centuries."

"And you didn't think that was worth mentioning after his people attacked us?" Ben asked, a shadow crossing his face. I had the vivid memory of him screaming in agony while a member of James' team tortured him.

"What good would it have done?"

"I think the people living inside this house had the right to know that one of the guys out there knew every single way in or out of Rosehill, including the secret tunnels that were meant to carry us to safety as a last resort."

"He couldn't get inside, or past the wall, not even on the grounds. The tunnel was the only place he could enter, but he couldn't come all the way, and I could cave it in if ever I needed to," I said calmly. I knew they would be upset that I never told them the extent of our relationship, but they needed to know I hadn't disregarded their safety.

"But you didn't. When would it have been enough? Clearly not when his people destroyed the front gate and tried to terrorize us. Maybe after they killed Alison? Once they'd brought in their own witch and that tunnel was our only way out, no matter how compromised?"

"Go easy on her, Ben," Caleb warned.

"Did you know about any of this?" He was infuriated.

"No, but we all knew she had a life before us. Centuries worth of relationships and experiences. What did you expect?" Etta joined in my defense.

I loved them for sticking up for me, but I deserved most of it. "I made a calculated decision. Lucy reinforced the barriers when she came into her power, and there is no witch more powerful than her, which means no one was getting through. And we needed that escape route. Whether he knew about it or not, that was how Sakina would get in if..." I stopped myself and took a deep breath to calm myself down, but I could feel the tears. Ben's look softened, because he wasn't angry enough to tell me her death was entirely my fault, even if we all knew it was.

"Did she know him too?" Etta asked gently.

"She did. Sakina felt safe on the grounds without needing to come inside because she knew James would never hurt her." I knew he wouldn't come alone if the Damned sent him. How could any other organization trust him without an insurance policy?

"He's the Knight who brought Christina and Laurel. And Jack." Etta named a few of the First Lifers that came our way after James encountered them.

"The Guardian," I corrected. "He left when it changed."

"No…" Chris perked up at that. "James Van Bergen?"

My look confirmed it, but it was only him and Caleb who knew the implications.

"Can someone start at the beginning?" Jackie asked. "Like what happened between you two and why does that name sound so familiar?"

"It's a long story…" I started, but Ben's look would have stopped me if Jackie hadn't.

"I won't be getting any sleep tonight, and maybe something you tell us can help prevent him from hurting anyone else?"

In their minds, all the mercenaries outside our walls were lumped together, so it didn't matter that James had helped me get Krishna out. He was just as responsible for their deaths as the ones who did it. And I couldn't blame them for that.

"Help us understand," Tristan added, looking like he was giving me the benefit of the doubt, but I was close to being found guilty.

I sighed and took a deep breath. "You all know I got my Gift when I was a child, and Sakina taught me how to control it. I did, eventually, but long before that, I changed my language, so I no longer gave any kind of command or order. I was safe and under the radar until the summer I turned sixteen. There was a lot of unrest with many Gifted wanting to use their power to torture humans and exert their supremacy. Fights would break out in the streets, Gifted taking out humans, or humans attacking those they suspected of being Gifted, to gain the upper hand. My father was known, in small circles, for welcoming Gifted to court, having them on his council, letting them tutor his children…he faced a lot of backlash and war was imminent, so he sounded the alarm and brought the Knights to London. Johannes Van Bergen was in charge, said to have more experience dealing with supernatural beings than anyone else in the world. My father refused to go into hiding, but he convinced Johannes to have his son, James, go into hiding with me and my siblings, to make sure we were safe."

"You expect us to believe James and his father came to your castle to save the villagers from people exactly like who he is now? That's preposterous, Delia." Ben was upset, but the fact that he was still there, listening, was a good sign.

"It's in the books in the Rosehill library. Gifted history, my ancestry, the Guardians, the Knights, and the New Order… every single volume will tell the same story as I am, with slightly different perspectives."

Ben looked to Chris, the one who reads history books for fun, and was taken aback when he nodded.

"Johannes had taught his son everything he knew, so he was the perfect soldier, with so many rules and restrictions. I absolutely hated him, for weeks, until one day, I didn't. I got to know the boy in the soldier's uniform and fell in love. We were staying at a family estate in the countryside, and he needed constant eyes on my siblings, so there were lots of walks in the garden where our hands brushed, glances across the room while he played chess with my brother, singing just for him on the pianoforte…it was a weird, scary time that also felt like we were in our own little world. Until the eclipse. One of the Gifted terrorizing the city could manipulate astronomical occurrences, so she dimmed the lights to make the riots easier. Not that we knew it at the time. We just lit candles and were going to continue playing games, until James locked us all in the cellar and went to see what was going on."

"I'm not sure how this fits in," Tristan said delicately. "Other than you look like you hated him again by that point."

"I did. I felt utterly betrayed, because he didn't bother to explain himself so much as lock the doors and run off. There was an escape route to a boat on the river, which my brother, Henry, wanted us to take to London, but we didn't have provisions or enough candles to survive the journey in pitch darkness. By the time we heard voices, Henry was ready to give James a piece of his mind, as he had never been treated so horribly in his entire life, but it wasn't James. The doors were fortified, and no one should have been able to get in, but there was an orange glow as a man roughly Caleb's size melted down the door in front of our very eyes. They were looking for my brother, a bargaining chip, but they paused when one of them sensed what I was."

"There are Gifted whose Gift is to suss out other Gifted?" Jackie asked. "Or do we have like a smell thing?"

"Lola could tell which life you're in by looking at you," Alison shared.

"And James can tell the difference between First Lifers, Gifted, and regular humans. But I don't know how this person knew, just that they did. We were prepared to fight – I hadn't even considered using my Gift – but a group of Knights who'd been following them from the city arrived with James and fought them off for us. Unfortunately, they'd heard what I was, and wanted to get rid of me as well. Many Knights believed the best way to stop the uprisings and ensure there would be no repeats was to eliminate all Gifted, whether they were a part of the riots or not. James stood between us to protect me, but he was outnumbered, and…"

"He gave a life for you," Caleb finished for me. He'd given many, both for me and for Etta, so he knew what it entailed. But he didn't grasp the magnitude of James' sacrifice.

"He gave *his* life," I corrected.

"He wasn't Gifted?" Tristan was shocked.

"Not that we knew of at that point. I was cradling his body, not even bothering to defend myself anymore, when his father showed up with more Knights. He was furious that his soldiers had taken to killing Gifted without discrimination, even before he discovered what happened to his son."

"But he woke up," Jackie said, looking on the bright side.

"The next day," I agreed. "The Knights had won, but there were council meetings and punishments to contend with. Johannes removed himself from the organization and created a new one, with the same purpose, only he judged based on actions, not abilities. They called themselves the Guardians, and spent the next few years going around the world, creating safe houses and teaching Gifted how to defend themselves, finding people like Sakina willing to show them how to control their Gifts so they no longer posed threats."

"And the rest of the Knights?" Alison asked.

"They disbanded. Many joined the Guardians, but a frighteningly large number became the New Order of the Night, who travelled the globe, hunting down Gifted and eliminating them."

"Did you go with James? Were you a Guardian?" Tristan asked.

"In all the ways that mattered." I smiled, remembering that time, where all we did was make a difference in people's lives. "But I didn't follow him until I died a few years later. From the plague, which I would not recommend."

"Then you went around for centuries, living happily ever after until he snapped?" Tristan asked.

"Not entirely. We spent centuries together, and we were ridiculously happy. I was a nurse, a teacher, a writer, a singer in New York for a bit…I tried everything. James, on the other hand, was a soldier, whether officially or off the record. He was always trying to save people, to protect the innocent." I condensed half my life into that simple statement.

"What changed?" Jackie asked, but I could see a shadow pass many of their faces, wondering if James was broken, or if they might snap as well.

"They ripped out his heart," I said simply.

CHAPTER TWENTY-FOUR

DELIA

"Literally?" Jackie shuddered.

"Probably not, but I wasn't there to see how it ended."

"How did it begin?"

"After a beautiful wedding with all the people we loved." I recounted the night I lost everything. "We couldn't have children of our own, but long before I opened Rosehill, James and I would take in orphans and raise them…"

"We could bring her some bread tomorrow. And a chicken or something, so she isn't too hungry," Cadence suggested while we walked along the harbor. She was only eight years old, but had more love and kindness in her heart than half the people we'd met during our stay in Boston. Not that we associated with bad people - most of them were wonderful – but she always wanted to give, expecting nothing in return, simply because she hoped it would make someone else happy. Even I often had ulterior motives when I helped someone these days.

"That sounds like a wonderful idea." I smiled before a dog barking in the distance woke Mackenzie, who'd fallen asleep in James' arms as

we were leaving the wedding. Maude was still on the dance floor, her smile just as bright as it had been this morning at the prospect of spending her life with Patrick, but her feet would not last much longer tonight. James had nearly offered to carry her to bed, like he used to when she was a child, but Patrick was more than capable. She'd found herself a guy almost as good as mine.

"Did someone have a good nap?" I gave Mackenzie my finger to hold on to as James rocked her, kissing the top of her head and warming my heart. He was the most handsome, thoughtful, and caring man I'd ever encountered in all my years, but it was the way he fathered our children that made me particularly weak in the knees. Mackenzie was barely a year old and had only been with us a couple of months since her parents passed, but her eyes lit up every time he walked into her room.

"She's probably overwhelmed because she doesn't recognize anything." Cadence came over and played peek-a-boo a couple of times before cuddling into me, so I could wrap my arm around her and hold her close.

"Is that how you feel?" I kissed the top of her head and looked around. The city changed every time we came back to it, not that James ever had trouble finding our way. When I came on my own, I used the waterfront as a reference, or the constellations, because the buildings changed faster than I could keep track of them.

"No, I think it's exciting to come here for the wedding and meet workers and soldiers and politicians...all the people who would never come to Rosehill."

"But," James pressed. He was doing an awkward walk that looked ridiculous, but Mackenzie was giggling like it was the most fun she'd ever had.

"I'm also eager to get home. Mrs. Potts must miss us terribly. And Mr. Brown."

"Who wouldn't miss you?" I agreed, giving her another hug. Mrs. Potts liked to mother us all, even though James and I were centuries older than her. She knew the truth, but still saw us as a young couple

in need of parenting advice. It could get annoying to be taught how to calm a sick infant when you'd done it for hundreds of them without issue, but she meant well, and it all came from a place of love. Mr. Brown, on the other hand, was our dog. He probably enjoyed being in the company of the woman who fed him table scraps without having to walk the grounds with James every morning.

"It is nice to see old friends," James agreed. "But I've got everything I need right here." He held Mackenzie in his left arm and wrapped the right around us, kissing the top of Cadence's head, and then my cheek.

"Me too," Cadence agreed.

IT WASN'T long until Mackenzie got fussy, so I took her in my arms while James and Cadence started singing and dancing to entertain her. James' eyes kept darting around to make sure no one was watching, but he would do absolutely anything for our girls, and I loved him all the more for it.

"I don't think that's age appropriate," I warned when they veered off into a drinking song.

"Jeremy and Mr. Potts sing it all the time," Cadence argued, then sang hats instead of ass, which got James and I to burst out laughing.

"Well. It's working on this one," I shared as Mackenzie went back to giggling.

Cadence sang the next verse of the song, using her own interpretation of the lyrics that made it very difficult to keep a straight face. I was dealing with Mackenzie's new game, which consisted of putting her fingers in my mouth while I pretended to munch on them, until a man's voice joined in with Cadence's song. I was going to reproach James for correcting her lyrics, especially when the real ones were unsavory, but I quickly realized it was not my husband's voice. I did recognize it, however, and it brought a chill to my bones.

"Good evening, your Ladyship." The man looked deranged as he said the words with disdain, almost spitting in my face.

"Good evening, Mr. X," I greeted him, holding Mackenzie closer to my chest as James came over, tucking Cadence behind us.

"But it isn't really, now is it?" He glared at me.

"Are you in need of assistance?" James asked. We'd met the man the day we arrived. He'd rushed to us in a panic, having heard we could help his brother, who'd been in an accident. He'd perished not long after they brought me to him, and judging by their attire, these men were coming from his funeral.

"I was, but you both saw to that, didn't you?"

"We're very sorry about your brother. We were just on our way to the inn with our daughters, but my wife and I would be happy to meet you afterward."

"Our adopted, human daughters," I specified. The look Cadence shot me was one of utter heartbreak. She'd been ours since she was three, and never once had we implied that she was anything other than my flesh and blood, except for when it came to honoring her birth parents, in which case we shared her.

"That's smart of you, but I'm afraid it doesn't make much of a difference. You see, there's this thing I discovered recently, of guilt by association."

"Who's guilt?" James asked, confused more than angry. "These are innocent children. If you'd like to air out your grievances with me, I would be happy to comply, but there's no need to involve them."

James still thought this was rage over losing his brother, which he saw as neither of our faults. I knew differently, but was not expecting the change in his look when Mr. X showed him his ring. I'd noticed it the other day, only briefly when he'd handed me a clean cloth, but he'd retrieved his hand and hidden the ring before I'd gotten the chance to get a good look at it.

"Lilah, get the girls out of here." James' tone was even, and his face betrayed no emotion, but I could tell he was afraid, which was not something I'd seen in him for centuries.

"Oh, they're not going anywhere," Mr. X argued as more men surrounded us, filling the street. While he wore plainclothes, most of *the men with him wore the insignia of the New Order of the Night. I'd warned James that bedtime stories were supposed to make children feel safe, but at least our daughter knew these men weren't our friends, or to be trusted.*

Cadence had always been strong-willed, just as her parents had been. She moved to the side so the men could hear her better while she shouted at them, "I'm not Gifted!" with her hands raised. "These are my parents and they're not evil. They don't use their Gifts on people. Unless it's to help them."

"Cadence," I warned, trying to push her back behind me, but James moved to cover her.

"Don't you understand?" she asked when that didn't deter them. "They help people."

James was between me and Mr. X, with Cadence standing behind him, so I put my hand on her shoulder and took a step back. If we could get away from his anger and into a busier street, he would have no choice but to come for us later, when the girls weren't with us.

"Why don't you—" The carefully planned instructions might not have activated my Gift, but I didn't get the chance to use them before a sharp pain pierced my back. I didn't realize it was a knife until whoever was behind me pulled it out and pushed it in again. He must have pierced my lungs or windpipe, because I couldn't get the air I needed to speak.

Mackenzie had been screaming, but she suddenly went quiet, as I felt a sickening warmth spreading through my dress. The knife had gone through my back, but I'd felt it deep in my chest, like it had come through the other side, which wouldn't matter except I was holding Mackenzie against me. I had never wanted so badly to hear a baby cry as I did in that moment, but she was heartbreakingly silent.

"That was for my brother." Mr. X was emotionless, but his words made James and Cadence turn back to look at me.

Cadence screamed in horror when she saw the blood. "You're the monsters!" she yelled at them. "She was just a little baby. You—"

I never got the chance to find out what else she thought they were.

The world had gone fuzzy for me by then. James had taken Cadence in his arms, encircling her with his own body as much as he could, but Mr. X had thrown the knife before he got to her. I'd stepped forward as well, not letting go of Mackenzie, or letting anyone near Cadence, but the attacks kept coming, speeding up my blood loss. James tried to fight, but there were so many of them, and he couldn't fight while holding Cadence at the same time. Not that it would have made a difference if he'd let her go. It was agony as more and more blades tore through my skin, but it was nothing compared to the pain in my heart when Cadence had stopped screaming. When James stopped fighting. When we died.

I woke up at home, *in my bed at Rosehill, but along with the hunger that came from resurrection, I felt an emptiness in my heart and in my soul.*

I expected James to be beside me, sleeping in a chair while he waited for me to wake up, like he had every other time, but I was alone in the room. There was noise coming from downstairs, but I went into the girls' rooms instead. Mackenzie slept in a crib in our bedroom, so there wasn't much to see, but Cadence's room was filled with dolls and teddy bears, ribbons, and paintings that made her happy. The curtains were open, letting in the early morning sun, but the room felt darker than ever before.

I took the faded yellow blanket she'd been given to us in and went to lie on the bed. I was convinced James would come back from whatever he was doing in the kitchens, see our room empty, and find me in there, where he would take me in his arms and hold me until the pain wasn't tearing me apart anymore.

Instead, I woke up and it was dark out. I was still clutching the blanket, a massive headache from the dehydration and lack of nutrition. James never took longer than me to wake up. He was down to just over an hour, whereas I was slightly less than a day.

I had assumed he was the one who brought me home, but what if he hadn't woken up at all? What if something he did recently made it so he would never wake up again?

I wanted nothing more than to stay in that bed forever, holding on to my memories, but I rushed downstairs instead, finding Mr. and Mrs. Potts at the table in the kitchen, talking over tea with their son, Jeremy.

"Is James..." I started, but I couldn't get the words out. Thinking them made me feel sick, but saying them out loud would destroy me.

"Miss Delilah, can we get you something? We prepared a feast for when you woke up."

"Where is James?" I asked.

"He'll be back presently," Mr. Potts assured me.

"He thought you would return this evening," Mrs. Potts added. Everyone in the household knew what we were, but few of them had witnessed our 'returns'. James had died so many times that he usually woke up before we made it home, and I'd been lucky to always have him there, to not only take the blade for me, but to eliminate all threats before succumbing to his injuries, so I would be safe to either bring him home, or wait there for him to wake up.

"Where did he go?"

I was expecting her to tell me he was arranging the funerals, or perhaps reporting Mr. X to an old contact still on the New Order's council, but Mrs. Potts just looked guilty.

She was saved from having to answer when James walked in, looking defeated and heartbroken.

I took in a huge gulp of air as the tears overwhelmed me and I rushed into his arms. He was surprised to see me vertical, but his arms wrapped around me out of habit, pulling me close as if I was his lifeline.

"I wanted to be by your side when you woke up." He held me tight, breathing in my hair, as I ran my fingers through his golden locks.

"It's okay, you were with our girls," I said, but it brought on another batch of tears as his body tensed.

"I'm so sorry."

I was vaguely aware of the Potts family leaving us, but it was like nothing existed outside of James' arms around me. For days, we were in a haze of grief. We had lost children before, to old age or sickness, but never to another human, especially not because of what we were.

When we buried Cadence and Mackenzie, it was as if we had died as well. James vowed to hunt down Mr. X and his family to get revenge. I thought it was the pain talking, so I didn't pay all that much attention. I put all my energy into helping others; patrolling at night and spending my days at the hospital. James patrolled with me, but we no longer spent more time together than apart. He wasn't protecting the innocent anymore, he was hunting the wicked.

When I realized he stuck to his work and got his revenge, eliminating every X he could find, I left. I couldn't look at him knowing how much blood he had on his hands from killing not just Mr. X, but his innocent wife and children as well. Vengeance reaped vengeance, and blood wars never ended. It was always the children who paid the price.

I came home after a few months of nursing for the army, hoping James would show remorse over what he'd done, that he would be the man I loved once more, but he was gone.

"Is that so we don't hate him? So we can understand that you're clearly still in love with him?" Jackie asked when I was done. It felt like a weight had been lifted, to have all those secrets out, but as much as I wanted to talk about Cadence and Mackenzie, and even James, the time I lost them all was not something I enjoyed remembering.

"It's my truth. It's messy, and it's not black and white, but I knew James better than I know myself, and I understand the pain that drives him because I sometimes feel like I'm drowning in it myself."

"And when he came after us, that was the only time you've seen him since?" Tristan asked. There was disappointment in his eyes, but he also looked at me pleadingly, like if that was my only offence, he could forgive me.

"That night in the woods was the first time, yes. He sent kids here with other people because he knew what I was doing, but he never came himself, or called or wrote…there was nothing."

"But since he's been here…" Jackie pressed, her voice small. "You've been meeting with him, haven't you?"

"I have," I admitted. I never wanted to lie to them. "But I never gave him information or let my guard down so he could hurt us. I needed to know what he was here for, and he told me. He also promised that he wouldn't use our past against us, and he hasn't. If anything, it's the reason Krishna made it back in one piece."

"If you say he isn't evil, and that he understands how much it hurts to lose someone at the hands of these organizations, then why is he coming after me? Why would he help you save Krishna, but still try to kill me?" Alison struggled to understand.

"For a multitude of reasons. When he has a target, that's the only person he allows to get hurt. He hates collateral damage. Plus, Sakina was his family once upon a time…but he is still coming after you despite all this, because of your blood."

"He's after the stupid cure?" Tristan was upset.

"No. I assume he took the job because of you, not what you might cure…." I took a deep breath, knowing how terrible I felt when I first learned my family's history. It was why I'd kept the killer's name out of my story. "He wants you because you are the descendant of the man who took everything he cared about away from him. The man whose brother I couldn't save, who cornered us in that alley…his name was Richard Carmichael."

"It could just be a coincidence," Tristan argued after moments went by with no one speaking.

"It isn't though."

"That's why you were so insistent that I was like the

Bennetts," Alison realized. "Do you hate me as much as he does?"

"No," I assured her. I took a step forward, yearning to take her hands in mine and let her know she was nothing like that man, but she took a step back, so I stopped. "I made peace with your family a long time ago, when Richard's grandson married the granddaughter of a woman I raised. He taught me a lot about forgiveness, and how children should never be held accountable for the sins of the father. It's a never-ending cycle of self-fulfilling prophecies that help no one."

It was getting late, and I'd given them a lot to think about, so after a few more questions that made it clear I didn't have the answers anymore, everyone headed off to bed, with the promise that we would figure things out in the morning.

"WHAT ARE YOU GOING TO DO?" Jackie asked me when she was the only one left.

"I'll call Ingrid. Hopefully, she can help us get everyone out safely." I wasn't sure how much I trusted her illusions against James' hunting, but we didn't really have much of a choice.

"I meant about everyone here." She put her hand on my shoulder.

"They'll come around," I said with as much certainty as I could muster. "And if they don't, it's okay, because I deserve it."

I patted her on the shoulder and went up to my bedroom. I knew Alison's Gift was more of a curse these days, but what I wouldn't give to touch the harp in the barn and see what she saw. To hear Cadence's laugh, Mackenzie's incoherent babbling...even their crying would be welcome. I had centuries worth of items whose memories I would trade millions to revisit.

CHAPTER TWENTY-FIVE

ALISON

My first thought when I woke up and saw the sun coming in through the window was that I'd overslept and needed to get down to the barn as soon as possible. It took me less time to remember yesterday's horrible events than it took to jump out of bed. Not that Tristan made that possible by pulling me closer to him. My body was conditioned to resist, to get up and get on with the day, but I had absolutely nothing to get out of bed for. Unless it was to leave Rosehill and let their lives go back to normal, but I'd ruined that possibility, and felt certain that the mercenaries outside would get to me before I slipped away, and everyone inside would either be drawn out by the commotion and tempted to help, or would eventually suffer by being force-fed the cure.

I knew I wasn't entirely to blame. I wasn't the one who'd done the actual killing, but I might as well have. Sakina and Mohinder would still be alive if it weren't for me. If I hadn't let myself get safe and comfortable at Rosehill instead of going off on my own like I knew I should have. Delia wouldn't be fighting her soulmate, Penny wouldn't be having nightmares, Krishna would still have her parents...That was another reason I wasn't eager to leave the bedroom. Sakina had implied Krishna's Gift was strong, so she might feel my guilt and hear all my thoughts, but there was the possibility that if I stayed far enough away, I wouldn't add to her burden.

The whole time Delia was being reproached and telling her story last night, a part of me was grateful, because as she shared her pain and heartbreak, everyone had something else to concentrate on rather than the fact that whether Delia should have warned us or not, none of it would have mattered if they weren't harboring me. I was relieved that they were focusing on someone else, until even Delia's story highlighted the fact that not only me, but my entire bloodline was made up of harbingers of death. I was up to eight now, with Dr. Richards, the five police officers, Sakina, and Mohinder, while my ancestor murdered innocent children and seemed to relish in their turmoil. And that was only the ultimate deaths of people who wouldn't be coming back. Tristan, Ben, and Caleb had all given lives to protect me – and the other Rosehill inhabitants – from the people who were after me.

"What I wouldn't give to know what's going on in your mind right now." Tristan had propped himself up on one arm and leaned down to kiss my temple. I looked up and saw he was troubled, which I knew was also because of me.

"I don't want to be ungrateful, or make their deaths be for nothing…"

"But you want to leave again."

"I just don't want to be responsible for all the bad things anymore."

"Allie, you know that none of this is your fault, right? No one blames you or wishes you were gone."

"But those mercenaries came here because they're after me. If I had gone somewhere else, no one would have bothered you."

"I would have been with you," he said in a way that left no room for discussion. "And if you think the blame falls on the person responsible for you being here, then that would be me or Delia. Everyone heard you trying to leave to protect us, but we all thought it was better to keep you here and protect you."

"Sakina and Mohinder weren't a part of that vote," I argued.

"She agreed to train you. And she refused to move into the manor. Not that I'm in any way blaming her, but we all made choices based on who we are and what we knew. I knew I loved you and would follow you wherever you went, but I didn't trust myself to protect you on my own, so I was selfishly glad we ended up here. Delia and Sakina would both rather die than believe that James guy would hurt them, which maybe they're right, but maybe we all have people we're willing to risk everything for. The people inside Rosehill are safe, and everyone who went out there and risked their lives to bring us here or to get Penny and Krishna back…none of that was on you."

I nodded with a sad smile because there was nothing he could say for me to accept that. Logically, I knew it wasn't my fault. But it was still all because of me.

TRISTAN GOT up and got ready, but I stayed in bed a little longer. I drafted my daily texts to Malcolm and Grace, who was back at work as if she hadn't recently been on life support, then texted with Sybill about potential outfits for her date with Damian. She'd tried to FaceTime, but I didn't feel up to pretending, or to telling her what was going on. She was under the impression that Rosehill was a fortress that kept everyone safe, and I didn't want to ruin that for her.

When I managed to drag myself out of bed, I quickly put on a pair of shorts and a t-shirt, then made my way back to the student dorms. I went past the trophy room and what appeared to be a teacher's lounge, then a study room, before I found the school library. It had thousands of books, many of them first editions worth more than my parents' house. I wasn't looking for a specific book, just information. Terrence hadn't been able to get much from interrogating Professor Mallory's crew, since they'd been in FBI custody ever since their original plan failed. My best bet was to figure out everything I could about myself, my ancestors, and the people we were up against, so *Knights: Old and New Orders* felt like it might provide some answers.

Out of curiosity, I scanned the index for mentions of a supernatural Eclipse or Henry VIII, and found a passage that supported Delia's story.

"I was so excited when I saw we had rescued the Prince of Wales, thinking of all the riches we would be given for the King's gratitude, but Milos and Edward turned their swords onto the princess. I was shocked, but thankfully Van Bergen's son was there to talk some sense into them. Or so I had hoped. They sliced at him with all their might, nothing like we do in practice, and I watched in horror as they forced him to take his weapon out as well. It was brother-upon-brother, and I couldn't stand it. I ran."

I FOUND another book called *The Night's Handbook* and flipped through the pages, more trying to find out how my ancestor justified being a part of the New Order than anything else, but the name Carmichael caught my eye. Apparently, Roxton Carmichael was president for a decade, after which his brother, Richard, took over for a few months, before his untimely murder at the hands of a deranged Gifted. As the elder son, he should have inherited the position from his father, but he was overly cruel and unstable, until his brother's death at the hands of a Gifted woman rallied the support he needed to write new laws and amend the old ones to be even harsher and more absolute. By the time his son, Aldrich Carmichael, ended his terms as president, the entire handbook had been rewritten. Whereas before, deadly force could be used upon suspicion of Giftedness – assuming reasonable doubt – after the Carmichaels were done with them, you could murder someone simply for associating with suspected Gifted. No proof necessary.

"How did you guys get something like this? It looks like it would be required reading for members and barred from everyone else," I asked Chris when he came in, completely forgetting my manners.

"Ah, the creed and manifesto." He sighed before coming over to take a seat. "Tristan was looking for you."

"You've read these books, haven't you?" His reluctance to tell me just made me more intrigued.

"The history books were my favorite," he agreed. "Especially if I knew some of the players."

"These rules are barbaric."

"I've heard they rebranded the textbook to focus more on how evil and dangerous the Gifted are, less on all the cruel and disgusting ways you can make them suffer."

"Because people are still joining?" I was horrified.

"It's like enlisting in the army, only they're always on the wrong side. They probably pay for your studies and healthcare, which would be enough to tempt anyone with loose or non-existent morals."

"And the person who brought this book to Rosehill?"

"Before becoming Gifted, my father was—" He put his hand out to stop me from jumping to conclusions. "Raised to follow in his father's footsteps. I was young when he died in his Last Life, but when I asked about the first time, he told me it was in a training accident. From offhand comments I've heard here, I'm assuming he wasn't cutting it, so they left him in a ditch wearing his training uniform, with the manifesto in his breast pocket. Hence the mud and bloodstains."

"I'm sorry." I didn't know if it was for his father's death, for what they did to him, or for having that as part of his legacy, but I felt it needed to be said.

"Most families have rotten apples in them. Luckily, you can throw away the rotten ones to save the tree, or you can pick the good ones before the rot spreads and plant a new tree. I like to think we're just the latter."

I had a million arguments as to how it wasn't that simple, and I wasn't just a good apple on a bad tree, I was literally killing everything around me, but he looked at me with such kindness and concern, like even though I'd only just met him, we were family. All my arguments disappeared, and no matter how wrong I knew he was, I just wanted to believe him.

"If your parents were both Gifted…"

"Eight-year-old me was pretty crushed when I was the only one of my friends who didn't get a superpower, but grown-up Chris is glad he dodged that bullet." He looked at me with sympathy. "How about we go find that boyfriend of yours and whip up something yummy?"

"I'm not sure even your cooking can fix this," I argued.

"Nonsense, comfort food makes everything better," he assured me, taking my hand in his and bringing me back to the rest of the Rosehill population, where not a single one of them treated me any differently.

CHAPTER TWENTY-SIX

DELIA

"Hey Ing, just leaving you another message. I know you're probably busy at the shop, but I could really use one of your illusions. You mentioned it works on all the senses, right? Either way, I would love to hear from you. It's been too long."

I hung up and brought my hand to my forehead, trying to rub out the tension. There were now six strangers crowding the house, with dozens waiting at every single opening in the wall.

"Where are you going?" Ben asked, following me down the stairs to the basement. There was no accusation in his tone, but I knew he no longer trusted me. He assumed I was going to meet up with James, which I wouldn't do with him.

"I'm trying to find an exit. A way out I haven't thought of that gets everyone out safely."

"And how is that going?" His look softened and his hand did that flex thing he did when he wanted to take my hand but stopped himself because he knew better.

"James and I built Rosehill together. The only advantage we have is the magical barrier, which is why our best bet is to just keep everyone inside until the mercenaries get bored and wander off." I sighed, knowing that would not happen, but I didn't have a better idea, and I'd been looking at the problem from every angle, non-stop.

"That's not really an option," Ben argued.

"It's the only place that's safe. Under this roof. That's it."

"And what about the next time they lure someone outside? If they know you at all, or bother to do any research, they'll know that the best way to get to you is to threaten your children. Not all of them are under this roof," he pointed out, an obvious reference to James, who knew that better than anyone. Even if we didn't have a history, James would never use innocent children as bait, but I couldn't say the same for every other person out there, lying in wait.

"The magic should hold, even if I'm outside." There was no confidence behind my words. I knew the barriers got weaker the farther I got from Rosehill, and God only knew what would happen if I died. Would it sever the magical protections, or was Rosehill bigger than one person? Would my administrative control pass on to someone else?

"We don't know that." Clearly, he wasn't in the mood to comfort me tonight. "What about Tristan and Alison? I don't know for sure if he would give up his girlfriend to save his sister, but Alison would, without a doubt, trade herself for hers. She didn't even want to stay here if it meant putting *us* in danger, which tells me she would walk right through that barrier if they so much as suggested they were going to go after her family."

"Her family is safe. We have people watching them around the clock, and Tristan wouldn't let her walk out." I used the arguments I could, because I knew he was right. Even the threat of trying to figure out where her family was would be enough to lure Alison away.

"Delia!" I was expecting his pain, but his anger shocked me. "Does he have such a hold on you that you can't even admit it? None of this is like you."

"You don't know me, Ben. You're blinded by your affections, and you put me on this pedestal, but I don't deserve it. I make mistakes and I misjudge people, but he wasn't one of them. I know that man. He would not break a promise to me, ever, and he cannot get in." I saw he was about to contradict me on that, so I kept going. "I chose to let Alison stay here with us, even after you warned me not to. I should have gone away with her and left Etta in charge here. Or Sakina. I should have forced them to come stay inside the manor, because I should have known James wouldn't be the only one they sent, and besides, he was there with a team of people I didn't know, people who hurt you without cause."

I could see him struggling not to comfort me as I fought the urge to cry. Part of me craved his reassurance, because he wasn't prone to lying, but I also knew that if he allowed himself to take me in his arms and tell me it wasn't my fault, I would fall apart, and I wasn't sure I could put myself back together.

"What's the plan then?" he asked instead.

"I reached out to Ingrid. She can alter the reality you see, hear, taste, smell, and feel, so as long as she blocks out any trace of Alison, we can all leave the manor safely until the mercenaries are gone. I'll bring Alison to a safe house somewhere with an army of Guardians ready to protect her, while you could take the children to another one, or possibly the plantation, because I trust you more than myself with them, and I wouldn't survive losing anyone else."

"For how long?"

"Until it's safe." I could hear the desperation in my voice as I said the word, putting so much weight on that ideal, that was proven wrong time and time again. "Maybe Alison can convince her entire bloodline to come with us. And someone can take up her training, so whoever travels with her won't be so vulnerable. Maybe the mercenaries will leave Rosehill and give up on it as soon as they see she's gone. My long-term plans aren't where they should be, but my priority is just to get everyone to somewhere no one is trying to kill them."

"Okay." He nodded.

"That's it?"

"I would follow you to the end of the world, Delia, not because I don't know you or I'm enamored with this perfect version of you I have in my head. You make mistakes and your plans are far from foolproof, but you do whatever it takes to keep the ones you love safe, and there is no one in this world I trust more than you, regardless of personal feelings."

Ben left once he was done, and as soon as I was alone in the basement, I let all the tears I'd been fighting pour out.

CHAPTER TWENTY-SEVEN

DELIA

Out of everyone at Rosehill, it was determined that I was best suited to take over Alison's training. I was the most experienced and had taught more lost children how to control their Gifts, but I'd handed the reins to Sakina as soon as she'd moved onto the grounds, because she was the one who taught me, and it was taxing to find creative ways to tell someone what to do without telling them what to do.

Alison was waiting in the training room when I arrived, looking subdued and nervous, the bags under her eyes mirroring Tristan's.

"How far did you get with Sakina?" I asked her with my best impression of business as usual, ruining it when I winced at the sound of my mentor's name, and the memories it brought up. Images of her laughing or rolling her eyes at me, but also how she looked at the end, the crime scene burned into my memory for eternity.

"I'm good with things, but we never got to people. She had me try not to take it from Tristan at night, but that was it."

"Did it ever work?" I turned to look at her, perhaps a little too eager.

"Not really," she admitted sheepishly. "But we did figure out it takes skin-to-skin contact for it to work."

"That's very helpful," I insisted. "Does it work every time with things?"

"Everything we ever tried in the barn," she agreed.

"What about something like this?" I took out my red velvet box and showed her the necklace she'd recognized from the painting; the one that called out to her before she even knew she had a Gift.

"I thought they kept it in a museum?" Her eyes went wide at the sight of it. I'd wondered if working in a museum dulled your awe the way living in a castle surrounded by them did, but apparently it hadn't, at least not for this.

"I lend it out sometimes with other relics from my past, especially to help an old friend, but mostly I like having it close," I argued, shutting the case. "I don't have your Gift, but I can feel the heartache mirroring my own whenever I get close to it." After I died, Henry had gifted it to Margaret so she could wear it to honor me, and as a calling card when she needed a friendly face, but once my siblings were all gone, it was returned to me, so I could wear it and mourn the generations of family I had loved and lost. I wore it sparingly, only for big occasions, but I often reached for it to feel close to them. Each time, it broke my heart and brought tears to my eyes. If I had Alison's Gift, I wouldn't want to go anywhere near it. "Did it call out to you just now?"

She nodded and looked at the box with apprehension. "Does that mean I would see something if I touched it, no matter how hard I tried not to?"

"It might. Or you might be stronger than that." I tried to convey how much faith I had in her, that she had mastered her Gift and would see absolutely nothing, but I also wanted to let her know it was more than okay if she couldn't silence the centuries of grief numerous members of my family had poured into the necklace.

Alison walked over with determination. It was what you needed in order to do something you knew was going to be painful, but you still had to try.

Even touching the case made her grit her teeth, as I'm sure I never once touched it without knowing exactly what was inside, feeling the same emotions. I wore the necklace every time James and I renewed our vows, reaching for it during the ceremony whenever I missed them…but in the mornings when I was getting ready, even if Cadence was the one who put the necklace on me and I smiled while she put flowers in my hair, getting the box from the back of my closet was always going to be painful; a constant reminder of the people I'd lost.

"You're doing excellent, Alison," I encouraged.

"It doesn't feel like it."

"Have you seen anything yet?"

"No, but I haven't even gotten to the necklace," she argued, her brow furrowed with intense concentration.

"The box is just as old and holds as many memories, so even that is an accomplishment. I believe you can do this."

She opened the case and closed her eyes before putting her hand down so her palm covered the ruby, and each finger grazed a pearl. Her lips pursed and her shoulders tensed for minutes that felt like hours, until she shook it all out and looked at me with shock.

"What did you see?" I took the case back from her as my mind went over every shocking memory she might have experienced.

"Nothing." She was surprised. "I'm still aching to see all the memories something like that holds, so many more than the one I saw the last time I touched it, but I thought of how much I didn't want to feel that pain again, or to keep killing my sister."

"What about if you didn't prepare yourself and try so hard?" I asked. "Like if I threw this at you, what would happen?"

All I had on me that was old, other than the case, was my signet ring, which I never removed, because it was part of a multiple step process I could use in order to communicate directly with the current royal families of Europe, to verify my identity. I let out a sigh of relief when she caught it, but her eyes went as blank as Jackie's before she looked at me with wide eyes and surprise.

"Was that Queen Victoria?" she asked me. "Like the original?"

"It wasn't Emily Blunt," I agreed. "Although that casting was excellent. I'm a sucker for those retellings. And books about them. It either reminds me of what they were like in a good, nostalgic way, or I spend days telling everyone who will listen how badly they got it all wrong. And yes, that's as annoying as it sounds." I gave her a moment to digest this new development. "But that means you aren't in control of it yet. You're repressing it. Which is incredible progress, but takes a toll on you."

"I don't care what it does to me. If I don't start working on people now, I don't know if I'll ever get the chance. Even if I have to repress it every time Tristan touches me, that's better than leaving him exposed."

She was upset, but also very smart, appealing to my motherly instincts. It worried me that accidentally touching any one of us during a fight would leave us defenseless, but it was better than losing Tristan entirely.

"You can start with me." I extended my hand for her to touch.

"Just try it out? Aren't you going to give me some pointers or something?"

"It should be the same concept as with the necklace. Either you're right and it works, or I'll have a few hours to boss people around and be able to teach you without spending most of it on my wording."

Alison didn't even graze the tip of my finger with how fast she zipped past it, so I cocked my head and used my eyes to tell her to try again.

She put her hand on top of mine, so our palms were touching, and kept it there for an entire second, during which she looked like I was pressing her hand onto the element of a stove. I did feel a heat, but it barely lasted an instant, and wasn't the least bit painful.

"Try to tell me to do something," she said as she moved her hand away.

"I wouldn't risk it. Not with a First Lifer," I argued, leaving the training room to walk down the hall.

"Do you want me to get Ben, or an animal, or…"

I got to the French doors that led to a balcony overlooking the courtyard and opened them so I could look over to the sleeping gargoyles on the roof.

"Lorcan, come to me," I called, looking straight at him and willing with every fiber of my being for him to obey.

"They have names?" Alison asked me cautiously, like she was worried about how I would react to this failure.

"Names, personalities, skills, and abilities…when you breathe life into something, it takes on a life of its own," I answered her question, but kept my eyes on Lorcan, who looked like any other inanimate statue on the estate. "I must admit, this breaks my heart a bit. I knew they listened to me because of my Gift, but I came to think that somewhere deep down, they just cared about me and wanted to help."

"Did they ever listen to anyone else?"

"When they were in their active phase, they'd listen to James." I could hear the guilt and pain in my voice, but hoped she couldn't, as Persephone flew to the ledge, sending angry looks to Lorcan for disobeying a direct order. "It was just a test.

You can return to your post," I assured her before turning to Alison. "How long does this usually last?"

"I don't know. Tristan says sometimes it's back by lunchtime, but other days it's after supper and he still can't make a spark."

"That's very interesting. If you were just another student here, we would make a fun science experiment out of it. If you wanted to, of course."

"That's kind of what the Damned want to do with me, isn't it?"

"Oh, God no. I meant I would let you touch me every morning and let the students keep track of how long it took me to get my Gift back. It would probably be safer for them than the explosions the boys were doing with Ben your first day here." I got a half-hearted smile in return. "You would never be treated like a test subject. Jackie wanted to know how far a person could be for her to use their eyes, so we tracked it whenever someone was travelling. The stronger the connection, the further the person could be, but I could go anywhere on the planet, and she could still find me. There were no tests or lab experiments, just doing what she normally does, because she wanted to know."

"Are you nervous?" Alison saw through my sharing.

"I haven't spoken freely since Noomi. She was a shield, like Mateo, in the sense that she was completely unaffected by Gifts, but dropping my guard with her made it easier to slip once the guard needed to be back up." I'd never even tried my Gift on Mateo, just in case.

"We can hold hands every time you speak," she teased.

"One day, I hope Penny can come behind you and put her hands on your eyes in one of those Guess Who games and get absolutely no reaction from your Gift. But to start, you need to be able to purposely touch someone without taking their Gift. I wouldn't recommend trying it out on other people, but like Sakina said, every time you touch Tristan, try not to activate it."

"And what do I do in the meantime?"

"You work on my soul."

Alison looked at me like I'd just told the least funny joke she'd ever heard; in the realm of murdering puppies.

"That's what you say you suck out of humans, right? You've removed my Giftedness, so the best we can do now is have you keep touching me while trying – and not trying – to suck that out."

"No." She shook her head, making connections I didn't want her to make, but she had to. "You're implying that Tristan is giving up more than just his Gift every time he touches me, and…"

She expected me to reassure her and say this was just to see if she could do it, but we didn't have the time to lie to each other.

"He hasn't said anything, and I think he's under the impression it's the stress and the worry that are getting to him, or maybe a bug that's going around, but Gifted don't get sick. We don't get colds or fevers, no cancer, or unexplained illnesses…if we're under the weather, it's an emotional thing, an infected wound, or it's supernatural."

"Tristan doesn't know that."

"A lot of Gifted don't. Colds, sore throats, headaches… they're things you're very aware of when they're happening, but it takes a long time to realize it when they're not. I used to get migraines in my First Life, so for decades I avoided harsh sunlight and overly loud noises, or massaged my temples when I got stressed, to keep them at bay."

"You've been letting me hurt him?" She was stuck on that point, not that I blamed her. I would never have mentioned it if it wasn't something I believed she could eventually stop doing.

"I didn't know for sure until his runny nose this morning. But now you can practice on me. I don't think you're sucking out anyone's soul, but I do think that, unintentionally, you weaken their immune system. Unconsciously you do it slowly, bit by bit, but I am told that when you mean to do it, you can knock out someone twice your size?"

"I feel like you're dismissing the fact that I've been slowly killing Tristan since the day I met him."

"I'm not dismissing it, Alison. Loving someone means taking the chance that they'll hurt you, and deciding it's worth the risk. Tristan knows you take away his Gift every time you touch him, and he's okay with that, because he would rather be powerless than without you. Etta can take care of us, but sharing my suspicions before now would only have made you feel bad for something you couldn't control. Now you can, so I want you to touch me like you do the objects, or those people at the Damned's satellite base."

She still didn't like it, or me at the moment, but she squared her jaw and closed her eyes before touching my hand again. At first, I felt nothing, but then it felt like...not like she was sucking the energy out of me – that was too literal – more like it was leaking away. There was no pain or discomfort, just a little warmth from her hand, and that woozy feeling you get after losing too much blood.

"I should have brought a chair," I said before moving away from the ledge. Alison took her hand away and jumped back, her arms and brain wrestling with whether she should come to my aid or stay away to do less damage. I wanted to pat her arm to let her know I was okay, but I sat down on the stone steps first, much less graceful than I had intended.

"ARE YOU OKAY? WHERE IS ETTA?" Alison crouched down to my level and kept coming close, then stopping just before touching me.

"That was you trying, right?" I verified.

"Like when I'm looking for a memory in an object that doesn't want to give me any," she agreed.

"That's really powerful," I told her, taking a deep breath to keep myself awake. "Don't be afraid to use it if you're in danger."

"You look like you're about to pass out."

"I'll be fine. I asked Etta to come find us once she was done with Tristan. She's telling him it's just about the cold, but I think you should tell him the truth. Or I can, but I'm leaving the decision up to you."

She cocked her head to look at me, like it was a test, which it kind of was, but even if she failed, I meant what I said.

"Did I go too far?"

"I've had worse." I gave her a weak smile. "I assume it will go away the longer I'm away from you, judging by your sister's recovery. When we're ready to call it a day, I won't let Etta fix it, so we can find out more about the duration, but my best comparison is that it's like bleeding out. I feel very weak, and cold, and like there should be so much blood on my hands, the literal kind, but there isn't."

"I'm so sorry."

"Don't be," I said, not skirting around it with the 'You shouldn't be,' I would have normally used if I still had my Gift. "When she was training me, Sakina had me tell so many people what to do, before I truly understood what I was doing."

"You were young, right?"

"Old enough to know better." I closed my eyes and rested my head on my hand. I knew I wasn't really losing blood, but it felt like if I let myself sleep, even for a moment, I wouldn't wake until the morning, another life older.

"What happened?" she asked.

"I shudder at the idea of what I might have become if I didn't have the Gift," I admitted something I often wondered about. "From the moment I could speak, my words held the power to make people do whatever I wanted. Every desire, every whim I had, I asked someone, and they made it happen, without fail," I shared.

"Because you were a princess." That part didn't seem real to her, but the ordering people around made sense.

"To be honest, no one realized the change when it happened. I was very sick, everyone thought I was going to die, they gave me my last rites, and then…I had a miraculous recovery. I think one of my mother's ladies-in-waiting was a healer who was afraid to tell us, but couldn't bear to see me die when it was happening. I went back to my life as if nothing happened." I paused, remembering that period of my life, though it was beyond fuzzy. It was like I could remember it, but had no actual recollection. "My parents were a little more protective and cautious with me, but other than that, things stayed the same. I got what I asked for, as did all my siblings, and we carried on. Until my mother died." I couldn't remember the specifics from those days, or the funeral, but even just mentioning it burrowed a hole in my chest that I had to reach up and try to put back together.

"I'm sorry," Alison said awkwardly.

"It was literally centuries ago," I assured her. "My father brought my sister to Scotland, so she could get married as planned, and while he was gone, I decided it didn't make sense that we could command people to do everything we pleased, but no one could save our mother, or bring her back, so I started demanding it of people. That they bring her to me, bring her back to life, sort of an 'I want my mommy' tantrum, only my position, my Gift, and the fact that she had died, gave it epic proportions."

"What happened to all the people who couldn't do it?" she asked, like she didn't really want to know.

"They tried." I sighed, remembering their many failed attempts, and the consequences for them and to my mother. "It went on for weeks until my father came home and had a heart to heart with me about death and how my mother was never coming back, no matter how badly we wanted her to. I stopped making insane demands and made requests of people more nicely, treating them like actual human beings. Other than the guilt, I put the entire thing behind me until Sakina showed up to teach me to control it. My father had experience with Gifted and was told of the lengths people had gone to in order to please me. He didn't want to make me feel bad about it, but he knew I needed help and couldn't risk a repeat once I was older and held more influence than simply the household staff."

"How long did it take you to control it?" Alison bit her bottom lip before adding, "Because it seems like you haven't really mastered your Gift, you just use the threat of it. Unless you were Gifted with the ability to control stone gargoyles, but I thought your Gift was to control all of us."

"That is roughly the ability I possess," I agreed. "And you're right, it took me longer than it should have, because I concentrated on changing my words instead of controlling my Gift. I'd seen the turmoil and the fear in the eyes of people I'd commanded, whether big or small, whether they would have done the task regardless. It was like I had violated their souls, down to the core, and I hated myself for it. I was afraid of my Gift, so I tried to bury it away instead of understanding it. But once I knew how to wield it, I was able to not wield it."

"I thought that if you say the words, people have to do it no matter what."

"It's about will. If I want someone to do something, even if I don't want them to be forced to, or even if I rephrase the sentence to make it sound like a choice, if I want it done, it will be."

"But you never do."

"Because the last few times I've used it on First Lifers, they've overreacted, hurting themselves and others," I admitted.

"What happened up here?" Etta asked, coming up the

balcony steps from the courtyard. I could have kissed her with how relieved I was to get out of that conversation.

"We were just admiring the view, having a pleasant picnic. We're all out of chocolate strawberries and champagne, I'm afraid."

"I have terrible timing." Etta played along, taking a seat beside me and placing my hands in hers.

The heat was like Alison's, only it went from her hands into mine, and through my entire body before leaving when she took her hand away. Her Gift took more or less time, depending on the severity of the injuries, and this time was more than long enough for Alison to look on with fear, worried it wouldn't work.

"Does it hurt you too?" she asked Etta.

"I feel it, but it's usually a dull pain that I mostly feel disappearing. With your friend Grace, I found the wound in her stomach and fixed it, knowing the rest would fall into place once that was taken care of. The same with Tristan. This time... I don't know, there wasn't a wound, it was somehow deeper."

"Soul magic is the most powerful." I squeezed Etta's hand to thank her, then stood up.

"Is Ingrid coming?" Etta asked of a woman who knew a thing or two about soul magic.

"I haven't reached her yet, but I called Lucy, and she says Ingrid was spending the year as a nineteen-year-old in Italy, so she doesn't expect her to be very reliable."

"Do you have a backup plan?"

"Working on it," I assured her.

Alison made the executive decision to go back to objects for the rest of the day, and while I resented the fact that she didn't think I could handle her Gift, I was also grateful I wouldn't have to feel myself slipping away like that until morning.

I specifically chose objects people clung to in their happiest or saddest moments, and watched Alison either struggle to see nothing, curse herself when she failed, or look at me with a cocky, 'is that all you've got?'

By the time we called it a day, anything she touched was innocuous, but if we touched her with something she wasn't expecting, she saw the memories until she pushed them out.

I PUT the necklace back in my room before going down to dinner, but Ben was waiting for me on the staircase.

"You let her touch you?" he asked in an angry whisper, though I didn't know who he didn't want to overhear.

"How else is she going to learn?"

"With objects. With someone else."

"I don't use my Gift anyway, and we don't know the long-term effects. I can't stop her from touching Tristan, but I can do my best to make sure no one else is hurt until we know more about it."

"I could grab someone from outside. Removing their Gifts would actually help us rather than leave us exposed, and I don't care what the long-term side effects are on them," he pointed out.

"We're not those people," I reminded him. "We do not experiment on people against their will, and we don't dehumanize them. Many of the people out there are Alisons who never had someone there to help them control their Gifts, or use them for good. I know a lot of Gifted and First Lifers who would have joined the Damned if it weren't for the families and support we've built."

"So your plan is to just adopt all the mercenaries who murdered Mohinder and Sakina so they can deliver Alison to her death?" he put it bluntly, but he was also right. I had been accused of being over-idealistic for as long as I could remember, misjudging how much people were willing to change for the people they cared about.

"I'm not welcoming them with open arms, but I won't become the people we're protecting Alison from either. I accept any harm that may come to me, but I won't inflict it upon others."

"And what happens if we're attacked? If someone makes it through the last barriers and we're left without gargoyles and without your Gift, that you don't use unless you have to, but sometimes you *have to*. And did you even see if removing your Gift removed the magical barriers? They are tied to you, aren't they?"

I wanted to keep defending myself. I had, after all, been trained over centuries by the best Knights and Guardians known to man...but that didn't matter against an army when I also had to protect innocent children. I hadn't intended to, but I'd inadvertently put everyone in Rosehill at risk.

"I'm sorry."

Ben had opened his mouth to argue some more, but then he shut it and looked at me with shock.

"I was only thinking of Alison, and of helping her. The greater consequences of my actions didn't occur to me, and I am sorry."

"Just don't do it again," he said with a shake of his head once the shock wore off, leaving me with my guilt.

CHAPTER TWENTY-EIGHT

DELIA

When Krishna didn't come down for dinner, I went up and found her still in Penny's bed, buried under the covers, with her palms pressed against her ears.

"How's it going, love?" I asked, taking her into my arms.

"It doesn't stop," she told me. "All the voices are screaming at me, but their pain…even when they're sleeping, it doesn't stop."

"Do you want to try to eat something? Or maybe I can make you some warm milk with cinnamon?" It broke my heart that there was nothing I could do to take her pain away, but there might be something I could do as far as her experiencing ours.

"Ice cream would be better," she said, following me to the kitchen for two scoops of strawberry ice cream. It wasn't even seven o'clock yet, but the skies outside were pitch black, possibly a new attempt at sensory deprivation from one of the Gifted outside. It didn't matter so much tonight, but I might plan activities in windowless rooms, or let Penny conjure up a little sunshine in the morning.

"People get brain freezes when they eat that fast," I warned, barely touching my scoop of vanilla while she took seconds.

"That's what helps," Krishna explained. "If I have a brain freeze, I can't hear as well."

"I might have a better idea for that. If it works, we can get you set up there permanently."

"Okay," she said, sounding so small and vulnerable I wanted to take her in my arms and shield her, but she took her bowl with her and kept swallowing ice cream by the spoonful.

The hallways reminded me of the ones I grew up in, and they were intimately familiar to me after centuries within them, but there was something about exploring places as a child that made you feel like you owned them, more than my years as an adult could possibly bring. There was a creepiness to the place in the dark, as with any large dwelling that doesn't have enough going on, but Krishna didn't seem the least bit afraid. She was preoccupied with her food, and when she finished, I took the bowl from her so she could cover her ears again. If I remembered correctly, Sakina told me the voices came from her brain, around her right temporal lobe, which meant the only relief blocking her ears could provide was psychological.

"This is where the classrooms are, isn't it? Are you going to teach me how to turn it off?" Her optimism crushed me, because I knew nothing more than what her mother had taught me, the same things she'd taught her, so I had no quick fix to turn it off. Plus, I knew how badly she'd wanted to come to school here, before she lost everything and was forced to.

"Hopefully, over time, the teachers and I will continue the work your parents started, but for now, we could turn this into a bedroom…if it works for you. We can have Lucy come over and put these spells on an upstairs bedroom as well, once everything is sorted."

I smiled encouragingly, praying this would work. We walked into the classroom, and I sealed the doors using both the regular lock and the one that activated the enchanted seal.

"You'll obviously be able to hear me while I'm inside with

you, but can you hear anyone else?" I asked, taking a seat beside her on the floor. There were chairs lined up against the padded blue walls, but she chose the pile of black mats in the corner, and I was in no position to argue with anything this kid might ask me.

"Your feelings are really loud," she warned.

"I'm trying very hard not to be."

"I think that makes it louder. Like you're wearing a neon sign that says, 'Don't Look Here!'"

"I'll work on that," I promised her.

"His were really loud as well." She played with the cotton from her pajama bottoms, staring at the ground in front of her.

"Who?" I asked, trying to catch her eye.

"The man who was there when they died. Who found me with the jars."

"James?" My breath caught before I processed what she said. "What do you mean by he was with them?"

"Appa screamed and then he was gone, but Amma was still there, and I wanted to go to her, but the man came, and his heart felt like mine, so I knew he wouldn't hurt her. He held her hand, but then she was gone, and he was so loud."

"I'm so sorry," I said instead of all the questions I had. It was one thing to want to pester Sakina and Mohinder, but another to make Krishna relive it.

"He loves you," she told me. "He's in a lot of pain, and it makes him angry, but most of his thoughts were about you."

"I'm guessing I don't help with the pain and anger." I don't know if I was fishing or apologizing.

"He's the one from the harp, isn't he? And the one you're in love with and thinking of whenever your heart hurts?"

"Were you listening in on Alison's lessons?" I asked, knowing she couldn't get memories from objects.

"Only sometimes. But she didn't figure it out, so I thought I would never know, until...until I met him."

"He is the one from the harp," I agreed. "And I'm sure my heart doesn't always hurt when I think of him."

"I'll have to pay more attention."

"No, love, you shouldn't have to feel any pain or sadness. It's much too big a burden." I kissed the top of her head. "Is this any better than Penny's room?" I brought us back on topic.

"Much better." She smiled and relief flooded through me. "But I don't really feel like sleeping all the way over here when everyone else is together upstairs."

"That's a fair point. I can stay here with you until we figure that out."

"What will happen to the classes?"

"There are more classrooms," I reminded her. "And maybe this will finally convince them to take a break for the summer."

"Why would you want to stop doing the things that are fun?" she asked like I was crazy. Perhaps it was because I'd already hurt people with my Gift by the time I started lessons to control it, but I never found them fun. They were always a necessary evil I had to face so that I wouldn't hurt more people. I loved the fact that the joy hadn't been sucked away from it for Krishna yet.

I LEFT Krishna in the quiet of the classroom, especially without my loud emotions, and went to find sleeping bags. I would have to set up something more permanent for her, but I didn't want tonight to feel like she was caged in a classroom, so I thought I could make it more like a slumber party, and less scary. Penny found out what I was doing and insisted on coming with me, then before long, nearly everyone came down and we each slept either alone or in small groups within the different classrooms, with the clear glass in between us. Brandon and Charlie provided more than enough entertainment, although the best parts were their unintentional mishaps. Even Lena, who'd come under the guise of making sure everyone hadn't been kidnapped but had yet to leave, cracked a few smiles. I wouldn't have called anyone particularly happy, but they were trying to be, and helping each other to become so, which was really all I could wish for.

CHAPTER TWENTY-NINE

ALISON

Delia brought me to an empty training room while everyone else helped move Krishna into her new bedroom. I'd tried to be a part of it and to help without touching anyone, but I could tell that I was in the way more than anything. Delia must have noticed as well, because she was the one who asked if I wanted to work on my Gift.

She looked as optimistic and healthy as ever, but her words from the other day hadn't left me. I was keeping my distance from Tristan a lot longer than I was before, and built a fortress of sheets to keep between us at night. It worked until my brain shut off and all I wanted to do was cuddle into him. As soon as I woke up, I made him off limits to myself, which was easier when he woke up first and went to make us breakfast, but a lot harder when he was still in bed, and I had to not only untangle myself from him but also turn him down when he suggested we stay under the covers a little longer. I'd told him I was the one making him sick, wracked with guilt, but he'd looked at me like he hadn't known for sure, but he'd had his suspicions, and didn't think that changed anything. While I begged to differ, it was hard to argue with someone who knew all the facts but didn't care, especially when his arms were the only thing that made me feel safe. Penny had suggested I find myself a cool pair of leather gloves to never take off, and although I originally laughed at her silly idea, I kept coming back to it. If my lessons kept going the way they were, a full body suit would be my best option. At least Delia didn't currently look any worse for the wear, and Tristan had been better since Etta worked her magic on him, pretty much back to his old self.

Delia took a seat, and I sat across from her without thinking, then almost jumped up when faced with a memory I had to push away.

"What was that?" I asked.

"I'm sorry, but I have to ambush you with powerful objects until you can resist even the most tempting of stories with absolutely no warning."

The chair had a throw blanket on top of it, which I had thought was for comfort, but was clearly a trick. It looked hand-knit and old, but more from my grandmother's childhood than Delia's.

"As far as I know, it should only have happy memories, but you blocked them out, didn't you?"

"Just like when the artefact kept me out," I agreed. "The Magnum Finis. I've been looking through the books in your library, but even if they mention it in the index, none of them have pictures, except one, but it's a terrible drawing that could be of anything."

"It's easier to protect something if no one knows what it looks like."

"And the ones who do don't share?"

"Precisely." She smiled. "But coming back to that blanket, unless you were expecting me to ambush you, that means your mind is putting up its own defenses now, and switching from showing you everything it can, to letting you decide." She looked so proud of me that I hoped she was right.

"I'm not getting any better with Tristan," I argued.

"Baby steps," she reminded me.

I sighed and closed my eyes, concentrating on both clearing my head and not reacting to whatever Delia was going to hand me. I opened my eyes and reached forward, just as the cell phone in my pocket alerted me to a FaceTime call.

"I'm sorry, I'll turn that off."

"Might as well answer," she said when I showed her it was my sister. "Family has a way of knowing when things aren't right."

I felt awkward answering in front of her, especially since Sybill had been forming opinions about the people at Rosehill and wasn't sure she trusted the magic school headmistress who shared a history with the villain. Luckily, Delia took out a box of training gloves and acted like she needed all her concentration to organize them.

"Hey, what's up?" I asked, putting on my everything-is-wonderful smile in case my parents were with her.

"Just waiting for Damian to get his final discharge, then we're hanging out until his flight leaves. Mom and dad are taking me out for a pick-me-up tonight." She rolled her eyes to imply she was too old for that sort of thing, but knowing my sister, she was mostly thrilled. "How's the lockdown?"

"They gave up on the constant nighttime, but the animals are getting stir crazy."

The old stables are a part of the main building that's still protected, so Ben encouraged them all to go there for their own safety, or disperse into the woods, but Rosehill had a lot more animals than I'd expected, and the old stables were not big enough for all of them.

"That sucks. Are you working on your curse?"

"I'm actually with Delia right now," I agreed, moving the phone to show Delia in the background.

"Oh," Sybill said, her eyes going wide to reproach me for not warning her we had company. "Nice to meet you, Miss Delia."

"You too, Miss Sybill." Delia came over and waved. "Your sister is working very hard and making incredible progress."

"She does that," Syb agreed. "Well, I won't keep you from your training, but be safe and I'll try to call you tomorrow."

"I look forward to it. Love you, Syb," I said before disconnecting.

I turned to Delia to resume our lesson, but her expression was desolate.

"What's wrong?" I asked, about to call my sister back. Delia had clearly seen something on the screen that didn't sit well with her.

"Nothing is wrong, exactly." She sighed as if mentally preparing herself to break some bad news to me. "Your sister is the Protector."

"Sybill?" I asked stupidly. "You can tell just by looking at her?"

"Not at her, but the necklace. That's the key. It wasn't in the books because it would be too dangerous to identify the Protectors to those who would use them to open the Magnum Finis, but I told you I witnessed a Ceremony, and I was quite close to a previous Protector. That was the necklace."

"Oh." I don't know why I'd thought there might be another branch on the family tree, some distant cousin who was more experienced and could help us once we found them, but now I knew we were truly alone.

"I can increase the number of people protecting her, but the best would be to convince her to go to a safe house. I know an old Guardian who runs a bed-and-breakfast in Ojai. I might be able to persuade her to take your family in for the foreseeable future..." Delia tried to reassure me.

"That isn't it," I argued. "Although yes, we should probably get them all the protection we can if they're walking around with the necklace someone else might recognize...but I'm the Protector."

"I know you want to protect her, but—"

"No, the necklace is mine," I stopped her. "They gave it to me when I was little, but Sybill really likes it, so I let her wear it when she goes for experimental trials or extended hospital stays. I didn't know I was putting a target on her back."

Delia digested this new information for a moment before assuring me, "Most people don't know what it looks like. All the texts refer to it simply as the key, which some assume is just blood from the Bennett bloodline."

"Still..."

"I'll send more protection," she promised. "Your grandfather said nothing when he gave it to you?"

"I was four, but I don't think my grandmother said anything about choosing me to protect an ancient artefact from being used for evil. Just that he wanted me to have it."

"Was your grandfather's death unexpected?"

"Car crash," I agreed.

"He must have thought he'd have more time," she said to herself.

"What does this mean for me?" I tried to remember everything she'd said, or that I'd read about the Protector.

"It means—"

Her words were drowned out by the loudest doorbell I'd ever heard. I could feel the fear coursing through my veins. I wouldn't expect the mercenaries outside to ring the doorbell for admittance, but anyone outside the front door was either an enemy, or in a lot of trouble.

"I'll go see who that is, but these rooms hold people and magic inside or out, as needed. If you lock it once I leave, no one will be able to come in unless they have my master code, or you let them."

"I'll stay safe," I assured her, but the fear in her eyes was anything but reassuring.

CHAPTER THIRTY

ALISON

I sealed the door as soon as Delia left. This was basically the plan I'd come up with when Delia had first shown me the school, but I'd learned a lot since then. In the short term, these rooms would keep us safe, but it was more like a waiting game, where we were just trapping ourselves into smaller and smaller places with fewer and fewer resources.

At first, I paced around, running through who could have been at the door. There were tons of options for regular people who meant us no harm. Or even mercenaries trying their hand. We knew they were out there, so ringing the doorbell shouldn't have been that scary. Next, I touched random objects in the room; trying to find a powerful memory in the plastic chair, to not see anything when I touched the gloves...I was just about to dig into the blanket and see which happy memories it held when my phone rang.

"Thank God," I started when I saw Sybill's face. "Someone—"

"Allie," my sister cried on the other end, the sobs making it hard for her to breathe.

"What's wrong Sybill? What happened?" I found myself

praying that Damian had dumped her, because it was the only non-life-threatening reason she would be this upset.

"They found us. I don't know how, but we got to the hotel room, and they were waiting for us…"

"Sybill, slow down and tell me exactly what happened? Where are you? Are mom and dad with you?"

"I don't know…they locked me in the closet, but…Allie, they said they'll kill us if you don't give yourself up. I don't know what to do, but I heard dad scream, and I don't know where Mom is…"

"Don't worry Syb, I'm coming, okay? I won't let them hurt you."

"I'm so scared, Allie—"

The line cut off, and I tried calling back at least a dozen times, but it kept going straight to voicemail.

I fumbled with the keypad to get myself out, having to try three times before it worked. I walked into the hallway and debated my next move, failing to steady my hands. And my breathing. If I went left, I could easily reach the front and back doors, but I would have to walk by the other classrooms, where Tristan would probably see me through the glass. Even if he didn't ask me what I was doing, I wouldn't be able to smile at him without his seeing right through me. I'm sure the guilt was already written all over my face. But Sybill was in danger and as much as he understood how much I loved my sister, there was no way he would let me give myself up to save her. I was probably walking into a trap, with absolutely no guarantee that they would let my family go, but if I stayed safe behind these walls while my sister died, I was better off dead.

I took a deep breath, turned right, and almost collided into Krishna, who had her arms full of paintbrushes and chalk.

"We thought it would be fun to add our own art to the walls," she explained.

"How much of that did you hear?" Her calm demeanor didn't fool me. She hid her emotions better than I did.

"Your phone call? Not a word," she assured me.

"And the deliberating I did in the hallway?"

She looked uncomfortably at her feet, giving me the answer I needed.

"Is there any chance this can be our little secret?" I tried, wishing I had something on me that could bribe a small child. Her giggle reminded me she could hear everything I was thinking.

"I can't lie to Miss Delia," she apologized. "And it's not safe outside. You shouldn't go there." The pain behind her eyes wrecked me, but not enough to change my mind.

"I know. But they have my sister, and I would do absolutely anything to protect her."

She nodded, and looked like she felt sorry for me, but she was still going to run to Delia the second I left her.

"What if you don't lie, but just wait until someone asks you where I am? That way, you aren't doing anything wrong, but I get a head start and a chance at saving my sister?"

She considered it, and I didn't have to be psychic to know she was picturing what happened to her parents and how she would give anything to have saved them.

"But as soon as they ask, I'm telling," she warned.

"That's all I'm asking," I assured her. "Thank you, so much."

"Just be careful though, okay? Don't let them catch you."

"Of course." I smiled, making it a point not to think that I was literally trying to get past these mercenaries so I could go surrender myself to a different group of mercenaries.

CHAPTER THIRTY-ONE

DELIA

I had always hated the doorbell. Whenever I was expecting guests, I always waited outside, or by a window so I could reach the door before they pressed it. The bell rang throughout the entire mansion; the sound repeated in every corner through tiny boxes I had once tried to disconnect before someone, probably Ben, reminded me I needed them for when I didn't know someone was coming and had to find out before they were sitting in the foyer. Because with so many people wandering in and out, the doors were never locked. Hopefully, that wasn't the case today.

"What is that?" Penny asked when I passed the other classrooms, the fear apparent in her voice. Charlie, Brandon, and Caleb had been moving the furniture from Krishna's parents' bedroom into the training room, while Etta was organizing the painting of the walls to make them more fun.

"The doorbell." Brandon was reassuring, until he realized it wasn't the sound that scared her, but whatever caused it.

"There's no one outside." Ben walked in calmly, but he was breathing heavy, as if he'd run from the front door.

"What do we do?" Jackie asked, standing tall like she was

ready to fight. I loved this newfound determination and confidence she was putting on, but not today. At least we could seal this entire section, and there was an escape tunnel from the science lab, as an absolute last resort.

"Do you remember Samuel Boyd?" I asked Jackie. "He lives in the manor beside Gabriel and Lucy?"

"Clara's father?" she asked.

"Do you think you would be able to see through his eyes if you tried? For me." I knew she hated doing it without asking, but I would take whatever consequences if my hunch wasn't right.

"I see our front door." She sounded confused. "And a bunch of people scattered around the front gate. He's here."

"There was no one outside," Penny reminded her.

"Sam's Gift is making himself invisible. When I couldn't reach Ingrid, I maybe asked around about her," I told the look Ben gave me. I wasn't sure if he was upset that I hadn't shared my plans with him, or because Sam was a Last Lifer, and I didn't usually call on them.

Everyone followed me to the front door, where I opened it as wide as it would go, and went to the edge of the stairs, which I hoped was still under the main building's enchantment. I counted the men and women I could see, stopping at fifteen – more because I was drawing attention than because there weren't dozens more to count.

"We heard you could use a hand?" Gabriel asked once I shut the door, appearing suddenly in the foyer between Lucy and Sam.

"I called for information, not for you to come risk your Last Lives for me," I reproached, taking them each in for a hug. I'd needed the one from Gabriel more than I cared to admit, but it hadn't felt right to call him and seek comfort over someone who was causing us so much grief.

"I was under the impression you could use someone to make a car invisible so the kids could get to somewhere safe," Sam shot my plan for Ingrid back at me.

"And these two?"

"She's stubborn as they come, and he wasn't going to let her fight alone."

"Tristan asked for my help." Gabriel raised his hands like he was just doing what he was told, and that's all there was to it.

"Sam said you weren't sure how strong my barriers were," Lucy explained her presence, but there was a playful edge to her voice, reproaching me for ever doubting her.

"So far, the house one is amazing, the loophole on the other one is rather inconvenient, and we let them blow up the wards. Although neither of you should have made it past the wall."

"I think I have a free pass since I made some of them. So, watch out if ever I turn evil."

"Do people just turn evil?" Penny asked me.

"Of course not," I assured her, lifting the little girl into my arms. "Lucy was joking."

"It wasn't very funny."

"She has a funny sense of humor," Gabriel told her with a wink.

"I take it you want to pile as many people as we can in a vehicle and get as far away as possible before they notice?" Sam verified.

"I'll stay back and make sure it looks like we're still here, maybe cause a distraction, but the safe house said they could take a boatload."

"Only pack the essentials," Ben warned as everyone headed for their rooms, though I assumed he was going to the war room. He would probably insist on staying with me as well, but I needed as many eyes on the kids as I could get.

. . .

I KNEW PACKING the essentials would not end well even before Penny asked me which bag her stuffed panda would fit in without being too claustrophobic.

"I'll send him to you once you're settled," I assured her, wrapping the gigantic bear in my arms to make sure her bag wouldn't consist solely of stuffed animals.

IT TOOK three attempts before Krishna and Penny were ready with a small backpack each. Jackie's duffel bag was bursting at the seams, while Charlie, Brandon, and Lena barely had anything. I knew she was used to not getting attached to things, but she hadn't packed more than a toothbrush and the weapons she'd arrived with, which worried me.

"Is Allie done packing?" I asked Tristan when he came down the stairs empty-handed. I was running interference between Penny and everyone who had room to pack some of her stuffed animals in their bags.

"I can't find her."

"Oh, I'm sorry. I forgot to tell you she was in the blue room." I felt terrible, but the worry on his face told me she was not in the blue room, and he wasn't surprised. "Was she taken?" Without waiting for an answer, I went to the classroom we'd been about to work on her Gift in, but it was empty. There didn't appear to have been a struggle, and she'd unlocked the doors from the inside.

"My guess would be that she left." Tristan sighed, looking at all the packed bags and resigned faces.

"Because she doesn't like us anymore?" Penny was absolutely crushed.

"She likes you so much that she didn't want you to get hurt," he argued. "She knew we weren't using the tunnels because your…James would find us the second we got out."

Tristan looked at me apologetically, because he knew as well as I that sacrificing herself wouldn't help anyone, but as much as I hated it, I couldn't blame her. At her age, I would have done the same, convinced James was sparing my feelings when he insisted it was safer for everyone if I went into hiding with my siblings than if I stayed at the palace and let them have me.

"Did you hear something?" I asked Krishna. While everyone else was either surprised or worried by this turn of events, Krishna had gone silent and wouldn't meet my eyes. "I know you don't share what you hear, but if you know what happened to her and can help us find her…"

"It wasn't like that." She looked down at her feet again and sighed. "She got a phone call from someone called Syb, who said they were in trouble and needed help. She asked me not to tell anyone, but I said I couldn't lie to you, so she said to wait until you asked, so she could have a head start."

"I thought you had people watching her family?" If looks could kill, the one Tristan sent me would have.

"We do. I talked to Jazmin this morning, and everything was fine. Alison and I were on the phone with Sybill right before the doorbell rang."

"Clearly something happened."

"Don't jump to conclusions," Ben warned, subtly placing himself between me and Tristan, but I knew the anger was directed at himself, not at me. Not that I would ever forgive myself if something happened to any of them. I'd make Ben stand aside and let Tristan do his worst.

"One of the mercenaries can alter their appearance," I remembered. "If they did their research, they easily could have pretended to be her sister to lure her out." I dialed Jazmin's number as I reassured him.

"Miss my sunny disposition?" she asked when she picked up.

"Is Sybill okay?"

"She's in grave danger of a killer brain freeze with the speed she's going through that slushie. But I do think she'll finish before the boyfriend. Loser's buying."

"You have eyes on her right now?" I verified.

"I do. And Collin is at the table with them, but he might not even finish his. Sybill made us after Alison told her someone was watching over them, so we take turns. It would have been a lot cheaper if I'd just taken a job at the ice cream shop. They've been here every day. Sometimes more than once. But the milkshakes are to die for."

"And there are no threats you can see? No one called us here?"

"They're worried about Alison, and Sybill isn't looking forward to her boyfriend going home today, but other than that, they're having the time of their lives."

"Thank you."

"Is everything okay?"

"It will be," I told her, but my eyes were focused on Tristan. "They're all safe," I said as I hung up.

"It was a trap?" he understood. "You can take the kids to safety; I'll stay here and find her."

"That's very sweet, but also stupid," Caleb argued.

"They're safe inside the building, especially with Lucy here to reinforce anything that might not be up to par. But I don't think our invisibility ruse would work more than once..." I looked to Sam.

"We ditched the car a ways back and walked, but even that was hard to navigate once we got close. They're all just lying around, waiting for you guys to come out. They're not even hiding."

"I think I know where she'll be." It was my turn to feel guilty. Again.

"You think your *friend* led her outside?" Ben asked like the word 'friend' was painful for him to use.

"No, that isn't his type. He would just wait her out. But as soon as she got past the wall, he would have sensed her."

"That's gross," Penny pointed out.

"More like scary," Krishna argued.

"Is it true that he always finds his prey?" Lucy asked me, checking with Gabriel. He clearly had more of a say in them coming here than Sam implied, and I got the impression Gabriel might have filled them in on James.

"Always," I agreed. "No matter who lured Alison outside, I would bet my life he has her by now."

"Isn't that a good thing?" Lucy pressed.

"Everyone else out there wants Alison so they can bring her back to the Damned – alive – and get their reward."

"Not James?"

"I need to get to him first," I said instead of answering.

"Where is he?" Ben asked.

"The old hunting cabin on the edge of the property?" I turned to Jackie, who nodded.

"It would have everything he needs and be easy enough to break into. I can't remember the last time anyone used it."

"He wouldn't need to break in." I sighed. "He built it. With his bare hands. The magical barriers are the only thing keeping him outside of Rosehill, because he knows every way in or out as well as I do. He might even know some that I don't, because I usually stayed home while he had adventures on the grounds," I admitted.

CHAPTER THIRTY-TWO

ALISON

I took the doors that led to the balcony, then the stairs down to the courtyard. There was a tiny gate that let out somewhere on the side of the building, with no mercenaries in sight. Probably because the wall was intact on this side, which meant I had nowhere to go. I'd tried rock climbing exactly once, at a friend's birthday party in junior high, and if I couldn't make it up a wall with a harness and rocks sticking out at regular intervals, no way was I going to scale this much larger one without grips. I tried to call Sybill again, praying she could tell me it was all some big misunderstanding, but it went straight to voicemail. Again.

I took a deep breath and hid among the bushes, crouching my way towards the back of the building.

There were mercenaries in the backyard, but most of them were trying to look inside the house windows or camped out on the lawn, waiting for one of us to venture outside. They looked bored out of their minds, which wasn't half as terrifying as they'd been when they were luring us out to attack us.

The bushes brought me to a greenhouse, so I slipped inside and was glad to find another door at the opposite end. I would have expected all kinds of exotic plants that wouldn't survive New England winters, but it was mostly filled with roses. A lot of the finishing touches and ornamental details made so much more sense now that I knew Delia's history. Even the name *Rosehill* had meaning.

I lingered for a moment behind the greenhouse. There was a clear delineation on the inside to show where the stone wall ended and the magical protections stopped, so there was a very good chance I would be killed once I stepped outside. Or at least kidnapped and taken to the Damned, which amounted to the same thing. I had to hope that I could make it to the road before then, or that the deal would work to not harm my family, even if another team caught me.

The forest was eerily quiet, devoid of birds or squirrels, nothing that made noise other than my running shoes on the damp leaves. I considered making a run for it, but I froze when the deafening sound of a twig breaking under my foot resounded throughout the woods.

"See, I told you she would buy it."

I turned around so fast I probably gave myself whiplash. I was face to face with Sybill. Every detail, down to her voice, was perfect, but there was a cruelty to her tone, and a deadness in her eyes that was very unlike my sister.

"Sybill?" I asked. Tristan had mentioned Gifted who could control other people, and it wasn't so far-fetched to believe that there were some who could teleport, or magically create portals to get her here from California, but my heart was sinking. I didn't think this was my sister, which meant I'd just left the safety of Rosehill, and put everyone I cared about in even more danger, for a stupid trap I wasn't smart enough to see through. Or ask for help.

"I'm afraid Sybill isn't going to make it today, but I'm sure she appreciates your sacrifice. We all do."

The woman's features shifted in front of me so she grew

taller, and her hair went from strawberry blonde to so blonde it was almost white, shaved off at the sides and hanging in dreadlock-type braids that made her look so much more intimidating than my sister ever could, even before I saw her battle axe.

"What did you do to her?" I asked, holding my hands up as if there was something I could do with them to protect myself. I added 'bring a weapon' to the list of things I should have done before venturing out.

"Oh, I haven't touched her. It's a decent play, going after your family to make you comply, but I figured it would be easier to do it this way, since you're right here."

As she spoke, she put on long leather gloves, and one of her friends brought her a bright yellow rain jacket, as if my Gift could seep through the fabric of her regular clothes. It couldn't pass through anything, but my best bet was to convince her I could reach her from all the way over here, so she might not try anything. Although even if I got close enough to touch someone, I wasn't sure my Gift could knock out a dozen people before one of them knocked me out.

She took a step towards me, then collapsed without warning. I thought she tripped, until I saw the knife in her neck. I was going to make a run for it while those closest to her rushed to her side, thinning the circle around me, but when I went to move, I caught my foot on a root and fell to the ground. It was when I went to untangle it that I saw I wasn't caught in a root so much as the roots sprung out from the ground to catch me.

Delia had mentioned James would find me the second I left Rosehill. I'm not sure if I thought she was exaggerating, or if it surprised me when he wasn't waiting outside the greenhouse, but this was clearly the doing of his green-haired friend.

"Van Bergen," one of the Viking woman's friends looked up and saw James standing a few feet out of my reach. The man was leaning down to check on the Viking woman, so I wasn't sure if he was bowing on purpose, but there were equal amounts of hatred and respect in his greeting.

"We'll take it from here, Knox," James assured him while more roots came out of the earth and guided me – not-so-gently – deeper into the woods, but at a safe distance so I couldn't touch anyone or anything other than the tree, who seemed perfectly immune to my soul-sucking.

"We lured her out here. She's ours."

"I'll be sure to tell Miss Cao how brilliant your ruse was next time I see her, but in the meantime, I have some business to attend to."

"You can't just take her from us," Knox warned, bringing his palms up like he was prepared to use them.

Another man moved forward as well, both hands holding up a sword roughly as tall as me, handling it like it weighed no more than the rolls of wrapping paper I used to fight my dad with.

"Stedman, I am warning you that as members of the Damned who specifically wish for death, I have no qualms about killing every one of you to have her."

"We're a dozen against two, and your second is otherwise occupied."

"Ray," James greeted another man who'd come forward, wearing the thickest sunglasses I'd ever seen. It literally looked like he'd put sheets of black marble the length of binoculars in front of his eyes.

James had a confidence that implied he was going to win no matter how many people they threw at him, especially since he seemed to know all of them, and I knew he had at least three other people with him somewhere.

The roots grew tighter around my arms and ankles, warning me not to try anything, but other than running back inside Rosehill before anyone caught up with me, I wasn't sure where to go. Or who I wanted to win. The now-dead shapeshifter had been pretty scary, and her friends looked menacing, but I'd seen what James and his people could do. Part of me hoped I would be safer with someone who had such strong ties to Delia, but then again, I knew what my ancestor had done to him. It might be better to die by his hand than to be used as a lab experiment to kill other Gifted.

I barely had time to conclude that I would let fate decide, with the strong hope that they would all kill each other and I could get away, before Stedman moved forward, swinging his blade. I'd seen the scabbard at James' back, so I knew he hadn't really conjured his sword out of thin air, but that's how fast he pulled it out. Stedman was blowing in James' direction, which looked ridiculous and useless, until I saw the trees bending behind him, while James stood tall.

Knox ran forward as James delivered a fatal blow to Stedman and two others who'd joined the fight. I considered warning James, but decided against it, remembering his vow to murder me, regardless of the contract on my life.

When Knox put his hand to the ground, it was like the forest floor was a rug that he pulled up. The once flat ground rose into a series of roving hills. The woman holding me prisoner used unaffected vines from neighboring trees to lift us out of its path, but I could see the ground collapsing on itself beneath me. If there had been a time for me to escape, it was gone now.

James ran across the tops of the hills, faring better than I would have imagined, but it slowed his progress, like trying to go up an escalator coming down. I would not want to be Knox once James reached him.

Ray, the man with the sunglasses, reached up to the sky and made everything so much brighter than it had been a minute ago. Warmer as well, but he didn't seem able to control his Gift to a specific location, which explained his glasses. I wondered if his name really was Ray, or if James was mocking him for being such a ray of sunshine.

While most of the group had gone after James, there were a couple of them who tried to retrieve me, but the woman handled them easily, as if she were annoyed by the interruption rather than ever in danger. She had twig bracelets on her wrists, so when someone shot a bolt of purple energy at her, she brought her arms up and the bracelets extended until they formed a shield of branches that the blast bounced off of.

James sent a knife to the middle of that person's forehead, as if he had eyes on the back of his head and wasn't preoccupied with half a dozen men trying to kill him.

When someone came for me with a knife and a vial, attempting to climb up the roots, the woman holding me threw one of her bracelets over to protect me, while James threw another knife. I tried to convince myself this was him protecting me, rather than ensuring that he would be the one to finish the job, but I had my doubts.

Within ten minutes from the woman who'd looked like Sybill approaching me, a dozen people were on the ground and the woman, who I found out was named Vanessa, had me follow James into the woods with my hands tied by vines, ready to scoop me up if I so much as thought of running away.

AFTER MAYBE THIRTY MINUTES, we arrived at a cabin. It was old, like probably as old as Rosehill, though I doubt anyone had used it in forever. The appliances were ancient, like the fridge from the sixties you could hide inside to avoid nuclear war, and a stove you had to feed wood into, but there was also electricity and motion sensors that lit the staircase when they brought me to the cellar.

I expected it to be old, damp, and covered in cobwebs, but it was probably the most modern part of the building. There was a couch from the eighties against one wall, and an old ice box I knew was for hunting, but I couldn't help but feel like it was waiting for me.

Vanessa brought me to a bed in the corner across from the stairs and conjured up way more branches and vines than was necessary for someone my size, but there was a draft down here, and the leaves were soft and warm, kind of like a nature-infused hug.

"Your sister is okay," she whispered when she came close enough to toss me a bottle of water and a granola bar.

"Says the woman who just tied me to a bed in an abandoned cellar."

"Valkyrie's group probably doesn't even know where your sister is, and James would never do something like that."

"Forgive me if that isn't reassuring."

"I'm just saying you don't have to worry about your family. It might not be much, but it would haunt me if I was in your shoes, and she played that trick on me."

She didn't wait for my response before going over to James and whispering something I couldn't hear, but the way she put her hand on his arm and gave his hand a squeeze before going up the stairs was enough for me to feel Delia's future heartbreak.

JAMES STAYED at the bottom of the stairs for a moment, then came over to check and make sure I was secure, careful not to get anywhere near me.

I knew this was my chance to plead with him to let me go. I could tell him how I was young and didn't deserve to die, how I didn't want any of this. I could bring up the Delia angle, tell him how hurt and disappointed she would be if he was the one who killed me. At least a dozen arguments popped into my head, not that any of them were likely to work, but when I opened my mouth, I settled on, "I'm sorry."

"For what?" His voice was gruff, and he didn't even look up from the bindings he was verifying.

"I'm so sorry for what happened to your daughters. What my…I am so sorry."

He didn't respond, but he froze for a moment, as tense as can be, before he forced himself to resume his task. There was anger and rigidity to it now.

"I know it's not the same, but just the thought that those people had taken my sister…I would have done absolutely anything to get her back, and if they'd hurt her…I can't imagine what I would do." As I said the words, I was once again reminded that I was the only one who'd been hurting Sybill, consistently, for over a decade. I deserved whatever horrible things he wanted to do to me. I didn't want to die, but if him killing me kept my family and everyone at Rosehill safe, then maybe it was the best-case scenario, and I should just let it happen.

"No one else will have to suffer that loss at the hands of your bloodline. I'll make sure of it," he promised.

"It's probably best," I agreed, surprising him. "When they took me the first time, I was going to help them. This Gift, it's a curse, and I don't want to hurt people. Not strangers, not Gifted against their will, not my sister, or anyone who loves me or gets close to me.… not Krishna, who has to grow up without her parents because they helped me. If you need to kill me, I won't be able to stop you. But it's okay, as long as you don't let them have me," I asked of him.

"I don't care what your wishes are," James argued before I saw Vanessa was back. "Don't let her touch you," he warned on his way up the stairs.

CHAPTER THIRTY-THREE

DELIA

"Why do you think you can get through to him? He obviously changed if he didn't hunt innocent children when he was with you," Ben warned in a whisper as we made our way through the escape tunnel that would leave us less than a hundred feet from the old hunting cabin. Even though he was questioning my judgment, he didn't want anyone else to see him doubt me.

"I know him, Ben. He stalked Richard Carmichael and his family for months before he did anything, to convince himself they weren't innocent." I could remember him trying to justify it afterwards, telling me how the older son tortured animals, and the younger one had nearly blinded a weaker classmate by throwing rocks at him simply because he was bored.

"Allie is," Tristan argued, listening closer than I'd expected.

"That's why I'm going to reason with him." I knew they were joining me on this expedition for two reasons. First was to protect me from my undying faith in someone they were convinced would hurt me, and second was to fight him for Alison once I understood I couldn't reason with him. I just hoped I could prove them wrong.

Caleb was looking at me with a cross between sympathy and pity.

"I'm his Etta. If I can't bring back his humanity, no one can." I hoped that wasn't the case, because I knew I would lose more people than I was willing to part with if it was. "If we can end this without bloodshed, it's worth a shot, isn't it?"

"It is," Tristan agreed. "You really think you can reach him? Even after centuries apart?"

"His heart still belongs to Delia."

I was shocked to hear Ben defend him, however reluctantly.

We'd arrived at the end of the tunnel, which was in the opening of a cave. It had taken forever to excavate it, but history had taught us to be prepared, and if ever anything had happened at the manor while James was on one of his bonding trips with the children, he was never more than twenty minutes away. It also provided cover for us now, as long as James didn't have anyone inside the cave. There were enough rocks and hiding places to run for help or hide amongst the trees. That being said, I knew he would sense me the moment I moved past the vestiges of the enchantments, which I probably already had.

I turned to the gang that came with me. This was the moment of truth, to see if they would let me reason with him, or take advantage of any surprise they could manage and rush in guns blazing.

"Be careful," Caleb said, taking a step back to show he trusted me.

Ben just looked at me, torn again, while Tristan's fists were clenched so tight, I wouldn't be surprised if he pounced out the opening.

"Alison is my priority," I assured Tristan. "If I can't reason with him, I will…I will do what I have to in order to save her," I promised him. I'd tried to tell him I would kill James if it came to it, with conviction, but I faltered. If the time came that I had to, I would do it...but James and I killed and died *for* one another. We didn't kill each other.

"Thank you," he managed, but his eyes showed nothing but fear.

"She's worth it," I told him. "And so are you."

"Do you want me to come with?" Gabriel offered, the only one who knew our rich history, who'd been there for the heartbreak of losing him.

"I think it's best if I go alone." I gave what I hoped was a reassuring smile.

"You've got ten minutes," Ben decided.

I nodded instead of arguing, then followed my heart to James.

I CONSIDERED SNEAKING up to the cabin, or calling him out into the woods, but I was more worried about other teams finding us than what his people would do to me. I raised both hands up in surrender and walked straight to the front door, not the least bit surprised when it opened before I even reached the steps.

"Lilah," James said, a sad smile welcoming me inside. Technically, the cabin belonged to me, but it would always be his. Guests had used it, both for fun and when they were passing through and wanted their privacy, but no one had stayed long enough to alter the decor, which was dark wood with white and red accents. The carvings of roses and mountains caught me by surprise, because I'd learned to avoid them at the mansion, but they were here, reminding me of when we were an *us*, without even a trace of the single entities we were on our own. "What are you doing here?" he asked.

"I came to see you," I told him, knowing it wasn't really an answer. There had been two of his men I didn't know sitting at the kitchen table, but he gestured with his hand and they both left without a word.

"To join me, or to kill me?" he asked.

"Neither," I admitted. "I thought I might try reasoning with you. We both know you have Alison—"

"I always find my target," he reminded me, his sadness breaking my heart as much as my own did.

"I'm pleading for her life, James, the way we pleaded for the girls in that alley. Do you really want to become the monster Cadence died to prove you weren't?" It was a low blow, and I would have preferred to ease into this part of it, but I only had ten minutes, or until Ben and Tristan tired of sitting around and waiting, which probably wouldn't be that long.

"Don't compare me to him," James warned through gritted teeth. "They were innocent children. She's the descendant of the monster, and she obviously has no regard for her own life if she was going to hand herself over to the Damned." He argued like he meant it, but he knew it wasn't justified.

"I would gladly have given up all my lives to save my sisters," I called him on it. Whether he lured her out or not, Alison wouldn't have gone quietly without making sure Sybill was safe.

"Why do you care so much about her? One life to save all those children you have inside, and every other unsuspecting casualty of these mercenaries' crosshairs."

"Because one life is worth it. You spent centuries with me, saving lives because you used to think every single one mattered," I shot back, getting upset. The idea that he'd truly changed, that my James was no longer inside, terrified me.

"Even the blood of that soulless monster who—"

I flinched, and he went quiet. I watched his hand reach for me before he stopped himself and took a breath, dropping his shoulders in a way that made him look so deflated.

"There's something I need to tell you about the day we lost… everything," I said before he could apologize for being blunt and remind me how naïve I could be. After centuries spent carrying this secret, I needed to get it out, even if I could already feel the tears.

"Lilah, we don't—"

"Mr. Carmichael's brother didn't just die because I wasn't able to save him," I cut James off.

"Mistakes happen, Lilah. He was going to blame you for it, no matter what you might have done. If it wasn't because his brother died, it would have been because of what we are. But he should never have taken it out on innocent children." He looked sick, so I couldn't tell if he was seeing what Mr. Carmichael did to our girls or what he did to the Carmichael family afterwards.

"I didn't make a mistake. Or I did, but…I used my Gift. Not on purpose, but I was giving instructions, careful as I always am, then I got flustered when I saw his ring, and I paused, and when I said we needed to stop the bleeding…"

"Someone stopped the bleeding."

"Or something. His heart stopped, and no matter what I did, what anyone did, massaging it with my bare hands…it wouldn't come back."

I thought the understanding on James' face would turn to anger as he realized I was the reason we lost them, but he tilted his head and all I saw was empathy.

"You've been blaming yourself for centuries?" he asked, reaching for my hand.

"It was my fault. He came to us for help, and I killed his brother with my Gift. No wonder he was afraid of it, of us, and…I know what he did was wrong, and he overreacted, but he wasn't unprovoked. I started it. I'm the reason he killed our girls, that you killed his entire family…" I couldn't see his expression through the warm tears blurring my vision, but it was probably a kindness. I didn't know if I could handle having his hatred directed at me.

"Not his entire family," he argued, the admission weighing heavily on him.

"Or there would be no Alison."

"No, I don't mean that I must have missed someone…The baby that you were so horrified that I'd…I watched the family for weeks. Whenever I wasn't with you, I was watching them become monsters. Maybe I should have given his sons time to become men, to see if they would change, but as teenagers, they spent their time bullying others and exerting their power over those less fortunate, and…it maybe wasn't my place, but I know without a doubt that the world was better off without them." He paused and saw that I did not agree with that assessment, having always believed that everyone can change if they have sufficient motivation to do so. "But I couldn't kill the child before giving him a chance, to see if he would turn as evil as his father, or become decent without his influence. I spared the child because I couldn't go through with it."

"I know," I assured him. "I met him in 1843."

"You knew?"

"Of course, I knew. You crossed a line I couldn't forgive you for, but even in a blind rage, you wouldn't kill an infant. I knew you couldn't have done it after months to think over the implications and consequences," I said with the utmost certainty. "Why do you look just as remorseful over sparing the child as you do for killing the teenagers?"

"Because I know what his line has done. What that infant grew into. Had I been strong enough to do what had to be done, we could have avoided the horrors caused by centuries of the New Order. Carmichael's son was responsible for almost all their most ruthless policies, eliminating not only Gifted, but anyone who associates with them, any family members who might also be infected, who harbor them or lie to protect them…if you saw all the bad his descendants put out into the world…you would regret it as well."

I winced, because it was an argument you could easily justify. Not so much killing the descendants for what their ancestors did, but had he kept a closer eye on that child and eliminated him before he obtained the top position in the New Order, it would have saved hundreds of thousands of lives. The greatest Gifted massacres wouldn't have happened. Retaliations wouldn't have been so fierce, because we are used to dying, but not to our loved ones being hunted as well. His death would have been a godsend to generations of other families that will never be…but living as long as I have, you see that a single death has far more consequences than you could imagine.

"I thought the same as you, James. That every Carmichael was evil and deserved to die a slow and painful death as penance. When Francis was waiting on my doorstep, begging for my help, I didn't care. I just wanted to turn him away."

"Carmichael's grandson went to you for help? And you agreed?" Both shocked him. Alison was one thing, as she knew nothing of her ancestry, but Francis had known every last reason why he shouldn't have knocked on my door.

"I don't know if he would have grown up to be as ruthless as his ancestors, but he fell in love with a girl. A sweet, kind, and innocent girl who talked to insects and dedicated her life to helping others. When Francis' father discovered her Gift and took her, he inadvertently created a Carmichael line that not only rejected the New Order's values, they protected Gifted and stood for everything we did. Alison is the descendant of Francis Carmichael and all the terrible things his family has done, but she is also the descendant of Francis' wife—"

"Who would choose to marry into—"

"Hannah Bennett." He'd tried to cut me off, but I kept going, knowing the last name would be enough to quiet him, even before I added, "Little Miss Maudie's granddaughter."

"No…" The shock on James' face would have been funny if it weren't also hauntingly sad. Maude had been our beloved granddaughter; her wedding to Patrick Bennett was the one we'd attended the day we lost everything.

"That not only makes Alison someone I would give all my lives to protect, she is also the current Protector of the Magnum Finis."

"They said they wanted her blood because it was the cure, not that..." James looked horrified as he digested all the new information I'd just given him.

"They do. Because her Gift temporarily sucks your Gift right out of you. But they also know that her blood is the key to getting inside the Magnum Finis. That's why they wanted you to bring her to them, so they could bleed her dry, while keeping her alive, in the name of their self-interest."

"Why didn't you tell me?" he asked. "That she was Maude's, that she was a Protector...any of it?"

"Because that information could get her killed and put the rest of her family in danger," I reminded him. "But also because her life was worth it, regardless. I hoped you would have come to that conclusion on your own. That you would look at the young woman in front of you and see she is nothing like the monster you associate her with, but everything like the girls we lost. I hoped that watching her as you would, seeing her...I hoped you would put an end to it on your own and prove that the man I fell in love with is still inside there somewhere. Buried very deep down, but still in there."

I waited for his response, for the guilt, betrayal, pain, and anger to turn into an answer before the guys barged in to rescue me and Alison. I felt confident his sense of duty would prevent him from turning her over to the Damned, but I wasn't sure if his love for Miss Maude outweighed his hatred for Mr. Carmichael. He looked like he was about to break my heart and tell me the man I loved was dead, or something equally painful, but the door behind him flew open to reveal Potts.

"Boss, we've got a problem," he said with an urgency that would have scared me if I didn't know my ten minutes were up.

"Miss Delilah." He nodded awkwardly in my direction, but there was also a smile behind his all-business attitude.

"It's nice to see you, Jeremy."

"You might want to take that back in a minute."

He left the room, expecting us to follow him. James looked at me like the conversation wasn't over, but he still went out after Potts.

"What's the issue, Potts?" James asked, letting him know he could say it in front of me, which either meant he trusted me, or was going to kill me.

"It's the Carmichael girl... She's gone."

I'd been expecting him to say they had company, that Caleb was spotted through the trees, but I hadn't planned for this. My heart sank to my stomach. I looked off to where Tristan and the others had been waiting, hoping to God they had her.

CHAPTER THIRTY-FOUR

ALISON

Darius and Mick, two of the men who'd attacked us the night I got to Rosehill, had come down with Vanessa and now sat at a table in the corner. They shot me occasional glances that were a cross between extreme judgment and unfathomable hatred, neither of which was warranted.

Two new guys joined them after a while, smoking cigarettes that one of them lit with his bare finger.

"You couldn't do that outside?" Vanessa asked, sitting across from me with a magazine. She wrinkled her nose as she put her feet up on the end table.

"You can leave if it bothers you." He purposely blew smoke in her direction, so she made a wall of plants between them.

"Don't antagonize her, Jeb. It's common decency," Mick warned, swiping at the smoke with his hand.

"No one has ever accused me of being decent."

Vanessa rolled her eyes and tried to concentrate on the celebrity gossip, but Jeb kept blowing smoke in her direction, and I could see her tensing up as she tried not to react.

"It's not like *we* have to worry about lung cancer." The other smoker laughed, but he still put his cigarette out – on the table.

I wasn't a fan of the smoke either, but it was pretty low on my list of worries, and the trees holding me to the bed had sprouted more leaves to compensate for the air pollution.

"How long do you think it takes to turn her into a cure?" Jeb asked Darius, leering at me in a way that made my skin crawl.

"Didn't he say she takes it when she touches us?" Darius shrugged.

"He said you lose your Gift if she touches you, but it comes back, and you're still—"

"Damned." The newcomer cut off Mick's explanation.

"Oh, get off of it, mate." Darius shook his head. "Kiss your old life goodbye and embrace your new one."

"Easy to say when you can control it," Mick argued. "You choose to look like that."

Darius' scales were visible on his neck and up his arms, like a tattoo sleeve that ended at his wrists.

"Jealous?" Darius raised his brows and took a shot of some amber liquid they found in a cupboard. The label was so faded I couldn't even tell you what color it used to be.

"Do you think she needs to be alive for it to work, or they just want the blood to be fresh when they cut her?"

"Jebediah!" Vanessa warned. "She's not deaf."

"She's not for long either, though, is she?"

"We only get the reward if she's alive," Mick reminded him.

"Probably be a relief when she dies. We won't need her, and we'll have the cure."

"Doesn't it take the government years to come up with vaccines?"

"That's because they make money off the diseases. The Damned don't need money."

"I always pictured them as homeless people wandering around and muttering about being cursed, but that house she had us in...that was legit." The newcomer sounded impressed, but also like he was trying to impress everyone. He'd put out the cigarette for Vanessa and Mick, but accepted another one when Jeb offered, as well as countless shots of alcohol, even if he choked on it each time.

"It's to be expected. What's the compound interest on a hundred years?" Jeb laughed.

"She didn't look that old," Darius argued. "Those eyes were young and bright. I've tried contacts, and they never work that well on me."

"That's because your eyes reflect the darkness of your soul." Jeb smiled.

"I won't argue with that." He raised his hands in surrender before reaching across the table for the bottle Jeb was refilling his glass with. "But why buy when you can take?" He took a swig from the bottle, nearly emptying it to prove his point, but his eyes were locked on me.

"Don't mind them," Vanessa assured me. She wasn't exactly whispering, but she didn't intend for the others to hear.

"It's okay, I know what happens once you bring me in. You can *not* talk about it if that makes you feel better, but they'll take my blood and kill me, regardless."

"I know it isn't pleasant to be poked and prodded, but I don't think anyone intends to kill you. People have done terrible things in the name of science, but it is during wars and great tragedies that we make the discoveries that save millions of lives."

"Whatever helps you to sleep at night."

"I thought you said you would have gone willingly?" She revealed she was listening earlier.

"To protect my sister. But you're not dying. This isn't research to save lives, it's to take them away. This Damned woman is building a weapon with empty promises and you're all falling for it."

"I'm not justifying what it could be used for in the wrong hands, but you have no idea—"

"How hard it is to have a purpose that the entire universe conspires to help you accomplish? To be able to sacrifice yourself a thousand times to save all the lives you can? I wanted to get rid of my Gift because it hurts people, but you could literally put an end to world hunger. Have you even tried figuring out what you're meant to do before resorting to science experiments?"

"You're right. I'm here because I go where James goes, and he said we'd find you. My Gift is wonderful as far as what it can do for others, but it wasn't always that way, and some people don't have it so easy. Even Mick. James taught him to focus it on specific people, but one sneeze and everyone in a half-mile radius is in agony."

"I'm glad I'm dying so he can endure allergy season."

"For most of them, it isn't about the Gift. It's the curse. The waking up no matter how many times you die. Watching everyone you love not only die, but become relics of the past that you can't even reminisce about because no one alive today was even an idea when they died. It's the no end in sight."

"If only there was a way to fix that..."

I agreed with her on some level. I knew it sucked to live forever alone...but I don't think I would stoop to killing innocent children to put an end to it. At least not until I'd spent centuries trying to help people and inventing things and doing all kinds of good in the world, hoping one of them would be my thing.

"And what if the thing they're supposed to do is terrible? Maybe you're right, and I was supposed to solve food shortages. But what if I was meant to cause an earthquake that decimates an entire village, but leads to some significant discovery? What if my purpose was to drive drunk and kill a family because it's the only way their daughter grows up to invent the seatbelt?"

"You just said you were okay with tragedies that lead to discoveries, as long as they benefit you."

"I have no interest in taking the cure," she argued.

"Then what's the point? Why are you going along with it?"

"Because let's say I grew tired of searching for my purpose and decided to wreak havoc on the world, terrorizing the entire planet with no one who can stop me, because I just keep coming back. Shouldn't there be some way to defeat me?"

"Is that the only instance they would use it? Because it seems to me the Damned believe every person with a Gift is an abomination who deserves to be put down."

"I guess it depends on who you leave in charge."

"Considering you chose someone who sent an army to terrorize little children and turn them into orphans, I'd say you're doing a great job."

"I didn't choose her. I follow James. I don't know that woman, but I trust him implicitly."

"He isn't a saint either."

"Only the dead get to be saints. The living make mistakes, lots of them, but I've been around for many years, and he's the only one I've met who takes you in, teaches you how to control your Gift, to defend yourself...and then you're family. Whether you stay and help him make the world safer, or go off to find your happiness, he's got your back. Even when I was alive, I never...His word is everything to him. If he makes a promise, he doesn't break it, no matter what."

"Like his promise to kill me?"

She didn't have an answer for that, but the one who seemed to be James' second in command came from upstairs to talk to her.

"Are we heading out?" She perked up.

"Soon. Everything okay down here?"

"Jerks are being jerks, but nothing I can't handle," she assured him.

I pretended to be engrossed in my sleeve, hoping he might

slip and reveal something useful if he thought I wasn't paying attention.

"The new ones, or…"

"It's a toss-up." She sighed. "So far, they're just running their mouths, but we need to get a move on."

"He's looking into something, but it shouldn't be long," he assured her. "Are you okay?"

It took me a minute of Vanessa not responding to realize he was talking to me. I wanted to be snarky and sarcastic, to ask why he cared if they were sending me to die anyway, but I looked up and his eyes were kind, as if he genuinely wanted me to be safe and happy.

"Now that you have me, everyone stops going after my family and Rosehill, right?"

"We would never hurt anyone who wasn't the person we were after," the man said soothingly. "And Rosehill is the last place I want any harm to come to."

"I meant all you people who were hired to bring me in. The ones who killed Sakina and Mohinder for no reason at all."

"Once Miss Cao has you, she should call everyone off," he agreed.

"Then ask me again once that happens."

"I'm really sorry about this, Alison. We're usually on the other side as well."

With that, he exchanged a look with Vanessa and walked back up the stairs. So far, the most annoying thing about all the people who kept kidnapping me was their insistence that deep down, they really were the good guys, too.

THE GUYS, or jerks as Vanessa called them, were oddly quiet while the man was downstairs, but the minute I heard the door shut, they exchanged a look and nodded their heads towards me. Mick shook his head and raised a finger, but fear rose in my throat, and I knew that whatever was coming, I would not like it.

"Vanessa…" I started, but she shook her head and put out an arm, as if she'd also witnessed the exchange, but wanted to see what they had planned before reacting to it.

I didn't know what anyone was waiting for, but I sure as hell didn't want to just sit there to find out. I couldn't reach anyone while tied to the bed, but I was literally wrapped up in an extension of Vanessa. I grabbed the thickest branch I could see, not sure if I was looking for a memory to help me, or to somehow weaken her, but I hoped my Gift might weaken my restraints the way it weakened people.

I had to dig deep, but all I got was a memory of a woman, not Vanessa, holding on to the branch for dear life, as it wrapped itself around her and two children, bringing them to what looked like a guardrail, where Vanessa helped them over. Vanessa's black eyes were full of tears and terror.

The memory wasn't much help in my current situation, although Vanessa was looking at me with confusion. I don't know if they knew I could see memories, or if they just cared about the part that impacted them. Not that it was much help when I couldn't get close to anything but the bed, which didn't even have a nightmare to show me. Clearly, I was the first person they handcuffed to it.

A chair scraping against the ground let me know someone stood up, but before I could even turn to see what happened, Vanessa built a wall of thick branches between us and them. I don't know what she was hoping to achieve by it, but Jeb quickly set it on fire, while Darius' scales punctured through layers of wood like it was warm butter. The trees must have been connected, because while she tried to build a stronger barrier in front of her, the flames were traveling to me.

My first instinct was to scream and let her know I was about to be burned alive, but she'd already flung an arm back, so the burning part shriveled up and fell off.

So much of her energy was focused on the front that – weakened by the flames – my restraints were no longer holding me in place. Most of the foliage had been put there for my comfort, but the bark and vines around my wrists had gone dry enough that I could snap it to slip my hands through. I definitely didn't want to be with the men without Vanessa, but given the choice, I would much rather be in the woods on my own. I knew they couldn't get past Rosehill's stone wall, so as long as I could run that far, I had a chance of making it back inside, to safety. Not to mention, if any of them wanted to recapture me, they would have to get close enough that I might touch them. Hopefully, they would avoid that, which would let me slip away.

It was far from the best plan, but Darius was breaking through the wall of trees, and I didn't know how long Mick would put off using his torture on us. It was now or never.

I slowly untangled myself from all the plants, took a deep breath, then started running before my feet hit the floor. I heard Vanessa yell after me when I reached the stairs, but I didn't look back. I kept running as if my life depended on it, because it did.

CHAPTER THIRTY-FIVE

DELIA

"What do you mean, she's gone?" I asked Potts, but he just looked to James, not sure how much he could share.

"The door was wide open and there was no one in the cellar," he shared after getting a nod.

"No one?"

I tried to ignore the tightening around my chest at James' concern for the woman he was with, because we had bigger problems to deal with than my feelings.

"Not even—"

"It looked like there was a struggle – things turned over and Gifts used – but no blood or bodies."

"Who did you leave her with?" It was becoming less likely that my people had rescued her, unless they were currently being hunted, which didn't comfort me in the least.

"I left her in the cellar with five members of my team to keep her safe from the others out here while I figured out what I wanted to do with her," James explained, reluctantly, because it meant that even before I showed up, there was a chance he wouldn't kill her.

"You can tell your friends to stop hiding behind those rocks. They don't have her." James had the decency to look desolate before he and Potts continued to the cabin's cellar.

I looked back, expecting Tristan, Caleb, Gabriel, and Ben, but Lena, Brandon, Charlie, and Lucy were also speed-walking towards me, with Tristan staring at the back of James' head with a hatred I could feel to my core. A blur went past, which I assumed was Gabriel scouting ahead.

"What's going on?" I asked, glaring at the underage First Lifers, expecting them to cower under my stare, but they each met it with a steady gaze, not one of them backing down.

"They followed us," Ben explained.

"I can see that. Why aren't they back with Etta and the others?"

"Because we're not little kids, and you're outnumbered," Lena made it sound both like she had my back, and like I was the irresponsible one who needed help from a fifteen-year-old.

"And Alison is one of us," Charlie added, making my heart swell with pride in addition to the fear. How could I convey that their sentiments were admirable, but the last thing I wanted was them acting on them?

I wanted to send them home, even if I knew it was a losing argument, but Tristan decided the matter was settled.

"I'm more concerned about the fact that he just said he lost Alison?"

Tristan puffed out his chest and went to charge James, but I put my hands on his chest while Caleb and Ben each held a shoulder.

"He's our best chance at getting Alison back, unless one of you saw something?"

They all shook their heads.

"Does that mean you convinced him?" Caleb was hopeful.

"We were interrupted, but I think he sees things differently now."

Ben's look showed me his clear disproval of my choices, as he would clearly rather get rid of James and find Alison on our own, but he wouldn't go against me.

WE PICKED up our pace and got to the cellar's entrance just after James had lifted what was left of the wooden doors. Ben stayed outside, and I could tell he wanted everyone else to do the same, that he didn't trust the man bringing us into a secret lair, but I not only trusted the man; I knew the cellar was hooked up to my security system. It was the old school, ancient one that couldn't be accessed remotely from a computer, but I wasn't the least bit worried about being trapped, especially when we outnumbered the two of them many times. Gabriel would have warned us if there was an army waiting inside, but even then, I knew how to set off the sprinklers.

AS POTTS HAD PREDICTED, we reached the bottom of the stairs and found it abandoned. James looked frantically in every nook and cranny of the underground fortress, but there was no one there. Furniture was overturned, and a mirror was smashed, not to mention a forest had sprouted up in the middle of the room. We'd made all our hideouts soundproof, so even James' hearing wouldn't have registered the disturbance unless he was listening for something, which he wouldn't have been if he thought he had his target safely tucked away. The bed seemed to be where they'd been keeping Alison, but it was now covered in dead branches and crumbled leaves, which upset James so much he crushed a branch between his fingers.

"I found something." Gabriel locked eyes with me from the staircase, shaking his head when Tristan tried, and failed, to ask if it was Alison. "She was about a mile that way, not far from the old mill," he explained, guiding us to the woman who controlled the trees, the one James was so worried about. There was a deep gash in her forehead, so Ben was trying to make sure she was okay without getting too close.

"Vanessa!" James said when he saw her. "What happened?" he asked, cradling her as she woke up. Caleb and Gabriel both looked over to me, to see if I was okay, but I dismissed them to focus on the woman.

"Mick didn't think you were going to honor the contract, and he wanted his money. He said his fight wasn't with me, it was just business."

"That doesn't look like business," Gabriel argued, unaware of her crimes, only that he'd found her injured and alone. I hadn't noticed him leaving, but he had the cabin's first aid kit in his hands as he knelt beside them. "It's okay, I'm a doctor," he assured her, but it was James who needed to be convinced. They had a staring contest with lots of head tilts before James finally stood up and let Gabriel take care of the woman's head.

"Darius felt I chose my side," Vanessa explained with a sigh.

"Where did they take her?" Tristan went up to James, using his full height, which was basically the same as James', but Tristan had his youthful disregard for the reality of the situation, and was one wrong answer away from shoving James into the wall. It would have been comical if I couldn't see how badly he meant it.

"What will they do with her?" I asked the more important question. Finding her wouldn't be an issue for James, but if the orders had changed, we wouldn't like what we found.

"Whoever gets her is supposed to bring her back to the Damned headquarters in Boston so they can run tests and confirm it's her. It wouldn't be hard to find a car with the collection at the edge of the estate, but they would have to get past every other person here who wants her."

James didn't say it out loud, but his look told me that was the actual concern. Not that Mick or Darius would hurt her, but that we would lose her in the crossfire.

"What kind of reward do you have to offer to make people kill and kidnap for you?" Brandon asked, his youth showing more than he realized, as James locked eyes with me once more.

"First dibs on ending it all," he shared.

"That's it?"

"And a few million dollars, but I doubt anyone here is motivated by that, especially not when a single painting or jewel from the mansion could get you five times that. It's just to cover expenses."

He was right. Rosehill was worth more than even I could imagine. Most of my keepsakes were considered lost or missing, which would fetch them ridiculous amounts at auctions, or even with museums. Everything I loaned out was priceless. I just kept it with me for sentimentality. If I had ever suspected that the mercenaries would leave for any amount of money, I would have given it to them. I was hoping, no matter how unlikely, that Darius and Mick were in this for the money, and were – as we speak – issuing a demand to Rosehill for an exorbitant amount in exchange for Alison. I would gladly pay it, but I feared it wasn't coming.

"I told him you never break a promise. That your word is your contract. But he thinks you never promised to bring her in, only that you would find her."

"And we did," James agreed.

"You had no intention of bringing the girl to the woman who hired us?" She looked shocked, and betrayed, like she'd never, in her wildest dreams, even suspected that the guys were right about his honor.

"No." At least he was honest. "I was going to make sure they never got her, whether that meant protecting her from the others Miss Cao hired, or killing her with my bare hands."

His confession shocked Lucy, as he avoided my gaze, but the other faces showed nothing but hatred and anger.

"And the rest of us?" Vanessa asked.

"Were you following me for the cure?"

"No, I obviously didn't want it, but…"

"I'm sorry I didn't tell you, but this was never a democracy," he told her before walking off into the woods, towards the old mill where Gabriel had found her.

"Where are they?" Potts asked when James perked up and took a sharp turn to the right.

Though I don't think he liked it, James knew we would all be following him, and did his best to ignore us, although he looked back a few times to make sure that Vanessa, who Gabriel had helped to her feet, was okay.

"Jackie said she saw trees. She couldn't tell which part of the forest, but Allie was alone," Tristan told me in a whisper, a cell phone pressed to his ear. He didn't understand that when James was tracking, he could hear the ants crawling miles away. Tristan, and nearly everyone who'd come from Rosehill, kept giving me looks like this was our chance to go find her on our own, since James clearly didn't have her, but Jackie's eyes and even Lucy's tracking magic were nothing compared to James' enhanced senses.

"They're near the bluffs," James said, getting that determined look on his face before picking up the pace.

WE HADN'T EVEN BEEN WALKING for ten minutes before the woman, Vanessa, made her way to the front, so she could talk to James in what she probably hoped was a private conversation, but I wasn't the only one listening intently to every word they exchanged about the guys who did that to her and what he was going to do when they found them. I found out that the one who'd tortured Ben was Mick, who she suspected just wanted to be near people without hurting them, a plea I knew well, and the other, with the scales, was Darius, who hadn't said much, but had come alive at the prospect of a fight. Being against him had scared her.

James apologized to her, probably for not being there when she got hurt, but he was much better at speaking under his breath, so I couldn't make out his words clearly.

"We follow you because you have a code. Because as far as all the other crews go, you don't leave people behind, you care about us, you don't double-cross, and you always keep your promises. I'll always follow you," Vanessa whispered, her face pressed with a sadness and loneliness I knew too well, and saw all too frequently when I caught Ben watching me from across the room, before he turned away and pretended he wasn't, so I wouldn't feel uncomfortable.

"I never promised to give her to them. She needed to die, but no one deserves what they want to do to her." James was either oblivious to her feelings, or pretending to be.

CHAPTER THIRTY-SIX

ALISON

I didn't slow down until my lungs were burning and I couldn't hear anything over the sound of my breathing. There'd been shouts and explosions a while back, but I kept going.

I rested my back against a tree and tried to catch my breath while taking in my surroundings, but I recognized nothing. There were a lot of trees, but nothing to tell me whether I'd been running towards Rosehill, or away from it.

I slowly heard the sounds of the forest; birds chirping and squirrels scurrying. I convinced myself the animals would be spooked if an army was marching close by, so I headed off again, this time at a fast-paced walk, but slow enough that I might hear if someone was following. Well, probably not if James was hunting me, but definitely if a group of people was running after me, which was what I was currently avoiding.

I had no clue how long it had been since I'd left the cabin, when I saw red plants in the distance. I'd only seen them arranged in the wild like that once before, on the path that led to Sakina's from Rosehill. Which meant that if I followed it, I would either end up back with Tristan, or at least with some kind of shelter. Which would probably be occupied, but there had to be some kind of alarm I could sound from there.

I shook my head and reminded myself that I left Rosehill to keep the people I cared about safe, not so that Tristan's family could rush into a trap to rescue me again. I would figure something out once I got there, but shelter couldn't hurt, and they had mentioned escape tunnels. Maybe I wouldn't go inside. I would just wander around until I found something that looked like it might be a door. Or I would die out here, but at least my blood couldn't be used as a weapon if I was dead.

That thought offered very little comfort, but I held on to it as I followed the path lined with red plants. I wish I'd asked what they were for, because there had to be a reason rows of red flowers grew in the middle of the woods, but I wasn't about to look into it now. Especially not with a mob after me, and the woods filled with mercenaries who would be thrilled to stumble upon me.

I saw the Patels' house in the distance, looking nothing like it had when I'd visited with Delia. Half the windows were smashed, and the door was off its hinges. There was a collection of furniture off to the side with a group of people sitting in them, gathered around a campfire, while I could make out loud voices and laughter coming from inside the house.

My eyes followed the path of red plants to see if there was a way I could meet up with it past these degenerates, but before I could even formulate a plan, searing pain spread through my body. It was like my bones were on fire and my flesh was trying to get as far away from them as possible, which was agony.

"There you are, puppet."

I wasn't even surprised to find Mick leering down at me. He was probably out of my reach, but I couldn't lift my finger, even if he'd been closer. I tried to speak, but Darius came and hit me over the head with something hard. Then everything went dark.

CHAPTER THIRTY-SEVEN

DELIA

It had been so long since I'd watched James work that I almost forgot how exciting it was. And beautiful, if there wasn't something dead at the end of it. He wasn't as animalistic as my saying he could smell her implied. It wasn't like he sniffed the air, howled, and ran after her, but his nose was more sensitive. He would touch a fallen leaf and rub the mud between his fingers, examine the bark on a tree, or just look up at the sky and get some clue where we should be going. Jackie was helping as much as she could over the phone, but even I found most of the trees looked the same, and Jackie had the least experience in these woods out of all of us. Back when James would do this for fun, or to help people, not just for a payday, he would take me along with him sometimes, and I would ask him so many questions until he just narrated everything for me, explaining which bark meant what, how moisture in the air meant rain, or fires smell different when they're dying versus when they're new. I used to find it all so fascinating, but today I just wished we were moving faster.

Vanessa watched James with the same awe and amazement I

used to. While it had been clear since the night of Alison's arrival that she was in love with James, watching them together now told me it was unrequited. The way I sometimes caught her looking at me was as if she finally understood the reason he didn't return her affections. Not that I meant to rob her of her happily ever after, but I'd always believed in soul mates. My parents came from opposing families, and you would have assumed they were just together to form an alliance and have children, to continue the royal bloodlines, but that couldn't have been further from the truth. My father was one of the rare kings who never took a mistress during their marriage, and when my mother died, his advisors spent years trying to convince him to remarry, but he staunchly refused. I'd always wanted a love like that, and I knew, the moment James first kissed me, that I'd found it.

AFTER A FEW MINUTES, James put a hand out to warn us to stay back, then continued around the cliff as if he actually expected us not to follow.

"Gentlemen." There was a warning in James' voice when he came upon the rest of his crew, but the smile at the corner of Darius' mouth told me he had no idea what was coming for him.

"I never thought I would see the day that James Van Bergen went soft, but I'm not putting my faith in a man who betrays the Damned and lets a woman talk him out of doing what's right."

While Darius got his scaly arm ready, Mick spoke as if he could still persuade James to go along with their original plan. I could see his hand trembling, but he stood his ground.

"This isn't what's right, Mick. Even if Miss Delilah had nothing to do with it, we couldn't give her to Miss Cao. Their plan was to do tests on her and keep drawing her blood until they found a cure for Giftedness," Potts spoke up because James looked like diplomacy left the table the second they attacked Vanessa and betrayed the team. 'Honor above all else,' used to be a part of the Knight's creed, words James held on to even after he branched off.

"You say that like it's a bad thing. Or have you forgotten what happens when you can't control your anger in time?"

Potts winced, and I painfully remembered a baby deer in a pool of blood while a teenage boy cried that he didn't mean to. We'd spent hours walking these woods together so he could calm down, because he never got so upset as when he hurt people, which just triggered more attacks.

"It is when a small group of people control this cure and decide who gets to, or rather has to, take it." James kept his voice even, but his hand was on the pommel of his sword, waiting to use it.

"I see no problem with that."

In other circumstances, the pain behind Mick's anger would have made me at least try to convince everyone to lay down their weapons so we could talk this through, so I could try to show this Mick person that Rosehill was a place where we trained Gifted, so he wouldn't have to hurt people anymore.

"That's because you think bringing them Alison puts you with the people who decide," I pointed out, but I was clearly the last person he wanted to hear from. The one who corrupted his fearless leader and all.

"That was the deal. Whoever brings her in gets first dibs once it's done."

"First dibs means you can use it on yourself and die, not that you can use it on whomever you choose, or whenever you want to," James argued.

"What does it matter who they use it on? None of it will be my problem anymore."

Three things happened in quick succession when he finished speaking. Mick clenched his hand into a fist, causing every muscle in James' body to tense up as the pain coursed through his veins. Thanks to being tortured way too many times without giving anything up, James fought through it and lunged at Mick, slicing into him at a speed I normally attributed to Gabriel. But, more importantly for the rest of us, the clenched fist must have been a warning that told Darius, and at least thirty men and women who appeared out of nowhere, to attack us.

Mick had allied himself to a group that looked terrifying and threatening even before they pulled out their weapons. One of them merely put his hands out to his sides in a sudden motion, but the sparks that erupted, like the ones from a saw on metal, warned me not to let anyone I cared about get anywhere near him.

The guys and Lucy all pushed forward to fend them off, while I found my way back to Lena, Brandon, and Charlie, who'd stayed behind, but were still intending to fight. Not that I could hold them back with these odds. I was needed as well.

"Please?" I asked of them, knowing I could use my Gift and make them run away from me, but I didn't know if they would ever forgive me. And I wanted them to have all their faculties intact, in case the way home was even more dangerous than what was going on out here.

"She's one of us," Lena repeated Charlie's sentiment. It made me unbelievably proud, especially coming from Lena, but this was a rare time when I wished my First Lifers had less love and compassion.

"Your Gifts work from a safe distance," I reminded them, knowing that most of the people attacking us probably had Gifts that worked the same way, but I intended to get in the way of any who tried to hurt them.

· · ·

I WAS deadly with my blades, and I knew it. Normally I would be worried about who I was killing, but faced with men who had kidnapped Alison and could kill the teenagers behind me, I couldn't think of them as people, only as enemies needing to be defeated.

One of them kept regenerating so fast that I couldn't be sure if that was his Gift, or if he had died so many times that it only took seconds for him to come back to life. I sliced his head off with a wince, hoping the kids hadn't seen, and that it might give me a few extra minutes to focus on someone else.

Lena kicked the dismembered head across the forest floor so the man would either have to grow a new one, or wait for a friend to come and reattach it for him. She nodded as if she was assessing my state, which just reminded me that in less than two decades, she'd seen things I wouldn't wish on my worst enemy.

As we got closer to the body-shaped tarp bundle the mercenaries were protecting, that I feared held Alison, the soldiers were more experienced and harder to fight, such as Darius, whose skin couldn't be pierced, but turned into a blade the second you got close to it.

James rushed in and distracted him, attempting to land a blow between the scales that knitted themselves closer together at will, so I could focus on the three men guarding the bundle. I pegged them as the other group's leader and his two best soldiers, since they fought like men who'd been extensively battle-trained, but neither of them exhibited any Gifts. I knew some mercenaries in the woods were humans trying to rid the world of Gifted, but these three kept flicking their wrists and pushing their palms towards us, then panicking when nothing happened. Wherever Alison was now, she'd recently touched these people.

One of them had clearly relied heavily on their Gift in previous fights, so he set off at full speed as soon as he realized he'd lost it, but the other two had been trained, probably on the streets, since their style was messy, with a lot of cheap shots that were questionable at best. Lena froze the one who was running away and tried to come help, but I fended off the other two until Tristan arrived and electrocuted one so I could dispatch the other.

Brandon opened the bundle with his Gift, so we could stand at the ready in case it was a well thought out trap, but Tristan rushed forward and took her in his arms as soon as we saw it was Alison.

"There's a—"

Whatever the device was that Alison broke away from the kiss to warn Tristan about, the point became moot when he fried it with his Gift.

The second we saw the blue light from Tristan's finger, Lena, Brandon, and I braced ourselves.

"Tristan," I called for him to step back to us. I wouldn't have been suspicious if I hadn't known there was a woman here who could change her appearance, who'd used her Gift to lure Alison out of Rosehill in the first place.

"It's her," Tristan said with conviction, looking into her eyes as he took a step back, keeping his hands protectively on the sleeves of her jacket so we couldn't do anything. I hated myself for thinking it, but at least I knew his Gift would work through her clothes if she tried anything.

I wanted to believe in his certainty, more than anything, but Alison had been nowhere remotely close to achieving that level of control at our last lesson.

"What do you see?" Lena asked, throwing her what looked like a bullet.

"Fear," Alison answered, barely grazing it. "A young girl holding on to a big gun, knowing she absolutely has to do something, but that there's no way in hell she can go through with it. Even if the price for disobeying is death."

"Welcome back." Lena stepped forward and let Alison toss the bullet back to her before Tristan took his girlfriend in his arms again. He was careful not to touch her skin, because now was not the time to take chances, but he looked like he would never let her go.

CHAPTER THIRTY-EIGHT

ALISON

We were surrounded by mercenaries, but Vanessa, James, and his second-in-command seemed to be on our side. Not that anyone was overly friendly with them, but they were facing the other mercenaries, braced for battle. I had no clue where we were, no idea which direction Rosehill was in, but it didn't really matter with their 360° coverage. Even the dead bodies were a threat, with five of them waking up to circle us.

"Take her away from here. I'll find you," James told Delia with a nod in my direction. I could still feel his anger towards me, but he didn't seem to want me dead anymore.

"Not so fast," Mick argued, though he'd been one of the dead bodies when I got out of the tarp. "Like I told Vanessa, my fight isn't with you. You're free to leave, but the girl is ours."

"We're not leaving without her," James warned, but Tristan and Delia had also stepped forward, probably to make the same claim.

It took everything in me not to reach forward for Tristan's hand, but I had no idea how I'd managed not to steal his Gift when he'd found me, and I couldn't risk it.

"Your army is made up of weaklings and children. And you're tired from fighting your way through us. What makes you think you'll even make it out?" Mick was spreading his fingers like he was just itching to use his Gift, which left a cold sweat down my back at the memory of the pain it brought.

"Because I trained the two of you, and I know exactly what you're capable of." James' words seemed to wound Mick, but Darius was smiling.

"We won't be that hard to cut down," he agreed. "But I wonder how many of the children we can take down with us?"

I looked around at Lena, Brandon, and Charlie, who were all ready to fight and die for me, just like Tristan and Gabriel and Delia and all these people who didn't deserve this. I ignored Delia's death stare and tried to step forward, to give them what they wanted. After all, I'd tried to give myself up for my sister, might as well do it for all of Tristan's family, but it was like invisible hands were wrapped around my shoulders, holding me back. I looked around to figure out who was responsible, and found Charlie and Brandon, who both shook their heads, furrowing their brows like there would be hell to pay if I did something that stupid.

"What do you want?" Delia asked, standing between us and Darius, her arms out to hold us back.

"The girl. James might enjoy making an enemy of the most powerful organization I've ever seen, but I would like to enjoy the next few centuries without spending them in a torture chamber."

The longer we spoke, the more time the dead ones had to regenerate, and the more attention we were drawing. So far, I saw one person watching from behind a tree, waiting to see who would win before running back for reinforcements, but it wouldn't be long until all of them came for us, and I couldn't imagine we would be able to face that.

"That's the one thing I can't let you have." Delia shook her head with a look to Lucy, who nodded before making a force field around us First Lifers.

Lena and the boys were pissed, since the force field worked both ways, but I was too busy trying to make sure I didn't accidentally touch anyone.

There were only about twice as many mercenaries as there were Rosehillians fighting, which almost seemed manageable with the determination and confidence our side was carrying. Lucy shot blasts of energy with one hand while keeping her force field around us with the other, which allowed everyone else to focus entirely on their own battles.

Gabriel rarely stood still long enough for me to see him, but the man he was fighting seemed to grow as many limbs as he wanted, and was now at eight arms fighting a nearly invisible enemy.

James threw his knife into the skull of a beast heading straight for Ben, who was preoccupied by Mick's agonizing torture. Throwing a second knife into Mick left him vulnerable to a blow in his own battle, but he quickly recovered with renewed anger. I wasn't even sure he saw the reluctant nod Ben gave to express his gratitude.

Darius was cutting through Vanessa's wall of trees just as quickly as she was putting it up. She managed to keep him at bay from everyone else, but he was furious, and I was glad the foliage was bearing the brunt of it.

Delia wielded daggers like a ninja assassin, retrieving them from the folds of her dress, her boot...it seemed like they were everywhere. Her fury was clear when one of them came up behind her and drew blood, but it wasn't as powerful at James' second in command's. As soon as he saw the man wound Delia, Potts clenched his fists; the man brought his hands to his temples, and then his head literally exploded. Delia had looked away when she realized what was coming, and I wish I had too.

Potts looked remorseful – and he had done it to protect Delia – but he was deadly.

So was Caleb. He mostly used his Gift on the trees, ripping them out of the ground to use as weapons, but I'd also seen him pick up an opponent and throw them into the woods. They hadn't returned.

It was incredible to watch.

They'd thinned them down to five mercenaries by the time someone shot a ball of energy straight at Lucy's stomach. I screamed to warn her and reached out to catch her, knowing it was useless and the force field would stop me, but she brought her hands down just in time to stop the ball from ripping through her, and the force field protecting us disappeared. Lena took advantage of the moment to shoot icicle daggers at the mercenaries, and I'm sure the boys were busy as well, but someone retaliated with red beams that looked uncomfortably like lasers, and even though I ducked and warned the others, it was still going to hit someone.

Lena turned, probably to freeze the laser beams, but before we could find out if that would work, however unlikely, a wooden shield sprung up around us from what I immediately recognized as one of Vanessa's bracelets.

Lucy brought her force field back around us as the wooden shield fell.

I turned to thank Vanessa, but she was on the ground, with Darius' spike arms buried in her chest, precariously close to her heart.

CHAPTER THIRTY-NINE

DELIA

"Vanessa!" James screamed, rushing forward and finishing Darius off before anyone else had the chance to react.

Gabriel, Caleb, and Ben took care of the remaining three while James sunk to the ground, clutching Vanessa in his arms. Once the threat was gone, Lucy dropped her force field, and Lena encased Mick and Darius' lifeless bodies in ice so they wouldn't be able to regenerate and come after us, at least not until the ice melted. Which should give us more than enough time to get back inside Rosehill.

"You shouldn't have done that," James said, brushing the hair from Vanessa's face with a tenderness that made my heart ache, though I hope I hid it well.

"They're safe now," Vanessa assured him. Each word was painful for her, like she was at the end of a marathon and even moving her lips was too much effort.

"We can bring her back to Rosehill." I offered, not wanting to intrude, but I could tell from Ben's uneasiness, and the way James' ears perked up, that more mercenaries were coming our way, and we had to get out of here, fast. I wasn't naïve enough to let this woman walk through the doors, to where Krishna and

Penny were hiding, but she'd given her life for my kids, and we had a healer who could easily come to the edge to help her.

"Don't let me slow you down," she argued. "Once I'm gone, I'm gone. And I am more than ready to go."

"She's in her Last Life," James explained with so much pain and sorrow in his voice.

"We had a good run," she told him, trying to smile, but it turned into a wince. "And you get to be with your Delilah now."

"Vanessa," he argued. I think he wanted to tell her he loved her, so I stepped away, but James wasn't the type to lie so you could feel better, even at the end. And although I could see, without a doubt, that he loved her, he wasn't in love with her like she was with him.

"I'll say hi to everyone for you." She tried to bring her hand up to his face, but it fell before reaching him. He caught it and brought it to his cheek, holding it there even though she was gone.

He took a deep breath that disguised a sob, then stood up. "Can you send Persephone back for her? Once everyone is safe?"

"Of course," I assured him.

"Then let's go." He walked off without looking back, but I could see the heartbreak in his eyes as we followed.

CHAPTER FORTY

ALISON

Once we got away from the mercenaries who'd kidnapped me and rolled me up in a tarp, I could see a road with abandoned cars in the distance, but my excitement was tempered by what sounded like hundreds of people stampeding towards us.

"You can leave with her while we hold the others off. If they know you're gone, they might leave Rosehill alone," James suggested with a pleading look to Delia.

"What happens to all the barriers if you leave?" I asked. Jackie had mentioned that every time Delia went away, she called in extra protection to compensate for weakening the barriers.

"They should hold," Lucy answered when Delia didn't, but it was a guess, not a certainty.

"They're stronger when I'm within range, controlling who gets in or not. But at their core, they shouldn't let any harm come to the residents within."

I could tell she was trying to reassure me, because the safest thing for me would be to get as far away from these people as possible, but the safest thing for the people inside was for

Delia to get back to them. And she needed all the help she could get.

"If we leave and they don't know where I went, they'll just go after my parents and my sister. Especially if they realize..." I stopped, not sure who in the vicinity might have James' super hearing, but I locked eyes with Delia and knew she understood.

"Even if we defeat these people, she'll just send more," James warned me that fighting our way back to Rosehill wasn't even close to the end of it.

"She'll keep sending more, and people will keep coming after everyone I care about, but I don't want people to keep getting hurt protecting me."

James looked at me like he wasn't sure how fighting them now prevented that from continuing, but I think I got points for not running away. Although I couldn't tell you when I started caring what James thought of me.

"Let's go out and meet them then, shall we?" Lucy suggested, rubbing her hands together as everyone prepared to fight.

I FOLLOWED them into the woods, staying close to Tristan, but careful not to touch him. I was incredibly proud that I managed to be in his arms without draining him of his Gift, but I wasn't willing to put it to the test while we were away from the protective barriers and about to face a bunch of mercenaries set on taking me. This summer was the first time I regretted giving up after one karate lesson, but at least I could take out anyone who tried to grab me. I trusted myself enough to remove their Gifts, but if I had to, I could also knock them out. I just wasn't sure how far I could go with that before the person never woke up.

I even felt confident about our chances. We were outnumbered, but they were spread out around Rosehill's estate, sandwiched between us and a stone wall most of them couldn't cross. If I based myself on the loud noises coming from the mansion, paired with Tristan's smile, the ones who'd stayed behind were giving the mercenaries there a run for their money as well.

Delia never mentioned martial arts classes on the curriculum, but she and Lena fought like they were trained assassins. I could barely see where they were going before their opponents fell to the ground and they moved on to their next victims.

Brandon and Charlie stayed back so they wouldn't be attacked while they concentrated on taking out groups of mercenaries, working together to drop boulders or make trees fall on anyone who got too close to the rest of us. I'd never seen them so focused.

It was like pulling teeth for Tristan to use his Gift against the nameless enemies, as if he'd much prefer if they attacked him first, but he looked at me and sighed before delivering each fatal charge.

"It's a bit much, isn't it?" Lucy asked me, creating some kind of glowing orb between her palms. "I was in awe the first time I saw them fighting, and I can't say it's any less impressive now."

She threw her orb, knocking a dozen assailants into the air before they each landed with a thud, all the while trying to comfort me.

"It's unexpected," I agreed, holding my hands up in fists as if that would dissuade anyone from coming after me.

"I don't know why they all love their medieval weapons. Even the newer Gifted, but it's all about honor and proving themselves." She rolled her eyes, shook her head, and sighed, with a worried glance at her fiancé.

"But you said you're not…"

"Gifted? No, just your average witch doctor. I was you a few years ago, though." She concentrated on her energy balls and threw them with an exact precision, bypassing everyone on our side and knocking out loads of mercenaries. Then she reinstated the energy shield thing, all the while carrying on a conversation like we were two ladies having brunch.

"I find that very hard to believe," I argued.

We were pushing forward, closer to Rosehill, so I took the opportunity to pick up a weird ax thing someone had abandoned when Lucy's magic hit them, the lightest weapon I could find. I was so busy thinking about her, and how I couldn't believe this fierce, strong woman in front of me was ever as helpless as I felt, that I wasn't able to stop the flash until I felt the memory of the blade slicing into my chest.

"You have no idea," Lucy said, catching me from behind as if she expected me to pass out.

I wanted to ask more, but I froze when an arrow flew past Lucy's right ear and landed in a tree in front of us. It wasn't the first projectile we'd had to avoid, but none of the others had come from behind us. We both turned back, and I saw what looked like an entire army battalion in military formation, making their presence known while waiting for the signal to attack.

"What is that?" I couldn't imagine the American Government showing up to rescue us, or sanctioning my kidnapping. But stranger things had happened, and it had been a secret branch of the FBI that showed up at the jam factory the last time I was in over my head.

"The New Order." It was James who said it with resignation, but everyone who wasn't a First Lifer had this look, like there was no way we were making it out alive. If we'd been outnumbered before, now we were outnumbered, out weaponed, and completely surrounded, with growing numbers of mercenaries and the New Order between us, Rosehill, and all potential exit routes.

We should have left when we had the chance.

CHAPTER FORTY-ONE

DELIA

"Looks like you were taking too long, brother," Edward called out to James. My breath caught at the sound of his voice; I hadn't heard it in ages, but every time I did, death and destruction followed.

"Is he—" I silenced Alison with a look as we all adjusted our positions, so we surrounded her within the greater circle of unfriendlies. No, he wasn't truly James' brother – not by blood – but they had trained side by side for decades before a group led by Edward murdered James while trying to get to me. He'd created the New Order with a few of their other brothers, and hunted Gifted until the day he died and became one of us. His self-loathing now fueled him just as much as his hatred of Gifted.

"If I knew you were invited, I would have ensured you a better welcome," James said through gritted teeth.

"You didn't think those Damned idiots were the only ones who wanted the Magnum Finis?" Edward smiled, which made him look even more menacing than he had with a scowl, accentuating the burgundy scar that ran the length of his right cheek, into his hairline. It was James' handiwork, from that day he first died, but Edward wore it like a badge of honor. Had it disappeared when he woke up Gifted, he probably would have sliced the cheek open himself.

"Should have known they didn't have the resources to come up with this on their own."

"Now be a good soldier and hand her over."

The men were circling each other, or as much as you could while surrounded by other people, with James making sure that he was always between us and Edward; not that it would make much of a difference once he started using his Gift.

"I'm afraid I can't do that." James held his gaze steady, but I could see his hand at the ready, every muscle in his body tense with anticipation.

"I figured the years would make you slower, but I didn't know they would make you dumb."

"You've never won against me before," James pointed out, referring both to their years of training and every attack Edward had waged since. Edward was unconscious by the time James succumbed to his injuries the first time, and we'd somehow held our own every time he'd come after us since, but barely, and not without casualties.

"There's a first time for everything." Edward shrugged. "Although it wouldn't be a fair fight, would it, attacking you while you're distracted by the dying screams of everyone you love? Good evening, your Royal Highness." He mock-bowed to me, making the incorrect assessment that James knew more than just me out of the bunch, but his words sent chills down my spine, the kind I couldn't shake, that settled in my bones. Because I loved every single person standing beside me.

"Lilah," James whispered to me under his breath. "I can take him. I can do a lot of damage…but I can't stop them all and keep everyone safe."

"I know." There were too many of them. Even if every one of us that could fight took on twenty men, there would still be a hundred that could slip past us and get to the children. The teenage, almost adult children who would never stay back unless I used my Gift to make them.

"We need you."

"I can't," I argued. Edward was Gifted, but most of the people following him wouldn't be. They would be human, or possibly First Lifers, the kind that were prone to overreacting and causing more damage than I'd ever intended.

"I trust you, Lilah, and I don't see any other way to keep them safe."

I looked around, both at the people standing with me and what we were up against. Gabriel nodded encouragingly, as did Tristan and Alison. They either trusted me as well, or didn't care about the consequences.

I weighed my options, but I saw Edward raising his arms and knew I didn't really have any. I made eye contact with Lucy, who nodded, then took a deep breath and looked right into Edward's eyes.

"All members of the Damned and New Order of the Night lay down your weapons and remove yourselves from Rosehill without harming anyone," I called out, with Lucy making sure it reached the very last row of soldiers.

James, Ben, and Gabriel had each moved around me, stopping attacks while I spoke, but by the time I finished, it was no longer necessary.

CHAPTER FORTY-TWO

ALISON

I'd never seen Delia use her Gift, and by the looks of everyone around me, most of them hadn't either. It was instantaneous. One minute they were preparing to attack us, to get her to stop talking, then suddenly, all our opponents abandoned their positions. Their faces showed confusion and fear, mixed in with determination and anger, as they dropped whatever weapons they were holding and turned around, all of them heading towards the main road that led away from Rosehill.

I let out a sigh of relief as the crowd around us thinned out, though the guys didn't take their eyes off James' 'brother'. I looked around at the faces on our side, and was relieved that none of them showed the agony and terror of the New Order. We were all still standing, still in one piece.

I was so focused on making sure everyone was okay, on smiling gratefully to Delia and Tristan, who'd saved me when I thought I was ready to die, that I didn't notice anything was wrong until I saw the flash of silver and felt the blade slice into me.

I let out a painful breath as it went in. My first thought was that this was the most painful memory I'd ever felt, but when I brought my hand to my chest to reassure myself that it was nothing but a memory, it came back bloody. I looked down, and all I saw was red.

CHAPTER FORTY-THREE

DELIA

"Alison!"

Gabriel was off in a blur, snapping the neck of the man who threw the knife before anyone else had the chance to react. The guttural cry Tristan made as he rushed to Alison, and the confused look on Alison's face did me in, but I was prevented from joining them by the fact that at least a dozen from the New Order had stayed behind after pretending to follow my orders. They were armed to the teeth and looked ready to kill each and every one of us who got in their way.

One of them actually snarled as he cocked his head and revealed metal earpieces. I hadn't noticed them before, or maybe I'd thought they were for communicating amongst each other, but it was now clear that the metal covered the entire ear, so they either couldn't hear anything, or more likely filtered out my Gift.

"You didn't actually think that would work, your Highness, did you?" Edward used my title mockingly. "That we would be dumb enough to come here unprepared like those fools?"

Instead of waiting for a reply, Edward lunged for James, while the others did the same, each of them choosing their target carefully. The only ones who were cautious were the ones who went after Brandon and Charlie, whose Gifts wouldn't have been observed by outsiders.

Everyone else was not only prepared for what they encountered and protected by shields specifically designed for our Gifts; it was like they knew our weaknesses. These were the best and brightest the New Order had to offer, and I was out here with a band of misfits, half-consisting of children I couldn't bear to see hurt.

Everyone that remained had the metal contraptions on their ears, which I thought was just for me, but then a woman opened her mouth and screamed. The sound that came out was anything but human. It grated on my eardrums and felt like every cell in my brain was vibrating against each other, so I couldn't do anything but bring my hands to my ears and scream in agony. It didn't even surprise me when I felt blood on my palms.

Tristan was still struggling to reach Alison, using his hands to create enough electricity to keep his opponents at bay, but not for long, as their shields seemed to absorb his Gift – not take it away from him, but they used it to power them.

The screeching stopped as suddenly as it had started and turned into a scream before the woman realized something was wrong. Alison was on the ground at her feet, with her hand firmly planted around the woman's bare ankle. She lashed out and tried to kick Alison away, but she held on with every ounce of strength she had until the woman collapsed beside her.

CHAPTER FORTY-FOUR

ALISON

My eyes were closed by the time Tristan reached me, but I knew it was him. I'd nodded when Delia explained to me what it felt like when I used my Gift on her, but I'd never lost so much blood that it made me pass out, so I hadn't known what she was talking about. Until now.

I struggled to open my eyes, but everything hurt. My lids felt like they were made of lead that required superhuman strength to open, and as much as I wanted to reach out to Tristan and make sure he wasn't a figment of my imagination, there was no way in hell I could lift my arms.

"You're okay, I've got you now."

I tried to reply, but my mouth was so dry, it felt like my lips might crumble if I spoke. I nodded instead, but I doubt my body complied.

"I love you so much Alison, I can't lose you. I need you to wake up, okay? Just wake up," he pleaded.

I wanted to tell him I was trying, that I wasn't really sleeping, my eyes were just so heavy that I couldn't open them, but I knew that even if I was aware of the sound of his voice, and of his arms holding me, I was nowhere near awake. I was dying, and as horrifying as the idea was, as long as it wasn't this freezing wherever I was headed, I would be okay.

My lack of a response only upset Tristan, which I gathered from the sob that wracked his body around mine.

He screamed and there was so much pain in it I thought someone had stabbed him in the heart. It was enough of a jolt that I opened my eyes and saw him screaming to the sky in anguish, with blue lights dancing all around him. On second thought, maybe it was the electricity that gave me the jolt, like a human defibrillator. Which would be great if I wasn't bleeding out.

CHAPTER FORTY-FIVE

DELIA

Tristan's anguished scream sent a blast of energy throughout the forest, leaving electrical pulses that made it feel like the surrounding air was sizzling and warm. The cell phone in my pocket burned my thigh, so I took it out and saw it was fried, which didn't bode well as far as calling for help, but when I looked around, all the New Order were clutching their ears like we had for the banshee scream. Apparently, their earpieces had fried as well.

I didn't know if the damage from their devices made them deaf, but I saw them ripping off their protective gear and took my chance.

"Leave here and never come back. You will never harm Alison, or any Rosehillian, ever again."

I didn't even bother with singling out who the message was intended for – I knew it would find its mark.

I watched as every last New Order member left, clearly against their will, including Edward, who now had a matching cut on his left cheek. I watched until every one of them was gone, not about to let them take us by surprise again. I nodded gratefully to Lucy, who sent some kind of energy after them, hopefully to reinstate the wards and make sure they didn't come back.

"Delia, come help her," Tristan called, the fear in his voice breaking my heart. I was used to being called to scenes because I'd trained extensively as a nurse, but this time it wasn't my medical training he wanted – he would have asked the doctors for that – he wanted a parental figure to fix it and tell him everything would be okay. Which I couldn't. Everyone else huddled close, staring at Alison, frozen, looking to me for an answer as to what they should do.

I knelt beside her and felt her pulse weakening.

"She needs blood," I said, applying pressure to her wound, but it wouldn't be enough.

"Will she make it?" Tristan asked, his voice cracking at the end, so I could hardly make out the last words.

"I don't know." I chose honesty. "We need to get her to Etta as fast as possible."

I looked over to where I had last seen Gabriel, but a blur came around my other side.

"Hey!" Tristan argued when he sensed someone trying to take Alison from him.

"He's the only one fast enough to give her a chance." I put my hand on Tristan's shoulder before he could use his Gift against Gabriel.

Tristan nodded, and Gabriel disappeared with Alison in another blur. I took Tristan in my arms, even though he was much too old for it. He needed the reassurance, and I needed something to focus on other than James and the lifetimes we had to make up for.

"What do we do now?" Lena asked me as Tristan ran after Gabriel back to Rosehill.

"We wait. And we pray she wakes up."

"Etta will save her, right?"

"If Gabriel got her there in time," I agreed. I wanted to take her in my arms and assure her everything would be okay now that the threat was gone, but I wasn't a fan of lying. I had no clue what was going to happen. Even my Gift would only last until their next lives, at which point they could easily circle back with a vengeance.

"Let's go see how she's doing," Lucy said, putting an arm around Lena that I was shocked she didn't shrug off. Ben looked at me like the last thing he wanted to do was leave me alone with James and Potts, but he nudged Charlie and Brandon to follow Lucy, leaving only Brutus behind.

"I should go make sure everyone's gone, then I'll head back to the cabin, and…"

James was in the middle of telling me he would leave, and if I was being logical, that was probably the best idea. He'd terrorized us and led all the mercenaries to Rosehill. He had a lot to make up for, but at the moment, I couldn't care less. I bridged the distance between us and just deflated in his arms. He was caught off guard for a split second before he wrapped his arms around me and held me close, letting me feel whole for the first time in centuries.

"I have to get back to the others," I told him, making no effort to leave the shelter of his arms.

"I know," he agreed. "And I can't come with you."

"Where does that leave us?"

"Same place we've always been." He sighed before taking a step back so he could look into my face. "I have loved you every minute of every day since I first laid eyes on you; I've just never deserved you."

"Does that mean you'll leave?" I was used to being without him, but the thought of having him so close only to lose him again tore my heart to shreds.

"Not until I know you're safe. Which, as long as you're harboring the Protector, you won't be."

"So, you'll live in the woods and spy on us?"

"It's nothing I haven't done before." The corner of his mouth went up in a smile, but it didn't reach his eyes.

"I noticed some renovations in the cabin I had nothing to do with."

"You never did like to go inside."

He brushed my curls behind my ear, then leaned close and kissed my forehead.

"We can talk tomorrow," I decided.

"I'm not going anywhere," he promised.

I nodded, not trusting myself to say more until I'd checked on Penny and Krishna. Until I talked to everyone. Until Alison woke up.

KRISHNA AND PENNY both ran into my arms as soon as I crossed the stone wall, but the remnants of a battle littered the lawn.

"I'm so glad you're both okay," I said, squeezing them both so tight I worried they might break.

"We helped," Penny told me. "Sam and Chris had actual weapons, and Mateo is really good at throwing things, but I made it storm and Krishna knew when people were coming, even if they were hiding. One of them was invisible, like Sam, and she was like, 'Right there!'"

"I couldn't leave with half of my passengers missing, and Jackie can be very persuasive," Sam explained, taking me in for a hug once I released the girls.

"Alison…"

"She'll be okay," Jackie assured me, coming close so I could take her in for a hug. "Etta's with her upstairs."

"Thank you. For everything you did, for staying behind when I know you wanted to come, for always fighting with everything you've got." I tried to hold back the tears, at least for the girls, but I felt like I hadn't breathed properly in years.

"I learned from the best." She winked at me before her eyes wandered, probably to Tristan.

"Is it over?" Krishna asked me as she and Penny each wrapped an arm around one of my legs to walk back to the house.

"For now." I put on my best reassuring smile.

I was beyond grateful that everyone agreed to spend the evening in Tristan's bedroom, eating a bunch of fancy finger foods Chris stress-cooked once the fighting was over. We'd started out in the sitting room, but Tristan wasn't going to leave Alison's side, and we all wanted to make sure she was okay. It was tight, but no one wanted to be alone, not even Mateo, who let me take him in my arms for a full second before he broke free and shook it off, choosing to sit on the desk where he was out of the way, but still in my sights. We were exhausted and there was so much to do and figure out, but for a couple of hours, I had eyes on my people, and could convince myself they were all going to be okay.

CHAPTER FORTY-SIX

ALISON

I woke up in what I recognized as Tristan's bedroom, but it was different. Instead of an office chair in front of the desk, there was a shrink's couch beside the bed, where Tristan was sleeping upright.

I tried to sit up, but I got a stabbing pain in my chest, which made sense, given the bandages covering my stab wound.

"And she's awake. Only took you thirty-six…no, thirty-seven hours."

I recognized Etta's voice, but she sounded exhausted.

"You were there, before I…"

"You held on just long enough for Gabriel to bring you to me. Which is good, because losing his Gift at that speed might have done you in for." Etta smiled, a warm but tired smile, like she had been by my side just as long as Tristan had.

"How much longer until I don't feel like I just got run over by a truck?"

"Well, I don't have to touch you to heal you, but as a reflex, you've reached out and grabbed on to me every time I've tried. The deeper the wound, the more it burns, and your subconscious doesn't like it."

"I'm sorry," I apologized.

"Don't worry about me, I only use my Gift when Caleb does something stupid, or to help others. In this case, I was just doing what I could whenever I got my Gift back, until we decided it would be best to wait until you woke up so you could see I'm not trying to hurt you."

"I'll keep my hands to myself," I promised, gripping the bedsheets to prove my point.

ETTA'S HEALING made me feel warm and fuzzy, so even though I had a million things to figure out, I cuddled up next to Tristan on the couch and was out.

CHAPTER FORTY-SEVEN

DELIA

"This one." Penny cut a white rose to add to the bouquet we were making for Alison.

"And this one." Krishna took a yellow one before turning to me with a look I now understood meant James was coming close. Apparently, we both had to work on being less loud with our emotions, but she didn't mind as much when it wasn't bad ones.

Penny looked at me when they knocked on the greenhouse's door, but Krishna yelled, "Come in!" before I could do anything.

Lucy had strengthened all the wards and enchantments, but it was James' own decision not to cross the stone wall. He and Potts had replaced the gates and were fixing up the Patels' house, but neither would cross the threshold until the people inside trusted them. I wasn't sure how long that would take, but I knew it wouldn't be before Alison was back on her feet, and her opinion would count the strongest.

"Did you find the book?" Potts asked the girls when James and I didn't get past 'Hello.'

"How did you know it would be there?" Penny asked. He'd been teaching them about the secret passageways, which

Krishna found exciting, but Penny had thought she was the expert, with only Chris knowing more than she did.

"I put it there." He shrugged his shoulders. "I told you I grew up here."

The three of them got into an animated discussion about the book and other treasures they might find, while James filled me in on his progress.

"How is Alison doing?" James flexed his hand, then balled it into a fist, which I knew was his way of stopping himself from reaching out to touch me. Penny and Krishna had decided they trusted him now, which worried me a little, given what Penny had seen of him, but we were taking things excruciatingly slow.

"Etta was finally able to heal her this morning, so she should wake up soon."

"That's good." He sighed with genuine relief. I searched his eyes to see if he still wanted her dead, but he almost looked like his old self.

Back to my James.

"Time to go home," I told the girls after a few more stories and lingering looks, with a goodbye smile to Potts.

"Can we come back tomorrow?" Penny asked as we headed to the other end of the greenhouse. Both girls turned back and waved to James and Potts before we headed for the house.

"We'll see," I said like I had every day, but so far, we kept going back.

"Ben!" Penny exclaimed, rushing into his arms when she saw him in the distance. He'd been working a lot on the grounds within the stone wall, repairing the guard post and avoiding me.

When he put the girls down, they immediately focused on Bear and Brutus while he kept his eyes on me.

"Haven't seen you in days." I tried to smile like I was teasing, but I had to clench my teeth together to keep the tears at bay.

Krishna was an excellent actress, because she didn't even look up from the dog she was petting, even though I knew my emotions were screaming at her.

"Wasn't sure you wanted to see me."

"I always want to see you," I said, hating myself because I knew that was probably the last thing he wanted to hear.

I noticed the dogs slowly made their way to the kitchen doors, with the girls following, just out of earshot.

"I'm sorry," I apologized.

"Don't be." Ben gave me a sad smile.

"There are a lot of things that I should have done differently. I depend on you more than I should, and I trust you with all that I am. I should have trusted you with the truth, instead of protecting—"

"My feelings," he finished for me. "My life, his life. Alpha male temper problems."

"Something like that," I agreed because he was smiling like it was water under the bridge, which I knew it couldn't be, but I wanted to believe it.

"I talked to Krishna," he explained. "Even my dogs trust him, which frustrates the hell out of me, but they're excellent judges of character."

"I don't know if we'll survive a bunch of teenagers living with Krishna." I tried to lighten the mood, because that girl listened to way more than she should, on top of all the things she couldn't block out.

"Maybe a little honesty isn't a bad thing."

"Probably not," I agreed.

"I can try not to avoid you so much." He smiled, but it didn't reach his eyes.

"If it's for you, I get it. And I deserve it. You're my best friend, and I miss you, but I know how selfish that is."

"I miss you too," he assured me.

"For what it's worth, if it were you on the other end, I would have defended you just as fiercely."

"I know." He wrapped an arm around my shoulders and placed a kiss on the top of my forehead. He'd never done that before, but it felt…right. And safe. "I know exactly how you feel about me Delia, I've always known. I just didn't know James was still alive."

"I wasn't sure either."

"I'm happy for you. Or at least I will be. Someday. I hope." He smiled, a genuine smile, and I couldn't help but reciprocate.

I heard a large truck engine and looked over to see Mr. Bosworth at the front gate.

I sighed before letting him in.

"I've got it," Ben assured me.

"I think I'll give it a try," I argued, picking up the pace while Ben followed, looking at me like I was crazy.

"Good afternoon, Mr. Bosworth," I called out once he was out of the truck.

"Miss Hill," he greeted.

"If you could please bring everything inside and put it all on the table beside the pantry rather than in the doorway, I would really appreciate it," I told him, a mix of relief and apprehension pooling in my shoulders. I wasn't worried that I'd done it wrong, but it was going to take some getting used to. "The check is on the counter when you're done."

Ben had watched me with his head tilted, looking mighty impressed.

"You just told someone to do something," he pointed out.

"I didn't use my Gift, I just asked nicely," I warned his look.

"I wasn't judging. Just proud of you," he assured me.

"I figured it was about time I stop letting people walk all over me because I'm afraid."

"Long overdue," he agreed.

CHAPTER FORTY-EIGHT

ALISON

"Are we just waiting for them to regroup and come find us?" I asked once Penny, Krishna, and Mateo had gone to bed so the rest of us could hold another family meeting in the sitting room. I hadn't been in any condition to travel, but I did not want to stay here and go through the events of the past few weeks again. I'd FaceTimed my parents, who were jealous of the surprise weekend getaway Tristan took me on, but the truth was that we were all sitting ducks, and I couldn't let anyone else die for me.

"I'll take the children – and anyone under eighteen – with me to the Owens plantation until this clears over," Delia shared, eyeing Lena, Jackie, Brandon, and Charlie, who thought sitting in on the meeting meant they would be a part of whatever came next.

"Even if they think you're dead, they'll still send someone to make sure. Lucky for us, they need to build a new army, because anyone who was here won't be coming back anytime soon." Ben smiled at Delia.

"I'll take you to a safe house. They're specifically designed to protect Gifted, even against other Gifted, and the only people at them are Guardians who are trained like *them*." Tristan nodded to Delia, Caleb, and Lena, who I'm pretty sure blushed.

"I'm not sure they'll be fooled by us all going into hiding. If I was really dead, there would be a funeral; you would show them proof. And I don't want to be dead."

"Of course not," Delia assured me. "Our immediate plans are to get everyone who is vulnerable to safety, but that's not the only plan."

"I want to be a part of whatever the other plan is," I insisted. "As long as they think I have this power, they are going to keep coming after me, and I have no interest in living like that."

"Of course not –"

"I want to fight," I said before she could tell me whatever they were planning. Whether James was going to be a double agent and lead them astray, or Ben was going to kill every one of them, it was only a matter of time before someone else figured it out and tried to use me, either as a weapon or as a cure.

"Exposing yourself doesn't help anyone," Lucy argued, looking at me like she completely understood, but still wasn't on board.

"I don't mean fight the people who come after me. I want to find the magnum fin-thing, get my necklace, and destroy them. That way, my family can be safe, for once and for all."

"Bring the fight to them," Caleb concluded.

"We can do that," Delia agreed.

"Me too," I told her. "I'm not underage, or even one of your kids," I reminded her of her rules. "We know where the necklace is, so we just need to find the artefact." It had called out to me before, so there had to be a way to draw it out again.

"I think I know where it might be," Jackie spoke up. "You said it's a gold blob with jewels in it?"

"It's definitely not here, not even in the stables." Delia looked at her like she was being ridiculous. From what I could tell,

Jackie hadn't left Rosehill since I'd been kidnapped, except to come find me and Tristan in the woods.

"They have it," Jackie admitted, looking guilty. "The people who are after Alison."

We all looked at her with confusion, and although she couldn't see us, she must have felt it as she recoiled and bit her bottom lip.

"I was monitoring the people in the woods, but there was also this girl. I think she's being held captive by the Damned. They have a gold blob on the table in the room they bring her to sometimes."

"Can you hear what's going on as well?" Gabriel asked.

"No, but they have a map on the wall of the area surrounding Rosehill, with rough blueprints and pictures of most of us."

"How can you see her?" I asked. Jackie needed some kind of connection to see through someone's eyes.

"I bumped into her in a park. Before she was taken." I felt Tristan tense beside me.

"Can you go back and describe the room, or the map, anything that might tell us where they are?" Ben asked, like he was ready to put on some tactical gear and storm the building.

"Most of the time I see her, she's in a cell. Well, it's a room, but the door's locked and she can't get out, but it's like a normal bedroom without a window."

"We can work on figuring that out while I get my necklace," I said, as if that settled things.

"We," Tristan corrected me.

"A much larger we," Caleb agreed.

"You're one of us now."

Coming from Lena, I thought I'd imagined it, but she nodded when I looked over. Delia probably wouldn't let her come, but looking around the room…it felt good to be among family.

EPILOGUE

"**Y**ou failed."

Each word oozed disgust and frustration as Monica rubbed her fingers together. Whatever Gift she was hoping to channel, nothing happened, so she dropped her hand to her side and went to confront the man, standing barely an inch from his face.

"Well, not exactly," Jebediah argued.

"Are you hiding a teenage girl in that backpack?"

"Not yet," he relented, as upset with himself as she was. "But I have her blood."

"How much of it?" She perked up.

"Enough to get you started." He pulled out a series of vials. "She was injured, and they just left it behind," he shared, not explaining that he'd bribed one of the Gifted mercenaries to aspirate her blood from the soil.

"Looks like you get to live another day." Monica sighed. Death was a better motivator when you didn't wake up afterwards, but she'd heard it could still be particularly painful. "But if you don't have her with you by the time these run out, you'll wish you could die."

"Understood." He swallowed, eyeing the exit like he wasn't sure if he trusted her not to do something as soon as he had his back turned, but also trying to decide if he had the balls to ask for at least part of the reward.

"Your men are returning." Howard came in and announced.

"Without the girl?"

"She compelled us to leave." A soldier stormed through the door. "My body acted of its own volition; I had no control."

"That would be Delilah," Jebediah shared. "She runs the school."

"Why didn't you go back?" Monica could see terror behind the anger in his eyes. She knew better than most what it felt like to have your body under someone else's control; she just hid it a lot better.

"We can't. Everyone who was there can no longer return or harm them."

"For how long?"

"Forever, I think."

"Your Gift is fire, yes?" Monica turned to Jebediah.

"Yes, ma'am," he hesitantly agreed.

"Kill him. See if that changes anything."

"What?" the soldier asked as Monica left the room and sealed it to contain the flames. "No!" he yelled, screaming her name, but Monica kept walking until the sound faded away.

❧

Find out what happens next in
Third Eye

ACKNOWLEDGMENTS

This book was possibly my hardest one yet. I so loved the characters and the world I was building that I was paralyzed by the fear that I could never measure up to the vision of it I had in my head. Not to mention a nasty bout with COVID.

Thankfully, I have the most incredible family who love and support me more than I could ever deserve. Rikki, Paul, mommy, and daddy...words could never express how grateful I am, not just for the help you give to my career, but that I get to have you in my life. I am eternally in your debt and I love you all tremendously.

A huge thank you as well to everyone who reads my books. It is an honour to share these stories with you, and I am so glad you enjoy them <3

ABOUT THE AUTHOR

Amanda Lynn Petrin is the YA author of *The Giftedverse,* which comprises *The Owens Chronicles* and *The Gifted Chronicles.* She studied History and Psychology at McGill University so she could write compelling heroines going on magical adventures in the past, and hopes to turn these para-normal books into movies she can act in. She currently lives in Montreal, where she enjoys spending time with her family and living vicariously through the characters in her urban fantasy series.

Find her at: www.amandalynnpetrin.com

GIFTEDVERSE
AMANDA LYNN PETRIN
THIRD EYE
THE GIFTED CHRONICLES
BOOK 3

THIRD EYE EXCERPT

JACKIE

I woke up and immediately knew I'd overslept by the brightness of the room. Not that I had a specific time or reason to be up, but you had a better chance of running into everyone at breakfast if you were there around eight.

I focused on Tristan, to see if he was already in the kitchen, but instead intruded on a tender moment of him brushing Alison's hair off her face so he could watch her sleep. I quickly shook myself out of there, my heart racing as I waited for him to yell at me from across the hall. I wasn't sure if it was romantic or creepy that my surrogate brother was watching his girlfriend sleep, but it was definitely disturbing for me to join in.

Without thinking, I focused on the girl from the park, something I'd been doing a lot lately. It started by accident, and I should have stopped, because I never asked her if it was okay, but I got the feeling she didn't mind. Or at least she didn't used to. I felt guiltier doing it now that I was technically spying on her, but it was more on the people holding her captive. And if it helped us free her and keep Alison's family safe, then she wouldn't be able to blame me for it. Right?

At first, I thought she was still sleeping, because I couldn't see anything, but when I looked closer, I could make out her hand on the pillow in front of her, and some furniture in the distance, but she was still in the dark. It looked like a different room than she was usually in, but I'd have to wait for her to turn on the lights to make sure. Her hand moved to pull the covers up over her head, drowning out any clues I might have found, so I let her go and went to get ready.

"I think we're all worried you'll leave us and try to go off on your own again." I heard Tristan on my way to the stairs.

"Although most people would appreciate me bringing the danger away from everyone, I'd rather not see what happens if they send James after me again. And the order isn't important as long as we find everything and make it so no one ever tries to hurt my family again."

"What's going on?" I asked, joining their conversation.

"Delia wanted to make sure Allie was okay with us staying a couple more days for James to look into something. A tip about the Magnum Finis, or a Damned compound…she didn't give me details, but—"

"She was worried Alison would go to her parents on her own." I understood.

"Once. I went off on my own once, and—"

"And no, you will never live it down." He stopped Alison's attempt at defending herself.

It sounded like he leaned in to kiss her, which was nice since it implied he'd forgiven her for leaving in the middle of a lockdown without telling anyone so she could give herself up to the very people we were trying to protect her from. Although I guess nearly dying from it should give her a blank slate.

I was about to walk off and leave them to it when a cell phone rang.

"It's Sybill. I promised I'd send her some pictures to show my parents...I'll be right back," Alison said before rushing back to Tristan's bedroom to talk to her sister. Mr. and Mrs. Carmichael were blissfully unaware that their daughter's life was in danger, so her sister –who knew everything – was helping her keep up the charade of being on a romantic getaway with her new boyfriend.

"Sorry about this morning," I blurted out once Alison was gone.

"You never have to apologize to me, Jack. I know how to keep you out if there's anything I don't want you to see," Tristan assured me.

"What about Alison?"

"She knows I'm your eyes."

He meant it to be reassuring, but knowing something and being okay with it weren't always the same thing.

I held onto the railing down the stairs, focusing once more on the Damned Prisoner. She was still on the bed in her windowless room, rocking back and forth while gnawing on her fingernails by the looks of it.

I'd never felt what it feels like when I use my Gift on some-one, though Tristan says it kind of just feels like you're opening your eyes underwater. In the ocean or a really chlorinated pool at first, but then you get used to it. Knowing that, I would expect her to react negatively to my presence, but I willed all the warmth and care into my Gift as I could, wishing it could feel more like a comforting hug than an assault on her eyeballs. Whether or not my intentions worked, she must have gotten used to the sting, because she eventually ran her fingers through her hair and stopped rocking. She went onto her side, with her legs pulled up to her chest in the fetal position, and let her eyes go blurry. Which could mean tears, or that she was staring into space without blinking. Either way, it wasn't a good sign.

"We'll find you, I promise," I said, knowing both that she couldn't hear me, and that I had little power in making it true.

. . .

"GOOD MORNING, JACKIE!" Penny and Krishna called out as soon as I walked into the kitchen, to let me know they were there, but the voices were so loud and varied that I just assumed everyone was. It felt nothing like the other summers since I'd moved to Rosehill, where the majority of the students went home and left us with a shadow crew of orphans.

"Morning Penny Bug, Krish." I made my way over to the table, following their voices, and helped myself to a bite of Penny's cinnamon-flavored Eggo. I'd learnt the hard way that while Penny liked them boring and dry, Krishna smothered hers in butter and syrup, which made for a sticky mess if you weren't expecting it. I tried to listen for Delia's voice, so I could ask her what James found, but it didn't sound like she was in the kitchen.

"Delia's outside." Krishna answered without waiting for me to ask.

"With which one?" I asked of Ben and James, the two men vying for Delia's affections, though Ben would deny it. I could look and see for myself, but while Tristan and Delia had always been my go-tos who never minded me using their eyes as my own, I was starting to feel like there were some things I wasn't meant to see, even if neither had the heart to tell me not to.

"Both," Penny answered with her mouth full.

"So I should probably wait a bit?" I directed the question to Krishna, who didn't have to be there to read the room. Just like she could hear my thoughts, she could also feel their emotions.

"Or she might appreciate the diversion," Chris suggested, putting a plate in front of me that smelled like a cinnamon bun, fresh out of the oven.

"I'm going to miss these," I told him, putting my hand over the one he placed it on my shoulder.

"I'm extending my trip for as long as I'm needed...but you

don't plan to join us at the Plantation," he understood. While the adults were planning on scouring the earth for the Magnum Finis, Sam was leaving today — in an invisible van — to bring the kids to a safe house protected by a couple of Gifted and a witch.

"For once I might actually be able to help." I shrugged like it was no big deal, then headed outside, where the voices were fewer, but nearly as loud.

We'd held a vote where we unanimously decided that James and Potts could come into Rosehill, but some of us were more reluctant than others, which they seemed aware of, so they stayed in the Patel house. Or the hunting cabin. I never checked, but I knew they hadn't come inside yet. It was considerate of them, especially since I definitely wouldn't want to find myself alone in a hallway with either of them, but I think Ben would have an easier time hating them if they'd just invaded our space and been insufferable. Instead, they kept the animosity buried and used clipped politeness with each other.

"I'm not saying I don't think you're capable, I just think—" Ben said carefully.

"That it would be better to have you there to make sure I can take care of myself?" Delia finished for him.

"It isn't just you, Del, he literally came here for Alison, and you told her she could come along..."

I waited until I was close enough to use Delia's eyes, more to let her know I was coming than because I needed their help to cover the last twenty feet, but I nearly jumped up and dropped the plate of baked goods when I saw that James was looking at me. Probably the reason why he was so quiet.

"Is everything okay?" Delia asked me, giving Ben a look like they would continue the conversation later, before coming over.

"Fresh out of the oven." I motioned to the plate as if that was why I was out here.

"We use the same recipe but mine never turn out half as

good." I could hear the smile in her words, but also the stress. She had the world on her shoulders, or at least my world, and none of us were making any of it easier on her. It almost made me want to leave it at that and forget about why I really came out. But I couldn't.

"Tristan said James thinks he found something?"

"We're looking for the facility you saw, James just has a hunch he wants to look into. An old Knight outpost that was abandoned centuries ago, but might have had some movement recently."

"And you're going with him?" I verified. I was determined, but not completely out of my mind.

"I am, but I would never leave you guys unprotected. Lucy and Gabriel will—"

"I know," I assured her, figuring that was one of the arguments Ben had given her. "I want to go with you."

"Sweetie…"

"My birthday is less than a month away. Which means I am basically eighteen, and I'm the only one who's seen what the place looks like. From the inside."

"Which is why I'm really glad that the Owens plantation has excellent cell service."

"Delia…" I squared my shoulders and tried to stand tall, as if that would convince her.

"This isn't like coming with us to find Tristan in the woods when his life is in imminent danger. We aren't saving anyone, we are going after something that someone else already has. Something they will kill to keep."

"I know." I swallowed like that knowledge didn't terrify me. "But the reason I've seen the inside, that we know the Magnum Finis was there, is because there is someone who needs to be rescued. Someone who is terrified and giving up. I'm really worried about her."

"Did something change?"

I was still using her eyes, so I caught the look she gave me, like she didn't think it was a good idea for me to keep finding the girl they'd locked up, but she wasn't going to tell me not to. For one, Delia made it a point to never tell any of us what to do, but she also trusted our judgment. Either to be right, or for us to make our own mistakes.

"I don't know if they've moved her or they're trying to punish her, but she's in a dark room and she won't get out of bed, she's barely moving…"

"Can she see through the eyes of someone who…" James didn't finish his question, but I knew what he was asking.

"If you can see through her eyes, you know she's alive," Delia answered him, and reminded me.

"But there are many ways to be alive and not okay."

"I'll keep an eye out for her." James spoke up. He still made me uneasy, but the intensity in his eyes wasn't as terrifying when he wasn't trying to kill you. It felt like a promise that his eyes, his nose…every part of his Gift would search for her. For me.

"But she's not your mission. The Magnum Finis is your priority." I wasn't naïve enough to think anyone would choose rescuing my prisoner over recovering a powerful artefact that could somehow remove Giftedness. Especially from the hands of people who thought of Gifted as abominations who should be eliminated at all costs. I shuddered at the thought of what would happen if the Damned figured out how to use it. I was lucky enough to find a second family that loved and protected me a lot better than the first, but most of them were Gifted, who would die if given that 'cure'.

"Have you ever known us to leave someone behind when they needed our help?" Ben asked me. "If she's there, we will get her out." I was clearly not doing well if I'd somehow managed to get the three of them to agree on something.

"Isn't it better to have me there to make sure it's the right place?"

"We're just going to scope it out, Jack. Sneak in, sneak out… recon so a more qualified team can go in with a better understanding of what they're getting themselves into, and make sure everyone makes it out okay."

"So isn't it better to have me on the recon mission, to make sure it's the right place, then watch from a safe location farther away, rather than to go into the lion's den for the actual rescue?"

"It's better if you go to neither," Delia argued.

"When you're relying on stealth, less people is always better," James agreed.

"This again?" Ben sighed, exasperated.

"I was merely stating a fact, but the matter wasn't settled."

I didn't argue when Delia gently pulled me away from their bickering. I assumed they'd been going around in circles for a while, or she would have tried to put an end to it.

"How stealth do you think you can be with the two of them?" I tried a different tactic.

"They'll be civil when we need them to be." She gave me a stern look I heard more than saw, but my face must have been revealing more of my emotions than I wanted it to, because she sighed and asked, "Why?"

"Because ever since you found me, I've had someone there to fight for me, to make sure I'm taken care of. But I remember what it was like when I had no one, and that's what she's going through."

There was silence, with not even the guys arguing anymore. After what felt like an eternity, Delia sighed. I focused on her eyes again to see that she was looking to James, who looked over at me, before looking back to Delia and nodding. "Our intel suggests the compound is empty, but James will be scoping it out and the instant he even suspects there might be someone, or something that could possibly get anywhere near you…I will bring you back to somewhere safe and you will follow without arguing. You would be a part of the search, but not the danger. It's the best I can do."

"I'll take it." My face broke into a smile, thrilled that I won, at least partially, before I remembered what winning actually entailed.

"And nice try, but you're allowed to come because I believe we can keep you safe, not because I would ever risk your life to protect someone else's. Especially not grown men who bring it on themselves." Delia said the last part in a whisper, but neither of us were fooled into thinking they didn't hear.

"We leave at dawn," James told me.

"I'll help you pack."

I was going to remind Ben that I wasn't incompetent and didn't need anyone's help, but then I understood, and followed him to the War Room.